The Battle Joined!

Hethe straightened abruptly, staring at the offending item as his mind tried to sort out what it meant. His gaze slid around the room, taking in the uncovered window, the lack of fire, the tub of hot water that had at first been scorching, then cold. He recalled the hag, the ale, the missing linen and even his betrothed's horrific breath. It was all coming together in his mind to make a sort of sense.

He released a laugh of relief. The wench wasn't as resigned to this wedding as she would have everyone believe! She could not refuse, or betray her displeasure openly, so she had used strategy and plotted against them all.

Aye, she was clever, so it seemed there were brains to go with her beauty. But what to do about that? He supposed he could confront her, tell her he couldn't refuse the king's order and that she was wasting her time by trying to get him to call off the wedding. He grimaced at the thought. He would likely flub that. He didn't like confrontations—at least not verbal ones. Despite having been married before, Hethe was not all that experienced a husband. Still, the way she was acting, this was war—and if there was one thing the Lord of Holden knew a lot about, it was war.

LYNSAY SANDS

Bliss

AVONBOOKS

An Imprint of HarperCollinsPublishers

This book was originally published as an e-book in July 2010 by HarperCollins Publishers.

First Avon Books mass market printing: August 2017

Print Edition ISBN: 978-0-06-201961-5
Digital Edition ISBN: 978-0-06-201323-1

FIRST EDITION

17 18 19   QGM   10 9 8 7 6 5 4 3 2 1

In loving memory of
Catherine A. Henderson
(Aug. 16, 1958–Dec. 17, 1999)
A lovely lady who made the world
a better place while she was in it.

Prologue

England, 1173

"DAMN!" King Henry crumpled the scroll he had been reading into a ball and threw it to the floor in disgust. He spent a moment muttering about the soft hearts and interfering ways of women, then sighed with resignation and held his hand out to Templetun. "You may as well give me Lord Holden's message, too."

The other man's eyebrows flew up in amazement at the request, a touch of fear mingling with suspicion in his eyes. "How did you know?"

"It is not conjuring or anything, Templetun, simply experience. I never receive a complaint from Lady Tiernay that I do not receive one from Lord Holden as well. Besides, I saw his man ride in earlier and assumed he bore a message. There have been a few small uprisings in Normandy, and I asked Hethe to tend them for me. No doubt he is waiting to tell me he has done so."

"Ah." Relaxing, the older fellow handed over the document in question.

Henry opened the scroll a bit irritably, displeased

at having to explain himself. Templetun had only worked in the capacity of his chaplain for the past couple of days—his usual chaplain was ill—but already Henry was wishing for the latter's speedy recovery. His replacement was entirely too nervous, superstitious, and seemed to be far too eager to lend credence to Henry's reputation of being the "Spawn of the Devil." Shaking his head, Henry focused his attention on the parchment he now held. A moment later, it was a crumpled mass on the floor not far from the first, and Henry had leapt up to pace before his throne.

As he had expected, Lord Holden had cleaned up the little revolts in Normandy and was on his way home. But he had also added a complaint or two about his neighbor. It seemed his chatelain was harassed mightily by the Lady of Tiernay and was beleaguering Hethe with letters regarding the woman. In his turn, the Hammer of Holden had respectfully requested that his king do something about the woman . . . or he, himself, would.

It sounded very much like a threat, and it displeased Henry greatly to be threatened by one of his vassals. In fact, if Hethe weren't such a valued warrior and had not aided him so often in the past ten years, he would have seen him punished. But, unlike his father before him, Hethe had been a great asset.

He grimaced at the thought of the previous Lord Holden, Hethe's father. Born the second son, Gerhard had expected to be allowed to join a monastery and live out his life amongst the musty old papal scribblings he so adored. Unfortunately, his eldest brother had died, forcing him to abandon those plans in favor of marriage and producing an heir. The man had taken out that displeasure on his son.

To be honest, in Henry's opinion, Gerhard had been a touch mad. Fortunately, Hethe had not yet shown the same tendency. Unfortunately—for Hethe, at least—he had not even shown the same love of learning his father had, and the two had not gotten along. Gerhard's hatred had driven the boy from his home and straight into Henry's service as soon as he earned his spurs.

Ah, well. Gerhard's loss had been his own gain, Henry decided. But that didn't relieve Hethe of his responsibility to show his king respect. "What the Devil am I to do with these two?" he asked in frustration.

"I am not sure, my liege. What appears to be the problem, exactly?" Templetun asked tentatively. "I do realize they are both complaining—and from your reaction, I would say quite frequently—but about what, exactly?"

Henry turned to scowl down at him, opening his mouth to explain rather acerbically that his question had been rhetorical, when he changed his mind. Instead, he said, "Each other. Lady Tiernay writes to 'warn me' of her neighbor's cruel and abusive behavior to his serfs and villeins, because she '*knows* I would not wish to see any of my subjects so sorely mistreated.'"

"Ah," Templetun said again, biting back a smile at his king's sarcastic imitation of a woman's high-pitched voice. "And Lord Holden?"

Henry gave a short laugh. "He writes to say that Lady Tiernay is a nosy, harping busybody who makes his life hell."

"Hmmm." The new chaplain was silent for a moment, then murmured, "Did not Lord Holden's wife die several years back?"

"Aye. Ten years ago. In childbirth. And Hethe has been my best warrior since. Always ready for a fight, always away on campaign for me. I don't know what I'd do without him."

"Did Lady Tiernay's husband not die four or five years ago as well?"

"What?" Henry scowled briefly, then his expression cleared. "Oh, nay. That was her father. Lady Tiernay is not married and has not been. Her father neglected to see to that ere his passing."

"She is of marriageable age, then?"

"Oh, aye. She is beyond old enough to marry, I should think. Why, she must be . . ." Henry paused, doing the math in his head. "I think she may be twenty or thereabouts." Groaning, he walked over and wearily rested his hand on his throne. "And there is another problem. I shall have to marry her off soon. How the Devil am I expected to find a husband for a harping wench like her?" Again, he began to pace.

"Perhaps you already have one, my liege," Templetun offered with some trepidation. When the king turned on him sharply, he shrugged. "Mayhap the solution is to have Lord Holden marry her. It will solve both problems at once. She will be married, and they will be forced to work out their difficulties between themselves."

"They will kill each other within the week!" Henry predicted with disgust.

"Mayhap." Templetun paused innocently. "But still—both problems would then be solved, would they not?"

Henry considered him with frank admiration. "Damn, Templetun," he finally breathed. "You have an evil mind." He rushed back to his throne and threw himself excitedly upon it. "You shall write two messages in my name . . . and take them forth yourself!" Then he turned to the chaplain with a dangerous look in his eye. "And, Templetun," he added. "Don't fail me."

Chapter 1

No one was more surprised than Helen when she kicked the ball. She had only paused on her way across the bailey to watch the children play for a moment when the ball suddenly rolled toward her, and she impulsively kicked it. It was a mistake.

Goliath, who'd stayed dutifully by her side as always until then, took it as a sign that they were going to play. He was off after the ball in a heartbeat, barking gaily and running like the wind. Helen tried to call him back, but her voice was easily drowned out by the squeals of the children who raced after the huge wolfhound. The dog reached the ball first, of course. Unfortunately, he didn't understand the rules of the game and, as a hunting animal, he did not fetch it back right away. Instead, he picked it up in his massive jaws and shook it viciously side to side.

Helen couldn't hear the material tear, but she knew it had happened when feathers suddenly filled the air around the beast. Satisfied that he had killed his prey, Goliath strode cheerfully back through the dismayed children to drop the ruined ball at his mistress's feet. He then sank to the ground and rested his head happily on his front paws in what Helen considered the very picture of male satisfaction. Shaking her head, she bent to pick up and examine the damaged toy.

"My lady?"

Helen turned her attention from the slightly damp-with-dog-drool ball and glanced at the two women who appeared beside her. "Aye?"

"This is Maggie," Ducky said quietly. Ducky was Helen's lady's maid, but also a friend. If she had brought this other woman to her, there had to be something the two needed. Surveying the slightly warty but kindly-looking crone, Helen decided she liked what she saw.

"Hello, Maggie," she greeted the woman, then tipped her head slightly. "You are not from Tiernay." It wasn't a question. Helen knew every one of her people; she made it her business to know them. This woman wasn't one.

"Nay, my lady. I come from Holden."

Helen's lips tightened at the news. It could only mean trouble of some sort. Her thoughts were distracted by a murmur of discontent as the children arrived to cluster around her. Their accusing little eyes moved unhappily from Goliath to their now mangled toy.

"I shall repair it at once," she assured them guiltily, relieved when the promise seemed to appease them. "Come."

The order was for Goliath, who immediately got to his feet to keep pace at Helen's side as she headed for the keep, but the humans obeyed as well. Ducky and Maggie promptly fell into step behind her while the children trailed at the back. The group made a small parade as it crossed the bailey, mounted the steps and entered Tiernay keep.

"I shall need some fresh feathers, Ducky," Helen announced as they crossed the great hall.

"Aye, my lady." The woman was off at once, heading for the kitchens where Cook had been plucking chickens all morning for that evening's meal.

"You children go wait at the table. I shall have Ducky bring you drinks and pasties while you wait." So saying, Helen led Maggie and Goliath over to two chairs by the fire. Seating herself in her usual spot, she gestured for the older woman to take the other, then began to search through the small chest nearby for her sewing needle and thread. Goliath settled on the floor by her feet.

Helen was aware of the way the woman hesitated, then perched uncomfortably on the edge of her chair, nervous and stiff as could be, but she ignored it as she sought what was needed. She had just gotten ahold of the necessary items when Ducky appeared at her side with a wooden bowl containing the requested feathers.

"Thank you." Helen accepted the bowl and smiled at the woman with appreciation. "Perhaps you could have someone fetch the children some refreshments and sweets while they wait?"

"Aye, my lady."

Helen began to thread her needle, her attention focused on the task as she asked Maggie, "So, you are from Holden?"

"Aye." The old woman cleared her throat and shifted uncomfortably on her perch. "I used to be in charge of the chambermaids there."

"Used to?" Helen inquired gently. She drew the thread through the needle's eye, then glanced up in time to note the bitterness that flashed across the servant's face.

"Aye. I was released last Christmastide," the woman admitted reluctantly. A moment later she blurted, "The lord wanted only young and pretty maids to serve in the chambers."

Helen's mouth thinned. Such news didn't surprise her. Very little could surprise her regarding the Hammer of Holden's behavior. Hard work and service were not often repaid kindly by the man. *Cruel bastard*, she thought with irritation, then forced herself to start mending the large jagged tear in the children's ball. After several stitches she felt calm enough to ask, "And what have you been doing for these last six months?"

The woman cleared her throat again. "Farmer White had been courting me up until then. He was a widow," she explained, blushing like a lass fresh out of a schoolroom. "When I was released, we married. I tended his home and helped on the farm." Her smile and blush faded, leaving her pale and weary looking. "He died these two weeks past."

"I am sorry," Helen said gently. Glimpsing the tears that sprang to the woman's eyes before Maggie lowered her head, she turned her attention back to her task. Deciding she had left just enough unsewn, she turned the ball back inside out and began to stuff it with feathers. She was nearly done with the chore when Maggie recovered enough to continue.

"I knew there would be trouble. I couldn't manage the farm on my own, of course. . . ."

"He evicted you and gave the farm to another couple," Helen guessed quietly. Such wasn't unheard of, but to her mind it was cruel to treat someone so shabbily when they had worked so hard and faithfully for so long.

Maggie nodded. "He sent poor young Stephen down as usual to do his dirty work."

Helen nodded. Stephen was Lord Holden's second, the man left in charge of Holden while the Hammer was away. Which appeared to be quite often. Lord Holden seemed forever off doing battle somewhere. But while Stephen was Holden Castle's chatelain, none of the decisions were his. Surely the Hammer kept up a steady discourse with the man, ordering him to do this or that—none of it very pleasant or kind—and from all accounts, young Stephen suffered horribly from being forced to carry out such wicked deeds.

"He had Stephen claim everything in the cottage for heriot," Maggie continued, drawing Helen's attention back to her. "Then he was ordered to burn it all before me and send me on my way."

Helen's eyes widened incredulously. Heriot was the equivalent of a death tax, a legal part of the feudal system. But claiming every last possession, then burning it all . . . well, that was just cruel. And deliberately so. "Did Stephen do it?"

Maggie grimaced. "Aye. He is a faithful servant. He apologized the whole while, but he did it."

Helen nodded solemnly as she stuffed the last of the feathers firmly into the ball and prepared to sew it closed. Of course young Stephen had done it. He would follow his lord's orders.

"His mother would have wept to see him forced to act so."

Helen glanced up questioningly at the woman's words and Maggie explained. "We were friends when she lived in the village. This would have broken her heart."

"She is dead?" she asked politely, knowing the old

servant needed the change of topic to help her maintain composure. If talking about Stephen's mother would help her distance herself from her recent losses, Helen saw no reason not to indulge her.

"Oh, nay. She is not dead. But when Stephen became chatelain and was forced to dole out such harsh punishments . . . Well, she could not bear to stand by and watch. She left the village. Most people think she is dead, but I think she is living on the border of Tiernay and Holden. Stephen often rides out this way for the afternoon. I think he is visiting her." She fell silent for a moment, then added, "He rode out here after seeing to burning my things. Probably went to visit her then as well."

Helen took in the lost expression on the old woman's face and the way she was slumping in her seat and said gently, "And so you came to Tiernay."

"Aye." Maggie sat a little straighter. "My daughter married the tavern keeper in the village ten years back."

Helen nodded. She knew the tavern owner and his wife, of course.

"And they have offered to take me in . . . but they must have your permission first."

Helen was silent for several moments. She was responsible for her land and everyone on it, and therefore, as the woman said, her permission was imperative before any new tenants were allowed to move in. Her first instinct was simply to nod and say certainly Maggie was welcome at Tiernay. But Helen had noted the woman's odd tone as she had spoken of her daughter's offer. There was no doubt that Maggie had worked her whole life. Losing her position in Holden Castle must have been extremely demoralizing. Her marriage and position as a farmer's wife had saved her pride somewhat, but now she was reduced to accepting charity from her own child. Helen suspected it rankled the old woman greatly, and now, considering the matter solemnly, she shook her head. "Nay."

"*Nay?*" Maggie looked fit to burst into tears, and Helen mentally kicked herself for speaking her thoughts aloud.

"There will be no charity for you, Maggie. You are still strong and healthy. You can work. As it happens, I am in need of someone with your skills."

Maggie lost her tragic look, hope slowly filling her withered face. "You do?"

"Aye. Edwith used to be in charge of my chambermaids here. She died a month ago and I have yet to replace her. Ducky has had to fill that job as well as tend to her own duties. You would be doing both of us a service should you take Edwith's place. It would relieve a great burden on Ducky."

"Oh!" Much to Helen's consternation, the woman burst into tears. For a moment, she feared she had erred and Maggie wished to stay with her daughter. Then the woman positively beamed at her through her tears, and Helen relaxed.

"Oh, my lady. Thank you," the new mistress of chambermaids breathed, positively glowing at the idea of being useful again.

"Thank *you*," Helen said firmly, then smiled at Ducky, who had appeared suddenly beside her. "Perhaps Ducky could show you around and introduce you to the girls who will be under your guidance."

"Certainly." Ducky beamed at the other woman, then glanced back to Helen. "Boswell says there is a party approaching."

"A party?" Helen raised an eyebrow in inquiry, and Ducky nodded.

"Aye. They bear the king's standard."

Helen paused briefly, then smiled widely. "Good, good. If you should see my aunt on your tour, pray tell her the news." With that, she quickly slipped the last stitch through the ball, tied it off and broke the thread. Standing as the other two women moved away, Helen carried the ball over to the table where its owners were still eating and drinking.

"Here you are," she said cheerfully, setting the ball on the table. "Good as ever. Hurry up with your treats, then get you outside to play. 'Tis too nice a day to be indoors."

Moving away to a chorus of the children's agreement and thank-yous, Helen scurried to the door of the keep, brushing down her skirt as she went.

The travelers were riding through the gates of the bailey as she stepped out into the light. She waited for Goliath to follow her through, then pulled the door closed behind the dog and quickly smoothed down her hair. She felt nervous. This was a party from the king, Ducky had said, and Helen could see that her servant was right. Henry II's standard fluttered there for all who cared to look—and Helen was looking. This was a banner day. The king was likely responding at last to the many letters she had sent him regarding Lord Holden. That was the only explanation for this visit.

It did her heart good. Helen had begun to fear that the king was entirely ambivalent toward the coldhearted and even cruel behavior of her neighbor. She had been left feeling frustrated and helpless by her inability to do more than to take in Holden's

serfs and villeins who fled or made their way to
Tiernay, and write letters of complaint. Why, once
or twice she'd even had to go as far as to purchase
Holden's prospective victims to save them from his
wrath. Lord Hethe, the Hammer of Holden, was
most certainly a devil in human guise.

But finally the king had sent someone to handle
the matter. At least, she assumed he had sent someone. This entourage was far too small to count the
king amongst it. Henry's own traveling party could
span for miles, as it included his lords and ladies, his
servants, his vassals and everything he might need
on his journey.

Nay. He had obviously sent a man in his stead to
tend the matter, and that was fine with her. This af-
fair was most likely beneath his attention anyway; it
affected only those whom the Hammer abused.
Compared to an entire country's hardships, this was
a small problem. In fact, the people of Holden were
very fortunate King Henry was looking into the
matter at all.

That thought cheering her, Helen waited patiently
until the group of men reached the bottom of the
stairs; then she made her way down to greet them,
Goliath at her side.

"Lady Tiernay?" It was the oldest of the train
who greeted her, his expensive robes rustling as he
dismounted and faced her. He wore a hopeful expression.

"Aye. You are from the king." She stated the obvious, and the gentleman nodded, a smile tugging at his
lips as he took her hand and bowed to press a kiss to
her knuckles. "Lord Templetun, at your service."

"You are welcome here at Tiernay, Lord Templetun," Helen said formally, then placed her hand on

his arm and turned toward the stairs. "Pray, you must be hungry and thirsty after your journey. Allow us to welcome you properly with a meal and drink."

Nodding, Lord Templetun started up the stairs with her, calling orders over his shoulder as they went. They had nearly reached the door to the keep when it burst open and the children poured out. Laughing and screaming one moment, they were wide-eyed and silent the next. At the sight of Helen and Lord Templetun, the group mumbled their excuses and moved solemnly down the stairs, only to burst into a noisy run once they were past. Headed back to the game she and Goliath had interrupted, Helen thought with amusement. She smiled and ignored the questioning glance Lord Templetun threw her.

Leading him inside, she urged the king's man to the table the children had just emptied. Helen saw him seated in the head chair that her father had always occupied, then excused herself for a quick trip to the kitchens. She returned moments later with a passel of servants trailing her, bearing the finest food and wine available in Tiernay keep, on its finest silver trays. After nervously supervising the serving of Lord Templetun, at last Helen seated herself beside him and sipped silently from a mug of mead while he ate. She was impatient to confirm his purpose in being there, but she knew it would be rude to do so before he had satisfied his hunger and thirst.

Fortunately for her state of mind, Templetun was not a man to waste time on savoring sustenance. He devoured a shocking amount of food—and even more of her finest wine—in a trice, then sat back with a satisfied sigh and beamed.

"I must compliment you on a fine table, my lady. That meal did you credit."

"Thank you, my lord," Helen murmured, wondering how to broach the subject of his purpose. Templetun soon put an end to that worry by tugging a scroll from his voluminous robes.

"I bring news from the king." He set the parchment before her, then began to dig at his not-so-shiny teeth with the longish nail of the baby finger on his right hand as he awaited her perusal of it.

Her hands suddenly shaking, Helen broke the seal and quickly unrolled the scroll, her mind racing over the possibilities of how the king intended to punish her neighbor for his rough treatment of his subjects. Appoint someone to watch over him? Fine him? Chastise him?

"*Marry him?*" The words seemed to scream out of the scroll at Helen as her eyes flew over its contents. "Nay!" Her head was suddenly light and fuzzy. Feeling herself sway, she shook her head determinedly and peered at Templetun. "Surely this is a jest?"

She was so upset, she didn't even notice that she was agitatedly tearing the scroll as she glared at Lord Templetun. Nor did she notice the sudden wary concern on the man's face as he slowly shook his head. "Nay, my lady. The king does not jest."

"Well, he must—He cannot—This is—" Helen's stumbling monologue died abruptly at the sound of approaching footsteps. She turned, relieved to spy her aunt entering the room. Aunt Nell was ever the voice of reason. She would know what to do about this . . . situation.

"Aunt Nell!" Even Helen was taken aback by the desperate tone of her voice as she launched out of her seat and rushed to greet the woman who had served as mother to her since her own mother's death some few years ago.

"What is it, my dear?" her aunt asked and caught her hands, her gaze sliding between the ripped and crumpled scroll Helen held and her niece's pallid face.

"The king, he sent Lord Templetun here." Helen gestured at the man at the table. "And he—" Unable to even say it, she shoved the remains of the scroll at her older relative, silently urging her to read it.

Taking the torn message, Lady Nell uncrumpled it and slowly read its contents. Helen watched as her aunt's eyes flew over the words on the page, then paused, went to the top, then flew over it again.

"Nay," the woman breathed with a horror as deep as Helen's own, then whirled on the man still seated at the table. "Is this a jest, my lord? Because if it is, 'tis a sad one indeed."

"Nay, my lady." The king's man shifted uncomfortably in his seat, looking oddly guilty. His gaze darted around the room, looking everywhere but its occupants, then he said, "The king dictated that missive himself and ordered me to bring it to you. I am to take another on to Lord Holden and bring him back here for the wedding. The king thought it would be good to allow your people time to prepare for the celebration."

"But—" Helen paused and shook her head, trying to gather her rather scattered wits. "But, this cannot be. Lord Holden is an evil, horrid, *cruel* man. The king cannot expect me to marry *him!*"

When Templetun remained silent, his head lowered, refusing to meet her eyes, Helen began to realize that she was indeed expected to do just that. Numbness crept over her, softening her horror, and she sank back onto the trestle table bench. She was to marry that horrid, cruel bastard neighbor of hers. Hethe.

The Hammer of Holden. The man who burned villeins out of their homes for no purpose. Dear God, what would he do when he was displeased with *her*?

"There must be a mistake," Aunt Nell announced firmly, drawing Helen from her miserable thoughts. "Surely the king would not be so cruel as to force my niece to marry *that* man. Perhaps he simply does not understand. We must travel to court and explain things to him. We must—"

"The king is no longer at court," Templetun interrupted solemnly. "He has gone to Chinon to see young Henry and remove some of the members of his court."

Helen and Nell exchanged startled glances at mention of the king's son. It was Helen who murmured uncertainly, "Remove some of his court?"

"Mmmm." Templetun's face was full of displeasure. "Aye. Henry wishes to arrange a marriage between the daughter of the Count of Maurienne and young John. The count seems interested, but wants to be sure John has prospects first. The king offered to invest him with the castles Loudon, Mirebeau and Chinon, but young Henry objects. He will only concede to this if his father allows him to rule either England, Normandy or Anjou in his own right."

"He wants more power." Nell sighed with disgust.

"Aye." Templetun nodded his head solemnly. "It was a mistake for the king to crown his son while he himself yet lives. The boy wants the power that goes with the title."

"But what has that to do with removing some of his court?" Nell asked impatiently.

"Ah, well, the king first thought to take Henry into custody as a warning, but he believes some of young Henry's courtiers are sparking these ideas in him and hopes that after the removal of their influence, his oldest son will settle down." He spoke candidly, then, seeming to realize that he was gossiping, frowned and changed the subject back to the matter at hand. "In any case, seeing him would make no difference. His mind was made up. He feels that you, Lady Helen, and Lord Holden should work your problems out between yourselves, and he wishes the wedding to take place at once. I am to see to it."

Helen lowered her head, her gaze landing on the scroll her aunt still held, proof of King Henry's intent in the matter. It had been written plainly in the message, but for a moment her aunt's words had given her hope. If she could but talk to the king, throw herself on his mercy—

Movement and a rustling just beyond her right shoulder drew Helen from her thoughts. Peering back, she spied Ducky. The maid was wringing her hands, grief and fear both twisting her face as she stared at her mistress. Obviously, the woman had heard enough to know what the message ordered, and she was no less horrified by the missive than her mistress. Straightening, Helen forced a reassuring smile to her face for the servant's benefit, then glanced around with a start when her aunt—the sweetest, gentlest of ladies—suddenly bellowed like the veriest fishmonger.

"Where the Devil did he get an asinine idea like this?"

Helen spared a moment to gape at her aunt briefly, then turned to hear Lord Templetun's answer. He did not appear eager to give it. In fact, he was looking quite reluctant. Guilty. The old man was nearly squirming in his seat with his discomfort. Helen was just starting to get the oddest inkling when her aunt suddenly spoke that suspicion aloud.

"You!"

Templetun froze abruptly, the expression on his face not unlike that of a child startled while raiding the pantry.

"It *was* you," Helen breathed in horror, unsure whether to ask why or simply go for the man's throat. Before she could do either, Templetun was on his feet and easing around the far end of the table.

"Well, I should be getting on now. The king doesn't like dawdling, and, while it is not a long ride to Holden, the day is waning and travel is so much more uncomfortable at night, is it not?"

The question was rhetorical, Helen was sure. At least, the man didn't appear to intend to stick around for the answer. He was sidling eagerly toward the main door now, moving fast, and talking faster still. She wished he'd choked on the food she had served him.

"I have been informed that Lord Holden is presently on his way home from performing a task for the king," he continued as Helen's aunt began to follow him slowly across the floor, eyes narrowed and furious. "So you will have plenty of time to prepare the celebratory feast. I would guess you should plan it for next week's end. That should be about right. I will send a messenger ahead, of course, so that you can see to any last-minute details." The last was said as he slid through the door.

"The little rat!" Nell said harshly once the keep door had slammed closed behind him.

Helen heartily agreed with the pronouncement, but had other concerns more pressing. "Why would he suggest to the king that Holden and I marry?"

"Why, indeed?" Aunt Nell muttered, then moved back to place her hands on Helen's shoulders to comfort her.

"Surely you are not going to actually marry him?" Ducky gasped, moving forward to join them. "Not the Hammer?"

"I hope not, Ducky. Truly I do." Helen's shoulders slumped miserably.

"But what will you do?"

Frowning, Helen began to twist her hands together as her mind flew over the possibilities. Flee? To where? Beg the king? How? He was away and the wedding was to take place at week's end. Kill the prospective groom? A nice thought, but not very practical, she admitted with a grimace.

"My lady?" Ducky prompted anxiously.

Helen sighed. "I am not sure what I *can* do," she admitted unhappily.

Ducky's eyes widened in horror. "Can you not refuse him? Just refuse and—"

"And have the king send me off to an abbey? I would rather marry the man and kill him than do that! Who would look after my people if that happened? The Hammer, that is who. Tiernay would be forfeit to him as my dower should I refuse the king's orders."

Ducky bit her lip at that, then leaned closer to whisper. "Maggie knows this and that about herbs. Or Old Joan the Healer. She might know of something we could give him to—"

"Bite your tongue," Helen hissed, covering the maid's mouth with her hand and glancing nervously about the empty great hall. "I never want to hear such a suggestion from you again, Ducky. It could get you strung up in the bailey."

"But then what will you do?" The servant looked miserable as Helen removed the hand covering her mouth. "You cannot marry the Hammer."

Helen sighed again. "It appears I will have to. I cannot refuse a direct order from the king."

"Why not?" Ducky asked frantically. "The Hammer does it often enough. Why, he—"

"That's it!" Aunt Nell, who had stood silent and thoughtful throughout the last few moments, suddenly grabbed Helen's arms excitedly, unconsciously giving her a shake.

"What?" Helen asked with a glimmer of hope.

"*You* cannot refuse. But the Hammer *can*. He is too powerful a lord for the king to force him, should he really wish to refuse."

Ducky snorted. "And do you really think for one minute that the Hammer will refuse to marry her? Look! She's as pretty as her mother ever was. And sweet as honeyed mead as well. Then there is her land. Who would refuse a dower like Tiernay?"

Helen sagged slightly, some of her hope leaving her, but Aunt Nell merely straightened her shoulders and spoke staunchly. "Then we shall have to make you and Tiernay less attractive."

Ducky looked doubtful. "Templetun has already seen her for the pretty lass she is. You can't suddenly blacken her teeth and shave her head."

"Nay," Helen agreed slowly, a small smile teasing the corners of her lips as an idea flared in her mind. "But there are other things we can do."

Chapter 2

*H*ETHE, Lord Holden, sat at the head of his table and gaped at the man before him. Hethe had just returned from several weeks of battle, fighting for his king. It was something he spent more time doing than anything else of late. Actually, it was almost all he had been doing since his wife's death ten years ago. Before that even. Henry II was forever extending his power, and Hethe had utilized his sovereign's ambition to provide an excuse to avoid the home he had shared first with his hypercritical parents, then with the sweet young Nerissa.

He rubbed the weariness from his eyes, wishing he could take the memories away as easily. Thoughts of his poor dead wife always made him contrite. They had been too young. *She* had been too young.

Turning away from the thoughts as he always did, he scowled at Lord Templetun. "Explain to me your presence here again if you please, my lord," he ordered carefully.

"The king sent me with this message." The man pushed the scroll at him again, no doubt hoping that this time it would be taken. "And ordered me to collect you and take you to Tiernay to marry Lady Helen."

"You cannot marry that hag!" William exclaimed as Hethe reluctantly took the proffered scroll and broke its seal.

"Lady Tiernay is not a hag," Templetun said with a reproving glance at Hethe's first—the man who, above all others, was supposed to look after his lord's best interests. "I just came from there, and she is quite lovely."

"Oh, aye. Well . . . you would say that, wouldn't you?" William muttered.

"Have you ever seen the lady in question?" Templetun asked irritably, then nodded in satisfaction when the man reluctantly shook his head. "Well, I have, and she is quite lovely. Quite." His mouth turned down then, and he added almost under his breath, "Though her aunt is something of a termagant."

"What was that about her aunt?" Hethe asked abruptly, handing the king's missive over so that William could do the actual reading. He himself was interested only in the signature, and had recognized it at once as the king's. He had received enough missives from the man to know Henry's hand by now. That was enough to tell him that Templetun's claims were probably true. Not that he had really doubted it. Why would the man lie about something like this?

Templetun's expression promptly turned testy at the question, but he merely shook his head and asked, "Well, what say you? Will you marry the lady or not?"

"Do I have a choice?" Hethe asked with a bark of laughter, but he glanced at William rather than

Templetun for the answer. His first glanced up from
the scroll he was reading and shook his head with
disgust.

"I thought not." Shifting, Hethe pushed a hand
wearily through his hair. The last thing he needed
right now was another wife to worry about. Even if
he had been looking for one, Tiernay's tyrant was
the last he would have chosen. Dear God! The
woman was an abominable busybody, forever sending messages berating him for the way he dealt with
his people. At least, so he had heard. He never read
the messages himself, but William reported to him
on the matter. His first received the news from Stephen, his second, whom Hethe left in command
while he was off fighting. The younger man was
horribly harassed by the woman.

Now it seemed that he himself would be the one
harassed—and not by impersonal messages. He
would have to deal with the woman personally.
Most personally, indeed. The thought was enough
to make him shove himself from his seat and hurry
toward the stairs. Templetun was immediately on
his feet and following.

"My lord? What are you doing?"

"I am going to take a bath," Hethe announced
without slowing his steps. "I trust I will be allowed
to bathe the stench of death off me and enjoy a
night's rest ere I must rush off to wed the wench? It
is not as if she is going anywhere."

"Oh. Nay." Templetun stopped at the foot of the
stairs and allowed Lord Holden to continue alone.
"I mean, aye—a bath and rest are fine. I will send a
messenger to warn Lady Tiernay that we will be
leaving on the morrow. After we break fast?" he
added hopefully.

"After the nooning meal," Hethe corrected. "I would hear how things go on my land ere I rush off to a new holding."

"Aye. After the nooning," Templetun agreed reluctantly.

Grunting in response, Hethe continued up the stairs and to his room. He was standing staring out the window several minutes later when a tap came at the door. Calling out for whomever it was to enter, he wasn't at all surprised to see the door open to reveal servants bearing a tub and numerous pails of hot water. He hadn't ordered the bath, but had spoken his desire to bathe aloud to Templetun. That was enough to see the deed done here. Holden's servants were well trained and swift about their duties. That was good; his men had chosen and trained these workers well.

Hethe watched silently as his bath was prepared; then he dismissed the servants. One of the maids stayed behind, prepared to assist him in the bath, but, buxom and pretty though she was, he waved her out, too. He wished to be alone. He had to consider this matter of his marriage. To be married again. To have another wife for whom he was responsible.

Feeling his muscles tense at the very thought, he quickly stripped off his clothes and stepped into the tub. The water closed around him as warm and inviting as a mistress, and he leaned his head back, his eyes closing as he felt his body slowly relax and his mind drift.

He had been a mere twelve years old and Nerissa seven when their marriage had been contracted. He was seventeen and she not quite twelve when their parents had grown weary of waiting and decided to hold the ceremony. Both sides had been greedy for the merger between the families—Holden offering his family name and title and Nerissa her father's wealth. Young though he had been, he had been old enough to suggest—rather sensibly, it turned out—that they delay the wedding until the girl was older. But neither side had wanted that.

Unfortunately, Nerissa was the one who had paid the price for their parents' ambitions. She had grown heavy with child right away, then been sacrificed on the birthing bed. She had not yet seen her thirteenth year.

Hethe would never forgive himself for failing to persuade his father to wait. Or perhaps he could have refused to consummate the marriage. He might have allowed them all to think it was consummated, then secretly waited until she was a year or two older. But he had not. Seventeen he had been, and as randy as any young man. And she had been a lovely girl—even at that age. A combination of drink and his father's firm instruction had ensured the deed was done. Nine months later he had listened to her screams as their child fought to make its way out of her. The child had failed, and Nerissa had bled to death with their babe still inside her.

And so Hethe had been fighting his demons and the king's enemies ever since. He spent weeks and even months covering battlefield after battlefield with blood. He would fight until he wearied of the stench and sight of death, then return home, always hoping that this time he would be able to rest. That this time, home would be the haven he sought. But he'd never found that haven. For him, Nerissa's screams still echoed through the castle halls as they had for nearly three days those many years ago. Quickly, sometimes even within hours he was eager to leave again. He could find no peace.

Today was no different, he thought grimly. Though this time it was not the screams of Nerissa that made him wish to flee Holden's cold stone walls. Nay. This time, the thing that would send him running back to the battlefields was the message which the king's man had just delivered. Marry again—and to the tyrant of Tiernay.

It was ironic, really. This time *he* would be the sacrifice, and to the king's whims. He couldn't say he was amused.

A tap at the door drew him from his unpleasant thoughts and he sat up slightly, calling "enter" as he began to splash water over his skin. He was no more surprised when William entered than he had been to see the servants appear with his bath. By now his first would have had a report from Stephen, and he would pass the news on to him. It was the usual routine.

"What news while we were gone?" Hethe asked, cupping his hands together to scoop water up and splash it over his head, dampening his hair.

"Nothing really. At least, nothing we had not heard from Stephen's missives." William shrugged, then sat on the end of the bed to consider Hethe unhappily. "You are not really going to marry her, are you?"

Hethe was silent for a moment, then asked, "Did the letter sound like a request or an order?"

"An order," the man admitted reluctantly.

Hethe made a face, then shrugged at his thoughts. "I suppose I have to. I had to marry again sometime," he added, trying to resolve himself to the matter.

"Aye, but . . . to Tiernay's tyrant. . . ." William looked pained, and Hethe laughed slightly at his expression.

"Aye, well. I'll marry her, bed her; then we shall see if the king can't use our services in subduing that son of his. If we leave my wife at Tiernay and I make infrequent visits, things should not change so much."

William's relief was palpable, and Hethe understood it. The other man had been a smallish boy, often picked on by others. But in his late teens, he had a growth spurt that had started him toward the tall, strong man he now was. That, plus his training at Hethe's side, had turned him into a skilled knight. Hethe knew that his friend hoped to gain glory, the king's attention, and perhaps a grant of land and his own demesne, by his sword. It was the reason the other man had never hesitated to ride into battle with him, why he even encouraged Hethe in volunteering himself and his men to Henry. Hethe suddenly settling down with a wife and avoiding warfare could hamper such ambitions. But William needed not fear; Hethe had no desire to settle.

"Bedding the tyrant of Tiernay," William said, the man's words drawing Hethe's attention to his feigned shudder. "Ugh. You have my utmost sympathies."

"And I appreciate those sympathies, William. Truly, I do." He spoke in arid tones, but his mind tried to recollect a picture of the woman. She had been a mere child the last time he saw her, perhaps ten. He had gone to Tiernay after his father's death to discuss and ensure the continuation of the treaties between Holden and Tiernay with this woman's father. It had been the year after Nerissa's death. Aye, she would have been about ten—only a year or so younger than his own bride had been when he had married her, but Tiernay's daughter had shown none of the curves or beauty of his Nerissa. She had been a scrawny little thing. All teeth and elbows, as he recalled. She had probably not improved with the passage of time, either. Helen of Tiernay probably resembled nothing more than a naggy old buck-toothed horse.

"Child! They are here! I saw them from the window of my bedchamber. They are arrived!"

Dropping her sewing, Helen stood abruptly, her hands suddenly tangling themselves in her skirts and clenching the fine material as her aunt flew down the stairs. For a moment she just stood there, panic blanketing her and stealing her thoughts; then she cast it off and regained her senses enough to shout for her maid.

Ducky must have heard Aunt Nell's anxious cries, because it was a bare heartbeat later that she came flying out of the kitchens. She carried a mug and looked just as panicked as Nell. The two women nearly collided as they rushed across the great hall toward Helen. For some reason, their frenzy had an immediate calming effect on Helen.

All was well. The messenger from Lord Temple-tun had arrived at mealtime last evening. They had been warned and thereby given time to finish the last of their preparations. She was ready, she reassured herself, but ticked off the checklist in her head anyway.

She was wearing her finest gown. Her hair was clean and lay in soft waves about her face. She looked as good as she possibly could. Helen almost wished she was filthy dirty and dressed in rags, yet, had she done anything of the like, Templetun would have realized right away that something was afoot. After all, his arrival had caught her unaware the first time. He had seen how she normally looked. Blackening her teeth and wearing an overlarge gown stuffed with cushioning did not seem a prudent or particularly intelligent approach to scaring her would-be husband into refusing the wedding decree. Her plan had to be more subtle than that, and it was. There were only two things left to do, but for the sake of potency they had to be left until the men's arrival.

"Do you have the garlic?" Helen asked Ducky as the servant and Aunt Nell came to a halt before her.

"Aye, my lady. I have it here." She handed her mug to Helen's aunt to hold, then dug in her pocket for the small stash she had been carrying since the messenger had informed them of the Lords Templetun and Holden's expected time of arrival. Retrieving a handful of them, she began to peel away the thin, dry, outer layer of one clove, then handed it to her mistress and turned her attention to peeling another.

Expression grim, Helen accepted the offering and promptly popped it into her mouth. She winced as she chewed the pungent herb. It felt as if it were burning her mouth, but she continued to chew and popped each newly peeled clove into her mouth until she had six of them in there and was alternately chewing and pushing them about with her tongue. Ducky and Aunt Nell grimaced sympathetically as they watched her work the garlic around. Once she finished, she swallowed the whole mess, then held out her hand for the mug her maid had given to Nell.

Her aunt lifted the mug first for a sniff, and her expression and the way she jerked her nose away warned Helen of the liquid's potency. Nell handed it over. Helen lifted the mug to her own nose then, only to jerk it away just as quickly. She had rather hoped that the garlic would temporarily kill her ability to smell, and aid in her consumption of the concoction they had brewed to strengthen their plan. Such was not the case. *Dear God, I cannot drink this*, she thought with horror as her nose was assaulted with the foulest scent it had ever been her displeasure to smell.

"Courage," Aunt Nell murmured almost under her breath, and Helen glanced over at her. The woman forced a bracing smile to her face and nodded. Realizing that there was nothing for it, Helen released a pent-up breath, then plugged her nose and tipped the mug's entire contents into her mouth. Her first instinct was to gag, her second to spit, but Helen clenched her fingers and even her toes and stood firm . . . waiting for those impulses to pass. They didn't.

Eyes beginning to water, she forced herself to hold the brew in and even to swish it around. It wasn't until she was sure it had coated every last inch of the inside of her mouth that she allowed herself to swallow the foul stuff. That act left her gasping as the liquid shot downward, seeming to take her breath with it.

"Oh, God!" She coughed as both Aunt Nell and Ducky thumped her heartily on the back. Their expressions were almost tragic with pity.

"Are you all right, dear?" Aunt Nell asked anxiously as the coughing began to subside.

Helen nodded, breathed in deeply, then realized

that her action wasn't really helping since the air came in tainted by the foul brew coating her mouth. She forced herself to breathe normally and handed Ducky the husks of the cloves she had consumed.

"Aye," she said at last, though she wasn't really sure. The potion was not lying lightly in her stomach, but seemed to be causing a terrible upset there. It was just as repugnant to her innards as to her mouth, it seemed.

"Then perhaps Ducky should get rid of the evidence and we should go greet your guests."

"Aye." Straightening, Helen gave her maid a reassuring smile. "Be sure the ale and food are ready too, please, Ducky. And don't forget to see to the baths." The woman nodded and moved reluctantly toward the kitchens, taking the remains of the garlic and the now empty mug with her.

Helen paused a moment to brush down her skirts, then started for the main door to the keep, her aunt at her side and Goliath at her heel. She ran through the plan in her head as she walked, and tried to reassure herself that it would work. The Hammer *would* cry off this marriage. It was the only hope to which she could cling. She had to believe it. If she allowed herself to consider the other possibility—

Helen cut her thoughts off right there as she reached the main doors. She reached out to open them when her aunt stopped her.

"Smile," Nell instructed gently. Helen immediately pasted a polite smile on her face, then awaited approval.

"Well," Nell said after a hesitation. "I suppose you shouldn't seem overjoyed at their arrival. That might make them suspicious. And it is not as if you are going to enjoy torturing the Hammer of Holden."

Her last words had the desired effect. While Helen's smile did not widen, it did become a little more natural, the tension in her face relaxing as she considered the scenario to come. Nodding her approval, Aunt Nell pulled the door open and ushered Helen outside.

Her eyes sought out and found the men riding into the bailey, and Helen knew at once which one was the Hammer. He and Lord Templetun were riding in the lead with a couple of dozen men following, and Helen gasped as she caught her first sight of him. He was terribly handsome. That was something she had not expected. She supposed she had always assumed that a person's nature was reflected in his looks, and she had expected him to be as ugly as his actions. This man was far from ugly. His head was turned and bent slightly toward Lord Templetun, who appeared to be speaking, so she wasn't getting a full picture, but what she was seeing was enough to take her breath away. She was almost sorry for a moment that she wasn't going to marry the man, but then the party reached the foot of the stairs and began to dismount, and Helen's breath caught in her throat again.

Dear God, now that the men were off their horses and standing, the very size of her would-be husband became obvious. He and the man who drew his mount up opposite Lord Templetun were the largest of the knights and soldiers in the group. They were both also twice as broad as the older, shrunken Lord Templetun. But it was Lord Holden with whom Helen was concerned, and he looked nothing less than the killer he was—strong, broad and grim.

Helen forced herself to recall with whom she was dealing: The Hammer. A cruel, angry man who she was sure could snap her in two with little effort. Up until then, she had been focused on nothing but getting out of this wedding. Now she focused firmly on the fact that her plans would probably infuriate the man who had come to collect her. What if he took that fury out on her? What if he—

"Courage." Apparently sensing the panic welling within her, Aunt Nell spoke the word quietly. It was enough. Helen firmly pushed her unpleasant worries and fears aside. Stiffening her determination, she forced her chin up a bit and pasted a smile firmly back on her face.

"There is still time to turn tail and run for your life."

Hethe's face cracked into a smile at his first's conspiratorial whisper. William had been making such comments all the way from Holden. Hethe just wished that they had not been half serious. The fact that William was as worried over this marriage as he himself was was not reassuring. But then, they had heard a great deal from this wench over the last several years since her father's death—most of it in the form of written reprimands. Ere that, he had known she existed but had not been forced to deal with her. It wasn't until her father's death that she had become a burr in his backside. Suddenly, Lady Helen of Tiernay had gone from being simply the daughter of his neighbor to a pain in the arse.

It had all come about quite swiftly, too, as he recalled. Where before then he had always had a good relationship with the neighboring estate, Hethe had found Tiernay suddenly releasing a barrage of nasty, berating letters, correspondence that chastised him for his treatment of his servants and villeins. *As if I have ever mistreated anyone under my rule*, he thought irritably. Only Lady Tiernay, now in charge of her father's estates, seemed to think he did. He supposed that, being a woman, she would see some of his punishments as a tad strong or unnecessary, but Hethe had always found that a firm hand produced good results and allowed everyone to know where they stood.

"Dear God." Those words, pushed out on an expelled breath by his first, drew Hethe away from his thoughts. Turning to the man curiously, he then followed William's enchanted gaze to the woman at the top of the steps before them.

"Sweet Jesu," he agreed on a breath of his own.

The woman was radiant. Her hair was long and wavy and a golden color that seemed to capture the sun and reflect it back at the world. Her face, what he could see of it from this distance, was pale and perfectly formed. And her figure . . . His gaze slid over her body, devouring the becoming blue gown she wore.

This was no hag. This woman did not at all fit the image he had painted in his mind of his soon-to-be bride. Nay, this could not be Helen of Tiernay. There was no way that the harping, nagging wench constantly besieging Stephen with shrewish letters was this angel of loveliness. It seemed he was not the only one who felt thusly, for he heard William ask Templetun in an undertone who the two ladies on the keep's steps were. It was only then that Hethe even noticed the older woman at the younger's side, or the large dog at her heels.

"Ah. That is Lady Tiernay and her aunt," the older man said, gazing up at their hostess with satisfaction and not a little relief. Hethe could only guess by the man's expression that he had feared she might not turn herself out well for their first meeting. He had gathered, from a comment or two Templetun had made, that she was no more pleased about this union than he himself had been at first.

Hethe gave a start at his own thoughts. Than he himself had been *at first?* Surely he was not now changing his mind just because the lass was comely? He sneered at the thought. But, much to his shame, while he might not be pleased to marry the tongue that had been carping at him for the last several years, he found himself quite eager to marry this body. Or at least to bed it. He allowed himself a brief moment of fantasy before he recalled his poor deceased wife and realized that if he married this woman, he would have to get her with child eventually. He could take precautions at first, of course—withdrawing, and all those other tiresome things he had learned in order to keep from getting with child the women he had bedded since his wife's death. But, eventually, he would have to produce an heir. Or try to. He winced as Nerissa's screams echoed through his head.

"Shall we?"

Templetun's prompt rescued Hethe from his less than happy thoughts. Straightening abruptly, he led the way up the stairs.

"Lady Tiernay," Templetun greeted, jogging up the last few steps to come abreast of Hethe as he paused before their two hostesses. "May I introduce Lord Hethe of Holden. Lord Holden, this is Lady Helen of Tiernay and her aunt Lady Nell Shambleau."

Hethe moved up another step so that his face and Helen's were on a level, and managed a smile as he gazed into his fiancée's sky blue eyes that matched her gown. Actually, his mouth was responding to his nether regions, and it fashioned itself into a beaming grin of pleasure for the woman—until she smiled back and said, "How do you do?"

His smile died an abrupt death, becoming a dismayed grimace. It wasn't the woman's words that affected him so, but her foul breath that blew at him as she spoke. The shock of it made Hethe take a hasty step backward. He would have tumbled down the stairs had William not steadied him with a fist at his back.

"God's teeth!" he gasped in horror, bringing a perplexed and even slightly offended look to their hostess's face. It also brought him a rather sharp and confused look from Templetun, reminding him of his manners. Forcing a false smile of apology to his lips, Hethe turned his face slightly to avoid the noxious fumes and excused himself by muttering, "Nearly lost my footing."

"Oh, well, you must be careful, my lord," his betrothed breathed at him sweetly. Leaning closer, she snatched his arm through her own, presumably to save him from losing his balance again. She then smiled brightly and sighed gustily into his face. "Such a handsome man. We would not wish you to tumble down the stairs and break your neck! At least, not before the wedding, hmmm?" she teased, her eyes sparkling.

Hethe nearly whimpered. His head was swimming under the onslaught of her poisonous exhalations. Sweet Saint Simon! He had never smelled anything quite so raw or putrid. He hadn't thought it possible for such a scent to come out of a human's mouth. And the fact that it was coming from the sweet bow-shaped lips of the lovely woman before him just seemed to make the horror of it that much worse.

"Shall we go inside?" the woman's aunt suggested cheerfully.

"Aye," Lady Tiernay agreed. "I am sure you gentlemen are ready for a nice mug of ale after your journey." She spoke the words to Hethe, her breath wafting over his face like an ill wind carrying the stench of death. Feeling his stomach roil, Hethe nodded faintly, more than eager for any excuse to move and avoid the situation he was in.

Lord love me, I have to marry this wench, he thought as he hurried rudely up the last step and into the keep, dragging her a step behind. She would be breathing this putrescence at him for the next fifty years or so, he thought faintly, too dismayed to even realize how rude he was being by pulling Lady Tiernay about and leaving her aunt and the others to follow.

"Oh, my! You are thirsty, are you not?" Lady Helen laughed a bit breathlessly, rushing to keep up with him as he led the way in to the trestle tables set up before him.

"Aye. It was a dusty ride," Hethe muttered, breathing in the sweet fresh air of the great hall. He supposed it wasn't really sweet; it carried the odor of fresh rushes and various other things, but to him it was as wondrous as the aroma from a rose.

Lady Helen put on a little speed and reached the table at the same time as Hethe. She immediately set about directing him to a seat, then plopped onto the one beside him and turned to face him.

She was about to speak again, Hethe realized, and he felt himself quiver in anticipation of the stench about to cloud his nostrils. It actually seemed to him as if time slowed down for a moment as the horrified premonition swept over him. He saw her lips part, her mouth open, caught a flash of nice white teeth, even a glimpse of her tongue as she inhaled deeply to propel her words. Then, as he waited helplessly, she blew all those horrid fumes out over him as she spoke.

Through the sudden buzzing in his ears, Hethe thought he heard her say, "I trust your journey was uneventful?" But he wasn't positive. His whole body, every sense he had, was writhing in agony from her fetid breath. Moaning, he turned his head away, sucking untainted air into his lungs as if his very life depended on it. Indeed, at that moment, he felt as if it very well might.

"Is something the matter, my lord?"

He could hear the concern in her voice. That concern was reflected in Templetun's expression as the rest of the party caught up to them. William was at his side at once, his face furrowed with dismay.

"What is it?" his first asked, watching in alarm as Hethe continued to suck in air, almost hyperventilating in an effort to clear his body of Lady Helen's repulsive exhalations. He could actually taste the scent, it was so strong and pungent. Dear God, it was as if she'd been sucking on a dead man's rotting arm.

"I shall go see about the ale," Lady Helen murmured, her voice tight with anxiety. "Perhaps that will help."

Hethe grunted something he hoped would be taken for an affirmative, and heard the rustle of her gown as she stood and moved off.

"I shall help," her aunt said promptly and chased off after her.

It wasn't until the older woman had disappeared into the kitchens behind her niece that Hethe allowed himself to relax. His shoulders immediately slumped, and he sagged at the table. Dear God, not only was he to marry this wench, he had to kiss her during the ceremony! Lord Holden began to gasp air into his lungs, positive he was suffocating to death.

Chapter 3

ELEN managed to contain herself until she had slid through the kitchen doors. Once the doors had closed behind her, however, her control snapped and she bent abruptly at the waist, covering her mouth as little sobbing sounds came from it.

"Oh, my lady!" Ducky, who had been waiting and watching from the kitchens, was at her side at once. "Is he so horrid? Did he say something cruel? He didn't hit you, did he?" She gasped in horror, clutching at Helen's shoulders.

"Nay," Nell assured the maid, having slipped into the kitchen in time to hear her concerned words. "I do not think she is crying."

Shaking her head, Helen slowly straightened, revealing that her aunt was right. Rather than tragic, her expression was filled with hilarity. She was laughing so hard that it was coming out as sobs, and tears of mirth were streaming down her face. "I vow he won't go through with it," she gasped. "The poor man is near dead simply from my breathing on him. Oh, God, Ducky! He went right green!"

The lady's maid's face lost its concern, and on it

hope slowly grew along with excitement. "It's working, then?"

"Working?" Aunt Nell gave a bark of laughter as an answer. "The man is beside himself. He nearly fell backward off the stairs when she spoke to him, and he appeared quite faint just now as I left." She grinned proudly at her niece, her arm sliding around the girl's waist. "Your plan was brilliant, dear. He *will* bow out of the wedding. He is probably telling Templetun so this minute."

"Aye." Helen's grin was full of glee. "And if this isn't enough to do it, then the other things in store for him surely will be. We have won ere the battle has even begun. I can feel it!" She hugged her aunt exuberantly, then stepped back and beamed around at the others in the room. She was so happy at that moment that it didn't even offend her when Ducky put a little distance between them once she was assured that all was well.

"We must move on to the next part of the plan," her aunt proclaimed and glanced at Ducky questioningly. "Are the refreshments ready?"

"Aye. I have seen to them. All is ready," Ducky said quickly, and Helen reached out to squeeze her arm affectionately.

"I knew you would. Now, I suppose we had best return." Her gaze moved to her aunt. "You remember your part?"

Aunt Nell nodded. "Aye. I am to keep Lord Templetun and Holden's first distracted while you torture the Hammer," she announced dutifully, a grin spreading across her face. "Oh, this is the most fun I have had in years. I feel so naughty!"

* * *

"Whatever is the matter?" Templetun cried in alarm, gaping at Hethe's slumped figure. "Are you taking the ague?"

Still swallowing great gulps of air, Hethe shook his head. "It is *her*."

"Her?"

Hethe straightened in time to see his first and the older man exchange befuddled glances. It was William who finally spoke. Moving between him and Lord Templetun, his first put a hand on Hethe's shoulder and murmured, "Well, she is lovely, 'tis true. But not so lovely it should take your breath away like this."

Hethe groaned at the man's words and shook his head. "'Tis her breath," he hissed grimly. "She has the foulest stench about her I have ever encountered. The woman smells as though she feasts on carrion."

Rather than appearing concerned, William actually looked amused. It took the man's knowing smile before Hethe realized that his first thought he was joking. It was one of the insults they had batted around about her over the years, as he recalled. Lady Tiernay was a hag who feasted on the carrion of warriors and tortured the living with her fetid tongue until she could devour them, too.

"Nay," he started to say, then paused on a sigh of despair as the door to the kitchens opened and Lady Helen and her aunt breezed back out.

"The refreshments shall be along directly," their hostess announced, her concerned gaze landing on Hethe. "Are you feeling better, my lord? You have regained some of your color, I see."

Hethe stiffened in his seat as she moved directly toward him. Pausing to stand on the side of him opposite William, she reached down to clasp his chin lightly and lift his face for her inspection. "Aye. You have your color back," she said into his face.

Hethe held his breath. He didn't know what else to do. He could not insult the woman by pulling back or turning away; she was their hostess. She was perfectly lovely and behaving beautifully and obviously didn't have a clue that her breath was so offensive. So he held his breath and waited . . . and waited. A frown began to pluck at her forehead.

"Now, my lord, you are becoming rather flushed."

Hethe's lungs were burning. If she did not let go of him soon and move away so that he could breathe . . .

"Almost blue, in fact. Dear me, you are not well at all," she said into his face.

He had to breathe. There was nothing he could do about it. He was getting light-headed from lack of air. If he could just time it so that he sucked air in when she did, rather than while she was speaking or breathing out, all would be well, he assured himself. He watched, and when she started to breathe in, he released the used air burning his lungs and started to suck in oxygen.

"Oh! That is better," she said at once, and Hethe groaned aloud, unable to stop from turning his head away and gagging. Fortunately, the arrival of the ale seemed to distract her from his insult. "Ah, here we are. Thank you, Ducky."

Hethe managed to regain his composure while she saw to her servants. When a mug of ale was placed before him, he reached automatically for it. It was an excuse not to face her again for a bit. Any excuse was more than welcome. Lifting the mug, he swallowed a mouthful, then promptly spat it out.

Silence fell around him briefly; then Lady Helen was at his side again, appearing quite distressed.

"Is there something amiss, my lord?" she asked. "The ale is not to your liking? Our alewife is usually quite good, but there are times when a batch goes bad and she doesn't catch it, and—"

"There was a bug in my drink," Hethe interrupted. She paused in mid-flutter, blinking at him with confusion.

"A bug?"

"Aye. A rather large, live bug."

"Oh, dear!" She turned to her servant with horror. "Ducky—"

"I'm so sorry, m'lady. I didn't notice any bug."

"Neither did I when I took it from you." She sighed, not seeming to really hold the woman responsible. "Please check the mugs to be sure they are empty in future."

"Of course, m'lady. I am sorry. Shall I fetch another?"

"Aye." Lady Helen turned her apologetic smile back on Hethe and pushed her own mug toward him. "Here, my lord. I can assure you that this mug is bug free and that the ale is fine. I have already tasted it."

Managing a rather tight smile, Hethe took the offered mug.

"I hope that did not put you off. We have the finest alewife in this part of England and are quite proud of that fact," she announced as he peered cautiously into her mug.

Assured that there appeared to be nothing alive in the vessel, Hethe raised it to take a swallow, then nearly spat that out as well. It was politeness alone that made him swallow the rancid beverage. Warm piss couldn't taste worse, he thought with horror, swallowing the flat, yeasty brew. If the lady thought this was good ale, he was in for a long, dry visit. Or perhaps a short, dry visit.

"It is fine ale and no mistaking it," Templetun complimented from behind her, and Hethe's head shot around in shock. The man had even managed a sincere expression as he uttered the lie, Hethe noted with amazement.

"Aye. I daresay your alewife could teach ours a thing or two," William agreed, and Hethe's startled gaze swung to his first. William was never polite. He was a warrior. He spoke plainly and didn't dress anything up with polite lies. Confused, Hethe decided the man was being sarcastic.

"Don't you think, my lord?" William asked.

Hethe nodded solemnly and muttered, "Aye. No doubt Lady Tiernay's alewife could teach ours a thing or two." He lowered his head to peer into his mug with distaste as he added under his breath, "Like how to poison us."

"What was that?" Lady Tiernay asked sweetly, and Hethe glanced up to see that while Lady Helen had not appeared to hear him, both Lord Templetun and William had, and both of them were now staring at him with a combination of dismay and censure.

Hethe shifted under their combined glare, the realization dawning on him slowly that they truly seemed to think the beverage quite tasty. He didn't get to consider that for long, however, because Lady Shambleau was speaking, drawing their attention.

"My lord, I know you wished to have the ceremony when you returned, but Father Purcell is away at the moment and shan't return until tomorrow afternoon. I am sorry. It was unexpected. He was needed to give last rites and—"

"Tomorrow will be soon enough, my lady. Please do not distress yourself. Besides, that gives us time to negotiate the wedding contract." Templetun meant to reassure the woman, but Hethe nearly gave thanks out loud. Another day. He had an extra day's grace. Mayhap in that time he could find a way out of this marriage.

"You must be weary from your journey," Lady Helen commented. "Would you like something to eat right away, or would you prefer to bathe and rest ere the sup?"

Hethe nearly turned to face her, then caught himself and picked up his ale. He pretended to sip at the horrid stuff as an excuse for not facing her while she was addressing him.

"That would be nice, I think," Templetun answered while Hethe busied himself with his tepid, sour drink. "It is not a long ride, but the weather has been exceptionally dry of late. The road was quite dusty. I, for one, should enjoy the chance to bathe some of the dust away and rest ere the meal."

Hethe nodded and grunted his acquiescence, then set his drink aside and stood. He avoided looking directly at either of his companions, but saw both of them gulping down their drinks where they stood. That fact made Hethe frown with confusion. How could they stand the brew? It was disgusting. Shaking his head, he turned to follow Lady Helen and her aunt as they moved to lead the way upstairs.

Tiernay was larger than it had first appeared to Hethe. As they had ridden in, he had noted that, contrary to what he'd suspected, the fiefdom hadn't seemed to suffer any under its new leader. It looked just as green and prosperous as it had when Helen's father had ruled. Its people were plump and apple-cheeked, its orchards in bloom. Still, he didn't expect much in the upper part of the keep. He assumed that there would only be two or three rooms, and that he and William would have to double up until the wedding was over. He was wrong. There were at least half a dozen rooms on the upper level.

"It has been unusually dry of late and I knew your journey would be a dusty one," Lady Helen commented as she started along the hall. "I suspected you might wish to wash some of the dust away on your arrival, so I instructed the maids to prepare baths for each of you when you were spotted by the guards on the wall."

Hethe grunted an unintelligible response as he followed his fiancée and her aunt along the passageway, trailed by William and the king's man.

"My Lord Templetun." Lady Helen smiled at the older man as she paused and opened a door. "This is your room, my lord."

Hethe peered curiously through the door as the older man moved eagerly forward. He peered around the large, well-appointed room, a small fire burning cozily in the fireplace and a steaming tub sitting before it. Then his gaze fell on the pretty young miss pouring water into the tub as Lady Helen announced, "Your maid is Ellie. Ask her, should you need anything, and she will see to it."

"Thank you, my lady." Templetun beamed at all three women as he slipped into the room. "I'm sure I shall be most comfortable."

Lady Helen smiled back, then pulled the door closed and gestured for the other men to follow as

she and her aunt continued sedately to the next
room. "This is your room, Sir William."

She opened the door and smiled encouragingly at
the pretty little maid standing patiently beside another steaming tub. This was another large room,
another cozy fire, and Hethe felt himself relaxing,
forgetting the unpalatable ale as his first started into
the room. William waited patiently as Lady Helen
introduced the maid and repeated the comment that
the girl would see to any needs.

Pulling that door closed, she turned and smiled at
Hethe. "Yours is the next room, my lord."

Hethe followed her eagerly, already anticipating
a soothing bath and the soft hands of a sweet young
girl to scrub his troubles away. He paused politely
when she stopped by the next door. Hethe could almost feel the warm water rinsing away the dust
coating his body. Then the door opened. The first
thing Hethe saw was the maid. It was no sweet
young girl waiting for him. His maid was as old as
Methuselah. A crone. A hag. And a bent, nasty-
looking old hag too, with a wart hanging off her
nose like an apple dangling from a tree branch.

"Dear God," he breathed in dismay.

"This is Maggie. But of course you will remember
her from Holden," Lady Helen said expectantly, and
he was positive he heard a reprimand in her tone.
Unfortunately, he didn't have a clue why, and didn't
really recognize the woman. She looked vaguely familiar, but he could not place her at Holden. He supposed that with that wart of hers he should be able
to, but he had spent little enough time there over the
years. Since she seemed to be waiting for some response, however, he grunted a vague agreement and
nodded to the witch.

"She is the head of the chambermaids here now," Lady Helen continued, and again he felt sure there was some reprimand for him in her words, though he had no idea why and had little time to worry over it as she moved on. "We are very grateful for her knowledge and experience. That experience is why she shall be seeing to your needs personally rather than one of the younger, less knowledgeable girls. We thought it suitable that she serve you, the most important of our guests."

Hethe could hardly fault his soon-to-be wife's reasoning. Still, he wished he could as he thought of the pretty young women now attending William and Lord Templetun.

"Your room is a little smaller than Lord Templetun's and William's," Lady Helen went on cheerfully, "but we felt that as it was only for one night, it would be best to put you here. After the wedding, of course, you will be moved to the master chamber. There seemed little purpose in giving one of the other men this room, then switching them about after the wedding."

Hethe tore his gaze away from the dangling-wart-faced old crone to see that the room was indeed small. Nearly as small as a privy, he saw with dismay. There was barely enough room for the tiny bed it held and the tub both.

"If you require anything, just ask Maggie and she will see to it." Lady Helen's words drew his gaze back to the crone, who offered him a snaggle-toothed smile. He closed his eyes briefly.

"Enjoy your bath, my lord," Lady Helen added with a good cheer that made the hair on the back of Hethe's neck prickle. He turned abruptly to search her expression, but was in time only to see the door close on her and her smiling aunt. The smile did nothing to relieve his sudden anxiety. There had been something almost feral about it, he decided.

Pushing his worries aside, Hethe straightened his shoulders and turned back to face the crone, only to have those shoulders slump again when the crone winked at him.

"Dear God," he breathed miserably to himself.

"There now, your bath is all ready, my lord. Shall I undress you?"

Hethe gave a start, his eyes widening on the old maid as she advanced eagerly toward him. He could have sworn there was a mischievous look in her eyes. Throwing his hands up instinctively, he eyed her warty hands and took a step back.

"Nay, nay. I can do it myself," he said quickly, suddenly wishing he had waited for his squire to come in from overseeing the care of his horse before allowing Lady Helen to urge them above stairs. Then he would have had an excuse to send the woman off.

"A shy one, are ye?" The hag cackled, then busied herself gathering soap and a strip of linen he presumed was for him to dry himself with afterward. He wouldn't want her help with that either, he thought, a shudder running through him at the idea of her hands on his skin. Forcing the thought away, Hethe reluctantly began to undress himself.

"Ye sure ye don't need my help there, my lord?" the hag asked, tossing the linen over her shoulder and turning to survey his slow progress.

Shaking his head, Hethe at last resigned himself to disrobing, removing his sword belt and dirk. The hag stood watching him silently, her eyes lighting with interest as he removed his tunic. With that distracting him, it was rather amazing that he noticed that the room wasn't as warm as it should have been. Scowling, he glanced around the small, cramped quarters until his gaze came up on the window. It was uncovered, allowing a cool afternoon breeze in to fan over him. "There is no covering on that window!"

The wench raised her eyebrows and peered at him in surprise. "On a fine day such as this? Nay, my lord. Besides, it was sent down to have the dust beaten out of it. In your honor," she added, making him feel churlish for complaining.

"Well, then you should have built a fire," he grumbled. "I shall catch a chill getting out of the bath if you do not."

Her eyebrows rose again and she repeated, "On a fine day like this? Well, I thought a strapping figure of a man like yourself wouldn't be needing such fuss. But, if it's a fire you're wantin', I'll build one as soon as I have you settled in your bath."

Mouth flattening in displeasure, Hethe quickly continued to undress. By the time he got to his breeches, her eyes were practically burning holes in his flesh.

Muttering under his breath, Hethe resisted the urge to cover himself like a timid virgin and pushed off his leggings. He left them puddled on the floor and strode quickly to the tub. Awareness that the old witch's eyes were roving over him as he moved, and mostly over the area below his waist, made him pick up speed as he headed for the water. This was ridiculous, really. He had never been shy before. But he could almost feel her eyes burning into his groin—and the sensation was not pleasant. At least not from her. Now, if it had been one of the merry young maids that had been sent to Templetun and William, that might have been a different story. However, this one's gaze just made him rush forward and nearly leap into the tub, slopping water everywhere in his eagerness to hide himself.

"*Yow!*" Hethe popped upward out of the tub with a roar. The water was scorching hot. Blistering. He would be lucky if his balls hadn't been boiled right off. It was hard to tell at that point; every inch of skin that had been submerged in that moment before his nerve endings had reacted was now screaming in agony. Hethe stumbled in his eagerness to get out of the hot water, but he had only pulled one foot out of the tub when the old hag suddenly rushed forward with a pail of cold water. He supposed she was trying for the tub, but her aim was off. The icy liquid sprayed over his still-heated skin, leaving him gasping in shock as it ran down his body, half splashing into the tub, half onto the floor.

"Sorry, my lord. It seemed fine to me. It's the way Her Ladyship likes it. Guess you're a little more delicate." She set down the one pail, grabbed up another, and splashed it too over him as she spoke. "We'll have it right in a minute, though."

A third pail splashed over him. Hethe heaved a resigned sigh and merely reached down to cover his more important bits as she rushed away for more water. *This is a test*, he told himself soothingly. *The good Lord is trying my patience as some sort of lesson.* Hethe feared he was going to fail the test. Putting up one hand defensively as the hag stooped to trade her empty pail for another full one, he roared, "Enough!"

"Cool enough now, is it?" she asked cheerfully, straightening and turning to peer at him.

"Aye." Hethe dropped his hand back to cover his lower regions when her gaze dropped there, then plopped down to sit in the water again. Aye, it was cool enough now. If anything, it was too cool. Tepid at best, he realized with disgust.

"Shall I wash your back for you, m'lord?" the hag asked solicitously.

Hethe's gaze snapped to her as she advanced, soap in one warty hand. "Nay," he said quickly. "In fact, I am quite sure I'll need no more help. You can go."

"Go?" Her eyes widened in surprise. "But who will help you out of the bath?"

"I can get out on my own," he assured her grimly. "Just go. Now."

Shrugging, the old woman sidled to the door, but her eyes never left his free hand once. Hethe supposed she feared he might hit her. He was rather proud that he hadn't.

"If there be anything else you're needing, m'lord."

"Out!" Hethe snapped. He would die of his needs ere calling on the old hag to do anything else for him.

Nodding, she bobbed a curtsy once she was safely beyond his reach and slid from the room.

Sighing, Hethe released the hold he had taken of his most private bits to prevent their further abuse, then peered around the room. It wasn't just smaller than those rooms he had watched Templetun and William disappear into, it was meaner too. There were no tapestries on the walls, nothing to sit on but the bed and a half-broken chair, and, of course, no coverings on the windows or fire in the fireplace. The air was unpleasantly cool on his damp skin.

It was only for one night, he reminded himself soothingly. Tomorrow night he would share the master chamber with his new bride. Lady Foul-Breath. Groaning, he closed his eyes briefly, then sat up with a sigh and glanced about for the soap. The water was not getting any warmer. The sooner he cleaned himself up, the sooner he could get out. Unfortunately, the soap was nowhere to be seen.

Frowning, he started to stand to look about, but just then an image of the hag popped into his mind. She had been still holding the soap when he had ordered her out. He had a very clear image of that soap in her hand as she had exited the room. He also saw, quite clearly, the linen for drying hanging over her shoulder.

Cursing, Hethe sank back into the tub miserably. Pissy ale. A bath hot enough to boil off his balls, then freeze them. No covering on the window. No fire to dry by. A nasty old hag to serve him. And now, no soap or drying linen. And a soon-to-be wife with dragon breath. Oh, he would have to be sure to send his thanks to the king for this.

Straightening from her bent position outside Lord Holden's door, Helen leaned against her aunt helplessly, doing her best to smother her giggles as the door opened before them. Eyes widening as she saw the two women, the exiting Maggie immediately tugged the door closed behind her and urged them all down the hall.

"What were you doing?" Maggie hissed as soon as they were far enough away not to fear being overheard. "Had he seen you—"

"We could not just walk off and leave you alone," Helen explained, her voice bubbling with excited victory. "I was not certain of this part of the plan, and I feared for your safety when you volunteered to do it. But you were *brilliant*," she praised. "And so swift, Maggie. I knew you still had some fire in you."

"Aye," Aunt Nell agreed with a chuckle. "And it was very clever of you to keep yourself out of hitting range."

Maggie wrinkled her nose. "Aye. But I don't think it was necessary. He didn't look moved to hit me. Well, not really," she added at Helen's doubtful look.

"Hmmm," Helen murmured, unconvinced. "Nevertheless, I think we should stick to our plan. It would probably be better if you were out of sight for a bit. A nice visit with your daughter in the village should do the trick. She *is* expecting you?"

"Aye. And she's grateful for it. She's far along with her baby now, you know, and finds working in that tavern of her husband's terribly wearing. She is looking forward to my help, and I to the visit."

"Good, good." Helen patted her hand, then paused and peered at the cloth she held. "Is that—"

Maggie peered down at the linen in her hands and gave a slightly evil grin. "His Lordship's toweling linen. I forgot I had it when he ordered me out," she said blithely. Her lips puckered into an all-out smile at the twinkle in her mistress's eyes.

"You are a wonder, Maggie," Helen marveled, then turned the servant toward the stairs once more. "Off you go now. Have a nice time."

"Aye, m'lady." Maggie started off toward the stairs only to pause and peer back suspiciously at the pair of noblewomen. "You'll not be going back to spy on him, will you? I don't think it would be good for the two of you to be caught lollygagging about outside his room. He isn't in the best of moods at the moment."

"Nay," Aunt Nell agreed with a disappointed sigh. She began to urge Helen after Tiernay's mistress of chambermaids. "It would be best if we steer clear of the man for a bit. We wouldn't want to give him any reason to suspect something is amiss."

"Aye." Helen acquiesced reluctantly and allowed herself to be dragged away. There was nothing she wanted to do more than to go kneel outside the Hammer's door and watch the rest of their plan unfold. She supposed it would be an unnecessary risk, however. "Aye. I suppose I should check on the meal preparations anyway."

"I wish I could be here to see the rest of the evening's plans play out," Maggie chuckled, relaxing now that the others were moving down the stairs with her. A grin split her withered face. "Especially that little trick you taught Goliath. It should be quite entertaining."

"Aye," Helen agreed, but with a little less certainty. She had spent the better part of the last two weeks teaching her dog a very special trick to use against Lord Holden. Now that he was here, however, she was a touch nervous about using it. She didn't think the man would take it at all well. In fact, she decided right there on the spot, she would use it only as a last resort. Her other plots and plans seemed to be doing the trick well enough. Yes, yes. They were doing quite well enough without resorting to *that*.

Chapter 4

HETHE washed himself the best he could with cold water and no soap. Once satisfied he had done all he could, he stood and stepped out of the tub, dripping on the floor until he spotted his tunic. Snatching it up, he used it to wipe most of the water off him, shivering in the breeze from the uncovered window as he did, then hurried to the bed. A nice rest and then a good meal would go a long way toward correcting his mood.

Reaching the bed, he tossed his now-soaked tunic aside with disgust and crawled quickly under the bedclothes, noting that there were no furs to warm him, just the lightest of linens. Muttering about that, he huddled there briefly, trying to warm up, then shifted around, trying to find a comfortable position. Then tried again. And again.

Hethe twisted this way, then that, shifting again and again, but there didn't appear to be a position that might make him comfortable. The damn bed was as lumpy as the old hag's chest had been. Also, it was obviously stuffed with straw. No matter what position he chose, he could feel the straw poking him. He continued to shift about briefly, then forced himself to stop. He had slept on worse beds and in worse conditions, he reminded himself grimly. He had slept on the cold, hard ground a time or two. On horseback. Even in the snow. This problem was not so heinous. Surprising, perhaps, considering the wealth of Tiernay, but nothing that would stop him from sleeping. He could suffer to nap on this lumpy old bed.

Finding his mounting irritation eased at these thoughts, Hethe sighed and forced himself to relax. Though it was only half over, it had been a long day full of disappointments and travail. A little rest would right his world. After some sleep, he would see all these things as the pesky little irritants they were—nothing for a warrior to get all upset about. All was well.

That little lecture allowed him to relax fully. He felt his body ease, his muscles giving up their tension, his mind beginning to drift. He actually even began to doze when he became aware of a mild irritating itch. Shifting sleepily, he scratched his hip, then settled again. A moment later he scratched the spot again, then drew his leg upward so that he could scratch a sudden itch in his calf as well. He had barely satisfied that itch when he was forced to draw his other leg upward to scratch at the ankle.

Hethe was fully awake now. No more dozing for him as he began to scratch the tender spot just above the big toe on his other foot. Dear God, now it was his wrist. Pulling the offending body part out from under the linens where his hand had been busy relieving his other itches, Hethe scratched at it irritably. His scratching slowed to a halt as he saw the small lump forming there with a bloody dot in the center. It was some sort of insect bite, he realized with dismay. He gaped at it briefly until other irritating itches drew his attention; then he stiffened abruptly and pulled the linens aside.

Hethe's eyes widened in horror as he stared at the small black dots hopping about. They were almost impossible to see until they moved. One leapt from the linen to his leg. Another leapt from his ankle to his calf. At first glance he could see more than a dozen of them, leaping and hopping everywhere.

Fleas! The bed was infested with them. And they were making a meal of him! Moved to action, he scrambled to remove himself from his berth, only to get his feet tangled in the linens. It didn't stop his momentum so much as slow it, and Hethe landed on the floor at the side of the bed with a crash.

Cursing, he shoved the linens away with disgust and sat up, his gaze moving warily to the bed as if he expected an entire army of the little hopping pests to be swarming toward him. The fleas were in hiding, however. All there was on the bed now was a small dark brown square. Easing to his feet, he leaned over the mattress to get a better look at the item and stilled. It was a small patch of fur—and it was positively crawling with fleas.

Hethe straightened abruptly but merely stared at the offending item as his mind tried to sort out what it meant. Then his gaze slid around the room, taking in the uncovered window, the lack of fire, the tub of water that had at first been scorching, then cold. He recalled the hag, the ale, the missing linen and even his betrothed's horrific breath. It was all coming together in his mind now to make a sort of sense.

Hethe released a laugh of disbelief. The wench Lady Tiernay wasn't as resigned to this wedding as she would have everyone believe, he realized. She could not refuse the order to marry, or betray her displeasure openly, so she had used strategy and plotted against them all.

Perhaps she had hoped that he would refuse the order. No doubt she hoped he could put an end to it, and she had done all she could to encourage him to do so. But she was wrong; he was as helpless in this as she herself was. Though the wench wasn't all that helpless, he considered wryly. The girl didn't just have a dragon's breath, she had its claws too. That fact actually made Hethe feel better. She was a clever little female.

Had he a choice, as she seemed to think, her plan probably would even have worked. He probably would have done whatever he could to avoid marrying her. She had chosen the best route to deter him. Really. An ugly wife? Well, a man could always blow out the candles or close his eyes. A fat wife? Well, again, one could close his eyes . . . besides, plump women had their benefits. They made a soft pillow for a man. A shrewish or abusive wife could be beaten or put in the dunking chair to encourage a more pleasant nature. But a beautiful bride with such an offensive odor? That was enough to make any man cry. Blowing the candles out and closing his eyes would never have fixed that. Nor would thirty gallons of rosewater.

Aye, she was clever, so it seemed there were brains to go with her beauty. But what to do about it? He supposed he could confront her, tell her he couldn't refuse the king's order and that she was wasting her time. Hethe grimaced at the thought. He would most likely flub that. Hethe didn't like confrontations—verbal ones anyway. He could handle a sword as if he had been born with it in his hand, and was never one to shirk from battle, but arguments were another matter. His tongue ever seemed to tangle when verbal conflicts erupted. Hethe's father had had a tongue as sharp as a knife and had lashed him with it repeatedly during his youth. And he had been beaten when he'd tried to respond in kind. By the time Hethe had become an adult, his tongue just seemed a flaccid piece of meat in his mouth when it came to arguing his case. He knew what he wanted to say, but his brain never seemed able to put it into words.

He had once found it terribly frustrating. He supposed he still did, but, mostly, he just avoided verbal confrontations as much as possible and relied on his battle skills. And that was what he would do now, he decided suddenly.

Despite having been married before, Hethe was not all that experienced a husband. But this—this was war, and if there was one thing the Lord of Holden knew a lot about, it was war.

Hethe began to chuckle to himself, until a constant irritating itching managed to make its way through his thoughts. Sighing, he turned away from the bed and moved to the broken chair. There he could itch in some mild comfort as he planned his strategy.

Helen was just coming out of the kitchens when she spotted Lord Holden descending the stairs to the great hall. She hesitated briefly, wishing her aunt were around, but the woman had retired for a small rest before "the real battle began," as she had put it. Managing to paste a surprised look on her face— something she had practiced during the days while they had been awaiting his arrival—she rushed to the bottom of the stairs, peering up at him in concerned amazement.

"Is there something wrong, my lord? Could you not sleep?"

Hethe smiled at her widely. "I did not even try. My bath invigorated me and I found myself wide awake."

Helen felt her smile slip, but she quickly forced it back into place. "Oh. Well . . . isn't that nice? Did you—? Would you—?" She glanced briefly around the empty great hall, struggling with her disappointment at his missing what she considered the best part of her plot—his flea-ridden bed. Still, that just meant he would encounter the fleas later this evening, she reassured herself, then tried to think up something to distract him until mealtime. "A drink?" she offered at last, it being the only thing to come to mind at the moment. Helen did hate when there were variations in her plans. In fact, it quite annoyed her that the man hadn't simply gone to bed as expected.

"My, yes. Some more of that fine ale would be wonderful."

Helen's head snapped around at her guest's claim. Fine ale? God's garters! Didn't the man have any taste? She was certain her plan had gone perfectly earlier. Both his mug and hers had held stuff that had turned and been allowed to go flat. The bug he'd found had been placed deliberately, though they had expected Lord Holden to see it, not nearly drink the thing. She had planned to offer him her mug, too, to make sure he didn't realize that Templetun and William were drinking a different brew entirely.

Now, the man was describing her nasty trick as fine ale, and, well—

"Is there something wrong, my lady?"

Giving a start, Helen flushed as she realized that she had been standing there ruminating for far too long. Clearing her throat, she forced a smile and started across the room. "Nay, my lord. Pray, seat yourself, and I shall call for servants to fetch you some ale."

She didn't watch to see if he listened; she simply hurried to the door to the kitchens and pushed her way inside. Vexed, she frowned mightily as soon as the door closed behind her.

"My lady?" Ducky was at her side in an instant, concern covering her face. "Has something happened?"

"Aye. Lord Holden wants some more of our *fine ale*." Her words were grim, and Ducky's eyes widened in amazement.

"Fine ale? And why is he not resting ere the sup?"

"He is not tired," Helen answered dryly, then suddenly asked, "Did you remove the fur from his bed?" When the servant merely looked uncertain, Helen sighed. Maybe it had been good fortune that he had not wanted to sleep; maybe they had been pushing things too far. Lord Holden might have discovered the fur and put things together had he tried to take a nap. "You had best go check on it. And have someone fetch him some ale. I shall see if I cannot convince him he is tired after all."

"How?" Ducky asked with amazement.

Helen grimaced. "How, indeed?" she muttered, and started to push her way back out of the kitchens, only to pause and glance back. Perhaps now was the time to resort to the trick she'd taught her dog. "Ducky," she began. "I let Goliath outside. Fetch him back and bring him to me."

The maid swallowed thickly at the order, her eyes round and worried. She knew what Helen planned. "Oh, my lady. Do you think you should—"

"Yes," Helen said firmly. "I do." She pasted a bright smile on her face, then she stepped back into the hall. Returning swiftly to the main table, she recalled her fetid breath, and her smile became a little more natural. Of course! She might not need to use her trick. She merely had to talk to Hethe for a few moments, then he would be as eager to escape to his room as he had been earlier. Perhaps she might even make him wish to flee the keep without unleashing Goliath.

But was her bad breath fading? she wondered. Ducky had not turned away in disgust during their conference. She could not expect to win a battle if her weapon was blunted. Spinning abruptly, she hurried back to the kitchens. She would only use the dog if it looked like there was no other way.

Hethe settled himself down to wait at the trestle tables. After a few minutes, the sound of the door to the kitchens swinging open made him glance over his shoulder. Lady Helen came out smiling brightly, then paused halfway to the tables, her smile fading. After the barest hesitation, she whirled away and hurried back into the kitchens. He had no idea what sent her running back out of the hall, but he suspected that it was something to do with this battle they were waging. And they *were* waging war now, though she might not realize that he had joined the fray rather than fallen victim to it.

Hethe's strategy was a simple one. Negate everything. He would tell her that the ale was fine, her breath was like the sweetest flower, and the maid she had chosen for him had proven as capable as she should be. Lying on his bed was like sleeping on a cloud, and he was truly enjoying the fresh air the lack of window covering allowed into his room. He was going to love everything if it killed him.

The worst of it was that he was going to have to keep from trying to escape the assault of her breath. No more turning his head away. No more holding his breath. He was a man. A warrior. He could do it, he encouraged himself grimly, then glanced over his shoulder at the sound of the kitchen door again opening.

Lady Helen, another brilliant smile widening her lips, hurried toward him as if she couldn't bear to be out of his presence. *Clever little witch*, he thought with amusement. *Two can play at this game.*

Standing abruptly, he hurried to meet her, smirking inwardly at her startled reaction before she controlled it. He supposed that, to anyone watching, they might have looked like eager lovers as he grasped her hand and smiled gently down on her. He was especially proud of the fact that his smile didn't falter when she lifted her gaze and very deliberately breathed into his face. *God's teeth!* She must have gone back to the kitchen for a refresher of whatever foul mixture she used to taint her breath. His eyes began to water from the assault. Ducking his head to hide his reaction, he brushed a kiss over his fiancée's knuckles that would have made a court gallant proud.

The action obviously caught her by surprise. He heard her swallow as he straightened, and her face held a rather stunned expression. Smiling widely, Hethe shifted and slid one arm around her waist, using it and the hand he still held her with to guide her to the table.

"I must tell you, my lady," he murmured as he saw her seated and cozied up next to him on the bench. "I am pleasantly surprised by all I have found here."

Her eyes widened in a sort of incredulous horror. "You are?"

"Aye. Such a fine holding and a lovely bride." He gave her one of those hot, smarmy looks he had seen other men turn on the women they loved or desired. He wasn't sure it was working, however. The woman blinked, certainly, swaying closer, but that could be just so that she could breathe at him more effectively. He struggled on, acting the swain. "I am the most fortunate of men. There cannot be a more perfect woman in England than you."

"No?" There definitely was suspicion in her eyes now, he realized and just managed to contain a grimace. He needed to distract her. Some flowery compliments would be needed, he decided. Unfortunately, Hethe was the direct sort. He had never bothered with such foolishness before. And wouldn't now, he decided suddenly, an idea taking form in his head. He would insult her with compliments. Oh, this would be fun.

"No. Your hair is . . . yellow," he began sweetly, his smile widening at her confused expression before he added, "Like those little plants my horse tramples in my meadow."

She made a choking sound that might have been disbelief, but might just as easily have been amusement. She was definitely distracted. The suspicion was fading from her eyes. With this success, he decided to press his attack. "And your eyes are big . . . like a cow's. Only they aren't the same color as a cow's, of course," he hurried on as she made a strangling sound in her throat. "Cows usually have brown eyes, and yours are a much nicer—er—"

He hesitated briefly as he gazed into her eyes. They had appeared as blue as the sky outside when he had first met her. Now they seemed to be a greenish blue. "Well, they aren't brown," he said at last.

"Really, my lord," she began, but Hethe jumped in with the killing blow.

"And your breath is as sweet as the sweetest wine."

He was quite pleased to see her face flush, a choked sound slipping from her lips before she bowed her head. He couldn't see her expression then, but he could see that her hands were clenched in her lap. Victory! He was just celebrating the success of his endeavor when she suddenly lifted her head again. His own gaze narrowed as he saw the fire shining in her eyes. She was mad, all right, he realized, and felt a new wariness creep over him. There was good reason for it, too, he realized, when she suddenly leaned closer and sighed gustily into his face.

"Oh, my lord, you are too kind. Do I *really* have breath like fine wine?"

Groaning inwardly, Hethe barely managed to keep down the spoiled ale he had drunk earlier and forced his smile to widen. "Aye. Like the finest aged wine." Old and moldering after having sat about for years, he added silently, but was pleased with how smoothly and easily he spouted his lies. He sat a little straighter. *Damn, I'm good*, he thought and nearly burst out laughing at the vexation that flashed across Lady Helen's face.

She was obviously displeased. Any last lingering doubt that everything he had encountered was part of some plan she had to rid herself of him was quickly squelched. Aye, this was war she was waging. But he was going to win it. Hethe had never lost a war. A battle, perhaps, but never a war. . . . Yet.

He had barely finished his self-congratulations when the main doors of the keep opened and Lady Helen's servant entered with the great mangy dog that had been sitting on the steps when they arrived. The maid glanced at where Hethe and Helen sat at the table with what Hethe judged to be trepidation, then released the wolfhound and quickly backed out of the keep, pulling the door closed behind her.

If the servant's expression had not warned him that something was amiss, the way Lady Helen instantly relaxed and began to smile as she spotted the animal was a warning in itself.

"Oh look! It is Goliath. You two should meet, my lord." She got to her feet, smiling as the dog started toward them, then moved forward herself to meet him. "Come."

Hethe hesitated, suspecting that he would be sorry should he follow her, but his plan called for him to be as sickeningly agreeable as he could. Deciding that if she had done something foul like train the beast to bite him on command, he would break the animal's thick neck, he got cautiously to his feet to join her. He knew his mistake the moment her smile widened in spiteful satisfaction.

"Look, Goliath! It is Lord Holden!" she cried brightly, reaching out to tap Hethe's arm. The dog gave an excited bark and raced forward. For one brief moment, Hethe was sure she had indeed trained the beast to attack him. The dog launched itself forward. Hethe was a bare breath away from grasping the dog's stupid, tongue-lolling head and breaking his neck with a twist when Helen cooed gleefully from beside him.

"Oh look, he likes you! Is that not nice?"

Hethe stilled then and focused on what the animal was doing. Goliath was not in the midst of attacking him at all. At least, not a snapping kind of attack. His betrothed's damned dog was humping him!

Chapter 5

HETHE was exhausted when he made his way below stairs the next morning. His plans had gone forward well enough the day before. At least they had after Goliath's show of affection, he thought with disgust. He had never been so angry in his life as he had been at that moment. Even now, he felt sure he would have given up his plans, gone against his nature, and throttled Lady Helen to within an inch of her life if Lord Templetun had not chosen that moment to make his way down to the great hall.

The first to spot him, Lady Helen had urged Goliath off Hethe's stiff leg and moved quickly to the tables to take a seat, her randy hellhound settling himself at her feet. Hethe had stood rigid and furious, glowering at her back as he tried to rein in his temper.

Templetun had nearly reached him by the time he composed himself. Promising himself he would get Lady Tiernay back for her nasty trick, he had greeted the king's man coldly, then returned to the table with a renewed determination to bury his betrothed under false sweetness. Which is exactly what he did:

Showered her with compliments of a sort on her breath, the food, the ale, and all the other disgusting weapons of this battle that he was sure was meant to drive him off. In the meantime, his "compliments" for everything else were poorly disguised insults.

The shine to her hair looked almost as if she greased it, he had claimed, watching with interest and anticipation as her eyes had flared. Her lips looked almost bee-stung they were so swollen and ripe. Overripe, even . . . like fruit about to fall off a tree . . . How old was she?

He chuckled wearily as he recalled her outrage at that. She had not taken comments on her age well at all. It seemed she was sensitive about that subject. In truth, she should have been married and had three or four babes by now. Such was the way of things. But she was still single at twenty years and apparently feeling her age. He had almost felt guilty using it against her—especially considering the irony regarding his own young wife's death—but then he'd realized he was scratching absently at a bite on his calf, and his guilt fled as he recalled the flea patch in his bed.

He grimaced now, thinking about it. He'd tossed the flea-bearing fur out the window before coming below after his bath, hoping that action would remove the problem, but when he had retired later and crept warily into bed, he had nonetheless found himself nearly driven mad with scratching. Whether the itching was due to any fleas still present in the bed or due to the earlier bites becoming more irritated now that they were free from his clothes and vulnerable to the open air, or because of his own imagination, he didn't know, but it had sent him

tripping quickly out of the bed. He had spent the
night sleeping dressed and seated in the cracked
chair by his cold fireplace, without even a linen or
fur to cover him since they were all likely as flea-
infested as the bed.

He had not slept well or comfortably. He was
tired, his neck was sore from being twisted at an
odd angle all night, and his mouth had a nasty taste
to it from all that rotten food he had been forced to
eat and the pissy ale he had drunk. Which had been
part of his plan as well, to eat and even seem to sa-
vor the rotten food they served him. His stomach
had reviled him for it ever since, threatening to rebel
and generally churning in displeasure. The only con-
solation Hethe could find was that his feigned pleasure had first stunned, then frustrated and infuriated
his adversary. Lady Helen had been clenching her
hands and teeth so tightly through most of last evening that he would not be surprised if she had
scourged the flesh of her palms and ground the tops
of her teeth away. Aye, his campaign was a complete
success, or would be if it weren't such a torture to
endure. But he had put some of his sleeplessness to
good use last night and come up with a new campaign, one that promised to be less punishing . . . on
himself at any rate.

Hethe had just reached the bottom step when the
door to the kitchens opened and Lady Helen came
out. Her appearance was brief. The moment she
spotted him, she spun about and hurried back to
the kitchens. Hethe heaved a sigh and headed for
the table where a goodly portion of the rest of the
castle appeared to be breaking their fast. He knew
without a doubt that she was refreshing herself
with whatever putrescence she used to make her

breath so bad. She had done so several times the night before, slipping away to the kitchens, only to return shortly, the potency of her breath reinforced.

At least, Hethe consoled himself, she seemed to find no more pleasure in the scent than he himself did. He was positive he had caught a glimpse of misery on her face a time or two when she had been slow to redon her ever-present smile on her way back out of the kitchens.

Preparing himself for the onslaught of her dragon breath when she returned, Hethe seated himself beside a gorging Templetun. The man had been doing little else but stuffing his skinny face since their arrival. That, if nothing else, reassured Hethe that the food here was not as bad as what he had been served. The king's man appeared to enjoy it greatly. Templetun was also completely oblivious to the silent struggle being waged beneath his very nose, and Lady Shambleau was the reason. It had not got past Hethe's notice that his fiancée's aunt was forever busy distracting the man, and William, too, from what went on at the table around them. And she was doing a fine job of it. Templetun was kept so knotted up and William so amused by her sharp-tongued comments to the king's man that neither of them had had a chance to catch even a whiff of Lady Helen's putrid breath, or to notice Hethe's insulting retaliations. Which was all for the best, he supposed. He really didn't wish everyone to be aware that she was so averse to marrying him that she would take such drastic measures. He had his pride, after all.

A pride that was rather tattered at the moment, he realized with some self-derision as he reached out to snag hunks of Templetun's cheese and bread while the man was distracted talking to Lady Shambleau. The courtier glanced back to his food just in time to catch him at his pilfering, but Hethe determinedly ignored the man's startled glance and raised the cheese eagerly to his mouth. This was the only chance he would have for real food for the rest of the day, he was sure. Once Lady Helen returned from the kitchens . . .

"Oh, nay, my lord!" The cheese was touching Hethe's lips when he heard the shriek, his tongue just catching the first hint of its sweet taste. He almost groaned aloud at the loss as she snatched away the first edible morsel he had laid hands on since arriving.

"Nay!" she went on, all happy concern. "There will be no bread and cheese for my lord. Nay. I have a special surprise for you."

"A surprise?" Hethe asked warily. He was hardly comforted to see that his reaction sparked some mysterious pleasure in her.

"Aye. I asked Sir William what your favorite breakfast was, and then I made it for you," she announced. She made a quick motion and plopped a tray of pastries before him.

Hethe blinked in surprise at the offering. They looked perfect. Absolutely delicious. They smelled good too. And these pastries were his favorite. He glanced warily from the food to her innocently smiling face. She had gone to the trouble of making them for him herself? For one desperately hungry moment, he allowed himself to believe that he might have been wrong about her intentions. Perhaps he had misunderstood, and she was not waging war against him. Perhaps she was truly trying to impress him!

The thought died an abrupt death as Hethe picked up one of the confections and bit into it. Or tried to bite into it. He nearly snapped a tooth off in the effort. Good God! It was as hard as a rock! It was also salty and dry, he learned as the bite he had taken began to slowly dissolve inside his mouth.

"How are they?" she asked with almost believable anxiety, then added uncertainly, "This was my first effort at baking. Cook did not like the idea of my fussing about in his kitchen, but he relented. Is it all right?" When Hethe hesitated, unable to answer because he was still rolling the bit of rock-hard pastry around in his mouth, afraid to swallow, she began to wring her hands in an excellent portrayal of an anxious betrothed. "You don't like them! Oh I knew it was a mistake, but I wanted so much to do something to please you and—"

"I *love* them," Hethe abruptly lied to silence her. The woman was carrying on so, Templetun had started to glare at him for upsetting her. Which no doubt had been her plan. She was trying to make him look bad in front of the king's chaplain. No doubt, should he not eat the damn things, she would manage to make him look like some sort of uncaring beast. Hethe made a face, then swallowed his first bite determinedly. A heartbeat later he was grabbing up the ale she had set on the table nearby. The pebble-like bite of sweet bread had got stuck halfway down his throat, and he was hoping to wash it down with the ale. The ale was warm, flat, and tasted like urine, of course, but it did the trick and loosened the bit of food lodged in his esophagus. He was almost sure he felt it splash in his stomach, rather like a stone dropping into a well.

"Really? You really like it?" she asked, but he

thought her irritation must be affecting her acting abilities, because she appeared to be overplaying her anxiety. Clearing his throat, he took a deep breath in preparation of facing her and turned to beam blindingly at her. "Aye, my lady. They are quite delicious. Just the way I like them, in fact."

"Oh." Her jaw tightened, and he caught a flash of fury in her eyes before she managed to cover it. That was when the idea struck him. He acted on it at once.

"But I mustn't be greedy and hog them all to myself. Surely you will join me? They are the result of your hard efforts, after all." He pushed the tray toward her.

"Oh, nay, my lord. I made them for you." She pushed the tray back.

"Oh, come now," he cajoled, taking one of the pastries and offering it up to her. "You should try your own handiwork."

"Oh, nay, I—" She floundered briefly, then suddenly smiled widely at him. "I have already eaten and am too full to have more. They are rather large."

Hethe's eyes narrowed. "Aye. They are," he agreed slowly, but he wasn't going to be put off. "Perhaps just a taste, then."

While she watched with growing consternation, he made a great show of attempting, and failing, to break a piece off. He saw her panicked glance toward her aunt and knew exactly what that woman intended when she began to babble at Lord Templetun, also drawing William's attention away from what Hethe was doing by pulling him into the conversation. Hethe let her get away with the distracting tactics and simply kept trying to snap the sweet bread in half. When he found he couldn't, he resorted to taking it in both hands and smashing the center of the roll violently and repeatedly against the table. It took three solid thumps before the item snapped in half. Helen was flushed bright red by the time he finished, though whether from anger or embarrassment, he couldn't say. He didn't much care, either; he just smiled sweetly and silently offered the larger half to her.

"Oh, I—" Lady Tiernay glanced around, obviously seeking an escape.

"Perhaps Lord Templetun would care to have some, then?" he suggested quietly, and Helen froze, her eyes going round as plates. Some of the color fading from her face, she reached out and snatched the food from his hand.

Hethe smiled in satisfaction as she attempted to bite off a chunk. None broke free, and she winced with the effort.

"You know, I find it quite amazing that a lady would trouble herself to cook," Hethe commented as she continued to gnaw grimly at the pastry.

Using the need to speak as an excuse to avoid ruining her teeth, his betrothed lowered the sweet roll and smiled at him coldly. "Well, it pleased me greatly to do so for you. In fact, I am hoping once we are married that I might get to cook for you often."

Hethe turned his head away and coughed to avoid laughing out loud at the obvious threat. For a moment, the false smiles had been dropped; she had shown her teeth. And he found them adorable. He had to bite his lip to keep from laughing again when he turned back to catch his betrothed attempting to pass off the rock-hard treat on her big, oafish dog—but the beast would have none of it.

Hethe was about to comment on her not eating

her pastry when a new idea struck him. While she was distracted by trying to bribe her pet into saving her from her own cooking, he quickly switched his ale mug for hers. He had barely finished the task when she turned back to the table, her expression one of utter annoyance.

"Something amiss?" he asked easily, taking in her irritation-flushed face with feigned concern.

Apparently too peeved to bother keeping up her charade of the dutiful bride-to-be, she ignored him, her mouth tightening with frustration as she reached for her ale.

Hethe bit his lip when she promptly choked on the liquid and gasped.

"Something wrong with your drink?" he asked, all concern as she turned narrowed eyes on him suspiciously. Smiling at her, Hethe raised his own mug to his lips and savored a sip. Much to his surprise, it really was excellent. "Mmmm. I know I told you this yesterday, but truly you have the finest alewife in northern England, I am sure."

"You—" she began angrily, only to pause when Lord Templetun rose from the table and turned to them to speak.

"Lady Shambleau and I are going to retire to the church to negotiate the marriage contracts. I trust you wish me to handle this on your side, Lord Holden? You shall have final approval, of course."

Hethe hesitated, then smiled suddenly. "Certainly. That will give Lady Tiernay and me the chance to become better acquainted. We could tour the estate and perhaps have a nice little picnic ere returning."

Lady Helen's eyes widened in horror at the suggestion, and she opened her mouth, probably to protest, but Lord Templetun forestalled her.

"A charming idea," he approved, nodding his head. "Aye. I doubt this will take all morning, but I see no reason why you shouldn't enjoy some time together. This afternoon is early enough for the wedding."

Helen's mouth snapped closed; then a somewhat forced smile stretched her lips as she stood. "Lovely. I shall just arrange with Cook to prepare a picnic."

She was gone before Hethe could suggest that something edible would be nice. Turning to glance at Lady Shambleau as Templetun urged the woman to her feet, Hethe caught the concerned expression on her face. He arched an eyebrow at the lady. Likely she was in on her niece's plot, but he offered her reassurance anyway. "Lady Helen will be perfectly safe with me, my lady. We shall ride about the estate, visit a tenant or two, then stop for a picnic. I may even pick a flower or two for her along the way."

Lady Shambleau's eyes widened at that and she seemed about to speak, but Lord Templetun was growing impatient and took her arm, turning her away from the table.

"Come along. They shall be fine," he said impatiently. He urged her toward the keep doors.

"Oh, but . . . I should tell him Helen has a terrible reaction to posies. They make her eyes puffy and her nose run."

"I am sure Lady Helen will inform him of that should the situation arise."

"Nay. She will not. She is far too stubborn to admit something like that to *him*."

"Nonsense." Lord Templetun continued determinedly toward the door. "Besides, I suspect Lord Holden was speaking in jest when he mentioned picking flowers. He doesn't seem to me to be the sort."

Hethe watched the couple disappear through the keep doors, his mind taken up with what he had heard. Templetun had been right, of course. Hethe had been speaking in jest when he had mentioned plucking flowers. He had never in his life done anything of the kind—not even as a child. But now he considered the possibility seriously.

"So, she is allergic to posies," he murmured to himself, tucking the information away for strategic consideration later, then spotted his first approaching the table. "William, I have a small task for you."

Chapter 6

"HE knows!" Helen cried as the kitchen doors swung closed behind her.

Ducky was at her side at once, alarm all over her face. "Nay!"

"Aye. He switched his ale for mine. He knows what we are about."

"Oh, dear," the lady's maid breathed, beginning to worry her lower lip. "Is he very angry?"

Helen hesitated, her eyebrows furrowing with confusion. "I do not know," she admitted at last on a sigh. "He doesn't seem angry. At least, I do not think he does. But now he is talking about getting acquainted and going on a tour, having a picnic."

"A picnic?" Ducky's eyes widened.

"Aye. Have Cook pack a picnic, but only enough for one. Tell him to make it vile, as vile as he can. Vile enough to have this wedding called off by the time Lord Holden has finished it."

"You are not going?"

"Aye. I'm going," Helen answered, but wasn't herself too certain it was a good idea.

"Alone?" Ducky asked anxiously.

Helen grimaced at the question, her fear growing.

If Lord Holden knew what they had been up to with the poor food, worse ale, and her bad breath, not to mention everything else—and she was sure he did know—the evil man might very well be taking her out to drown her in the river. That would remove the necessity of his refusing to marry her.

For a moment, Helen considered the possibility of taking nice food along on the picnic, a veritable feast, and of being sweet and simpering. But, in truth, that wasn't her style. Besides, it was too late to stray from her plan now. He would recognize any retreat as fear of his reaction, and that would give him an advantage. Nay, she would maintain her resolve. For good or ill, she would follow her plan to whatever final battle it brought about. She just hoped she survived.

"And this, of course, is little Nelly. Her real name is Helen—she was named after me—but everyone uses the nickname Nelly for her, just as they do my aunt."

Hethe caught the baby Lady Helen gaily shoved at him, then held it out at arm's length, staring at it with a sort of horrified disgust. Little Nelly was a horror to behold. Her face was a mess of some sort of jam, her diaper, which was giving off a smell not too dissimilar to that of his betrothed at the moment, was slipping from her chubby little body, and she was reaching out with sticky, grasping little fingers at anything she could get her hands on. Fortunately, holding her as he was, the little beggar's options were limited. Hethe had learned after the first two babies Helen had thrust upon him that they seemed to like to hold his hair and yank for all they were worth. That had been about ten cottages and ten infants ago.

It seemed to Hethe that either Tiernay was amazingly prolific in producing babies or Lady Tiernay was only stopping at those cottages with babies in them so she could torture him. For that was what she was doing. He supposed it was his own fault. He had been unprepared for the first child she had forced on him and had let his horror and discomfort show. A good battle strategist, Lady Helen had promptly made use of his weakness. He had to admire her for that. In fact, if he hadn't been piddled, spat and vomited upon repeatedly during this hellish tour, he surely would have admired her. However, right at the moment, all he wanted was revenge. And he had decided on how to get it, too.

"Time for our picnic!" he announced abruptly, thrusting the baby at its mother and turning to remount his horse.

"Oh! But we have so many more cottages to visit," Helen protested.

"Another time. It is growing late."

"It is only mid-morning," she pointed out dryly.

Hethe reluctantly followed her gesture at the sun in the sky and grimaced. It wasn't yet overhead, only halfway there. Which made it about ten. He could have sworn it was nearly the supper hour. The short while since they had left the castle had certainly passed slowly enough for it to be. With nothing else to say, he offered the only excuse he had. "I am hungry."

It silenced her. In fact, the declaration seemed to please her mightily. Smiling suddenly, she moved to her horse and mounted. "Well, then surely we must feed you."

Hethe's gaze narrowed. Her smug expression made it quite plain that she did not plan for him to enjoy the upcoming meal. Considering that he had only one petrified bite of pastry rolling about in his empty stomach, the idea did not much please him.

If it was true that the way to a man's heart was through his stomach, then it was also true that a surefire way to rile a man up was to stand between him and sustenance. Hethe was hungry, and mean with it. If there had been any guilt attached to the next strategy in his plan, it evaporated right there on the spot. Lady Tiernay deserved what she was about to get.

"Here will do, I imagine. What do you think?"

"Hmm. Fine," Helen murmured absently, busy with the task that had consumed her since leaving the last cottage: trying to think up another way to torture the man on the horse beside her. Using the babies had been inspired. She had noticed his discomfort around the children at the first cottage they had stopped at, and she had used that to her advantage from then on. But his decision to stop for their picnic put an end to her fun, and she required something else to make the bastard miserable. Of course, the food she'd brought would go a long way toward that, but she wanted something more impressive and memorable for this excursion. She needed something that would finally push him into refusing to marry her, yet not make him angry enough to do her bodily harm. Even better would be to find something for which he could not blame her, something he could not be sure she had done on purpose. It was a tricky business, and it was consuming her thoughts as she dismounted and removed the blanket she had brought for them to sit on.

Hethe was there at once to take it from her.

Relinquishing the covering, Helen turned back to unhook the sack of food the cook had prepared, then followed her fiancé silently to the center of the clearing. She waited patiently as he unfolded the blanket and shook it out several times before finishing with his fussing and allowing it to lie flat. He stood back then, to let her settle on it, before easing down to sit across from her, his expression full of expectation. Helen felt her eyes narrow briefly, then shrugged inwardly and forced a smile. He wanted to eat? Let him eat.

Her smile becoming more natural, Helen opened the chef's sack and reached inside. The first thing she drew out appeared to be a small hunk of cheese wrapped in thin linen. It was only as she pulled it fully out of the bag that she noticed the scent wafting from it—one with which she was becoming quite familiar. The smell made Helen wonder what the contents of that special brew Ducky had concocted for her included. Not this cheese itself, she didn't think, because she hadn't noticed any chunks in the liquid Ducky had kept handing to her, though the beverage was thick in consistency. Perhaps she used the oil off of it, Helen considered as she set the cheese out on the blanket between herself and Hethe. Or perhaps it was cream gone bad. If that was the case, no wonder her stomach roiled after she drank it.

Forgetting her role, Helen wrinkled her nose briefly, then forced the expression away, determinedly plastering a smile back on her face. The next thing out of the bag was one of the sweet rolls she had claimed to have made. Really, Cook had made them, complaining the whole while.

The next thing she came up with was some rancid

cooked meat. Not a very large piece, just an edge really, probably one of the bits Cook cut off some slab of meat before serving it. Helen laid that on the blanket, too, then made a big deal of digging about expectantly inside the now empty bag.

"Oh, dear," she murmured with poorly feigned dismay.

Acting concerned, Hethe raised his eyebrows. "Is something the matter?"

"Well, it looks as if Cook misunder—achoo!" Caught by surprise by her sneeze, Helen covered her mouth belatedly and blinked several times before shaking her head and continuing. "Cook must have thought I meant to picnic alone. He sent only enough for—achoo!"

"For one?" Hethe suggested, solicitously producing a small square of linen for her to blow her nose.

"Aye." Taking the linen, Helen paused to do so.

"Oh, dear, oh, dear," Hethe murmured, adding a "Bless you" when she sneezed again.

"Fortunately," Helen began, frowning as she noticed that her eyes were becoming agitated and itchy. "Fortunately, I am not—achoo!"

"Hungry?" Hethe murmured, sounding unsurprised.

"Aye," she muttered, her voice coming out thick as she became aware of a scratchiness in it. "So you must go ahead—achoo! And eat—achoo! I shall just—achoo!"

Hethe was silent through another round of her nose-blowing before saying, "You appear to be suffering somewhat. Perhaps we should return to the keep rather than picnic."

Helen seriously considered his offer for a moment. She was having a terrible reaction to something. She only reacted this way to posies as a rule, but when she glanced around she did not see any. Still, there must be some nearby, she thought unhappily as another round of sneezing overtook her. Her gaze fell on the vile meal she had spread out between them, and she stiffened her back. She would see him suffer through it before they returned. Her itchy, irritated eyes and a couple of sneezes were nothing next to the intestinal discomfort he was about to suffer.

"Nay," she said, then turned her head to sneeze before continuing. "It would be a pity to let this f-f-f—achoo!—fine meal go to—achoo!—waste. I am content to watch you eat before we re—achoo!—turn."

"How sweet of you, Lady Helen. But there is no need for you to simply sit and watch. I could not leave you hungry while I ate."

"Oh, I—" Helen began quickly to make excuses, but he overrode her words.

"Is it not fortunate, therefore, that I thought to send William down to the village tavern to fetch a meal just in case something of the like occurred?" Presenting her with a smile as sweet as any she herself had produced, he tugged a much larger sack she had not noticed from the edge of their blanket. Then, while Helen watched in wide-eyed horror, he began to pull item after item out of the bag. The first item was roast chicken. And not just a leg or a breast, but an entire roast chicken, golden brown and succulent. Helen's mouth actually began to water at the sight of it. Next came a hunk of cheese that looked solid and sweet compared to her oily, crumbling mess. A loaf of bread followed, soft and fresh, then three roasted potatoes all cooked to perfection.

"I am sure they will not be as tasty as your chef's fine meal," he went on as Helen peered at the food and licked her lips. "But I shall suffer this lesser fare while you enjoy your own cook's repast."

Hearing the mocking tone of his voice, Helen slowly raised her eyes to his. There was no mistaking the triumph in his gaze.

The great hall was full of people eating their midday meal when Hethe escorted Helen back to Tiernay Castle. He led her, because by that time her eyes were quite puffy, which obstructed her vision somewhat. They were arriving in the middle of the meal, despite having stopped to eat some two hours before, because it had taken Hethe that long to consume every last scrap of the food William had purchased from the tavern. And he *had* consumed it all. There hadn't been a chicken bone with a nibble of meat left on it, or even a crumb from the loaf of bread left by the time he was done.

The glutton, Helen thought bitterly. He hadn't offered her even a bite of cheese from his feast, but had encouraged her to eat her own fare, stating that he just *knew* her chef must cook to her preferences, that he would not *think* of denying her the pleasure of enjoying it. Helen had spent the past two hours spitting moldy old cheese and bad meat out of her mouth under the cover of her sneezes, which had grown more violent and persistent with each passing moment.

"Would you care to join the table?"

Helen stiffened at that solicitous voice near her ear. She wasn't at all fooled by it. The man was an ogre. A beast. He was as cruel as they came. And she'd be damned if she was going to display her present state before all—a state he was wholly responsible for, she knew. She realized how neatly he had set her up when they'd finally finished and gathered everything together to leave. He hadn't even bothered to try to prevent her from seeing what lay beneath the blanket when he picked it up. As he'd refolded it, Helen had stood squinting in horror at the compressed patch of posies beneath. Then, she had recalled the way he had fussed over laying out the blanket. He had snapped it out several times over the ground, picked it up and turned it over to snap it out one last time before being satisfied. No doubt the side upon which they had sat had been covered with the essence of posies. Hence her violent reaction.

Oh, Lord Holden was an evil one, all right. Even his offer to return to the keep when she had begun to sneeze had been staged. He had asked her before presenting his sack of food from the village tavern. Had Helen known about that, she surely would have agreed to return to the keep at once, knowing that her plot had been foiled. But, nay, he had elicited her assurance that she would stay before revealing his master stroke, leaving her little choice but to remain and pretend to eat her own rancid food.

"My lady?"

Helen tugged her arm free from his guiding hand, then shook her head. "Nay, I think I shall just go lie down and rest, thank you," she announced stiffly. She waited for him to disappear, relieved when, after a hesitation, he released her arm and stepped away.

"What a gentleman," she sneered as she listened to his footsteps move away toward the trestle tables. Heaving a sigh, she squinted hard in an effort to see where she was going and made her way in the general direction of the stairs. She had only taken a few steps when she heard the pitter-patter of hurried footsteps approaching.

"Helen?"

"Aunt Nell?" she breathed with relief.

"Aye, dear. Lord Holden said that you might be in need of my assistance. Is something wrong—oh, dear Lord!" the woman gasped, apparently having caught a glimpse of her face. "What happened?"

"Help me upstairs and I shall explain."

"Wait. Just let me fetch Duck—Oh, Lord Holden is sending her after us now. Just a moment."

There was a rustle as her aunt moved several feet away to meet Ducky, then a brief murmured conversation before a rustling announced Nell's return. She took Helen's arm to lead her to the stairs.

"What is happening with the marriage negotiations?" Helen asked as they started up the stairs.

"Oh. I am delaying them as much as possible," her aunt murmured, then tightened her hold on Helen's shoulder. "That is what you want, is it not?"

"Aye. I shall need more time. We need another plan. He has discovered this one."

"What? Oh, no. How?"

"I do not know how," she admitted on a sigh as they reached the top of the stairs and started along the hall toward her bedchamber. "I first began to suspect he knew on his first night here, and I am positive he knows now."

"What happened today? How did you end up like this?" Aunt Nell's voice was full of concern as they reached Helen's room and she escorted her niece inside. "He did not hit you?"

"Nay." Helen grimaced with displeasure. "He had us picnic on a patch of posies."

"What?" she cried in alarm. "But why did you allow it?"

"I did not know they were there," Helen admitted with vexation as she eased over to lie on the bed. "I was distracted, and he placed the blanket over them. Actually, he wiped one side of the blanket over them repeatedly and, well, then he turned it over and laid it over them. I sat right down without realizing, and could not figure out why I was reacting so." Her admission was bitter.

"But when you began to sneeze and your eyes began to irritate you, why did you not ask him to bring you back to the castle?"

"I wanted to force him to eat those pastries and bad cheese ere we returned," she admitted with disgruntlement. "By the time I realized that he had fouled up that plan, too, it was too late. I was stuck there."

"How did he—"

Helen waved her aunt impatiently to silence. She had no desire to even think about the humiliation that morning, let alone explain it. She was more interested in other things. "We have a traitor in our midst."

"What!" Aunt Nell cried. Then they both fell silent as the door to the bedchamber opened. Helen turned her head and squinted at the person who entered. Her vision was rather impaired, but it appeared to be a woman in a dark gown. Ducky, she guessed as the blur rushed to the bedside.

"I brought cool water and a cloth as you asked me to, Lady Shambleau." Ducky's voice was easily recognizable, and Helen relaxed somewhat. Then the servant gasped in horror and Helen tensed up again, her head swiveling this way and that, trying to peer about the room for the source of Ducky's upset.

"What is it?"

"Your face. You are all swelled up," her lady's maid breathed in dismay. Helen sank back in the bed miserably. It did feel all swollen and tight. She had a pounding headache behind her eyes, and she was fighting the urge to rub away their puffiness—something she had not been able to keep from doing in the clearing where they had picnicked. She probably would not be in as bad a way had she managed to restrain herself there, but she had felt so itchy and irritated . . .

"Give me the bowl of water, Ducky," Helen heard her aunt request softly. Then there was the sound of water splashing gently, and a cool cloth was laid across her face. Helen gave a start at the sensation, then breathed a sigh of relief. The cool damp had an immediate soothing effect and gave her the first relief from irritation she had known for two hours. It was heavenly.

"What happened?" Ducky's anxious voice sounded, and Helen's lips twisted bitterly.

"He had us picnic on a patch of posies."

"Posies? But you are allergic to posies."

"Aye. And he knew it, the blighter."

"But how?"

Helen sniffled miserably. "We have a traitor."

"I fear I may be the traitor," Nell announced quietly. Helen reached up to snatch the cloth away from her face and gape at her aunt's blurry image.

"What?"

"Well, there is no need to look at me like that. I

did not mean to . . ." She paused and took the cloth from Helen, and there was the sound of water splashing again as she wrung it out. Turning back, she laid it back across Helen's eyes. "He mentioned a picnic, and I thought to tell him to *avoid* posies—as you are allergic to them. But Lord Templetun dragged me off before I could." She quieted briefly, and Helen could almost hear the frown in her voice when she continued with vexation. "He must have overheard me telling Lord Templetun." She made a clucking sound. "It was truly awful of him to use it against you. Not very chivalrous at all."

Helen gave a snort at that. "This is the Hammer of Holden. He has no chivalry."

There was silence for a moment; then Nell asked, "What do you plan to do now?"

"I do not know," Helen admitted miserably.

"Well." Aunt Nell heaved a breath out, then patted Helen's hand. "I have to get back below; Templetun is probably done stuffing himself by now and ready to get back to negotiations. You just rest awhile and relax. Mayhap something will come to you."

Helen gave a slight nod to that suggestion and listened to the rustle of material as her relative moved away to the door and left the room.

"Is there something I can get for you before I return below?"

Helen blinked her eyes open as the cloth was taken away to be soaked and wrung out again. Much to her relief, the cold cloths were already working. Some of the swelling must have gone down, because she could actually almost see properly. Her headache was still there, however. "Perhaps something for my aching head. And something to eat, too, please," Helen asked, closing her eyes as the cloth was placed back over them. "And maybe you could bring Goliath when you return, to keep me company?"

"Aye, my lady. Is there anything special you would like to eat?"

"Roast chicken," Helen said firmly. "If Cook doesn't have any, send down to the village tavern and Maggie for some."

"Is there anything amiss with Lady Helen?"

Hethe stiffened at Lord Templetun's question, then shook his head and finished sinking onto the trestle table bench beside him.

"Why has she not joined us, then? And why did you send her aunt off to tend to her?" the older man persisted as Hethe snatched a mug of ale from a passing serving wench.

Hethe took some time to sample the ale and release a breath of relief at its fresh taste before saying, "She is fine. Or she will be," he added with irritation, trying to shrug off his guilt. He hoped she would be all right. She really had suffered a violent reaction to those posies he had purposely laid their blanket on. He hadn't meant to cause her so much discomfort. A couple of sneezes, a little irritation, were all he had expected. Now, the woman's face was bloated like a corpse after being in the water a week. He grimaced at the thought, then shook his head and drank some more ale.

"Or she will be?" Templetun echoed slowly, his gaze narrowing. "What is wrong with her?"

Hethe supposed it had been too much to hope the man would let that pass. Shrugging with feigned nonchalance, he took another swallow before saying, "She appears to have reacted badly to the spot I chose for our picnic."

Templetun was silent for a moment, pondering that; then his eyes suddenly widened. "You did not picnic by posies, did you?"

"Nay," Hethe answered and watched the older man relax before admitting, "But I set the blanket out on top of some."

"On top of some? Out on—You set the blanket out on—But, Lady Helen is allergic to posies! Her aunt was fretting about it this morning. Oh dear, she—" He paused abruptly, his gaze moving past Hethe's shoulder. "How is she?"

Hethe glanced around in surprise, then shrank back guiltily under Lady Shambleau's hard-eyed glare as she paused behind him.

"She will recover, no thanks to you," the woman said coldly, and Hethe shifted again, feeling like a louse. Then irritation filled him. Reminding himself that Lady Tiernay would not be feeling guilty were *he* the one suffering right now, and that she, along with the woman standing scowling at him, had actually plotted that it should be so, he straightened and mildly shrugged.

"I did try to get her to come back sooner," he announced, adding when she looked doubtful, "when she first began to sneeze, in fact. I suggested it might be good if we returned to the keep. But she did so wish for me to enjoy the food she had had prepared . . ." He stared up at the woman with a meaningful look and was gratified to see her self-righteous attitude disappear, replaced by slight discomfort.

Turning away from him, Lady Shambleau glanced at Lord Templetun. "Shall we get back to the negotiations?"

"Yes, yes. Let us get back to them," the older man murmured, rising eagerly to his feet to lead the lady away. It seemed obvious to Hethe that the king's man was unsure what the undercurrents to this conversation were, and was unwilling to explore them. *Coward*, he thought dryly as he watched the pair disappear from the great hall.

"Well, let us hope that they complete the negotiations this time," William said suddenly, drawing Hethe's attention to his first. The man raised his ale to drink from it. He had been sitting silently since Hethe's return, merely listening to the conversations around him.

"Eager to have it done, are you?" Hethe asked.

His friend smiled wryly. "Well, you must be ready for it to be over, too. It will surely not be a trial for you to bed the wench; then we can get out of here and head back to battle." He scowled into his mug briefly. "The men are growing restless."

"We have only been here a little more than a day," Hethe pointed out with exasperation.

"Aye, well. We rarely last a full day and night at Holden, either. Why should here be any different? The men are not used to sitting about for so long."

Hethe contemplated his first's words unhappily but could not argue. This was the longest they had been away from the excitement and activity of battle for some time. Well, his men were away from it . . .

"No. No. You cannot come in. Goliath!"

Helen turned from peering out her window at those hissed words to see Ducky struggling to get into the room without the large wolfhound accompanying her. Her lips quirking with humor, she put an end to the quiet struggle. "Let him in, Ducky. He spent the night up here, but I let him out to do his business this morning."

"Oh! You're awake." Ducky gave up struggling with the beast and straightened, a smile of relief on her face. "You're looking much better today."

"Aye. I am fully recovered I think." She greeted Goliath with a pat on the head when he loped across the room to her, but her expression was grim. Helen had spent every waking moment since returning from yesterday's picnic trying to come up with another strategy to convince Lord Holden to abandon the wedding. Nothing brilliant had come to mind. Not even during the bath she had ordered brought to her—and Helen always thought best in the bath.

"Lord Templetun sent me up to see how you were doing today. He and your aunt are finished with negotiations. Lord Holden and his man are looking them over right now. Templetun claims if both of you agree, then there is nothing else to hold up the wedding."

Helen grimaced at her maid's words, though she had expected them. Her aunt had slipped in to see her late the night before, telling her apologetically that she had delayed things as long as she could, but the negotiations were done. Helen had known then that Templetun would not dally about finishing this business. The marriage would occur today unless she found some way to stop it. She had not found one.

There were so few acceptable reasons to refuse a marriage. Consanguinity was one of them—but Lord Holden was not even a cousin of a cousin. They were no relation at all, that she knew of, so she could not use that. Another reason was if one of the parties was a criminal, had committed rape or murder. However, while she felt he raped his land and murdered his people through insensitivity, no one else would see it

that way, so that option would not help. The final
escape was if one of the parties had made a religious
vow. Unfortunately, that was not the case, either,
though she suddenly wished she had had the fore-
thought to do so.

"My Billy was talking to Edwin last night," Ducky
announced suddenly. Helen glanced at her blankly,
confused by the change of topic. "My youngest son,
Billy," Ducky explained. "He was talking with Lord
Holden's squire Edwin yestereve . . ."

"Oh?" Helen murmured, still unsure what that
had to do with the matter at hand.

"Aye. Billy says that young Edwin mentioned as
how Lord Holden don't like water much."

"He doesn't?" Helen's interest was caught.

"Aye. He said as how His Lordship will ride hours
longer than necessary just to avoid crossing a river or
such. He said one of the other fellers told him that
Lord Holden nearly drowned as a boy, hasn't gone
near water ever since."

Helen's eyes sparkled briefly with devilment; then
the glint died and her shoulders slumped. "Well,
thank Billy for finding that out, Ducky. But I doubt
it will be of much use to us now. The negotiations
are over. No doubt Templetun has already sent for
Father Purcell." She made a face, then sighed and
moved toward the door. "I suppose I may as well go
below and see what is about. There is no sense trying to put off the unpleasantness any longer."

Chapter 7

"THIS will not do."

Helen gave a start at the sharp announcement from Lord Holden as he led his first back to the trestle table where she was seated between Lord Templetun and her aunt, perusing the contracts they had spent so much time drawing up. The contracts looked depressingly fine to her. Aunt Nell had certainly not allowed everything to go Lord Holden's way. Helen supposed it was the fact that she didn't really want to marry him that had allowed her aunt to be so demanding. Now, at the man's complaint, Helen felt a spark of hope that the wedding might at least be delayed a bit longer.

Hethe drew Lord Templetun aside, and Helen practically held her breath as she watched their discussion taking place. Lord Holden was grim and determined; Lord Templetun was waving his arms around and looking dismayed. Whatever Holden wanted was not impressing the man, she noted with interest and a touch of trepidation. At last, Templetun gave in and turned back to the table, his expression highly annoyed as he sought out her aunt.

"It would appear we have some more work to do," he announced.

Aunt Nell hesitated, her gaze veering to Helen; then she rose with a shrug. "Very well, my lord. Shall we?"

Helen was still watching the two walk away when Hethe dropped onto the trestle table bench beside her and said cheerfully, "Well, it would appear we have a little more time to get acquainted. What shall we do this morning? Another picnic?"

Helen turned slowly to glare at him, her eyes narrowing on his cheerful grin. "I think you should go to—"

Catching herself, she abruptly stood, her gaze going to the door to the kitchens. She considered making a quick detour there for garlic, but then she changed her mind. What was the use? Hethe had obviously already seen through that ploy. What she needed was time alone to figure out some new stratagem.

"Come, Goliath," she ordered, turning away from the table. She was halfway to the main doors before she realized that she was not alone. Lord Holden had stood and was now keeping pace with her.

"Where are we going?" he asked.

"*We* are not going anywhere. *I* am going for a walk to get some fresh air," she said grimly.

"A walk sounds nice. It will give us the chance to become better acquainted."

Helen merely gritted her teeth and held her tongue. The last thing she wanted was to walk anywhere with him. But she suspected that telling Lord Holden that would only please him. Glancing down at the dog keeping pace on her left side, she reached down to pat his head affectionately. She had missed the beast during his defection, but could hardly blame him. She hadn't been able to bear being around herself.

Doing her best to ignore the presence looming on her right, Helen stepped through the main doors, descended the stairs and started across the bailey at a quick clip, but Holden had no problem keeping up. They had left the bailey and started along a path through the trees surrounding the castle when an idea struck. They were not far from the river! She could hear its faint rush over the sounds of birds and other animals. She doubted Hethe knew what it was.

A smile suddenly bloomed on her face and she turned down a side path, chuckling softly when Goliath gave a bark of excitement and ran ahead before returning to her side, then doing it again. As the path broke through to the small clearing on the river's edge, Helen's smile widened, spilling across her face. She was halfway across the small clearing, heading for the small dugout boat tied to a post driven into the shore, before she realized that she had lost one of her companions: the tall, almost human one. Pausing, she turned to find him standing at the edge of the clearing, his narrow-eyed gaze surveying the boat and the water.

"Something wrong, my lord?" she asked sweetly.

His eyes fell upon her, full of suspicion. "What are we doing here?"

"I thought a nice little boat ride on the river would be pleasant. Would it not?" she challenged.

Hethe's mouth tightened. "I do not think—"

"Or, are you afraid?" she taunted. He straightened, growing at least an inch in height, and his expression darkened, but he didn't say anything. He just moved grimly forward, leading the way to the small vessel at the river's edge. Once there, he paused, looking uncertain.

Enjoying his discomfort, Helen joined him and peered into the boat, then smiled and held out her hand. His brow furrowing, he took it, then tightened his hold when she promptly used him for balance as she stepped into the small craft. Releasing his hand, she then held her arms out for equilibrium and stepped to the far seat where she settled herself comfortably, then turned and gave him a look of expectation.

Muttering under his breath, Hethe clasped the post the boat was tied to, then followed, clambering into the watercraft, not looking at all happy. Helen waited until he was seated opposite her before saying, "You have to untie the boat."

He stared at her blankly for a moment, then turned to stare at the post and the rope leading to it from a metal hook inside the boat. She had meant for him to have to stand up to untie the end attached to the post, but instead he untied the end in the boat and tossed it over the side where it would drag in the water. He turned to her with a shark-like smile, knowing he had confounded her plan to watch his discomfort.

Helen's gaze narrowed slightly, but all she said was, "You have to push off now."

For a moment she thought that she'd won, that he would storm out of the boat and head for home. The thought made her giddy. She needed time to think. There had to be something she could still do to prevent this marriage. But while he did clamber out of the boat, it was only to push the craft out into the water.

"Goliath!" Helen called, and the dog, who had been nosing around something a little further up the riverbank, turned and raced back to them, leaping into the boat as Hethe shoved off and managed to lumber clumsily into the craft without getting too wet. Dropping promptly onto his rear, Hethe grabbed for both sides of the boat, holding on for dear life as Goliath settled by Helen's feet in the bottom of the boat.

"There now, isn't this nice?" she breathed, beaming at him as he peered at the water moving past and gulped.

"Hmmm," he grunted, then glared with displeasure from her to the oars lying in the bottom of the boat. Seeming to realize that he was expected to row them about, he picked up one, examined it briefly, then set it in its mooring. The second quickly followed, and he began a clumsy attempt at propulsion. It was more than obvious that he had not done this before, but Helen wasn't too concerned. They wouldn't go far. There really wasn't much of a current here. This part of the river, while wide, was extremely slow and shallow. She wouldn't tell him that, of course. She could hardly play on his supposed fear of water if he knew they were really in nothing more than a wide puddle—at least compared to some of the deeper and swifter-running rivers around these parts.

Leaning slightly to the side, she trailed her fingers in the cool water. Helen had walked down here often with Goliath, but had rarely been rowing. She wondered now why she hadn't done so a time or two before. This was no one's boat, really—and everyone's. It had been here for as long as she could remember, something of a makeshift ferry, used by whomever was looking for a shortcut across the river rather than having to walk around or through it—providing it was on the appropriate side.

"Mayhap you shouldn't lean over like that," Hethe said suddenly, drawing her gaze. "The boat seems to be dipping rather low on that side when you do."

There was no mistaking the tense edge to his voice; the man was nervous and there was no doubting it. Helen felt herself smiling. After what he had put her through yesterday, it was nice to see him suffer a bit. More would be nicer still, she decided. Rather than straightening as he obviously wished, she leaned over further. The boat tipped precariously under her weight, until bare inches divided the boat's edge and the river's surface. She smiled as she did so, watching Hethe's expression tighten with anxiety.

Teeth clenching, he shifted to the opposite side of his seat, balancing out the boat somewhat and spoiling her fun. Heaving a sigh, Helen straightened and glanced around. He had been clumsy at rowing in the beginning but was getting the hang of it. They were sliding under a canopy of trees that had grown up on each side of the river, whose branches stretched overhead like a bower. The place would be terribly romantic if it weren't for the fact that she was with *him*.

It was Goliath's bark that set off the calamity. The dog had been lying calm and silent in the bottom of the boat, but suddenly shifted restlessly and sat up to peer over the side at the shore gliding past. Helen noticed the ducks paddling past at about the same moment that Goliath did, so she wasn't prepared for his sudden excitement. Leaping to his feet, the hound began to bark excitedly, then to romp first to the right, then to the left, then paused and put his paws on the edge of the boat as if to leap out after the birds. The ducks immediately began quacking frantically and flying off.

"Goliath! No!" Helen shouted, unable to enjoy Hethe's suddenly green visage; the way the dog had set the boat teetering in the water was alarming her as well. She started to rise from her seat, to catch and calm the excited beast, when he turned and romped her way again. This time, he crashed right into her in his excitement. She lost her balance in the bouncing boat, and the next thing she knew she was tumbling over the side and into the icy water. Goliath barked, Hethe shouted, and Helen shrieked for all she was worth. Then the water closed over her head, swallowing her in silence.

She surfaced a moment later, frantically coughing and spitting up the water that had filled her open mouth.

The idea came to her like a bolt of lightning. Still coughing and sputtering, she sank back into the water, jerking her arms about for effect as she did. She bobbed back up a moment later, calling weakly for help, then slid below the surface once more. After waiting a few seconds, she popped out again, her gaze frantically seeking and finding Hethe, who was now sitting in the boat several feet away, an odd expression on his face as he watched her floundering about.

Helen's jaw tightened. "I am drowning, you churl. Are you not going to rescue me?"

Her fiancé's mouth trembled; then he gestured. Helen swiveled in the water to see Goliath romping about right behind her, chasing ducks that were quacking and flapping madly from the water each time he approached. The water only came up to his shoulders. Thanks to the hound, she had not fooled Holden for a moment.

Grinding her teeth together as Hethe suddenly burst out laughing, Helen stood up. She was soaked, of course. Her gown was heavy with the river, her hair a damp mass about her head and shoulders, and she was freezing. Her dignity in shreds, she lifted her head grimly and strode out of the water, her gown slapping wetly against her legs, her slippers squishing with each step.

"Helen! What happened? Are you all right?"

Helen paused on the way to the stairs leading to the second level of Tiernay keep and had to wonder what had made her think she could slip inside and escape to her room before anyone became aware of her humiliation. She should have known better. Nothing had gone right since Lord Holden's arrival. Why should this time be any different? *Of course* her aunt and Templetun would be sitting in the great hall, just waiting to witness the consequences of her stupidity.

"Whatever happened to you, dear?" Aunt Nell cried as she reached her side and took in her sodden state.

"I had a little accident," Helen answered succinctly, continuing toward the stairs and wincing at the squishing sounds she made with every step.

"I can see that," Aunt Nell snapped, chasing after her. "But what happened?"

"Hear, hear. And where is Lord Holden?" Lord Templetun added, catching up to them as they reached the stairs.

"I am hoping he is floating facedown in the river, but doubt I could be so lucky," Helen returned in a sweet voice, starting up the stairs and ignoring Templetun's shocked gasp. Let him make what he wanted of her words. She didn't care. Leaving them gaping after her, she squished up the stairs to her room. She managed to strip away the sodden gown and was drying herself off with the top bed linen when Ducky rushed into the room.

The maid took one look at Helen's thunderous expression and apparently decided to keep her questions to herself. The two women worked silently to get her hair as dry as they could. Ducky then brushed it out and pulled it back into something of an acceptable style before helping Helen don a fresh gown, a green one to replace the sodden blue mess she had removed.

Still silent, Helen then led the way back down to the great hall. She would not hide in her room again today, as she had the day after the picnic! she determined. But she regretted that decision the moment she stepped off the stairs onto the great hall floor. Well, perhaps not the very moment, but it was then that the keep doors opened and Hethe strode in with an excited Goliath at his heels. Tail wagging wildly, the dog spotted his mistress at once and raced forward to launch himself at her.

Helen heard Ducky gasp in horror before she crashed backward under her dog's weight; then she pushed Goliath's wet body away to gape down at her newly soaked and muddied green gown.

"So sorry." Hethe strode cheerfully forward. "I suppose I should have left him outside, but I find I am becoming rather attached to the beast. Such a clever animal. Did you train him to do that little trick in the boat too?" he asked with a grin that rubbed Helen raw.

"No," she snarled at the reminder of what she had trained Goliath to do. The man wasn't even trying to hide his amusement, and she didn't appreciate that it was at her expense.

"Ah well, he is still clever." Lord Holden scratched an ecstatic Goliath about the ears, grinning at Helen the whole while, then straightened and turned toward the door. "I'll put him outside to dry while you change again."

Much to her fury all he had to do was slap his hand against his leg and Goliath, the traitor, rushed to follow him to the door. Helen had the childish urge to call the dog back to her side to prove just whose dog he was, but was prevented from doing so when Lord Templetun spoke up.

"Aye. You had best change," the king's man said, eyeing her wet and muddied attire with a wince. "The negotiations are complete. We are ready to proceed with the wedding. I have sent for your priest."

"I cannot believe it did not work."

Helen shifted irritably at Ducky's mournful words. "I can. The man is a dunce. He is also tasteless. I have never met a more annoying oaf," she snapped as the other woman continued to dress her hair with small flowers.

"Aye, but the garlic and—"

"He claims my breath is as sweet as flowers," Helen growled.

Ducky gaped at her briefly then shook her head. "Mayhap he has a poor sense of smell."

"Poor sense of smell, my eye! He figured out exactly what we were up to and has been doing everything he can to confound me."

"Are you sure? I mean, I know you thought that the picnic on the posies was on purpose . . . but perhaps it wasn't. Perhaps he truly did not see the patch when he set the blanket out. And perhaps he didn't hear your aunt when she told Lord Templetun of your allergy."

"Aye, and perhaps he truly does like that awful ale I have been giving him, and thinks it is some of the finest he has ever enjoyed," Helen muttered.

"He said that?" Ducky looked taken aback, then bit her lip. "What did he say about the lack of covering or fire in his room?"

Helen's mouth tightened. "He finds the cool breezes invigorating."

"The fleas?" Ducky asked almost hopelessly.

"His tough hide must be immune to the little pests. He has said naught about them."

Ducky was silent for a moment as she braided flowers into Helen's golden hair, then murmured unhappily, "I noticed he has been eating heartily of the food we serve him."

"Aye." Helen's head ached with remembered irritation. "He claims I have the finest cook in Christendom."

"Oh." Ducky looked terribly disappointed at the news. But she could not be more disappointed than Helen herself, who had truly convinced herself that he would step forward and refuse the king's ridiculous order that they marry. The man had failed her, and now it was her wedding day.

Dear God! My wedding day, she thought with

despair. Father Purcell was probably already waiting in the church. They would hold the ceremony as soon as she was ready.

And she had little choice but to obey Templetun. Unfortunately, there was nothing left to delay the inevitable. All else was in readiness. Helen's servants were all experienced and excellent at their jobs. Even as they had carried out her plot to bring an end to this travesty, she had made certain they were preparing the keep for the wedding she had never believed would happen. Decorations, a fine feast— all was ready. She had gone ahead with the preparations mostly to keep her guests from suspecting anything was amiss; now they would be needed. The wedding was not canceled. In fact, despite all their efforts, Lord Holden appeared distressingly complacent about the entire arrangement.

Helen winced as Ducky accidentally stuck her scalp with a stem.

"Sorry," the maid murmured, concentrating harder on her task.

"Enough! This is good enough," Helen snapped, waving her away impatiently and standing. Turning to her maid, she held out her hand. "Did you bring the garlic and—"

"Aye, but you said he liked it." Ducky moved to collect the cloves and the mug holding their vile breath enhancer. "Why torture yourself with this if it has no effect on him?"

"Because I am not sure it is *not* having an effect on him." She shook her head. "I cannot forget his reaction when he first arrived. I swear the man was fit to die from the odor."

"But then why is he claiming to like it?" the servant asked in confusion. "Surely he does not wish to wed a woman who so despises the idea of marrying him?"

Helen shrugged helplessly and took the garlic, speaking as she began to peel several cloves. "Mayhap we overestimated his ability to refuse. Mayhap it is no more possible for him to flout the king's orders than I."

"Then you think he has no more desire to marry you than you have to marry him? That he has no choice?"

"That about sums it up," she muttered resignedly, lifting the first clove to her mouth.

"Nay!" Nell screeched from the door. Helen turned to stare at the woman in amazement as she rushed forward and snatched away the cloves of garlic.

"What?" Helen asked in bewilderment, then gaped at her relative as the woman threw her cloves out into the courtyard. "Whatever are you doing?"

"Getting rid of those." Nell turned back from the window and surveyed her niece with a sigh. "That was one of the addenda Lord Holden insisted on being added to the contracts. It is why we had to negotiate further. You are never to eat garlic again."

"What?" Helen screeched. "But Cook puts them in—"

"That is fine, according to the contract, but you are not to eat cloves whole and raw."

"And you agreed to this?"

"Well, what else could I do?" Nell asked with exasperation. "The very fact that Lord Holden was demanding it had Templetun questioning why. I had to agree just to stop his curiosity. I had to agree to it all."

"All?" Helen had a sinking feeling in her stomach. "What else?"

Nell shifted and grimaced. "You are never to cook for him again. You must eat from the same plate as he. You must drink the same ale as he. There shall always be coverings on the window unless he demands otherwise. A fire is to be built in his bedchamber every night, and you personally are to attend his baths."

Helen stood silent and still at the news, her mind not seeming to work. It was Ducky who muttered, "It seems he didn't find the food or your breath so pleasing after all."

"Damn," Helen hissed, and her maid peered at her with concern.

"Surely it doesn't matter so much, my lady? Does it?"

"It cannot matter now, Helen," Nell agreed, moving to sit beside her. "We gave it a good try, but the king ordered this marriage and it appears it is going to go through."

"The king may be able to order us to marry, but he can't make us like it. Besides, I had hoped that if I made myself stink enough, Holden might refuse to consummate the marriage. That would give me more time to come up with a way out."

"Oh." Ducky nodded slowly. "You always were quick-witted, my lady."

"Not quick-witted enough, I am afraid," Helen said mournfully.

Hethe glanced toward the door of his room as William hurried inside. Standing, he raised an eyebrow questioningly at his first. "Did you get them?"

"Aye. Though I still have no idea why you would want garlic," the man admitted. He handed over several cloves of the fragrant herb.

"Aye. Well, I have rather stumbled upon a new strategy in war," he muttered, beginning to peel the items.

William looked querulous. "And what is it?"

"Sometimes the best way to beat the enemy, is to join them at their own game." Ignoring William's bemused gaze, he popped the garlic cloves into his mouth, ignoring the way they burned his tongue and the insides of his cheeks as he grimly chewed.

"And what enemy exactly are we vanquishing with garlic?" William asked carefully.

Hethe swallowed, hesitated, then shook his head. He had not told his first of all the petty little tricks his intended had been trying in her struggle to avoid marrying him. It was far too humiliating to admit that she so disliked the idea of being his wife—regardless of the fact that he himself had not originally been eager for this union, either. His pride was sorely tried by the fact that while he, upon first seeing her, had decided that this marriage might not be such a trial after all, she had not had a similar change of heart. Nay, this was a silent and private war, and he intended to keep it that way. Which was the reason for the garlic. He didn't trust the little witch not to ignore the contract and continue with her dragon-breath tactics. She was trying to avoid marriage to him, after all, and surely she would see that breaking the contract would be grounds to end it. His own breath freshening was simply insurance against such an occurrence.

Hethe smiled to himself as he swallowed the pungent mess. He had no idea what else she'd inflicted on herself to make the stench that assaulted him every time they met, but the garlic really was the worst of it. Which his own would cancel out.

"Let us go below. She should be ready soon," he said to his friend. He had finished changing into his freshest tunic and leggings while awaiting the man's return with the garlic. Now he reached the door and glanced back at William only to find him staring around the room with distaste.

"You have no coverings on your window."

Hethe shrugged at the observation. "They are being cleaned at the moment."

"But 'tis drafty in here. You should have had a fire built up. And really, Hethe, this room is half the size of mine. Even Templetun's room is—"

"Aye, but this was only meant for one night. We did not expect the delay in the ceremony. Lady Helen thought it best that I sleep in here for one night than for you to be stuck in here for one night, then moved to a more comfortable room later. I agreed," he lied through clenched teeth. "Come, or I shall be late for my own wedding."

"Aye." William moved toward him, but he did not look pleased. "Are you sure you want to go through with this? Lovely she may be, but she is still the 'Tyrant of Tiernay.'"

Hethe grimaced at the name. She *was* a little tyrant, too. A sneaky little tyrant. A beautiful, sneaky little tyrant with a sweet voice, enchanting smile, and quite the most delectable little body he had seen in ages. Clearing his throat, he pushed those thoughts away. "I am a lord with some power, William. Still, I will not refuse a direct order from the king without a very good cause."

"Aye, but if you told him how she has harassed and insulted you over the years—"

"He knows," Hethe reminded him quietly. "I dictated enough messages to you informing him of that."

"Oh, aye." William scowled. "Of course."

"Come." Hethe slapped him on the shoulder affectionately and steered him out of the room. "Have a little faith in me. I am your liege and a warrior. I can manage one little wife, don't you think?"

"I suppose," William said doubtfully. Hethe grimaced at the lack of confidence his man showed in him. Unfortunately, he himself had some doubts as well. The wench had proven herself to be quite clever. And there was nothing more dangerous than a clever woman.

Chapter 8

$\mathcal{Y}$OU may kiss the bride."

Frozen in place, Helen watched unhappily as her new husband turned to bestow upon her the bridal kiss. This was the worst day of her life. She was sure of it.

She stood stiff and unresponsive as his mouth closed over hers, expecting a quick peck. She got much more. His lips brushed hers lightly; then his tongue slid out to lave her mouth, startling her lips into parting. Immediately, his tongue swept in, and Helen's eyes widened abruptly at the pungent taste that assaulted her.

"You!" she gasped accusingly, pulling back. The man had the nerve to give her a slow, satisfied smile.

"Fire with fire," he murmured, to the confusion of those near enough to hear him. Then, leaning forward, he put a finger to her chin and pushed it upward, closing her mouth so that he could brush it again lightly with his own in a more proper kiss. Straightening, he turned back to face the priest and finish the ceremony.

Helen did not turn. She simply stood staring at the monster beside her. She had seen the look of victory shining in his eyes. He was getting what he wanted. He *wanted* this wedding. The realization sank in slowly and painfully. She had been fighting this battle assuming that he would not care either way, that he merely needed to be shown how unpleasant this marriage could be. But nothing was going as she had planned. First, he'd claimed to love all that she had created for him to hate, then he'd turned the tables on her at that picnic, then she had fallen in the river rather than he, and now he had turned her own weapon back on her. *Garlic!* she thought angrily. *I should have had a backup plan*, she realized. Something in case the first plan did not work. Poison in his porridge, perhaps, or a knife in his heart.

Or, she realized suddenly, *I should have thought out more thoroughly why he had not promptly refused the wedding*. She had not exactly endeared herself to the man with her complaints to the king over the years, surely. Why had he not refused outright? Why had he come here entirely ready to carry out the wedding?

The answer to that was so simple and obvious, Helen nearly groaned aloud. Tiernay, of course. She had forgotten how rich and prosperous the fiefdom was, how attractive it would be to him. Helen herself was just a small part of what he gained through this marriage. Tiernay was the prize. And one well worth having. Suddenly, she realized where she had gone wrong. It was Tiernay she should have made appear as unattractive as possible. It was Tiernay she should have made smell and painted black.

For a moment, she was terribly excited at the realization, but then she realized that it was too late in coming. Or was it? Could she still delay the consummation of the marriage? Could she still find a method to escape? She had to!

She spent the celebration that followed in a tizzy, her mind racing about like a crazed mouse. She had to do something. She had to think of a way to put him off long enough for her to make Tiernay unattractive. Something he could not combat. Around her, the festivities continued. There was much toasting and cheering. Much ribald teasing and laughter. But she was oblivious to the lot.

It was not until the last course of the feast that inspiration finally came to her. Standing abruptly, Helen ignored her new husband's startled and questioning glance and hurried toward the kitchens. As she had expected, Ducky was there.

Hethe rubbed his stomach absently and watched his new bride disappear into the kitchens, a sense of foreboding overtaking him. His gaze slid to her aunt to find the woman looking after her niece with a concerned expression. He had a feeling it was not a good thing. He had been aware of his new wife's silence throughout the meal. She had not touched a single bite of the food set before her. He had almost been able to see her mind working over the problem of his having combated her bad breath with some oral stench of his own. And it had worked. At least, he assumed it worked. With his own mouth garlic-drenched, he had not really been able to tell if she had flouted the directives of their contract and chomped on the stuff herself. It mattered little, he supposed. What mattered now was that with the garlic filling his own breath, hers had not been the least bit offensive. For a moment, before she had pulled away, he had found himself enjoying that kiss more than he expected. The wedding night would not be a trial for him.

In fact, now that the problem of her offensive breath was out of the way, he was anticipating the coming night with great hopes.

The opening of the kitchen door drew Hethe from his thoughts, and he watched curiously as his new bride returned to the table. She looked slightly anxious and distracted, he noted with a frown, and he arched an eyebrow as she reclaimed her seat. If she saw his questioning look, she ignored it, merely picking up the quail drumstick in her trencher to handle it with an obvious lack of interest.

"Is the food not to your liking?" he asked solicitously, knowing that was not the problem, but unable to keep from teasing her a bit after the torments she had put him through. Not to mention for what he had been forced to do to combat it. Eating the garlic himself, for instance. It was a terribly clever idea, but now his stomach was roiling rather ominously. He would have liked to blame it on the meal he had just eaten, but as per the contract, he and his wife were eating out of the same trencher. As he had hoped, that had greatly improved the flavor of his meal. Dinner was delicious. It was certainly not the cause of his stomach upset. The garlic he had consumed was wholly to blame for that. It didn't seem to be sitting well with him, and he had been burping it up ever since.

"Nay," Helen at last answered, managing to produce for him a somewhat stiff smile. "I mean, aye. It is quite good. I just find I am not very hungry."

"Ah. Too excited for the night ahead," he suggested, a smile coming to his face. He nearly burst out laughing at her reaction to his gibe. The woman blanched, her expression twisting into one of incredulous annoyance before she seemed to realize what she was doing. Forcing a smile that held only a tinge of sarcasm, she spoke dryly.

"Aye. That must be it," she muttered, then glanced to the side where her maid had suddenly appeared.

Hethe watched curiously as the woman leaned down to whisper something in her mistress's ear, then the woman rushed off toward the stairs, and Helen turned to beam at him.

Hethe blinked. His wife was absolutely lovely. A beautiful creature. He had been so distracted of late, he had quite forgotten that.

"Yes, husband. In fact, I am so excited I think I shall go above stairs now and spend a little extra time preparing for you. Will you excuse me?"

"Aye," Hethe murmured, helpless to keep from smiling in return. Helen was such a lovely thing— eyes sparkling, lips curving, just for him! He watched her stand, gesture for her aunt to follow her, then hurry off toward the stairs. His gaze dropped, and he watched her hips sway as she walked away.

"Where are they off to?" Lord Templetun asked in a curious voice.

"Hmm?" Hethe tore his gaze away from his retreating bride reluctantly.

"Lady Helen and her aunt," the man repeated. "Where are they going?"

"Oh. They are going off to prepare for the bedding." Various images flashed through his head as he heard his own words. He pictured Helen stepping naked into a tub of water with rose petals floating on its surface.

"Already?"

Templetun's question startled Hethe back to reality. He glanced blankly at the old man, then around the room. The meal was not yet even over. Most people were only half done. The feast had been arranged to follow hard on the heels of the wedding, so it was still extremely early. Too early for the bedding, or preparing for it. Suddenly the picture that had risen to his mind's eye a moment before returned. This time, however, instead of stepping into a tub of warm water with rose petals, his wife was stepping into a tub with large brown things floating in it. If he concentrated hard, Hethe could tell they were cow patties.

"Sweet Jesu!" He popped up from the bench as if a spring were under his arse, but before he could move away, Templetun caught his arm and pulled him back.

"Now, now, there is no use in being overeager. It may be early for the bedding, but if she wishes to prepare herself special for you, you should let her. Now that I think on it, it is rather marvelous the way she has resigned herself to this union. I probably shouldn't tell you this, but when I first came with the king's order that the two of you were to marry . . . Well, let's just say she was not the most eager of brides," he confided with some amusement. He added, "In fact, by the time I left for Holden to collect you, I feared I might very well have a war on my hands."

Hethe groaned in response. Had no one else yet become aware of the silent war that had been taking place since his arrival? No, of course not. She had never breathed her putrid breath on them, and neither Templetun nor William had had to suffer the cold, the scalding or the fleas. And Hethe had not told them of the incidents, either; his pride would not let him.

"Now, now." Taking his groan the wrong way, Templetun patted him on the back encouragingly. "As you can see, she got over it quite quickly. It was most likely simply nerves. She is obviously quite pleased with the situation now. Look how she's preparing."

Hethe's only response was to loose another moan and drop his head on the table in despair, barely missing his trencher. His mind was filling with a variety of ways that she could be preparing right that moment. Not one of them was good.

"Ugh! Oh, Gawd! Oh, this is just horrible . . . Oh!"

"Aye," Aunt Nell agreed from her position near the door—a safe distance from her niece and poor Ducky, who was helping.

"Oooooh . . . I cannot—This is—It is good I did not eat, else I would surely be tossing it up right now," Helen muttered with vexation, then groaned and sighed before crying out, "Oh, God! 'Tis unbearable!"

"Aye. 'Tis," Ducky agreed, her nose wrinkling with distaste under the strip of linen she had tied around her face to cover her nose. However, catching the tears sparkling in Helen's eyes, she decided a bit of encouragement was needed. "But that is all to the good. It means this plan of yours should work. I mean, he'll not touch you when you're like this. Of course," she added a bit worriedly, "now that the wedding is over, there's no telling how he'll react. What if he beats you, or—" She paused, her concern fading abruptly to be replaced by a sly smile. "Nay. He'll not wish to get close enough to beat you."

Helen's answer was another groan. She did not wish to be close to herself just now. This was just awful, the best and worst idea she had ever had.

A knock at the door made all three women freeze, their gazes clashing. It wasn't until the second knock that anyone moved.

Dropping to her haunches, Helen instinctively huddled behind the bed, then peered over it to hiss at Ducky, "See who it is. But do not let them in."

When the maid nodded, Helen dropped a little lower, taking the opportunity to peel and pop into her mouth one of the cloves of garlic Ducky had smuggled in earlier without her aunt seeing. The contract be damned, he had consumed garlic, and she would not be caught again without it. She glanced over the side of the bed as she chewed to see that Ducky had reached the door. The maid hesitated as Aunt Nell shifted to one side to be out of the way, then opened the door the barest crack to peer out. Helen heard the low murmur of a man's voice, then Ducky's higher response. The maid had barely answered before she shut the door with a snap and whirled.

"'Tis Lord Holden's first. He says Lord Templetun sent him to see if you are ready. The Hammer is eager to come above, but Templetun wanted to be sure you were ready first."

Helen hesitated. Her first reaction was an emphatic "*No!*" But the truth was, she *was* ready. Or as ready as she would ever be. Biting her lip, she nodded. Ducky flashed her a sympathetic look, then turned back and started to open the door.

"Wait!" Helen cried, and Ducky promptly slammed the door she had just started to open.

"What is it?" Aunt Nell asked with concern, taking several steps toward her niece before freezing, her nose twisting in distaste. She promptly scuttled back to her spot beside the door. "What?"

"We need to air out the room, else all will know what we're about," Helen explained to her aunt, then instructed Ducky, "Tell them I shall be ready in just a moment, that you shall come fetch them when I am."

"Aye, my lady." Ducky nodded and turned quickly to open the door and pass on the message.

"I am going up there." Hethe got to his feet determinedly, only to be yanked back down rather abruptly by both Lord Templetun and William.

"So impatient, my lord," Templetun chastised gently. "She will be ready soon. William said that he thought they were going to have you go up already, but that your wife forgot something. No doubt the maid will be down any—"

"Here she comes," William interrupted.

Hethe followed his gaze to see the maid crossing the hall toward them. Nothing could have held him in his seat then. Popping off the trestle table bench, he started across the hall toward the stairs at once. The others were a little slower to react. He heard Templetun mutter in frustration then the sudden scuffling of feet as all the men in the keep scrambled after him. He winced inwardly. He had already tried to convince them that there was no need for a bedding *ceremony*. After all, he'd pointed out, his wife had taken only her maid and her aunt to see *her* above stairs, so they should just forgo any men taking *him* up. But the men had all, every one of them, merely laughed at that suggestion. Especially his own warriors. He was not to escape without their interference.

Hethe would not have minded except that he was not sure what he would find once they got up there. He was beginning to get an unsettled feeling, a sense of doom's approach. He had given up his brief fantasies that she was bathing and perfuming herself for his pleasure. Instead, Hethe very much suspected she was preparing another battle tactic, and was not overeager for the public to know that his wife was not pleased with their marriage. He had not kept silent about her tricks and stink warfare only to have it revealed at this juncture, and quite so publicly.

"Just a minute," Templetun hissed, catching up to Hethe in the hall outside the master bedchamber, drawing him to a halt. "We are supposed to carry you in, not follow you like lackeys."

Before he could protest, Hethe found himself hoisted on the shoulders of his first and another of his warriors. He grimaced. On the night of his wedding to Nerissa, he had had to be carried because he was too drunk to walk. He suspected his father had known that drunk was the only way he would carry out his husbandly duty on the young bride. Now he was reluctantly being carried into this room because he feared what awaited him. It was the last thought Hethe had before Templetun opened the door and he was carted forward.

"Here he is. Your groom," Templetun called out cheerfully as he led the small crowd of half-drunk men into the room.

Knotting his fingers in the hair of the warrior whose shoulder was under his right arse cheek, Hethe

tried to keep from toppling backward off their makeshift chair as he peered quickly and suspiciously
around the room. All seemed fine at first glance. His
wife's aunt stood out of the way by the covered window. There was a bed, a fire, two chairs, several
chests, and his bride in the bed, her hair spread
around her in golden glory. That was all Hethe caught
a glimpse of before he was lifted from the shoulders
of the men carrying him and set on the floor. His feet
had barely hit the ground when the group converged
on him. Ribald jokes and his clothes were suddenly
flying through the air; then he was naked. And cold.
Once his clothes were missing, he realized that the
room was oddly chill. His gaze shot to the fireplace,
but as he had seen, there was a raging blaze there.
Before he could consider the matter further, Hethe
was being dragged to the bed, where he was tucked
in. Then, still laughing and tossing around some vul-
gar remarks, the men allowed themselves to be
herded from the room by a beaming Templetun. Lady
Shambleau, who had stood by silently throughout,
left at a more dignified pace.

Hethe watched the door close with amazement.
His entry had come off without a hitch. There had
been no public humiliation, no sign that his bride
wished him anywhere but here. Speaking of his
bride . . .

He turned to peer at the woman in the bed beside
him. The men had sat him on the mattress, and
Helen lay there flat on her back. She had been silent
and serene throughout his men's rude jokes and
gibes. She had merely lain calmly under the covers
waiting. She was still lying serene and calm, waiting,
he saw as he peered down at her.

"Well." He cleared his throat. She wasn't even

looking at him but staring at the drapings over the bed, her cheeks pink with embarrassment. Hethe cleared his throat again, realizing for the first time that this was a damned uncomfortable situation. He tried to recall his first wedding night, to remember what it had been like, but truthfully, he had been young and nervous that first time and had drunk quite a bit as a result. It was all rather a blur. He had the vague recollection of merely pouncing on his first wife.

But he had been young and unskilled then. It had been forgivable. It was not now. He sure wished he could, though, he admitted with a sigh. Worse, Wee Hethe was wide awake and urging him to do so. He could feel the way the linen on his lap was tenting with his excitement. But he had to show some finesse here. It would be shameful to just pounce.

Instead, he tried for some conversation. "Well, that was not so bad. I had feared they may get carried away."

Lady Helen squeaked something of an agreement, but didn't move. Hethe sighed. "I—"

"Shall we get to it, my lord?" she asked in a voice that was not quite steady. Hethe paused, his eyes widening. Dear Lord! She had just given him permission to pounce!

A smile of relief splashing across his face, Hethe turned in the bed and leaned over to press a kiss to his new wife's lips.

Helen stiffened as his mouth covered hers, her body going rigid with shock at his touch. She hadn't expected him to start like this! Well, she really hadn't considered how he would start, else she would have realized that a kiss was the most natural beginning.

He would hardly just rip the linens aside and go at her like a dog after a bitch in heat.

His lips moved over hers, infinitely gentle yet firm. Much to her dismay, she had the most amazing desire to soften beneath the caress. That was enough to panic her, and Helen began to shift beneath the linens, intent on pulling her arms out from where they were pressed to her sides under the bedclothes. The moment she began to shift, however, Hethe lowered his body on top of hers, effectively trapping her where she lay.

Helen promptly opened her mouth to ask him to let her up, but the moment her lips opened, some-thing filled them. His tongue, she realized a bit dazedly as it swept inside. Her next thought was a rather incoherent *Oh, dear* as she felt her body begin to churn out sensations she had never before experi-enced. There was an odd sort of warm hum going through her blood as he kissed her. It was creating the oddest instinct in her to arch beneath the linens, to press herself closer to him, though they really couldn't get any closer with him lying half atop her as he was. Then she felt one of his hands cresting over the heavy fur beneath the linens covering her, smoothing over one mound that was her breast and closing there briefly, giving a gentle squeeze, then a firmer one that made her moan into his mouth.

The sound of her own pleasure grated in her ears. Shock, embarrassment and panic swelling inside her, Helen began to struggle. She was suddenly desper-ate to get her arms out, but she was well and truly trapped and knew it was all her own fault. Then his hand moved away from her breast. It slid over the linens, across her stomach, tracing the impression of her body to the mound between her legs. He paused there to press gently, and this time Helen couldn't stop herself from arching up. She actually lifted him slightly with her reaction, a combination of startled surprise at both the touch and the heat that it ignited deep inside her.

Shocked as she was, Helen's legs parted of their own volition beneath the linens. Not much. Just the few inches the tight bedclothes binding her allowed. But it was enough for Hethe to ease his hand between her legs and press the bedclothes against her more intimately.

As she felt the spark within her deepen into a fiery ache, Helen stopped lying quiescent beneath him and began to kiss back hungrily; her mouth widened under his, her head shifting slightly, her tongue braving out to meet his. She wasn't sure she was doing this right, but didn't much care—she was just doing what felt good. And, God, did it feel good. Without realizing it, she closed her legs around his hand, trapping it there briefly as she kissed him, pressing it tighter against herself. Then she felt him pull his hand free and moaned her disappointment into his mouth.

Chuckling softly, Hethe broke the kiss and smiled at her. "Don't worry, little one. I—"

Helen blinked and glanced down when he stopped talking so abruptly. His gaze had traveled downward and he appeared confused. Glancing down at herself as well, she saw the fur he had revealed by removing the upper linen while she was distracted. The desire inside her died a quick death. *Uh-oh*, some part of her brain cried out like a child. Helen steeled herself against what was to come.

* * *

Hethe stared rather blankly. It was not a cold night. Fur was not needed; a simple linen would have done. But his wife was swathed in a fur that was tucked tightly around her body, covering her from the neck down. Even her arms were under it. He hadn't noticed it when they had hustled him into the bed, but now, as he stared at it, he felt the passion inside him fading away to be replaced with apprehension. All of his earlier suspicions regarding her "preparations" returned. This fur, he suspected, did not bode well. Part of him wanted to think she had covered up out of shyness, to prevent any of the men from seeing anything that only he should see, but he very much feared that wasn't the case. Deciding he had best look and get it over with, Hethe reached out grimly and pulled the fur aside.

Helen waited for the explosion. She fully expected one. Shrieking, shouting, roaring, bellowing. Perhaps even hitting. She had known it was a good possibility; this was the Hammer, after all. But she got none of that. In fact, at first she got no response from him at all. The man just sat, frozen beside her, as the odious scent of the plant Ducky had called stinkweed began to waft out into the room around them. Helen had rubbed the plant over every inch of her skin as if she were putting on some lotion.

It was terribly potent, she knew, but Hethe was not responding as she had expected. He just sat. Then she chanced a glance at his face and realized that his eyes had gone round with horror, his mouth opening and closing silently, and his nose had pinched closed all on its own. He was pale, but quickly gaining a greenish tint.

"Is something amiss, my lord?" she asked when

she couldn't stand the silence any longer. She hoped she managed to infuse complete innocence into her voice. "Are we not going to consummate the marriage now?"

Just to add to the moment, she brazenly whipped the covering away from her body completely, revealing herself, but also fanning the odor outward at him. The trap was sprung! She watched with interest as he blanched, gagging under the assault, then made a mad scramble off the bed.

He backed away from her, his eyes shooting wildly about the room until they settled on the chamber pot. The next thing Helen knew, her new husband was hanging over it, heaving out his meal.

Surely this would push him over the edge and send the man running to the king to have this wedding annulled, she thought with satisfaction. More importantly, so much for the wedding night, she thought with an amusement impeded only somewhat by the misery her own scent was causing her. The amusement fled her face and she eyed him warily as her new husband's retching finally ended, and he straightened to glare at her.

He was not pleased.

Actually, she would say he was furious. Enraged. Yes, she had certainly gained his attention with this stunt. This was no longer a silent war. It was out in the open.

"What is that?" he asked grimly.

Helen didn't even bother to pretend not to know what he was talking about. "Ducky calls it stink-weed. It grows in a marshy area not far from here." She smiled sweetly and asked, "Did you wish to try it on, like you did the garlic? I am sure Ducky could fetch some more, should you wish."

She felt immense satisfaction when he blanched in horror. There was no need to fear consummation tonight. She had won. Helen had barely formed that satisfying thought when Hethe suddenly strode to the door and flung it open. She wasn't all that surprised to see Ducky and her aunt outside, having huddled by the door to await his reaction. They had probably both feared he would kill her; Helen suspected he may just have done so, had he been able to bear coming near her. He was *furious*.

For a moment, Helen feared he may take that fury out on the trembling maid and her aunt, but he didn't.

His voice was cold with rage, but controlled, as he ignored her aunt and snapped at Ducky. "You will fetch a bath up here. You will also fetch every ounce of perfume, every flower petal, every *anything* that smells pleasant and bring it up here as well! Do you understand me?"

"Aye, my lord." Ducky scurried away as quickly as her feet would take her. Helen saw the woman crossing herself as she rushed toward the stairs. Her husband's gaze then turned to Aunt Nell, who took a wary step back.

"I think I shall just . . ." She waved vaguely and made a quick escape under his glower.

Helen shifted in the bed, tugging back the fur to cover herself. The action immediately drew her husband's gaze back to the bed. If looks could do harm, his would have burnt her to a cinder on the spot.

Helen peered down at the fur covering her and began to pluck at it nervously to avoid his gaze. Much to her amazement, she was suddenly suffering guilt. It was a wife's duty to submit, and she wasn't exactly submitting.

Irritated by the discomfort her own conscience was causing her, Helen reminded herself that this man was a cruel, heartless bastard, and that she didn't want to be his wife. The fact that none of his behavior since arriving at Tiernay really backed up the bad opinion she had gained of him these past few years was somewhat damping to her sense of righteousness, but she forced her chin up grimly anyway. There was *nothing* for her to feel guilty about.

Chapter 9

*H*ETHE'S eyes narrowed dangerously on his bride. For a moment, he thought he had seen a glimmer of shame on her face. That fact had soothed his temper somewhat, but then her expression turned defiant and she glared at him as if this situation were all his fault. Pushing the door closed, he moved toward the bed; his hands clenching in fury. He only got halfway across the room before his bride's eyes widened in alarm. Without further warning, she tossed the fur covering her aside, once again fanning the scent out at him.

"Did you wish to try, after all, my lord?" she squeaked.

Hethe paused abruptly and gagged again, then charged for the window. He had already befouled the chamber pot. This time he tossed the rest of the first good meal he had been served at Tiernay out the window and into the courtyard below. A muffled laugh sounded from the bed behind him, and Hethe silently vowed his wife would pay for this. Aye. She would pay.

Hethe was still hanging out the window when a

knock sounded at the door several moments later. His stomach empty now, he was no longer tossing up its contents. He was simply breathing in the sweet fresh air that the position offered him. Straightening reluctantly, he turned to shout, "Enter," then watched from his relatively safe location by the window as the door opened and a slew of servants filed in carrying a tub and pail after pail of water.

Hethe watched grimly as the tub was set down and water poured into it. It was amazing, really, how swiftly they worked, he thought with amusement. His wife's servants could not seem to finish their chores and leave quickly enough. He did not miss how each of them stumbled in their step, or cringed as they caught wind of the sickly sweet odor that perfumed the air. Without fail, each servant glanced to their mistress, then to him. He had no doubt that they knew what was about, and Hethe grew grimmer with each humiliating moment that passed. It seemed this had not been a silent war of wills at all. He was beginning to suspect that every person in Tiernay Castle knew about the battle their mistress had waged. It seemed the only people left ignorant were his men and Lord Templetun.

Hethe supposed he should be grateful that they, at least, were unaware of the humiliating fact that he was an unwanted groom. But he wasn't feeling particularly thankful at the moment.

His wife's maid was the last to enter. Ducky. A basket full of bottles and vials hung over her arm. Hethe gestured for her to approach. Taking the basket from her, he then bent a glare on the servant. Ducky wasn't a stupid woman. Heeding his silent order, she threw her mistress an anxious, apologetic look, then fled the room. She pulled the door closed behind herself and the last of the other servants. Hethe and his wife were alone.

He immediately turned his glare on her. Apparently, she wasn't as bright as Ducky. Either that, or she was stubbornly playing dense. Eyebrows arching, she asked innocently, "What?"

"Get in the bath," he ordered.

She hesitated briefly. Then, apparently deciding not to risk open rebellion, she gathered the fur around her in an awkward sort of toga and eased carefully off the bed. Raising her chin, she crossed the room, walking in a sort of arc so that she passed close by him.

He nearly whimpered when he found himself briefly adrift in the odoriferous if invisible cloud that surrounded her. His stomach churned ominously. Closing his eyes, he concentrated on keeping what was left in his stomach, in his stomach. Her scent, on top of the garlic that had been plaguing his digestion ever since he consumed it, made a rotten combination.

The sickening aroma faded. Hethe opened his eyes to see with some relief that she now stood before the bath. Rather than drop the fur and get in, however, she simply stood shifting from one foot to the other. He was confused by her hesitation until she began to open the fur covering, then paused to glance over her shoulder at him unhappily. It came to him then that she was reluctant to disrobe in front of him.

Not surprising, really. Despite the fact that they were married, they were nearly strangers. He would have wondered had she not showed some reticence. In fact, had this been a normal wedding night, and

she a normal, shy, innocent young bride, he might
have given her privacy—at least until she had dis-
robed and entered the bath. This, however, was
nothing near a normal wedding night, and Lady
Helen was far from the normal, shy and innocent
bride. The Good Lord alone knew what she might
get up to while his back was turned. He was not going to turn it.

"In!" he snapped.

Lady Helen's eyes narrowed on him in impotent
fury; then she turned away, straightening her shoulders grimly and dropping the fur. Hethe's mouth
curved up in slight amusement at the flash of pink
skin he caught as she leapt for the cover of the bath.
He was positive the fur hadn't even hit the rushes
before she had settled herself in the water, knees
drawn up, and arms wrapped grimly about them in
as modest a position as one could manage in a tub.

As fast as she had been, he had still caught a titil-
lating glimpse of her shapely legs and behind. Had
his stomach not still been roiling, he was not sure he
would have appreciated it more. As it was, he merely
noted that her arse was as generous as her bosom.
That pleased him. He straightened grimly and began
to root through the basket Ducky had provided. She
had taken his order seriously and brought anything
that might be thought pleasing in scent. Dried herbs
usually used for cooking lay nestled among the des-
iccated petals of various flowers. There were also
several different oils and tinctures. Hethe opened
one or two bottles, sniffing the contents suspiciously.

They were all pleasant enough, Hethe supposed.
But then, next to his wife, cow dung probably would
have smelled like heaven at the moment. That
thought made him pause and glare briefly at her

slender, curved back. Which was, of course, a waste of time. She was wholly unaware of his stare. Giving up, he turned his attention back to deciding what to try first.

His wife's putrid stink drifted across the room to him now that the fur no longer cloaked it. One whiff was enough to make him decide that he would use the largest container of scented oil first, and if that wasn't sufficient, would add another. Straightening determinedly, he sucked in a deep breath and held it as he strode forward.

Pausing beside the tub, Hethe dug through the basket of containers for the largest. He snatched it out, opened it and tipped its contents into the bathwater between his wife's pink back and the rim of the tub. She stiffened, but neither spoke nor looked around.

Hethe hesitated a moment, then replaced the container in the basket and bent to swish the water around with one hand, splashing some onto her back, over her shoulders, and even onto her head. She squawked in protest as the water ran down her hair and face; then she turned her head to snarl at him over her shoulder.

Ignoring the look, Hethe straightened, hesitated, then risked a quick breath of air. A noise of disgust nearly slid from his lips, but he caught it back. The one container of oil, of course, had not been enough. Hethe retrieved the next bottle, opened it, and dumped the contents in as well.

Holding his newest foul breath, he dug another container out of the basket and quickly dumped it in. His lady wife jerked around to stare as he was dumping in that third container. Her eyes widened briefly in horror; then she set to squawking.

Hethe thought she was shrieking something about mixing the scents and not to use all of them, but he wasn't sure. He was growing a bit light-headed— though he didn't know whether it was from holding his breath so long or from having the revolting stench of her trapped in his lungs. Whatever the case, he was not going to be deterred. Ignoring her protestations, he quickly emptied the last of the containers into the bathwater; then, holding the empty containers awkwardly in one hand, he upended the basket over her, raining flower petals and herbs over her hair and shoulders into the water. She stopped squawking then and quickly lowered her head to avoid getting any dried goods in her eyes or mouth.

Hethe gave the basket a good shake to make sure that every last flower petal and bit of herb was in the bath with her, then staggered away from the tub, dropping the now empty containers back in the basket as he did. Once a good distance away, he released the foul air trapped in his lungs and took a tentative breath. Much to his horror, despite his efforts, there was no lovely perfume to the air. If anything, the smell now was worse than it had been. And he was standing further away than before.

"What?" he choked out in horror. His wife's head swiveled, her eyes fastening on him with murder in their depths as she glared out from beneath the bits of dried flowers and herbs that had caught in her hair.

"As I was telling you, my lord. One should never haphazardly mix perfumes and herbs. They do not always blend well."

Hethe closed his eyes with a groan. Not only had they not mixed well together, it seemed to him they didn't mix with her at all. At least not with the *eau de stink-weed* clinging to her. If anything, adding the herbs, flowers and oils had only accentuated her original stench, amplifying it. Rather than defeating, he had aided her. The realization was rather galling.

A sudden solid mass at his back brought Hethe's attention to the fact that while he had been thinking, he had also been unconsciously backing away from his bride. He now stood against the wall next to the window. Even there he could not escape her stench. His eyes were beginning to sting and fill with tears as they were assaulted by the pungent air.

Hethe cursed under his breath. It looked as if consummating the marriage was definitely out of the question, now. The only positive thing about the situation was that his bride looked about as miserable as he had been since arriving at Tiernay.

Aye, this definitely made up for his cold, mean room, ancient maid, frigid bath, horrid food, awful ale, flea-ridden bed and his bride's unbearable breath. Not to mention her little scheme to get him in the water today. And whereas he had been able to at least escape his flea-ridden bed and room, she could not escape her own stink. Aye. Had he planned this, it would have been a brilliant strategy.

"Oh, no!"

Drawn from his thoughts, Hethe glanced at his wife sharply, noting with dismay that her face was turning a bright red. "What?"

"Those flower petals. What were they?" she asked urgently.

Hethe stared at her blankly for a moment, then noticed that her eyes were growing puffy and turning red—rather like they had that day they had picnicked in the field. His eyes widened incredulously. Was it his imagination, or did he vaguely smell . . . ? Peering down at the basket he held, he lifted one vial after another out to briefly sniff. It was a whiff of the largest one that made him pause. This was the bottle he had poured in first. The one he had mixed about in the water before splashing it over her head and shoulders. His eyes turned to his bride in horror. She didn't notice. She had raised her arms out of the water and was peering at them in dismay. Even from where he stood, Hethe could see the angry rash beginning to form on her skin.

"Posies!" she shrieked, suddenly leaping from the water as though it were acid. That was when he saw that the irritation did not just cover her arms. Every inch of her that had been submerged in the water was now growing a dark red rash. Oh, dear, this definitely made up for everything she had done or tried to do to him, he thought faintly as she held her arms away from her body and turned slowly to face him.

"You threw posies in here with me?" she cried in disbelief.

Unable to speak, Hethe merely held up the empty vial. It hadn't been petals, he was sure; it had been the oil. Her howl of misery nearly deafened him. Guilt suddenly enveloping him, Hethe began to ease his way toward the door. This was not good. Not good at all. Nope. He had never meant for something like this to happen. This was . . . Well, it was awful, he decided as he reached the door and scrambled to open it.

Just seeming to notice his attempt to flee, Helen stopped howling and transfixed him with her eyes. "Where are you going?"

"Going?" Hethe gave a guilty start, then hesitated briefly, his hand pausing on the doorknob.

"Aye. You are not just going to leave me like this, are you?" she cried miserably.

"Leave you? Nay, nay." He began to scrabble at the door latch again as she started forward, her scent billowing forward in a noxious cloud.

"Nay, of course not," he assured her solemnly, but the humor of the situation and the way her plans had backfired were suddenly striking him as terribly amusing, and he was having trouble keeping a smile off his face. He knew his lips were twitching, and that only seemed to infuriate the woman before him more.

"Nay. I merely thought to fetch your maid up to attend to you . . . and perhaps your aunt, too," he murmured, then pulled the door open and slid through it while he could. Hethe barely got the door closed before a frustrated screech sounded and something crashed against the door.

His amusement dying, replaced by concern now that she was no longer standing before him, arms outstretched, hair and body littered with bits of herbs and dried flowers, he hurried for the stairs to the great hall in search of assistance.

Helen was rolling on the bed scratching herself like mad by the time her aunt and Ducky appeared. Their arrival didn't stop her, though. She didn't even look around to see who it was. She simply continued to writhe on the mattress scratching whatever she could reach with her hands. What she could not reach with her nails was chafed against the rough fur with her wriggling and writhing.

"Oh, dear God! Helen!" Her aunt rushed to the bedside and put a restraining hand on her shoulder. Helen flinched and immediately nudged the hand away to scratch, even as Nell got a first whiff of her and jerked back in horror. "What has he *done* to you?"

"The oils and flowers didn't mix well with the stink-weed," Helen cried out between little gasps for breath.

"I can smell that much," Nell muttered, pinching her nose closed with a thumb and finger. "But the itching, Helen. What happened to cause the itching?"

Helen curled into a fetal position to scratch her legs, feet and between her toes before answering. "There was essence of posies in one of the vials Ducky gave him!"

"Oh, no!" the maid cried in horror when Aunt Nell turned on her. "I didn't know. I swear. He said to fetch everything that smelled good. I raided the kitchen, then went to Old Joan the Healer and told her to give me anything she had that was pleasant smelling. I did not even think to check what each was." She turned to peer guiltily at her writhing mistress. "Oh, my lady, I am so sorry."

Too agonized to answer, Helen merely continued writhing and twisting, aware that her two friends were watching helplessly. Then her aunt turned to Ducky and said, "Go find Old Joan. Explain what's happened. She must have a salve or something that will help. Bring her here."

Nodding, the maid hurried from the room. Aunt Nell waited until she had gone, then turned her concern back upon her niece. "Helen. You must try to stop scratching. You will cause scars. Please." She moved close enough to lay her free hand gently on Helen's shoulder. This time, when Helen reached up to nudge her hand away, Nell caught her fingers and held them firmly. "You must try to stop."

"No," Helen moaned, trying to pull her hand free. "This rash is driving me mad."

Nell's mouth tightened, and she was silent for a moment. To Helen it seemed that she was listening for something. She understood what when Nell said, "You are wheezing, girl. Are you having trouble breathing? Damn! I should have told Ducky to have the others bring up a fresh bath. We should be trying to wash the posy essence off you." Releasing Helen's hand, she whirled away and hurried out of the room.

Helen promptly resumed scratching herself. She knew she shouldn't, even wanted to stop, but she felt as if her skin were crawling with hundreds of spiders, their little legs tickling across her flesh.

It seemed like hours that her aunt was gone, though in reality it was probably only moments. The woman returned with a battery of servants bearing Lady Shambleau's own private tub and fresh bathwater. Ducky was hard on her heels, leading the old woman from whom she'd gotten the scented oils.

The healer took one look at Helen and rushed to the bed to grab her hands and hold them. "No," she said firmly when Helen tried to struggle. "Don't let her scratch," she ordered Ducky. The maid rushed forward to take the healer's place, but it required Nell's added strength to restrain Helen enough so that the healer was free to begin mixing her salves and ointments.

"Try not to remove the smell," Helen ordered spitefully, writhing so that the fur would scratch her back since she could not use her fingers.

Joan turned an exasperated glance on her, but it was Nell who spoke up: "Surely you do not think he will try to consummate the marriage now?" she cried in disbelief.

Helen's thoughts at that moment were more along the lines of revenge. She could no longer discern the foul stench clinging to her. She was positive it had killed her ability to smell. But she could tell by the reaction of the others that it was still strong upon her, and as she lay there, desperate to relieve an all-over body itch that would not be relieved, she was thinking that she and her husband should spend a lot more time together. Should get better acquainted. She was going to cling to him as English ivy did a wall, she decided grimly.

"Just try to not remove the smell," she hissed when she realized they were still waiting for her answer.

Shaking her head, Old Joan tossed aside the herbs she had been mixing and started afresh.

Hethe crept down the hall, mostly feeling his way in the darkness. The sun had not yet risen, though he had spied the orange and pink streaks of dawn on the horizon from the window of the small, cold bedchamber he had been given. It had not been a comfortable night. He had shunned the bed so as to avoid the fleas and had again slept huddled in the cracked chair by the cold fireless hearth. Even so, it had been better than sleeping in the room his bride had poisoned with the odors of posy and stinkweed.

Dear God, just the idea of returning there now made him wince. But it must be done. Lord Templetun had retired directly after he and the other men had seen Hethe to his bridal bed. At least, the man had not been below when Hethe had gone down to find Lady Shambleau and his wife's maid. Templetun had also apparently managed to sleep through the disturbance that had followed the bedding ceremony. That being the case, the man was ignorant of what had gone on last night, and Hethe was hoping to keep him that way. Which meant that when the king's man arrived to demand proof of the consummation, Hethe would provide it. He doubted if his bride was in any state to do so. From all accounts, she had had a rough night.

There would surely be hell to pay if the king's man wasn't provided with proof, and Hethe had had just about enough hell of late. So, as the first streaks of light peeked over the horizon, he'd ripped a strip of linen off the top of the bed—as far from where the flea-ridden fur had been as possible—shook it out, then tied it around his face to cover his nose and mouth. Then he had inflicted a small cut on his hand, bloodied the center of the linen, and tugged it off his bed. He now crept down the hall of Tiernay Castle, headed for his wife's room. He should have shaken it out better, he realized as a sudden itching began beneath his arm, right where the bundled linen rested. The sheet was still infested.

Picking up his pace a bit, he was relieved when he felt the wall give way to another door. Pausing, he took a deep breath, then eased the door open and slid into the room. While the windowless hallway had been pitch-black, the sun had risen quickly during Hethe's slow journey and his wife's bedchamber was already filling with an orangish golden glow. Taking a reluctant step away from the door, Hethe peered toward the bed and the woman sleeping in it. The light really wasn't very complimentary to her present state. It just accentuated the blotchy red rash covering her once flawless skin.

Hethe had the grace to feel guilt wash over him. He truly hadn't meant to cause this. He had lost his temper and acted rashly, not even thinking before dumping the vials of oils and such into the bath with her. He knew better than that. Acting rashly could be terribly dangerous. It often got men killed and, apparently, caused rashes on women.

He was grimacing over that fact when a rapping sounded at the door, startling him. Head jerking around, he started toward it only to pause partway there. He could hardly answer the door as he was. He reached up to tug the linen off his face, scowling and scooting closer to the door as the room's foul atmosphere assailed him. Trying not to gag, he released the linens long enough to tug his tunic off over his head, then drop it to the side. Retrieving the linens, he stood so that the door would block him and opened it a crack to shove the linens out at whomever had knocked.

"Here. Go away. We are still sleeping," he hissed, then after a bare glimpse of the priest and Templetun's startled expression, and Lady Shambleau's shocked one, he pulled the door closed.

"What is about?" That sleepy question from the bed drew Hethe's gaze, and he turned to gape at his bride. Oh . . . this light really was not flattering to her at all. No, sir. She was sitting up in bed now, clutching the linen to her breasts and squinting out of her red, swollen eyes toward him. It seemed obvious that she couldn't see a damn thing. Which was probably for the best, for if she were able to see what she looked like just now . . . Well, she would probably be screaming her head off.

"Nothing. Go back to sleep," he hissed at her in a hoarse whisper, then turned away to open the door a crack and peer out. Lord Templetun, Lady Shambleau and the priest were all moving down the hall toward the stairs, taking the linens with them. It seemed they were satisfied, he realized with relief. At least, Lord Templetun and the priest were. Lady Shambleau was glancing back over her shoulder and, when she saw the door had cracked open again, eyed Hethe with suspicion.

"What are you doing?" There was suspicion in Helen's voice, too, behind him. The sleepiness was completely gone for she had recognized her husband by his voice.

Sighing, Hethe eased the door closed and started back toward the bed, only to be brought up short by the smell. Retrieving from the floor the scrap of linen he had been using to filter the stink, he quickly retied it around his face, then quickly snatched up his tunic and replaced it as well. He took another step toward the bed, but again paused. It appeared his mask was only effective from a distance.

"Who was at the door?"

"That was Lord Templetun, your aunt and the priest," Hethe admitted reluctantly.

"What did you shove out at them?" she asked, squinting even harder in his general direction. Her eyes were nearly swollen shut, and he had to wonder how much she was seeing, if anything at all.

"A bloodied linen," he explained gently. "I realized they would come looking for it this morning, so I crept in here to give it to them," he announced. He awaited her praise for his thoughtfulness, but he should have known better.

"You *what*?" She was out of the bed and charging around it at him in a trice, apparently so mad she forgot that she wasn't wearing a stitch of clothing.

Unfortunately, it wasn't a pretty sight. Dear God, he had never seen skin so mottled, he thought as he backed away, not out of fear of a physical attack but to avoid her intensifying smell.

"I thought to save you any embarrassment," he said quickly, his feet moving faster than his mouth as he scrambled back toward the door.

"Save me embarrassment?" she snapped, her forward momentum briefly halting—much to his relief. "What you did was trap me in this marriage! They will not annul it if they think it was consummated."

Hethe felt himself stiffen. He had suspected that this was the purpose behind his bride's actions of last night, but suspecting and knowing were not the same thing. A man's pride could only take so much.

Forcing himself to remain calm, he tried to reason with her. "We were trapped the moment the king decided we should wed. All I have done is—"

"*We?*" Her head reared back, and she gave a short laugh. "As if *you* are unhappy about this! Ha! You get Tiernay, a fine, prosperous estate!"

Hethe's eyes narrowed on her; he was losing his temper quickly. "Aye," he agreed. "I get Tiernay. Unfortunately, it comes with you! A stinking, blotchy, rash-covered wench who doesn't have the sense to know when to be grateful."

A shocked gasp flew from her lips then, her mouth opening and closing like that of a fish. She shut it a moment later, and he could see her winding up to release an insult or two in return, but he forestalled her by adding, "And if you are trying to lure me to your bed, you would do better to put some clothes *on*. I fear this light does not do a thing for you."

His wife glanced down at herself, her eyes widening

as she realized she was standing there as naked as the day she was born. Then she raced back to bed with a squeal. Hethe took the opportunity to leave the battlefield, sliding quickly out of the room and pulling the door closed with a snap. He was pretty sure he had won this round, but it gave him little pleasure. He didn't feel that he had really fought fair, picking on her rash as he had.

And he hadn't been completely honest, either. While the rash detracted somewhat from her looks, it had not hidden the lusciousness of her curves, or the pertness of her breasts. Damned if he wasn't a little excited. If it weren't for her smell, rash or no, he would be very tempted to go back and make the fake consummation a reality.

Damn! Real war was so much easier than this one raging between him and his bride. At least in real war he did not run about aching to make love to the enemy.

Chapter 10

"WHAT are you doing?"

Helen straightened from rifling through her chest at the dismayed cry from the doorway. Turning to see her aunt rushing into the room and closing the door behind her, Helen gave her a nod of greeting, then turned back to her search.

"I am looking for a dress," she explained. "An older one. One I will not mind losing should this stench not wash out—Aha!" She straightened, a suitable garment in hand.

"Oh, nay, Helen. You cannot go below like this," Nell protested, covering her nose with her hand as she hurried to her niece's side and urged her to her feet. "You should stay up here for a while. Give your rash the opportunity to heal, to go away and—" She paused mid-sentence to turn her head away and gasp for fresh air. "Dear Lord!"

Trying not to be offended by her aunt's reaction, Helen shrugged her relative off and shook out the gown she held, trying to remove the worst of its wrinkles from being stored in the chest. "I must speak to Templetun. Tell him that the marriage isn't consummated, that it must be annulled."

"Nay." Her aunt snatched the gown away, then, using it to cover her nose and mouth, began to urge Helen back to bed. The woman's voice was muffled as she said, "Not as you are, Helen. You cannot let the man see you this way. He will know at once what you have been up to. Mayhap if you are . . . better tomorrow, you may see him then."

"But—"

"Do you really think the king will be pleased to know what we have been up to here? Why, the Good Lord knows what he would do if he should hear of our behavior. He certainly would not congratulate you on the idea. He's having enough trouble with a disobedient son; do you think he will be pleased with a disobedient vassal?"

"Nay," Helen agreed reluctantly. Shoulders slumping, she stopped resisting and allowed herself to be marched back to her bed. "I shall wait till the morrow. But you must not let Templetun leave before I can speak to him."

"I won't," Aunt Nell promised through the gown still pressed to her face. She used her free hand to tug the linens up around Helen's shoulders. "Now, you just rest," she instructed, then made a quick exit, still covering her nose with the dress as she slipped out of the room.

Sighing miserably, Helen lay back on the mattress and tried to ignore the fact that every single inch of her body seemed to be begging for her to scratch it. Which was all *his* fault, of course. The oaf. The ass. The . . . She gave up on maligning him with a sigh. There simply weren't enough words to describe the man. At least, not words nasty enough.

Her mind drifted back to their earlier argument and the things he had said. "*A stinking, blotchy, rash-covered wench who doesn't have the sense to know when to be grateful.*" Ha! What had she to be grateful for? Marriage to him? The Hammer of Holden? The cruelest bastard in northern England? A man whose people crawled to Helen begging for charity?

Realizing she was scratching her arm, she stopped and peered at the ugly red blisters covering her skin. They really were ugly. She must look a mess. Perfectly horrid. The thought was terribly lowering. Helen had never thought of herself as vain, and she had always considered looks unimportant, but right at that moment, she felt horrid. Ugly and itchy . . . and miserable. Something ran down her cheek and she lifted a hand to find wetness there. Tears. She was crying. Oh, great.

She sniffled miserably, then winced as her own odor offended her. She had been compelled to breathe through her mouth to avoid her own stench through the last miserable night, and had not slept a wink. While she had been numb to the odor at first, after a while it was as if the scent changed, leaving her inhaling a new form of stink with every breath. The only way to avoid it had been to cover herself with the furs. But those were so warm they had merely irritated her rash, driving her mad with itchiness. Neither state—nauseated or covered in hives— was conducive to sleeping. The first streaks of light were creeping into the sky before Helen had finally drifted off due to sheer exhaustion.

She had been woken mere moments later by that oaf she had married the day before, that buffoon who had the gall to call her blotchy and stinky. Her tears were starting to come in earnest now, and Helen sniffled once more, but this time it was not due to the olfactory assault. Her nose was plugged up from weeping. Which just went to show that there truly was a bright side to everything, she supposed miserably, then proceeded to cry herself to sleep.

"It is a larger estate than I had thought."

Hethe tore his gaze from the land they were riding through to glance at his first. "Aye," William agreed quietly. They were just returning from surveying the Tiernay estates. They had not managed to cover them all, but had covered a good portion of the fiefdom.

Lady Helen was an excellent manager; she knew what she was about and appeared to be doing an excellent job. Hethe's gaze slid to Boswell, Lady Helen's man, whom he had enlisted to guide them on this tour. The man had proven himself extremely knowledgeable. He had also been extremely polite all throughout this trip, but his resentment and dislike had shown. As had the resentment and dislike of most of the villeins they had come into contact with, that day. Admittedly, those were few. While Lady Helen had dragged him to every cottage with a baby in it, and while the people he had met with her had been quiet but not openly antagonistic, Boswell had seemed to deliberately steer them clear of the majority of Tiernay's people. And those few they had come in contact with had been surly and resentful.

The open and apparent distrust of his newest subjects was a tad disturbing to Hethe. He was used to spending his time around his warriors on the battlefield, and every last one of them was faithful and respectful. Not only that, they also liked him.

Hethe did not understand, and he did not care for this animosity being directed his way. He would have liked to blame it on Helen, but since her presence on the day of their picnic had seemed to prevent this very behavior, he did not know what to think.

"You slept late this morning." There was a touch of teasing in his friend's comment, and Hethe nearly wore down his teeth grinding them together. It was not that he was angry with his first; it was that thoughts of the night before—his wedding night—made him want to smash something. God! What a debacle.

It had not started out badly. He had a vivid recollection of his bride's body soft beneath him, her lips opening beneath his like a flower to the sun. Her tongue stroking his. Her moans and sighs. The way she had arched into him. The way his body had responded to her eagerness, turning hard and demanding.

Unfortunately, he also had vivid recollections of the scent of her once that fur had been stripped aside, and of puking up his dinner out the window before forcing her into the perfume-laden bath. Damn, one memory made him hot for her, the other made him want to throttle her. But the memory of her initial response to his touch gave him hope. He was sure that if it had not been for her rude scent intruding on them, he would have consummated the wedding last night—and with Lady Helen's blessing. She had certainly moaned and sighed and arched and shuddered beneath him like a willing wench. Until her trick had called them both back from their passion.

"Long sleepless night?" William teased now,

making Hethe realize that he had not responded to the earlier comment.

"It was my wedding night," he pointed out, somewhat uncomfortable regarding the dishonesty of that implication. "One is not expected to sleep much on his wedding night."

"Nay." The other man grinned, then shook his head and sighed. "I must admit, I envy you. She is a beautiful woman."

"Aye. She is."

"And she has a sweet voice. I find it hard to believe she is the Tyrant of Tiernay."

"I don't," Hethe muttered artlessly, then scowled. "I mean, I don't believe it myself," he lied to cover up that there was anything wrong with his marriage. Much to his relief, the group left the woods then and began to cross the open land that circled the castle.

Hethe immediately spurred his horse to a trot, grateful for the excuse to avoid his man's questions.

Helen was pleased to find the great hall relatively empty when she crept downstairs. She had hoped it would be so, since it was late morning and there was a while yet until the people would congregate to enjoy their midday meal. Still, the way her luck was going lately, she would not have been surprised to arrive to find the room crawling with people. There were just half a dozen servants moving about, though, each seeing to his chores.

Helen went in search of food. She had not eaten much at the wedding celebration the night before, then had cried herself to sleep this morning instead of breaking her fast, so when she had woken up several moments ago, she was famished. She had dressed, brushed her hair and made her way below questing for sustenance hoping to get something to eat and drink, then slink away before the hall started to fill up.

With that thought in mind, Helen approached the nearest servant, grimacing when the woman glanced up to see her and briefly smile. Very briefly. The look was quickly replaced with one of horror as Helen drew nearer and her stench became apparent.

Muttering rather desperately that she would fetch Ducky, the servant whirled away and hurried toward the kitchens. She was followed quickly by all the other servants as the stench surrounding Helen slowly began to fill the hall. No one wished to be near her.

Trying to convince herself not to take it personally, Helen moved to sit at the trestle tables with a sigh. They had already been cleared, of course. There was not a scrap of bread, a bit of cheese or a mug of mead about for her to partake of while she waited. It wasn't long, though, before the sound of the kitchen door opening drew Helen's attention away from her hunger.

Glancing over her shoulder, she saw Ducky moving cautiously closer, and she stood to greet her. The maid paused several feet away, her nose wrinkling briefly before she controlled the instinct and managed a smile.

"Good morn, my lady," Ducky began, then bit her lip. "Your lady aunt said that you would not be coming below today. She seemed to think it would be best if you remain in your room until the worst of . . ." She gestured vaguely toward Helen, a gesture that might have referred to her smell or to the angry red rash covering her once pearl-white skin. "Until it had passed."

"I know, but I woke up and was hungry. I came in search of food."

"Oh. Of course. Well, I can bring something up to your room for you and—"

"There is no need for that, Ducky. I would rather eat here. It will be less trouble for you." When the maid looked doubtful of her plan, Helen sighed. "I am sick unto death of sitting in my room. There is no one around right now. If I eat quickly, I can be done and return above stairs before anyone comes."

"But your aunt—"

"Where *is* my aunt?" Helen interrupted impatiently.

"She went down to the village. Lucy had her baby and—"

"Lucy had her child? Oh, I should go see her!" Helen's excitement died abruptly at her maid's horrified expression, and melancholy took its place. "Oh. No, I suppose that wouldn't be a good idea, would it?"

"Why do you not just sit down, my lady, and I shall bring you something to eat and drink," Ducky murmured. She'd evidently relented on forcing her mistress to return to her room, and she was eyeing Helen now pityingly.

Nodding despondently, Helen sank back onto a trestle table bench and sighed miserably as her maid hurried off to do as she'd promised.

Hethe's relief upon returning to Tiernay Castle was short-lived. He had barely taken two steps inside the keep when his nose was assailed by the most godawful smell. He knew at once that his wife was somewhere about. Still, it took him a moment to place her as the woman seated at the trestle table. Mostly, he supposed, because he could not believe that her stench could reach so far. She must have just come below, he decided, leaving a trail of foul air to drift in the atmosphere behind her. He took in her forlorn pose with a weary sigh.

"Dear God, what is that smell?" William exclaimed, a step behind his master.

Hethe promptly turned to face both him and the men who had accompanied him on the tour. They had all been eagerly looking forward to a drink to wet their dust-filled mouths. "You and the rest of the men go down to the village tavern for a drink, William," he instructed grimly. "I shall follow directly."

His first hesitated a moment, then shrugged and turned to herd the men back out of the keep.

Hethe waited until the door closed behind him, then cautiously approached his wife. He found he could only manage to get within ten feet of her before the smell became completely unbearable. Taking a seat on a bench some distance from her, he turned about to eye her. He was positive she was aware of his presence, but she did not trouble herself to address him or even look his way.

She was pushing meat and cheese around in a trencher, looking completely miserable. Hethe felt his heart soften somewhat for how she must be suffering. She could not get away from herself. Also, he experienced some guilt because he was responsible for worsening her state. Yet, he remembered, she had brought it on herself with that damnable weed. He frowned over at her.

"Is there something wrong with your food?" he asked. As an opening gambit it left much to be desired, but it did make his wife raise her head to look at him. Hethe nearly winced at the sight. Her face was pale, the only color being dark shadows beneath her eyes and those damnable patches of raw skin. Her hair was pulled sharply back from her face, leaving it looking somewhat hawkish.

"Nay."

"Then why are you not eating? If the fare isn't acceptable, you should let Cook know."

She heaved a sigh at that. "There is nothing wrong with the food. It is me."

"You?"

"I cannot smell anything but myself, and therefore can taste nothing I eat," she explained quietly.

Hethe grimaced. He could understand that completely. The smell was certainly killing the appetite with which he had returned from his tour. Unfortunately, there was nothing he could do to rectify the stink, so he struggled for something with which to change the subject. He suddenly noticed that she was wearing the ugliest damn dress he had ever seen. Not just ugly, it was faded and tattered and even a bit too small. He scowled as he peered at it. "What the Devil are you wearing?"

At her husband's words, Helen glanced down at herself with disinterest. "A dress."

"Well, I can see that. But why are you not wearing something more befitting a lady? You have better gowns than this. I have seen at least two of them on you."

"Those are my good gowns," she explained patiently. "I thought I should save them—" She paused abruptly as a servant suddenly appeared at the table with a mug and a pitcher of ale. The serving maid set the mug before Lord Holden and poured drink into it, then hesitated, her gaze shooting reluctantly to Helen. "Did you wish for some ale, too, my lady?"

It was obvious the girl was hoping that Helen would say no, and Helen almost did out of pity, but she had awoken with a terrible thirst and had quickly consumed the mug of mead Ducky had brought with her meal. Grimacing apologetically, she pushed her mug as far along the table as she could in answer.

The servant bit her lip unhappily, then straightened her shoulders like a soldier going into battle, sucked in a deep breath, held it, and raced forward. She filled the mug with more speed than care, slopping much onto the table in her rush. In an effort to redeem herself, Helen supposed, she then pushed the mug halfway back toward her mistress before whirling to rush away. Her gasp as she released the air she had been holding was quite plain in the silence of the room as she rushed toward the kitchens, sucking in great gulps of air.

Helen sighed, her gaze sliding to the Hammer. The man was gazing after the servant and, even as she watched, amusement began to curve his lips. A laugh bubbled up inside him, until he caught her glare. He straightened his face at once.

"Hmmm," he said, clearing his throat and grimacing in an obvious effort to kill his desire to laugh. Surely he knew she would never forgive him, or allow him into her bed, should he laugh. He'd be lucky if she ever—

"Yes, well . . . We shall have to get you some more dresses, then," he announced, distracting her from her ire. His humor contained, his gaze slid over her again. "I do not wish you to wear your hair like that, either. I prefer it down. Do not dress it so again."

Helen's hand went to her hair at once. She had pulled it back tightly and tied it with a bit of leather Ducky had fetched. As it was, she'd been too weary and miserable to fix her hair properly. Now, she let her hand drop a bit irritably. What did she care if he did not find her attractive?

"I took a tour of our estates today."

Helen glanced sharply. "Our," not "my"? The choice of words surprised her, for everything she'd owned was now his by law, or would be once the marriage was consummated. She experienced a quick memory of last night. For a moment, she was back in bed with her husband's body pressing down on her, his mouth delighting hers, his hands caressing her. She felt her nipples harden, heat pooling low in her stomach at the memory, and she flushed with embarrassment at her body's betrayal. Turning, she picked up her ale to hide her reaction and took a quick drink.

"I get the feeling that I am not well liked by your people."

Helen swallowed with a vaguely amused grimace. His saying that he was not well liked was an understatement. Everyone at Tiernay feared and hated him. And with good reason. Crofters who built too close to the border of his land had been known to find themselves burnt out. Cows who wandered onto his soil were kept. And everyone knew how he treated his people, especially since some of the Tiernay villeins and servants had once been Holden people but had fled here for protection.

"I blame you."

Helen nearly spit out the ale she had just begun to swallow. Forcing it down her throat, she turned to gape at him with disbelief. "Me? You blame me because the people around here—your own included—fear and despise you?"

"My people do not fear and despise me," he argued, obviously affronted.

She grunted. "You could have fooled me, my lord. I have taken in enough of your people who claim that they do."

"What?" It was his turn to gape at her. "None of my people have come here."

"They certainly have. I have paid a fortune purchasing your serfs and—" She paused abruptly and stood. There was no sense telling him what he already knew. Lord knew, she had added to his wealth by buying away those servants he would otherwise abuse.

"Where are you going?" her husband snapped, turning on his bench to glare at her as she headed for the stairs. "I am not finished talking to you."

Helen turned around at once. She could be a dutiful wife when the occasion called for it, she thought grimly, enjoying the way he blanched and rose abruptly to fall back from her approach. Continuing forward, she widened her eyes innocently. "Why, my lord, I thought you wished to continue speaking to me? Was I wrong?"

Covering his nose, Lord Holden retreated desperately. She could see the thoughts in his head. A good warrior knew when to attack and when to retreat. This discussion was one best kept for another time. In a few days perhaps. Or a week. When his wife was not quite so ripe. Turning abruptly, he rushed for the keep doors. "I am going to the village tavern to join my men. I want the hall aired while I am gone. See to it."

The door slammed on his last word and Helen sneered at it.

"See to it," she muttered, turning toward the stairs. He could see to it himself when he returned. She was going to her room for a good cry. Perhaps if she cried hard and long enough, her nose would stuff up again and she would be free of her stink long enough to get some more rest. Sighing despondently, she started up the stairs.

"We should have eaten at the keep. I thought you said the food at your picnic from here was good."

Hethe glanced up at William's miserable comment. He couldn't blame the man for making it, though. He had thought the meals placed before him at the keep unpleasant, but this tavern's salty stew, tough and blackened meat, and watered-down ale were worse than anything he had been served by Helen's cook. William had not been treated to the same awful fare that his master himself had suffered. And this was nothing like the chicken he'd had the other day from this tavern. Ah well, perhaps they were waiting for more supplies . . . or something.

Sighing, Hethe chewed determinedly at the black meat he'd been given. He could not even hazard a guess as to its nature. It may have been beef; then again it may have been chicken. It was charred and dried out to the point that he could not tell.

The tavern owner's wife came forward, slamming a pitcher with more diluted ale on the table, spared a moment to glare at her guests, then marched away.

Well, she tried to march, but it was really more of a
waddle. The woman was pregnant, obviously so,
and very far along, and Hethe was surprised she
was still waiting tables in her advanced condition.
He watched her waddle through the kitchen door,
his eyes sharpening as they landed on an old woman
waiting on the other side. Hethe stopped his chewing at once, stiffening where he sat.

It was the old hag who had nearly boiled his balls
off with his bathwater the day he arrived. Dear God,
the old harpy was following him around, making
his life miserable, he realized with dismay. First she
was in the castle, now she was here—and he didn't
doubt for a minute that she was behind this horren-
dous meal.

Standing abruptly, he spat the inedible meat on the
floor and made his way grimly toward the kitchen. A
sudden silence fell over the room as he did. Hethe ignored the sudden absence of conversation, his focus
on the kitchen door and the old hag behind it.

The women in the kitchen must have been warned
by the silence in the common room, for both of
them stood frozen inside the door, huddled together
and watching warily when Hethe appeared. He
paused just inside the room, his gaze moving from
one woman to the other. The younger of the two
looked terrified, her eyes great round holes of panic.
The older just looked grim and resigned. She shifted,
placing herself before the younger in a protective
gesture.

"Is there something wrong with your meal,
m'lord?" The old hag had the audacity to sneer as
she spoke the title, Hethe noted, greatly taken aback.

"You're not afraid of me," he realized with
amazement. The silly old witch *should* be afraid of

him. Any commoner with any sense—especially one who had just served her liege a meal unfit for dogs—would have been terrified of his temper. The old hag wasn't.

"I'm an old woman," she pointed out with a smile. "The worst ye can do is beat and kill me, and how many years of my life would you really be taking?"

Hethe stiffened. "I do not beat or kill old people," he snapped impatiently.

"Sure ye do. Old Bets was eighty if she was a day when ye had her killed. And ye've done worse than that, too. Ye'd do it to me easy enough, I'd wager."

"Old Bets? Who the Devil is she? And who filled your head with these black lies?" Hethe asked with disgust.

The old hag tilted her head slightly, eyeing him with consideration, but it was the younger woman who spoke, her voice quavering with fear as she did. "He's right, Mom. He never beat or killed any of the servants himself. He always had that other feller of his do it. He just gave the order."

Before Hethe could respond to such defamatory accusations, the door opened behind him. Glancing over his shoulder, he saw William standing there, his expression grim. The man was obviously prepared to back him up in whatever way necessary. But Hethe didn't need any backup. This wasn't a battle. He was just talking to two deluded village women. And he didn't want the situation to get out of hand—which it surely would if his first witnessed the insolence of these two peasants. He turned to leave, then paused, dug out a coin and tossed it at the feet of his accusers. "For my meal."

With that, he led William out of the kitchen and then out of the inn.

"What happened?" his first asked once they were outside, mounting up to return to the keep.

"Nothing," Hethe muttered, but his mind was on what the women had said. Lies, all of it. He had never in his life beaten or killed, or ordered to be beaten or killed, an old servant or villein. Or a young one. But both those women believed he had, with all their heart. "Who is Old Bets?"

William glanced over sharply at the question. "Old Bets?" he asked with confusion. "I do not—"

"Never mind," Hethe interrupted with a sigh. He would find out about the woman on his own. He would get to the bottom of this if it was the last thing he did. Someone was spreading horrific lies about him.

No wonder Lady Helen had struggled so hard against being his wife. Unless *she* was behind the slander . . . He considered that as they rode silently back to the castle. He didn't like the idea, but supposed it was possible. That would explain why the lies had been easily accepted by Lady Helen's tenants as God's own truth. They wouldn't expect their lady to lie about such a thing. Still, why would she dislike him enough to spread such foul tales?

He would get to the bottom of that, too, he assured himself. If he could ever get close enough to the woman to question her. If she had any more tricks like that stinkweed of hers—

"When do you think we will be able to return to the fighting? I'm sure Henry could use us by now."

Hethe glanced over at his first. He wasn't too surprised by the man's question. He and William had rarely stayed in one place for long these last ten years. No doubt the man was growing extremely restless, as his men surely were.

In truth, Hethe was growing a mite restless as well, though he knew where to lay that blame: his wife. His desire for her had been sharp and biting all through the meal after the wedding, and then once he was in bed with her . . . Her breath hadn't bothered him in the least once he had dosed himself with those garlic cloves, and he had nearly drowned in the softness of her mouth. She had responded to his kisses, too, making his passion even hotter. He had been like a randy lad, wet behind the ears. He could still taste that desire.

Of course, it had died an abrupt death once he had pulled the furs aside and gotten a whiff of her. His nose twitched now just recalling it. Damn, where she had come up with that stinkweed was a question he would like answered. The bogs, no doubt.

"Hethe?"

Startled out of his thoughts once again, Hethe realized that he had not answered his first's question. When would they head back to war? In truth, he wouldn't mind leaving right away. He was weary of this battling to bed his bride, and the Good Lord alone knew what next she would come up with to forestall him. Maybe his best bet was simply to go back to war and give the Lady Helen time to get used to being married to him. Perhaps once Templetun was out of the way, once things had settled down again, she would give up her ridiculous resistance and resign herself.

"And maybe pigs will fly," he muttered derisively.

"What was that?" William asked.

Hethe shook his head. "Nothing. I am thinking that we should go to the fighting soon. Very soon. Tomorrow morning, even," he announced firmly. There was nothing really to hold him here.

Chapter 11

"H E'S gone!"

Helen forced her eyes open as her aunt rushed into the room; then she pushed her hair out of the way and sat up slowly as the older woman rushed to her chest and began to rifle through it. Confusion overwhelming her, she asked sleepily, "What? What is going on?"

"Your husband is gone. Richard de Lucy sent for him in the king's name. The earl of Leicester has put ashore at the mouth of Deben in Suffolk with Flemish mercenaries. Bigod has joined him."

"The earl of Norfolk?" Helen asked faintly, beginning to wake up now.

"Aye. They plan to invade and overthrow in Henry's son's name. Holden has been called to help fight them off."

"Really?"

"Aye. Get up! We must hurry."

"Hurry to do what?" Helen asked, feeling her confusion return.

"Lord Templetun plans to leave, too," Nell explained, holding up a dress, examining it briefly, then tossing it aside. "He is breaking his fast right now, but plans to leave directly afterward. If you wish to talk to him before he does so, you must hurry."

Releasing a panicked squawk, Helen shoved the linens aside and leapt from her bed. Her aunt tossed at her the gown she had apparently chosen, then scuttled around the bed and back toward the door. She paused there, turning back to watch as Helen began to pull the dress on over the thin chemise in which she had slept.

"We shall have to do something about your hair," she announced as her niece's garment settled into place and Helen began to tie her laces.

Catching the concerned tone, Helen reached up to feel her hair, grimacing at the knotted mess it had become. She had ordered a bath brought up the night before, but hadn't had the heart to demand Ducky's assistance; the smell had been still very strong. She had sent the maid away and done the best she could at washing her own hair, finding the task difficult in the small tub. Afterward, she had been relaxed but rather weary. She had fallen asleep without even thinking of brushing out the long strands. Now, her hair was a wild mess about her head.

"I shall fetch your maid," her aunt decided and turned to the door.

"Nay, I shall brush it out as best I can and tie it back. There is no time to have Ducky tend it." Helen grabbed a brush and began dragging it viciously through her hair.

After watching Helen struggle to tug the brush through her hair for several moments, her aunt said with exasperation, "Here. Let me help, then."

"I—" Helen began, then paused when she caught

sight of Nell. Rather than approach her, her aunt had moved to the chest and pulled out a clean chemise, which she was presently tying around her face. That finished, Nell moved to Helen's side and held her hand out for the brush.

Helen gave the object up silently and turned her back to hide the shame on her face. It was humiliating being a pariah. If she had known she would have so little chance to inflict herself on Hethe, she would have had Joan fully remove the scent. The thought made her frown.

"Mayhap I should bathe before I see Lord Templetun," she suggested.

Aunt Nell hesitated briefly, then shook her head while continuing to work on Helen's hair. "There is no time for that, now. You will have to go as you are and hope he does not notice."

Helen snorted at that possibility, then realized she was scratching one hand with the other and forced herself to stop. She would send for Joan after this meeting, she decided. She would cleanse the stinkweed away and get more salve. Perhaps then she would feel more human.

"There. That is the best we can do for now," Aunt Nell announced, pulling Helen's hair into a ponytail and tying it back. Once her relative had finished and stepped away, Helen turned and hurried for the door, aware that her aunt was on her heels. They were starting down the stairs before Helen glanced over and saw that her aunt had not removed the chemise from around her face. Grimacing, she gave the bottom of it a tug to remind the woman, shaking her head when Nell paused abruptly to remove it.

"Go ahead," her aunt said. "I shall just return this, then catch up to you."

Helen continued down the stairs. Much to her relief, Lord Templetun was still seated at the trestle table finishing the last of his meal.

He wasn't the only one, of course. A good half of her subjects had already finished and returned to their work, but that left many still breaking their fast as she started across the great hall. They did not stay long. As soon as she was spotted, the talk in the room died, each person nudging the person beside them to point out her presence. News of her little problem must have spread, because Helen was barely halfway across the great hall when there was a sudden mass exodus. Rising almost as one, her people left their meals behind and fled as if for their very lives.

Helen thought, a bit irritably, that she had never seen them so eager to get back to their work. Not that her people were sluggards, but they enjoyed the morning meal as much as the next person. Not to-day, apparently. At least not if they had to suffer her ill wind. . . .

Glancing up with a start at the sudden sound of shuffling feet and hurried whispers, Lord Templetun watched with amazement as the great hall cleared. Helen was halfway across the chamber before he glanced around and spotted her. The man immediately got to his feet, a smile of greeting replacing his confusion.

"Ah, good morn, my lady. I am glad you decided to join me ere I leave. I—" He hesitated, his nose twitching; then his eyes widened incredulously as she drew nearer. When he took a nervous step back, Helen promptly stopped, aware that an embarrassed flush was rising along her throat and spreading across her cheeks.

They were both silent for a moment; then a high-pitched whine sounded behind her. Glancing over her shoulder, Helen spotted Goliath asleep by the fireplace. Ducky had warned her the dog had taken up position there since the little stinkweed incident. Now he whimpered in his sleep, covering his nose with both paws.

Heaving a sigh, she turned back to Templetun. He had a sympathetic expression on his face . . . for the dog. "My lord?"

Giving a start, the old man turned to her politely, then seemed to hold his breath and take another step backward. Realizing that she had unconsciously advanced again as she spoke, Helen made herself stop and gave the king's messenger a crooked smile. She meant it to be reassuring, but she suspected it came out as pitiful.

"Uh . . . I was just breaking my fast," Lord Templetun announced stupidly, using that excuse to move back to the table and take his seat—a good distance from her. Helen hesitated, then moved to the table as well, sitting what she thought would be far enough away to avoid overwhelming him with her stench. She'd thought wrong, apparently. The man promptly shifted to sit sideways, then perched his elbow on the table and moved his hand before his nose in as nonchalant a manner as possible while he eyed her.

"Er . . . You appear . . . Is that a rash?" he asked suddenly, his hand lowering briefly to reveal a concerned expression. After one breath, though, he replaced his hand over his nose.

"Aye." Helen sighed. "I had a bad reaction to something in my bath."

"Your bath?" he asked with surprise, then realized

what he had said and grimaced. "I mean, you reacted badly to something you bathed in?" He tried to make his words sound like a legitimate question, but it was a poor save. She supposed she shouldn't be surprised that he found it difficult to believe she had bathed. The facts did not exactly support that assumption.

Deciding it was best to leave the subject alone for now, she cleared her throat and said, "My aunt tells me that you are leaving us today."

"Aye." He seemed to cheer somewhat at that thought. Helen tried not to be insulted.

"Aye, well . . ." She hesitated, unsure, now that she was talking to him, exactly how to state what she had to say. After a moment of consideration, during which Lord Templetun turned his face to the side to breathe in deeply through his mouth, she decided that the fastest way possible was her best bet. Perhaps he would appreciate her consideration regarding the trauma through which she was putting him, and he would be more sympathetic to her cause.

"I want you to petition an annulment from the king," she blurted.

Lord Templetun stiffened at the request and began to frown. "I do not understand, my lady. Surely you realize that a marriage cannot be annulled once it is consummated."

"Aye. But the wedding wasn't consummated."

Templetun blinked at her pronouncement, then shook his head. "But I was given the proof. Lord Holden gave me the bed linen."

"He gave you *a* bed linen," she corrected. "It was not from *my* bed. And it was not my blood on it."

Helen did not really know what reaction she expected, but it surely wasn't what she got. Lord

Templetun froze up entirely at her claim, his expression tightening, his eyes narrowing to slits that examined her rather icily. She had never really thought of him as intimidating, but for one moment, she had a sudden urge to run away and hide. Instead, she began to babble.

"I am sorry, my lord. But I simply cannot stay married to him. He is—Well, just smell me! *He* did this to me," she announced with sudden inspiration. "And he caused the rash, too. The other day, he laughed when I fell out of the boat and into the river. He—"

"The river?" Templetun interrupted sharply.

Helen felt herself flush guiltily. "Aye. We . . . er . . . He thought a little row about in the river would be nice, and—"

"Lord Holden does not like water. He has not since he was a child." Templetun repeated what she already knew. "I do not see why he would suggest a row about in the river."

"Ah, well . . . Perhaps it was my idea," she mumbled, peering down at her hands.

Templetun was silent for a moment, then asked, "And this odor you exude? How did he cause that?"

"Hmmm? Um . . ." She shifted guiltily on the bench, her gaze shooting everywhere but on him. "He . . . er . . . put a lot of different scented oils in the bath with me. Conflicting scented oils."

"On your wedding night?"

Helen's eyebrows shot up with her surprise. She hadn't seen Lord Templetun since the wedding night. The alleged stinkifying by her husband could have occurred anytime since then. "Yes. How did you know?"

He stared at her silently for a moment, then proved

he was no fool. "I noticed a faint unpleasant odor when Lord Holden opened the door to shove the linens out on the morning after your wedding. It was *this odor*." He waved his hand vaguely to indicate the invisible cloud surrounding him; then his eyes narrowed. "There was also an odor the night before, when we brought him above to place him in your bed. I wondered about it then, and the fact that you were wearing furs under the linen, but the room was chill and everything seemed fine the next morning." He shrugged impatiently, then fixed his eyes upon her. "The odor in the room the night of the wedding was faint. Still, I am sure it was not this one."

"Oh?" she murmured nervously.

"Why did he pour oils and such in your bath?"

Helen struggled briefly for a viable lie, then sighed and confessed the truth. "I rubbed stinkweed all over myself to dissuade him from consummating the wedding." Seeing the outrage and fury appear on the king's man's face, Helen went on the defensive. "I did not want this marriage. I still don't. I will do anything to get it annulled. I—"

"Enough!" Lord Templetun stood. "I suggest you find your maid and have her pack a small satchel. Enough for a day or two, I should think. Then come back down here and be ready to leave."

"Leave?" Helen peered at him in alarm. "Leave for where?"

"For Holden. It is closer to where the king and his men are fighting the earl of Leicester and his Flemish mercenaries. I shall leave you there, then go on to fetch Lord Holden back to complete what should have been done on your wedding night. If we leave quickly enough, we may catch him before he joins the battle."

"Oh, but—"

"There will be no buts, my lady," the old man snapped, silencing her. "The king entrusted me with seeing to this, and I will see the deed done—whether you like it or not."

"Damn him!" Helen cursed, pacing her room furiously as her aunt and Ducky looked on sympathetically. "The stupid, stubborn, irritating old man!"

Pausing before one of her chests, she kicked it viciously and began to pace again. "This time, Lord Templetun will not be satisfied until he has seen for himself that the marriage has been consummated. He is leaving me no way to annul this union. I shall be stuck with that . . . *man* till death parts us!"

"Perhaps you will be lucky and he will die during this campaign against the earl of Leicester."

Helen paused and whirled on her aunt at that suggestion. "Do you think so?" she asked with pitiable hope, then just as quickly shook the thought away. "Nay, I should not be so lucky. The man has survived too many battles to hope that this one will do him in. It would seem that God has seen fit to see me firmly married to the bastard."

She paced the room again. "Templetun will force him to bed me this time and nothing will stop it. No smell, no rash—" She paused at that thought to scratch irritably at her arm, and Aunt Nell took the opportunity to interrupt.

"Then perhaps we had best prepare you for that," she suggested calmly, moving forward to take Helen's arm and urge her to sit on the end of the bed.

Helen gave up on scratching herself to snort with disgust. "If by 'prepare' you mean that I should bathe and powder myself for his pleasure, you can forget that! I am not preparing. Let him suffer my smell. The odious man."

"I do not know if that is a smart decision, dear. It might be best if you made yourself as amenable as possible."

"What?" Helen gaped at her aunt. "Do not tell me that you think I should just surrender gracefully? Because I will not. I will go down fighting. I will—"

"Nothing can be gained by further battle now," Nell interrupted, giving her arm an impatient shake that startled her niece into silence long enough for her to try to explain the situation. "My dear, I have supported you in each of your endeavors to avoid this marriage before now, but it would appear that there simply is no evading it. Templetun will see this marriage consummated. Any further resistance on your part will only see you hurt."

Rising, Helen waved such concerns impatiently away and resumed her pacing. "I am not afraid of Templetun or—"

"I mean physically hurt—by the joining," Nell interrupted again.

Helen stilled at that, uncertainty covering her face. "What?"

Nell opened her mouth to speak, then hesitated, her gaze moving helplessly to Ducky. The two exchanged a glance, then the lady's maid cleared her throat and tried to help. "You know the essentials of joining, my lady. I know her ladyship explained them to you."

"Aye." Helen's lips twisted in disgust as she recalled the lecture Nell had given her when she had reached marriageable age. It had all sounded vaguely revolting at the time. It didn't seem much more appealing now despite those exciting kisses she had exchanged with her husband on their wedding night. She preferred to think that her response to him had been some sort of aberration. A reaction to the stinkweed. Perhaps it had caused some odd effects. "He will stick his poker in my—"

"Yes, well," her aunt cut her off quickly and cleared her throat. "That is true, and usually you see there is some, er . . . The woman is prepared, and without that preparation, there is horrible pain. There is pain anyway the first time of course, but damage can be done if . . . she is not prepared."

Helen considered her aunt's words carefully, then asked slowly, "So if I do not bathe and powder myself for him I could be damaged?"

"Not . . . No, I—" Nell gave up and turned to Ducky for help.

"She means that if you fight him, if you don't bathe yourself and make nice, he may not be gentle with you and will not trouble to prepare you," the maid explained.

"*He* has to prepare me?" Helen squawked.

"He has to . . ." Nell began, but apparently couldn't bring herself to say it.

"You remember last summer and the May Day games?" Ducky asked suddenly. Helen and her aunt both turned on her with bewilderment.

"Aye. What of it?" Helen asked at last.

"Do you remember how the blacksmith wrestled the greased pig?"

Helen nodded her head with a smile. "The pig kept slipping free of his arms."

"Well!" Ducky smiled at her brightly. "You're the blacksmith and Lord Holden's poker is the pig and if there isn't any grease, his pig's likely to pain you when he pokes you."

Both women were silent as they stared at her satisfied expression, then Helen squealed, "What?"

"Oh dear, Ducky. Please do not help any more," Nell hurried to say as the maid frowned and opened her mouth again. Helen's aunt then rubbed her forehead briefly, then turned to take her niece's hands in her own. "For all that Ducky's explanation is flawed, perhaps we can use it. You see, a man prepares a woman with his kisses and touch. It causes the woman to produce some of the—er—grease, as Ducky referred to it, down there." She gestured vaguely to Helen's lap, then struggled on. "This eases the way for his, er, pig to—"

"I understand," Helen interrupted, flushing bright red. "And you are saying that if I do not bathe and encourage some kindness in Lord Holden, he may not trouble to—"

"Exactly!" Nell cut her off, then she heaved a breath out and said, "As there is no longer any use to fighting this, I really think it behooves you to try to encourage some gentler feelings in his lordship. For your own sake."

Helen stared at her aunt despondently, the blood draining from her face as she considered the news. "Do you really think that my bathing and being amenable will make him forget all we have done to him ere this?"

She could tell by the older woman's expression that she very much doubted that such would be the case, and Helen suddenly wished that she had shown a little more restraint in her battle, or not bothered at all. It seemed to her that all she had managed to do was make her situation worse.

"There are ways to encourage softer feelings in a

man." Ducky drew the gaze of both women again with her words.

"There are?" Helen asked hopefully.

"Aye. Seeing you naked should help. Men forget a lot of things at the sight of a naked woman. You've a good figure and that should be a good start at distracting him."

Helen goggled at the suggestion, the blood returning to wash through her face at the idea of stripping bare before the man.

"And if that doesn't work, jiggling your breasts at him should."

"Jiggling my breasts?" Helen cried in disbelief, but the maid nodded firmly.

"That worked real good with my Albert when he was still alive. Any time we had an argument, one little jiggle and he forgot he was mad at me. Nothing raised his poker faster than a jiggle."

"Ducky, I really think—" Aunt Nell began, getting to her feet, but was stopped from finishing her thought by a knock at the door.

"Enter," Helen called, standing as well, then wished she hadn't when Lord Templetun stepped into the room. The king's man took one look at the three of them standing huddled together and his pinched face tightened even further.

"I knew you would be up to no good. You haven't even begun to pack," he berated.

Slipping past her aunt and Ducky, Helen tried to appease the man, but he didn't give her a chance. Grabbing her wrist, he turned for the door. "Throw an extra gown in a bag and bring it below!" he ordered over his shoulder, dragging her out into the hall.

"But I haven't bathed yet," Helen protested as he tugged her along.

"And you will not. If you think for one moment that I am going to give you the chance to plot more nasty little tricks to play on Lord Holden, you are very much mistaken, my lady."

"But we were not plotting," Helen protested, tugging at the hand he held as he started down the stairs, pulling her behind him. After that little chat in her room, she was desperate to wash some of the stench off of her. Helen was a realistic girl: if she was going to have to go through with this, she would rather not be injured in the bargain. "I really do need to bathe and prepare, my lord. I—"

"As you bathed and prepared on your wedding night?" the old man interrupted with an angry laugh, tightening his grip. "Not likely. Holden hardly needs you to smell worse than you do now. We shall be lucky if he can accomplish the task as it is. Nay, you are not leaving my sight until I have you safely away from here and at Holden. And you can be sure that if we do not catch up to Hethe before that, I shall be ordering his second to keep an eye on you and not bring you anything you request, so do not think that you shall be able to do anything there to worsen your state and put off this matter."

That little speech carried them across the hall and outside. He was leading her down the stairs to the bailey when a breathless Ducky burst out of the keep behind them. The woman caught up to them as they reached the saddled horses that the men who had accompanied Lord Templetun held for them.

The king's man took the bag Ducky held and handed it to one of his men, then urged Helen toward a horse, but the maid suddenly threw her arms around Helen and hugged her hard.

Helen was a bit startled by the desperate display, until she heard the woman hiss in her ear, "Jiggle the breasts, my lady. Jiggle 'em good."

Helen didn't get the chance to respond to her maid's advice. She caught a glimpse of her anxious-looking aunt hurrying down the keep steps toward them, then Templetun tugged her from the servant's embrace and forced her to mount.

"That rash is obviously a judgment from God. He is punishing you for your disobedience."

Helen's hands clenched a little tighter around the reins of her mount. Lord Templetun had been lecturing her since leaving Tiernay. She was an evil, naughty, disobedient female. She had flouted an order from her king. She had gone against her husband. And if that were not bad enough, she had disobeyed God when she had taken the vow of obedience during the wedding ceremony, then turned around and broken it by not heeding her husband. She was an evil, nasty little sinner, and even God had judged her so by punishing her with the rash and horrific smell she was forced to endure. The smell, of course, reflected the putrescence of her soul.

Lord Templetun's sympathies were most definitely with Lord Holden at this point. Still, Helen could not help but notice, a little cynically perhaps, that his sympathies were not enough to make him annul the marriage and save Holden from her corrupting influence.

"Here we are."

Helen glanced up at the walls of the castle looming ahead. Holden. She had thought they would never reach it. Lord Templetun had forced them to ride at a slow trot so that he might lash her with his tongue along the way; thus the trip had taken much longer than it should have. It was past the midday meal now, she was sure.

The king's man fell blessedly silent as they passed through the bailey, and Helen took the opportunity to take in her surroundings. She had never been to Holden. Or if she had, she had been quite young, for she did not recall it.

Curious, she peered around at the people going about their business. She felt the difference at once, of course. At Tiernay, there were children playing, dogs running about, and laughter echoing in the air as her healthy, happy people worked. Such was not the case here. She did not see a single child or smile, and the majority of people here seemed lean, pale and grim.

Much to her surprise, that fact actually caused Helen some relief, and it took her a moment to realize why. Lord Holden's behavior since meeting him had been something of a shock. The man had been nothing like she had expected. Rather than being a big, ugly ogre as she had always presumed, Hethe had been handsome and hale. Rather than stomping around, glaring ferociously at everyone and ordering servants and serfs punished for the smallest misdemeanors, he had been smiling and almost charming. And despite his treatment—bad food, a cold room, the bath his first day and everything that had taken place since—he had not once demanded punishment of anyone.

True, he had played that trick on her in the

clearing, setting up the picnic on the posies, but he had also given her an escape from that, offering to return to the castle before they sat down. It had been she, bent on forcing him to suffer the unpalatable fare she had brought for their picnic, who had insisted on staying.

All of those facts had combined to make her fear that she had been mistaken, that perhaps she had been taken in by some very clever serfs and villeins from Holden who had spun a sad tale to gain her charity. She'd begun to imagine that perhaps he wasn't really the cruel, heartless bastard she thought, and that she had played those awful pranks on a blameless man. Which would have made her feel just awful.

But the atmosphere of the people of Holden seemed to indicate that she'd been correct. These people were miserable. They were also full of fear. There had been a flicker of relief on nearly every face they passed as the people saw who was come to their village, and she suspected that relief was because it wasn't their master.

They reached the front door of the keep, and Helen automatically began to dismount, but she was stopped by Lord Templetun's hand on her arm. Turning, she peered at him reluctantly, suspecting he had more to say on her disobedience. She was not wrong.

"I will be heading out to hunt up Lord Holden as soon as I find His Lordship's second and place you in his hands. I suggest that while you await our return, you repent and seriously consider changing your ways—else you will end up in a nunnery or the pillory."

Helen felt herself pale at his threat. She was very

glad for the sudden distraction of the door before them opening . . . until her husband stepped out. At least, for one brief moment she thought he was her husband. Then the man stepped out of the shadows and she saw that it wasn't him at all.

The warrior was as tall and strong-looking as her husband—in fact he, like Sir William, had the same shape as Hethe, which was the reason for her brief mistake, she supposed—but that was where the resemblance ended. Where her husband's hair was dark, this man's was a deep red. Where her husband's skin was tanned from being out of doors so much of the time, this man's was paler. And his facial features were softer, his forehead more lined with worry.

"Ah, Stephen," Lord Templetun greeted the younger man and quickly dismounted. "I have brought Lady Holden here to await your master."

Helen gave a start at the old man's words. In truth, it was the first time anyone had addressed her by her new married title: Lady Holden. She didn't think she liked it. Holden was a name she had reviled too long to wish to bear it as her own. Still, she forced a smile for her husband's second, who was now moving quickly forward; then she nearly groaned aloud with the realization that he was moving to her side to help her dismount. Unless the man had no sense of smell at all, he would—

Aye. He had a sense of smell, she thought with a sigh as the man stumbled abruptly to a halt, his eyes widening in incredulity even as his nose tried to pinch itself closed. Helen offered an apologetic smile and started to dismount unaided, but Hethe's second was too chivalrous to allow such a thing. He turned his head to the side, and she saw his chest expand as he sucked in some fresh air; then he rushed forward and caught her as she would have leapt from her mount.

"Thank you," Helen murmured, then realized by his panicked look that she had put him in a deplorable spot. The man was holding his breath, trying not to be overcome, but by thanking him, she had made it rude for him not to release his breath and respond in kind. Trying to save him the trouble, she struggled free and started moving toward the keep, babbling as she went. "Well, I am sure you will be off now, Lord Templetun. I shall just go inside and see if there is anything left from the midday meal so that I might eat. Have a safe journey."

If Templetun answered her, Helen didn't hear it. Her little speech carried her all the way to and in through the keep's doors. She bustled across her husband's great hall toward the trestle tables. Stephen stayed behind, presumably to have a talk with Lord Templetun. It wasn't a very long talk. Helen had barely reached the trestle tables when she heard the door open behind her and glanced around to spot the man entering and hurrying after her. She shook her head at his anxious expression. He really should have taken the opportunity to remain outside a bit longer. She would have, had she been him.

"Lord Templetun is here."

"What?" Hethe stopped his horse abruptly at the news from his squire as he rode into camp. "What does he want?"

"I do not know, my lord. He just said that he had come to collect you to take you back to Holden, to do something you had not finished."

Hethe cursed at that, suspecting he knew what that "something" was. No doubt his wife had gone

running to Templetun as soon as he himself had left
Tiernay. Why was it that women could never keep
their mouths shut? If she had just done that and
waited for his return, they might have sorted things
out without dragging Templetun and the king into
it. But, nay, not her. She had to—

"Did you say back to Holden?" Hethe asked suddenly as the boy's words fully sank in.

"Aye, my lord."

He frowned. He had left his bride at Tiernay.
Holden was closer, though. Perhaps Templetun had
taken her there, then ridden on to collect him. Unless
he was mistaken about what the man wanted. Mayhap he had forgotten to sign some papers or something. That thought raised his hopes somewhat.

A moan from the wounded man slouched in the
saddle before him drew Hethe from his thoughts.
He urged his horse forward again, riding to the center of camp before easing the unconscious knight
from his saddle, then following him down. "Have
someone tend to this man, Edwin. I shall go see
Lord Templetun."

"Aye, my lord."

Hethe started to lead his horse away, then paused
to glance back at the squire now kneeling over the
wounded soldier. "Where is he?"

"I showed him to your tent to rest until your return, my lord."

"Good." Turning away, he continued on toward
his tent, handing his reins over to one of his men as
he went.

"Lord Holden." Templetun got to his feet as Hethe
entered the tent. The king's man looked terribly relieved at his arrival. "How goes the battle?"

"They burnt down Haughley. But the king has them on the run."

"Haughley?" He frowned. "That was an old Norman keep. Built of wood."

"Aye," Hethe agreed. "It went up like tinder."

Templetun nodded, ruminating, then cleared his throat. "I am here because of Lady Tier—Holden," he corrected himself impatiently. "She said the wedding was not consummated."

Hethe grimaced. Surely enough, she had blabbed. Now it was up to him to try to save the situation. "You saw the proof of the consummation."

"She claims you faked that proof."

"Well, I say *she* is lying," Hethe countered with a pointed look. He really wasn't eager to bed the silly woman. If she didn't smell so much . . . well, that would be one thing. Unfortunately, she did. He did his best not to squirm guiltily under Lord Templetun's narrowing gaze.

"Will you really force me to have her examined and then come back?" the king's chaplain asked wearily.

Hethe considered. There was a good possibility that if he put this off long enough, his wife's smell might fade enough that it wouldn't be such a chore to bed her. On the other hand, he could get in trouble with the king for lying if he was caught. Shifting impatiently, he shook his head. "I will tend to it once I return—"

"I am afraid that will not do," Templetun interrupted. "The king instructed me to see the marriage done, and I intend to do so. You will have to return to Holden with me. I left Lady Helen waiting there."

Hethe opened his mouth to argue, then merely shrugged. Arguing would not get him anywhere. He may as well just go back and do his duty so that he could quickly return here to the battle. "Oh, hell! When do we leave?"

Templetun's eyebrows rose in surprise. Apparently, he had expected more of a fight. "Oh. Well . . . er . . . Now?" he asked hopefully.

Hethe's response was to turn and duck back out of his tent. "Edwin, bring my horse," he yelled, aware that Templetun followed right behind.

"I will just go see that my own horse is ready," the older man murmured, hurrying off. Hethe watched him go, then smiled at his squire as the young boy hurried up with his mount still saddled.

"Are Sir William and the others back yet?" he asked as he remounted. He had ridden ahead to get the wounded soldier to treatment as quickly as possible. William and the others had stayed behind to see if any of the other men sprawled on the battle-field still lived.

"Nay, my lord."

"Well, tell him when he gets back that I have gone back to Holden, and assure him I will return as soon as I can."

"Aye, my lord."

Nodding, Hethe settled in his seat and glanced around. Templetun was waiting impatiently for his horse to be saddled. Hethe took the opportunity to give a few more orders and instructions and to ask how the man he had brought back was doing, then urged his mount over to join the king's man for the journey back to Holden.

Chapter 12

HETHE dismounted with great relief. It had been a long day, and Lord Templetun had managed to make it even longer. The man had spent the entire ride back to Holden lecturing him on his duty as a husband, as a servant to the king, and as a man. It appeared he had let all of mankind down by neglecting to bed his wife. He was a warrior. A man. A superior being. She was only a woman—less intelligent, a lesser being. He mustn't let the king down again.

Hethe had managed to keep from plowing his fist into the chaplain's face only by a supreme act of will. Now he ignored the man, dismounted and made his way into the keep, leaving Templetun to follow or not as he wished. Of course, he knew the man would follow. This time, Templetun surely wasn't going to leave until he was wholly satisfied that the marriage was well and truly consummated.

The first person Hethe spotted as he entered his great hall was his second. A quick glance around showed that his bride was nowhere to be seen. If she had any sense, she was hiding, he decided as he crossed to the table.

"Hethe!" Stephen leapt to his feet, a smile of greeting covering his face. "I was beginning to worry that you would not return."

Hethe grimaced, then glanced irritably over his shoulder at his shadow—the king's chaplain. "We had already joined the king's men when Lord Templetun arrived. He had to wait until the day's battle was done for our return."

"Ah." Stephen glanced from Hethe to the older man, then cleared his throat. "Lady Helen is in your chamber."

Hethe couldn't help but notice the way the younger warrior avoided his eyes. It was obvious the man had noticed his wife's odor. Hethe hadn't expected any less.

"You should go up and—" Templetun began.

"My lord," Hethe interrupted irritably. "I do know my duty. Yet would it be possible for me to enjoy some wine first? It has been a long day."

Templetun hesitated, then gave in unhappily. "Very well. A drink first, my lord. But we really must get this finished up."

"We?" Hethe asked dryly. He doubted the man would be so anxious to see this accomplished were he the one having to do the *do*ing.

It was growing late, and Helen was pacing the master bedchamber when a disturbance drew her to the window. Peering outside, she heaved a long drawn-out sigh when she saw that Lord Templetun had returned with her husband. She had spent the afternoon biting her lip and peering sympathetically at Lord Holden's second as the man bravely tried to keep her company while doing his best not to show how offensive was her smell. He had been incredibly grateful to be relieved of the duty when she had come up here, but it had left Helen with nothing to do but ponder what was to come. Which had quickly become a tiresome exercise. There was nothing to do to put off what was to come, and seemingly, nothing she could do to prepare for it.

Templetun had kept his word; Helen had been unable to persuade Stephen to allow her to do anything about her odiferous state, refusing even to send up a bath. The man had been apologetic, had explained in pained tones that he wished he could—which she didn't doubt at all since he had had to suffer her stench—but, he had explained, Templetun had ordered him to supply nothing but food and drink and to watch while she consumed it. A bath was out of the question.

In the end, Helen had asked to be shown to the master's bedchamber so that she might look around. That request had, at least, been allowed, but not before Stephen had examined the room. Presumably to be sure there was nothing inside that might go against Templetun's orders. She had spent the rest of her time alone in this room, and she was not terribly impressed with what she found.

Hethe's chambers were large, and they had obviously once been opulent, but everything in the bedchamber was now old, threadbare and screaming of neglect. It seemed very obvious to her that Hethe did not spend much time here. Indeed, poking about revealed that there was not one of the man's personal items in the room.

With nothing else to do but worry about what was to come, and fret over the fact that she was unable to make herself presentable enough that Hethe might be gentle with her, Helen had decided she would do better to lie down for a rest. She had lain on his large bed, wide awake and anxious, until a servant came to ask if she wished to go below for the sup, or would wish a tray brought to her.

Helen had chosen the tray. It would have been nice to have company to distract her from her fretting, but she had not been willing to inflict herself on Lord Holden's second or the rest of his people, and so she had eaten by herself. Well, really she had been too nervous to eat, had merely pushed the food around. Then she'd spent the rest of her time pacing and waiting. Now, she grimaced at the sight of her husband dismounting below. It was time.

For a moment, she was overwhelmed by panic. She actually even peered around wildly, looking for someplace to hide or a way to escape. Then she realized there was nowhere to run, and she forced herself to calm down and stop acting like a ninny.

She was a grown-up woman. This was nothing of which to be so frightened. Every woman went through this. At least, every woman who married. Although she supposed they needed not fear it being quite as unpleasant as it was likely to be for her, especially since she had angered her husband repeatedly. That, along with her stench, would probably see her with a painful, ungreased pig. But, then, she had brought it on herself, and it would have all been over by now if she had not tried to put off her wedding night. It seemed that she had brought a lot down on herself lately.

If she was the superstitious sort, she might think that someone had cursed her. If she believed God was the cruel, punishing deity of Lord Templetun's beliefs, she might believe he really was punishing her for her disobedience. But Helen knew that this was just pure and simple bad luck. She also believed she could do with some good luck about now, and perhaps it was time to start making her own. Her aunt and Ducky's advice that morning came to mind.

Be "amenable" and "try to encourage some gentler feeling" in the man, her aunt had suggested. "Get naked and jiggle" had been Ducky's advice. Helen considered the matter briefly. She didn't think that she could manage the getting naked part, at least not fully. But she could be amenable and encouraging.

Hethe mounted the stairs, growing angrier with every step he took. Lord Templetun had "allowed" him one drink, and one drink only, then had sent him up to bed like a child. Hethe was not used to being ordered about so, and appreciated it even less in this instance. Of course, this was all Lady Helen's fault. If she had not gone yapping to the king's man—hell, if she hadn't gone and pulled that ridiculous stunt with the stinkweed—they would not be in this fix! Now, he was expected to make his way to his room and plow a field that reeked like a graveyard. Aye, he was a poorly done-by man. What great sin had he ever committed to deserve this?

Reaching his bedchamber door, he paused and briefly glared at it. Beyond that strip of wood waited a woman whose scent could curl a man's hair. And whose body could curl a man's toes, some part of him reminded. Hethe considered that thought briefly, his mind returning to the various sights he had been shown of that body. Aye, Lady Helen was a fine figure of a woman. And she had a face lovely enough to stir any man's soul. Perhaps he could find a way to overcome the smell . . . It would not last forever.

On that cheerful note, he opened the door and strode into the master bedchamber. He used the room very rarely on those rare occasions that he was at Holden, but he knew what it contained. Still, this time, he wasn't sure what to expect. A snarling and angry bride, perhaps? Or an anxious and nervous one as Nerissa had been? What he surely did not expect to find was a woman sitting naked before the fire, brushing her hair with long, serene strokes.

Well, she wasn't really naked; she still wore her chemise. But the scrap of clothing was extremely thin, and the way she was positioned before the fire made it so that he could see entirely through the fabric to the lush curves beneath.

For a moment, Hethe was enchanted; then he pushed the door closed and started forward—only to be forcefully reminded that she did not wish to be his bride by the familiar and foul perfume wafting across the room.

That was when he realized the whole situation was surely part of some new trick, some new plan to bedevil him. His disappointment at the realization was keen. Pausing, he glanced around the room warily, but he could find nothing amiss. Everything looked as it always did when he stayed here—except for her, of course.

"What new game is this?" he asked, moving back to lounge against the door. He could still smell her from there, but his desire to gag wasn't as strong.

Pausing in her hair-brushing, she turned slowly to peer at him, and he could have sworn that the uncertain expression on her face was sincere. "'Tis no game, my lord. No more tricks or plots. It would appear there is no way out of this marriage, so I thought to make it easier."

Setting the brush down, his wife stood slowly and turned to face him, the fire backlighting her so that her face and front were in shadow, but her body was outlined beneath the thin gown she wore. Hethe felt his body stir with interest as he peered at her and nearly sighed with relief. Perhaps they could get this consummation done after all. The question was, how?

With Wee Hethe showing interest, it was quite possible that he could just order her on the bed, rush over, whip up her chemise, pull himself out and thrust into her. He imagined he could hold his breath that long. That would see the deed done, but Hethe had never used a woman so brutally, and despite all she had done to him since their meeting, he could not treat her so. On the other hand, preparing her properly for this, her first time, would take time and finesse, and he suspected Wee Hethe would not stand up to the endeavor. Which left him in a bit of a conundrum.

Grimacing, he shifted from one foot to the other and glanced around the room, pondering the best solution.

"Shall I help you remove your armor?"

Hethe gave a start at the quiet question, and glanced at his wife sharply, then down at the mail he still wore. It was dirty and bloody, and he really should have removed it before coming above, but he had been so upset he had forgotten all about it. "Nay!" He nearly shrieked when she started to move toward him, then softened his voice to add, "J-just go lie down and wait. I shall tend to it myself."

Nodding, she moved to the end of the bed, then hesitated. As she was no longer cast in shadow by the fire, he could see the extent of her rash. In truth, while it was not as angry as it had been the night before, it still looked painful and slightly blotchy. He could overlook the blotches, he decided, though he had to wonder if it hurt. He did not wish his touch to pain her. Caught up by such concerns, he was completely taken by surprise when she began to remove her chemise. That was unexpected; he had not thought her to be so brazen.

The blush that followed the trail of the gown told him she was not quite as brazen as the action suggested. Still, it had been a brilliant move on her part. Wee Hethe had been stirring lazily, but it now sprang to immediate life. Aye, they just might get this done, he decided as she turned and sat on the end of the bed, then lay back on it, her legs still draped off the edge of the mattress, her body supine.

All he had to do was step up to the bed, move between her legs and—

He stopped that thought right there. He could not just plow into her like some rutting dog; he would have to prepare her first. Annoyed with himself, he set to work at removing his sword belt, then his mail hauberk. Hethe usually had his squire to help with such tasks, so was surprised at how heavy the metal tunic was. Grunting as he tugged and pulled and pushed and wriggled his way out of it, he decided that, in future, he would be sure the boy was around to help.

"Are you sure you would not like me to assist you with that?"

"Nay, stay there," Hethe said quickly, sighing in relief as he finally finished pulling the heavy armor off. Straightening, he gave his wife a triumphant grin and let the mail shirt drop to the floor, wincing at the clatter it made. The sight of Lady Helen, pushing herself up on her elbows and smiling uncertainly back, made Hethe swallow. Damn, but she was a beautiful picture, despite her blotchy skin.

Hethe immediately bent to set to work at undoing the laces of the mail chaussures on his legs. Within minutes, he was panting, twisting and contorting himself about in an effort to reach behind his knees to unfasten the blasted things. It appeared that Edwin had tied the straps in rather nasty knots when he had dressed his master this morning, for Hethe could not seem to get them undone. Cursing in vexation, he snatched for his dirk.

"Do you wish my help now?" his wife asked again.

"Nay," Hethe snapped, then sighed and straightened to eye her in annoyance. He would either have to let her help him, or ruin a pair of perfectly good chaussures by slicing through their leather ties.

"Oh, aye. All right." He slumped in defeat, then quickly sucked in a breath as she scooted off the bed and rushed toward him. She flushed deeply as his gaze slid over her, but picked up speed and hurried to move around him to kneel at his back. Hethe craned his neck and peered back over his shoulder and down, getting a lovely picture of her prettily flushed back.

The straps of the chaussures must have been knotted as he had suspected, for she was bent at the task for an inordinate amount of time and seemed to struggle to untie them. Or, on the other hand, mayhap it only seemed like a long time because Hethe was holding his breath.

He held that breath until his head began to spin

and his lungs burned. Every time he weakened and wished to take a new breath, he recalled her odor and forced himself to hold out longer. But, by the time she finally managed to undo one chaussure and it dropped to the floor with a clang, Hethe could stand it no longer. He let his breath out in a gasp, then sucked another lungful up, nearly fainting from its polluted state. He prayed vigorously as she set to work at the other chaussure. This one seemed to go much quicker, and Helen released a murmur of triumph as it fell. Then she straightened behind him, hesitated before skittering back to the bed and lunging into it.

"Thank you," Hethe gasped, expelling the breath he had been holding and drawing in a fresh one. This time he allowed himself a groan of disgust. Her scent stayed behind like an invisible sulfur cloud and its effect on Wee Hethe was devastating to say the least. The wee warrior suffered a sudden death, dropping as fast as any man struck down on the battlefield. Much to Hethe's dismay, even peering at his wife where she again lay prone on the bed could not reverse the effect.

"Is there something else you need help with?"

Hethe grimaced at the question and shook his head. "Nay. J-just . . . just stay there. I have to . . ." Backing toward the door, he searched his mind for a likely excuse to leave, but none was forthcoming. Settling on a vague shake of his head, he opened the door and slipped from the room. He really needed a drink.

Helen gaped at the closing door in shock. Where was he going? What about the bedding? What had she done wrong? Helen wondered with dismay. She had done everything she could think of to be amenable and encouraging. She had even got naked as Ducky had suggested. And hadn't that been one of the hardest things she had ever done? But none of it seemed to have worked. She had encouraged him right out the door.

Shaking her head, she dropped back on the mattress and stared at the bed draperies overhead, mystified.

Hethe took the stairs two at a time, then stormed across the great hall as if he were riding off to battle. His arrival, and in such a state, was enough to make Stephen and Lord Templetun, who were seated at the trestle tables, gape at him in wonder. They continued to do so as he reached first for Stephen's ale, then changed his mind and instead grabbed up the half-empty pitcher between him and the king's chaplain. Raising it to his mouth, Hethe downed the entire contents in one long, loud series of gulps, then lowered it and bellowed for more.

"Lord Holden," Templetun finally began. "What—"

"I am thirsty. Cannot a man drink in his own castle?" Hethe snapped, shifting impatiently from foot to foot as he awaited the arrival of more ale. Losing his patience, he started for the kitchens himself.

"My lord!" Templetun was on his feet and trailing him at once. "I hope you do not expect me to believe you have accomplished—"

"I do not expect anything from you, Lord Templetun. I am merely . . ." He paused abruptly halfway to the kitchens, then turned on the man and hissed, "She *smells*."

Templetun managed to catch himself before crashing into Hethe, then regarded him sympathetically. "Oh, aye . . . Well . . . I had noticed that, my lord." He heaved a deep sigh and pondered a moment, his wrinkled old face twisting and contorting and tugging this way then that before he shook his head. "You have my deepest sympathies, my lord, but this must be done. Surely you can bear her smell long enough to . . . er . . . accomplish the necessary deed? Or . . ." He brightened suddenly and suggested, "Perhaps you can hold your breath?"

"Hold my breath?" Hethe scowled. "I tried doing that while removing my armor. It took so bloody long that I had to breathe in and—"

"But your armor is off now," the man pointed out cheerfully. He clapped Hethe on the back and turned him back toward the stairs he had just descended. "All you need do now is cross the room and finish the job. Surely you can hold your breath that long?"

"Hmmm." Hethe considered the possibility. If he took a deep breath before opening the door, then rushed across the room . . . *Let's see*, he thought. There were perhaps ten good strides from the door to the bed. He'd need another moment to push down his breeches and position himself between her legs—

"Here we are."

Hethe glanced around with a start to realize that while he had been thinking, Templetun had led him back upstairs. They were now back outside his bedchamber door.

"Just take a nice, deep breath," Templetun instructed, sounding inordinately pleased with his plan. "That's it," he said when Hethe dutifully inhaled. "Now hold it and get in there and do your duty!"

With that encouraging hiss, the king's chaplain pulled the door open, gave Hethe a shove that sent him stumbling into the room, then promptly closed the door behind him.

Hethe shuffled to a halt a few bare steps into the room, then glanced toward the woman on the bed. She still lay exactly where she had lain when he left her. Apparently, she had decided to obey him for once.

He wasn't really fooled by this sudden turn in her behavior. If she was playing nice now, it was for a reason. Perhaps she had finally realized that she could not win against him and was hoping for good terms of surrender. Too bad she hadn't tried that tactic earlier. . . . Suddenly realizing that he was wasting time, something that definitely wasn't endless at this point, Hethe hurried forward, tugging his tunic off as he went.

He found his wife's eyes were wide and anxious when he reached the bed. Hethe tried to give her a reassuring smile, but it was difficult with his cheeks all puffed out like a chipmunk's. Tossing his tunic aside, he paused to consider her briefly, unsure where he should start. Despite what Templetun had said, he could not simply leap upon her without any preparation. No matter that she probably deserved it after all her stunts, he simply could not do it. Besides, he needed a little time to ready himself. His own flesh wasn't exactly throbbing with desire at this juncture.

So, should he caress her breasts? Fondle her feet? He usually started with kissing, but that, of course, was out. His thinking had barely got that far when he realized he had used up his breath. A puffy-cheeked frown tugging at his face, he turned and hurried back to the door to gasp out the air he had sucked in. He dragged in another breath.

"Is something wrong, my lord?"

Hethe had trouble formulating a response to his wife's anxious question. Was something wrong? Nay, nay. Nothing was wrong. Except that this was impossible!

"Is there something I can do to help?" she asked.

Hethe rolled his eyes. Now, she wants to help? She could not have been more biddable on their wedding night, waited abed for him all sweet and perfumed then? Nay! Then, she had made herself as unappealing as possible. Now that she smelled like stinkweed and posies, she was eager to be helpful? Women!

"Should I jiggle my breasts or something?"

"What?" He whirled on her, his eyes wide and incredulous.

"Well," she said with obvious embarrassment. "Ducky said that when her Albert was alive, all she had to do was jiggle her breasts at him and he would—"

"Oh, please," Hethe interrupted faintly, trying to banish the sudden image of the plump, middle-aged maid jiggling her not-unimpressive breasts. "I really do not want to know such things."

She was silent for a moment, then asked, "What should I do, then?"

"Just lie there," he ordered grimly. "Just—I need another drink."

Turning on his heel, he strode back out of the room without even bothering to retrieve his tunic. He walked down the corridor, straight down the stairs and across the great hall with the same grim strides as before. Reaching the table, he picked up the ale pitcher—it still rested on the table, and he was relieved to find that it had been refilled—and began to gulp down its contents.

"Oh, dear," he heard Lord Templetun mutter somewhere behind him. "This isn't going at all well."

"Well, the first time, he was minus his armor, and now he is minus his tunic. At least he is making progress," Stephen pointed out, his voice sounding suspiciously amused.

"My lord," Templetun began at last as Hethe lowered the emptied ale pitcher. "I really think—"

"I do not want to hear any more of your thinking," Hethe interrupted.

"But you must—"

"Tell it to Wee Hethe, Templetun. *He's* the one not cooperating."

"Oh, dear." Templetun's gaze dropped briefly below Hethe's waist with speculation. "What appears to be the problem with, er, Wee Hethe?" Was there laughter in the old man's voice?

Hethe rolled his eyes at that and bellowed the obvious: "She reeks!"

"Well, aye. But wee Hethe has no nose. How would he know?"

A guttural growl sounding deep in his throat, Hethe started toward the man. He would be mocked no longer! Luckily, Stephen jumped to his feet and moved between them. "A mask!"

Hethe glanced distractedly at his second. "What?"

"Can you not wear something over your nose to dull the scent?"

Hethe made a face at the suggestion. "I tried that the morning after the wedding. It blunted the smell, but did not keep it entirely out."

"Oh." Stephen and Templetun sagged with disappointment, then seemed to chew the matter over again. After a moment, his second perked up and suggested, "Perhaps, if you perfumed the mask—"

"A brilliant idea!" Templetun decided, nodding excitedly. "That will do the trick!"

Hethe didn't know whether to laugh or cry.

Helen sat up on the bed, her gaze moving resentfully to the door. Really, this was too much. How many times was the man going to flee the room like that? She would almost think it was funny, were it not for the fact that she was so anxious.

What with the conversation she had with her aunt and Ducky that morning, Helen was as nervous as the virgin she was, and her husband's constant retreats were not helping much with her anxiety. Not to mention the discomfort and embarrassment. Lying here on the bed, splayed out and awaiting his pleasure, was humiliating. Helen was not used to being passive . . . in anything.

She glanced toward the door again, her mind considering what was to come. What her husband's . . . She couldn't help but wonder what *it* looked like. She had a vague idea, but she hadn't had the sense to look on their wedding night. Now, she wished she had. How big was it? she wondered. The concern seemed a valid one. The man had colossal shoulders. Was his . . . was *it* just as colossal? Her legs slid together at the thought. She wished he would get this damn act over with. It was like awaiting stitches, or having a tooth pulled.

A rattle from the door warned of Hethe's return, and Helen promptly fell back on the bed. She heard the door open but refused to look up. Perhaps if she pretended she wasn't here and this wasn't happening . . .

"Sweet Jesu!" she shrieked suddenly, scrambling up the bed as a masked figure stepped up before her.

"It is I, Lord Hethe," it said. The muffled voice slightly ruffled what she saw was a strip of linen tied around the figure's head.

Helen merely stared. Surely her husband did not intend to wear that while he . . . Dear Lord, yes, he did. Biting her lip, she immediately dropped her head.

"This was Stephen's idea," he explained, untying the laces of his breeches and beginning to shove them down. "This way, your smell should not prevent the . . . You are trembling. Your shoulders are shaking. Do not be frightened; I will not hurt you."

Helen managed to subdue the dismayed laughter making her body shake, and she raised her head. The first thing she saw was his manhood, and it had a detrimental effect on her composure. She had been so terrified all day, so frightened of the object before her that actually seeing the wrinkled little bit of flesh sagging between his legs now was rather anticlimactic. She was expecting something huge, something terrifying. But, nay . . . *This* was the great hog? *This* could cause her damage? "Not bloody likely," she muttered aloud and burst out in gales of rather hysterical laughter.

Catching the stricken look that immediately filled Hethe's eyes, she tried to stem the flow of her amusement, but really, she had been so tense and anxious for so long, she could not seem to stop the sudden outpour.

"I am sorry. Truly," she gasped out as sincerely as she could while laughing uproariously. "It is just that you look—" Her voice died on a sigh as he tugged his breeches up and whirled away from the bed with disgust.

Chapter 13

HETHE stormed across the room toward the fireplace. He could not do this. How was he supposed to do this with her laughing? With her smell? Not to mention that blasted rash. Every time he looked at her red, blotchy skin, guilt consumed him—and annoyance. And both had a detrimental effect on an erection, it seemed. He had never considered it before.

Pausing by the fire, he turned to face her, half expecting to find her gloating and triumphant at her success in preventing the consummation. Instead, his wife looked absolutely miserable. Her laughter had died, leaving her sitting forlornly on the bed, her nose wrinkled against her own smell, and her hands clenched in her lap—probably to keep from scratching the angry red rash covering her. For some reason, the wrinkled look of displeasure on her face reminded him of the old hag Maggie. Of the fact that he hadn't looked into that matter yet.

Sighing, he sank into one of the chairs before the fire, his mind wandering to the old woman and her accusations. She claimed to be from Holden, but he didn't recall her. Still, that didn't mean much. He was never here. What he *did* recall, though, were her bitter words about him burning old ladies out of their homes.

Restless, Hethe frowned, got to his feet and strode to the door. He pulled it open abruptly and started to step into the hall, but he was immediately confronted by Templetun, who stepped out of the shadows. It appeared the old man had followed him upstairs, this time. The king's chaplain opened his mouth to lecture, but Hethe cut him off sharply. "Make yourself useful, man. Send for some wine." He glanced back toward the woman in his bed. "Have you eaten?" he asked her.

Lady Helen's eyes widened in surprise. She hesitated briefly, suspicion rife on her face, but then she shook her head.

Nodding, Hethe turned back to Templetun. "Have some food brought up as well."

The king's man looked a bit affronted at being ordered around so, but he must have realized that doing as Hethe asked might get the deed done. After heaving a sigh, he nodded, turned on his heel and started away.

"Have a bath brought up, too," Hethe called after him. Then another thought struck. "And someone who knows something about herbs and such," he added, scowling as he realized he had no idea of the name of the healer in his castle.

Lord Templetun raised a hand in acknowledgement as he moved down the stairs. Satisfied, Hethe closed the door and turned to peer at the berashed woman in his bed—his wife. He felt as if he should say something, but didn't have any idea what. Instead, he merely returned to his seat by the fire.

They were both silent as they waited. Hethe felt

her curious gaze on him, but he ignored it. He didn't feel like explaining himself. Besides, he himself wasn't sure exactly what he was about. He was following his instincts, that was all, and he had no idea where they would lead.

Helen was still trying to figure out what her husband was up to when the first tap sounded on the door. Hethe pushed himself up from his seat and moved to answer it, his bulk blocking her view as he carried on a whispered conversation with whomever stood on the other side of the door.

After several moments, during which Helen strained to hear what was being said and failed, Hethe suddenly stepped aside, allowing a woman to enter. Like every other servant at Holden, she was quite young and lovely. She also had the sweetest, most sympathetic eyes Helen had ever seen. Those eyes found her sitting miserable in the bed.

"Oh, dear, you must be suffering horribly," the young woman exclaimed as she approached the bed and eyed the rash covering Helen's once lily-white skin. She did not even wince at the odor, but smiled gently as she paused by the bed. Both the girl's kind concern and her not flinching in disgust combined to nearly put Helen in tears.

Telling herself her sudden emotionally turbulent state was all the result of the stress she had suffered since the arrival of the king's messenger, Helen blinked her eyes against the tears suddenly pooling there. She sniffled miserably and nodded that, yes, she was suffering horribly.

"May I?" The woman waited for a nod, then took Helen's hand, raising her arm to inspect the rash. After a moment, she asked, "An allergic reaction?"

"Aye." Helen's gaze shot accusingly toward Hethe. "To night-scented posies. A vial of their essence was poured into my bath."

"Oh, dear." The healer's gaze slid to Hethe, who was looking uncomfortable under a mantle of guilt, then back to Helen. She offered a reassuring smile and produced a small bag from the folds of her skirt. "Well, I have something that should help. I shall need some water."

She glanced at Hethe expectantly, and he shifted, his gaze moving around the room. Then there was another tap at the door and his expression brightened. "I ordered a bath to be brought up," he said.

"Good. I was going to suggest one as well, and that will take care of my need for water, too." The young woman moved off toward a chest against the wall beside the bed. Kneeling before it, she produced a small wooden bowl from her sack, and various herbs, too, and began to mix them as Hethe walked over to open the door.

Helen shrank under the linens as her husband swung the door wide, allowing the servants to enter. He ordered the food and wine to be set on the chest by the chairs in front of the fire, the tub to be set by the bed, then waited until all was prepared and the servants gone before glancing uncertainly at her. After a brief hesitation, he moved over to sit in one of the chairs by the fire. He poured himself some wine, then seemed to ignore the women's presence as he lifted the bottom of the linen surrounding his face to drink. Helen nearly giggled at the silly sight, but she managed to restrain herself.

Retrieving some more herbs, the healer moved to place them in the warm bathwater. She stirred them in, then turned to smile invitingly at Helen. "This should help soothe the itching. And we shall add some ointment to help you heal."

Helen hesitated, her gaze sliding toward Hethe. He was seated in his chair, half turned toward the fire, his feet on a log before it, his gaze firmly on the flames. It appeared that this was all the privacy she was likely to get. She supposed she should be grateful for this much, since he had already watched her bathe once. Quickly shoving the linens aside, Helen scooted out of bed, rushed to the tub, and stepped in to sit in the water.

Much to her amazement, the water, while cooler than she had expected, had an immediate soothing effect on every patch of skin it covered. Murmuring her relief and pleasure, she began to splash the liquid up eagerly over her arms and chest.

"Better?" the healer inquired gently as she began to splash the treated water over Helen's back.

"Aye." Helen sighed, then glanced over at her savior. "What is your name?"

"Mary, my lady."

"Mary." Helen leaned forward, submerging as much of her arms as she could under the water to ease their irritation as well. "*Thank you*, Mary."

"You are more than welcome, my lady."

"Where did you learn your skills?"

"My mother," the girl admitted reluctantly, picking up a strip of linen to dunk it in the tub and use it to continue to draw water up over Helen's shoulders and back.

"And where is your mother now?" Helen asked, suspecting she already knew the answer. No doubt the woman had gone the way of Maggie.

"She was the healer here till last year. But . . ."

"But?" Helen prompted.

The other woman's reluctance was apparent, for it took her a few moments to speak, and when she did, it was in a hushed whisper. "She was dismissed. Fortunately, she is able to advise me on things still, for I haven't the knowledge she does." There was no doubting the resentment in her tone. It was more than obvious the girl felt her mother should be here in her place.

Helen felt goose bumps rise on her back and knew that Hethe's eyes had turned their way. He was listening to them.

Well, let him listen, she thought. He should be ashamed of himself. Perhaps hearing about his own behavior from another's lips would make him see how ridiculous and cruel his misdeeds were.

"I have noticed there are only pretty young servants in the castle. I was told that the older women are released once they are no longer deemed attractive, no matter their skills. Is that what happened to your mother?" Helen asked loud enough to be sure her husband would hear.

Mary went still. The silence in the room seemed to draw out to infinity, until at last she sighed and said, "Aye. Lord Holden ordered her out of the keep. He prefers only young, pretty women here."

There was a crash as Hethe's feet hit the floor, then the stomp of his crossing the room.

"The hell I did dismiss that woman!" he snapped, towering furiously over them both. "And I have never, *ever* ordered that only pretty, young women serve me."

Helen glanced over her shoulder at her husband's looming presence, then toward the healer's pale and frightened face. Scowling at Hethe for bellowing and stomping about and scaring the girl, Helen protested, "Well, that is what Maggie was told when she was tossed out on her ear. She was too old and ugly to work in the keep."

"Maggie . . ." Hethe frowned. His eyes took on a faraway look. "No. She claimed she was burned out of her home for being too old, not thrown out of the keep."

"She was mistress of chambermaids here," Helen snapped. How could he not recall that? "She was tossed out on her ear for being too old. Fortunately, she had been seeing a farmer named White, and he asked her to marry him. She spent six happy months being a farmer's wife. Then he died, and you had her thrown out of their small cottage and all her belongings burned as heriot. She came to me for permission to accept charity from her daughter. Instead, I put her in charge of my chambermaids. She is still sharp-witted and skilled. She has value. Yet you tossed her aside like—"

"Get out."

Helen blinked at the interruption. It took a moment to realize that the grim order was not for her, but for Mary. She sensed the young woman's hesitation, so glanced over her shoulder to give her a reassuring nod. "Go on. 'Tis all right."

Mary stood reluctantly, then hesitated. "But the ointment . . . It must be applied to every inch of you after your bath."

"I shall attend my wife. Leave us," Hethe said, sounding less angry this time. Nodding, the girl handed him the damp linen she had been using to bathe Helen's back and turned to slip silently out of the room.

Helen eyed Hethe warily, then turned to peer down into the water, hunching her shoulders and

leaning forward in the tub to try to hide her nakedness. It seemed silly to be shy after all they had been
through, but something seemed different now. After
a moment of silence, she heard a rustle as her husband knelt at the side of the tub. He dipped the
linen into the water. They were both silent as he began to run the dripping cloth over her back. After
the third stroke, he began to speak.

"I dined in the tavern at Tiernay while we were
there."

Helen nodded but said nothing, waiting for him
to continue. He ran the damp cloth gently over her
back twice more before he did.

"I was served the vilest meal and ale it has ever
been my pleasure to suffer—outside of Tiernay Castle itself."

Helen bit her lip at those words. Much to her
amazement, there was a hint of humor in his voice
as he spoke. Had he forgiven her for the horrid food
she had served him as part of her efforts to convince
him to refuse the marriage?

"I happened to glance up as the maid who served
me—a maid very heavy with child, by the way—
waddled back to the kitchen. When the door swung
open, the old woman who served me at my bath
that first day was inside."

"Maggie," Helen murmured, beginning to relax
under the soothing scrubbing motion of the linen on
her back.

"Aye. Well, I stormed in there all indignant and
angry at such service, and the old woman tore into
me. It scared her daughter silly. She nearly dropped
the baby right there, I think," he said wryly, then
sighed. "She accused me of all sorts of things. Tossing her out on her ear. Stealing all her possessions.

Having those possessions burned." He paused briefly, and she sensed rather than saw that he shook his head. "I didn't know what the Devil she was talking about. But before I could straighten the matter out, William came in to see what I was doing. I didn't want to question the old woman in front of him . . . for several reasons. One, he's always had a rather nasty temper, and two, I didn't want our silent war to reach his or anyone else's ear. It was between you and me alone, as far as I was concerned. Getting into it with that old woman would have revealed far too much of what had been going on."

Helen shifted slightly, turning her head to look at him. He had removed the cloth from around his face. There was no longer any need for it. Whatever Mary had put in the bath had at last removed the odor of stinkweed. Her husband's expression seemed sincere, she saw, and for a moment she was perplexed. "Are you saying that you did not order Maggie removed as head of your chambermaids?"

He met her gaze straight on and shook his head solemnly. "As ashamed as I am to admit it, I didn't even realize that she ever *was* head of Holden's chambermaids."

When Helen gaped at him, he sighed and returned his attention to her back, running the cool, wet linen over it again. "I have not been at Holden much these last ten years. I have been wandering about, fighting one battle or another for the king. I was in Wales two years, then Normandy and Acquitaire. I spent another two years in Ireland—"

"Anywhere but Holden," Helen finished for him. Her doubts faded. She had known that he was away a great deal, of course, but she had not realized just how much. Now that she thought about it, though, every time a servant from Holden had come to her, it was Hethe's second, Stephen, who was said to have done the dirty work.

Remembering the man in question and how nice he had been, she shook her head. It was practically impossible to imagine that he had not simply been following orders. He had an open smile and kind eyes, his face freckled and friendly under carrot-red hair. And he had tried so hard to not let her know how offensive her odor was when she arrived here. As if she had not noticed herself.

"And when Maggie's husband died?" Helen asked, determined to get to the bottom of this. "When she could no longer bring in the harvest on her own, you didn't order her turfed and her belongings burned?"

Hethe raised his hand which held the dripping linen, the other covering the spot above his heart. "I swear to you here and now that I never gave either order. I never demanded that only pretty, young women work in the castle, that Maggie be removed—or Mary's mother, for that matter—and I never ordered Maggie tossed out when her husband died." He lowered his hands, his eyebrows lowering with them. "A pretty face, while nice, is useless on its own. I value skill and ability more."

He gave her a pointed look. "Wife, I intend to see that this situation is rectified. Mary is skilled, but her mother should be here, too. It is obvious, from what she said, that the girl is still apprenticing. The two of them should both be here—the mother to heal and to teach Mary to take her place, and Mary to assist and learn. That is only sensible. I have not won battles by keeping only the strong and fair young men about. My veterans are less impulsive and therefore often more valuable. It is not brawn that wins a battle, but skill."

"Aye," Helen murmured, actually believing him. "But if you have not been giving Stephen these orders . . ." She let the sentence trail off, unwilling to voice the implication of his second's perfidy. "How long has he been in charge of Holden while you were away?"

Hethe paused and calculated silently. "About five years, now. Aye." He nodded. "It was shortly after your father died, I think. That was five years ago, was it not?"

"Aye," Helen said thoughtfully. "That is also approximately when I began to hear news of the unpleasantness at Holden."

Hethe's mouth twisted. "And soon after that, you started berating me with letters." He was silent for a minute, continuing to wash her back, then suddenly said, "We should wash your hair, too."

"Oh, I—" Helen began nervously, only to gasp in shock when a pail of water was suddenly poured over her.

"Lean your head back," Hethe instructed.

After a hesitation, she crossed her arms over her breasts and tilted her head back, remaining silent as he began to wash her hair. His hands were gentle and soothing as they massaged her scalp. Helen felt herself slowly relax, her eyes closing, her mind beginning to drift.

"What other problems have you heard of at Holden? What unpleasantness?"

Helen's eyes slid open, a sigh escaping her lips. She really didn't want to think about such things just now—his hands felt so good—but she supposed there was no hope for it. Hethe began to rinse her hair. She closed her eyes again and considered the matter. There had been much unpleasantness over the years.

"Well." She opened her eyes, staring at the shadowed ceiling above. "There was the incident with that Adam boy. He started a fight in church. His hand was cut off for punishment. That was the first atrocity I heard of at Holden. It was shortly after my father died."

"I see." Hethe was silent for a moment, then cleared his throat and said, "Well, I do not remember ordering that, but it *is* the punishment suggested by the church. Fighting in church is—"

"He was seven years old," Helen interrupted grimly. "He and his brother were arguing and—"

"Seven?"

Helen twisted her head slightly to peer at him. There was no way he could be feigning his shock at this news. He was truly horrified, as she had been. Helen felt some of her years of anger against the man ease the teensiest bit. He truly hadn't known about this. She turned her face forward again, merely waiting, and after a moment he returned to rinsing her hair.

"Did he survive?" His voice was husky and tight.

"Barely. He is twelve now and helps out in the stables at Tiernay."

"At Tiernay?" Hethe repeated in surprise.

Helen nodded. "His mother brought him to me after the incident. She begged me to buy him and his brother from you ere something else could happen. They were both serfs."

"And you did." There was no doubt in his voice.

"Aye. I bought them all, including the mother.

Paid a pretty penny, too," she added sharply, and felt his breath against her bare damp shoulder as he sighed.

"As far as I know, I have sold no serfs since becoming Lord of Holden."

Helen said nothing to that. She had purchased quite a few of his serfs over the years, sometimes after a punishment, sometimes to save them from one. Sometimes she didn't hear news of trouble soon enough and was unable to save them. Like with Bertha.

"Bertha?"

His question made her realize she had murmured the name aloud. Swallowing, she nodded and glanced back at him. "Old Bertha had her breasts severed."

Hethe recoiled at his wife's words. "Her breasts? Isn't she my alewife?" he asked, not missing the irony of the fact that she was one of the few servants he could recall. He had liked to drink when he was younger. But he had cut back on that since taking up the responsibilities of the lordship of Holden.

"She was." Lady Helen nodded her head awkwardly. "Her wound became infected. She didn't recover."

"Jesu," Hethe breathed. "What was her offense?"

"She was caught money-lending."

Hethe shook his head, furious. "I did not order these things done. I did not even know about them."

His wife peered up at him silently for a moment over her shoulder, then turned to face front again. He wasn't sure if she believed him. He didn't like the idea that she might not. He truly hadn't been aware of these things happening.

But whose fault was that? his conscience asked. Hethe winced. He was lord here; he should be aware of all. He was responsible for his people. Ultimately, he was culpable for young Adam's severed hand and Old Bertha's lost breasts and life. Which were hard things to accept. He should have spent more time here, should have been more aware of his duty. Instead, he'd been off licking his wounds from the death of his first wife. The woman before him had been forced to protect his people.

"George lost his legs for poaching."

Hethe stilled, his hand unconsciously squeezing the damp linen he held and drizzling water down her back. He had no idea who George was, but that mattered little. "Poaching?"

"Aye. He was caught with a deer he said he found dead. From what I understand, there were no signs of injury to the animal; his story was most likely true. Still, the man's legs were cut off for trespassing in your forest and taking Your Lordship's game."

Hethe was silent. Removing a poacher's legs was an acceptable punishment by law, but . . . "Was it a first offense?"

"Aye. So it was said."

Hethe would never have ordered a man's legs cut off for his first offense. Hell, he probably wouldn't have for a second or third offense, either. Neither would he have cut off a child's hand for fighting in church, or severed a woman's breasts for *any* offense.

"I needs must have a talk with Stephen. Something is not right here," he announced, straightening abruptly and heading for the door, only to pause and swing back.

"What is it?"

"If I go out there now, with no proof, Templetun will be on me about consummating the marriage," he answered with a scowl. All these questions about who had been taking the rulership of Holden and its land into their own hands, and Hethe had to worry about the irritating interference of the king's chaplain.

He was not pleased, but what could he do?

Helen stiffened in the water. She had forgotten all about Templetun and his insistence that the marriage be consummated. He would not leave without being sure it was complete. Which meant they had to . . .

Her gaze slid over Hethe's naked chest, taking in the width and strength of him, the hard muscles, the flat stomach, the narrow waist, the breeches that covered him. He had started to remove them earlier, but she had been so busy laughing she had missed seeing much of what they hid. Now her gaze focused on the bulge of his manhood, and she shuddered at the thought of what he was supposed to do with it.

"You are shivering," he said to her. Hethe's scowl slid away, and he moved back to the tub. "No doubt the water has gone cold. We should get you out of there before you catch the ague." Bending, he picked up the linen the servants had left behind for her to dry herself. Unfolding it, he held it out.

Helen hesitated, feeling herself flush with embarrassment. Then she stood quickly and huddled into the linen, letting out a breath of relief when he quickly wrapped it around her. She let out a squeal of surprise a moment later when he scooped her up in his arms and carried her across the room to the fireplace. Setting her down before it, to warm and dry herself, he turned away and moved back to the bedside chest to collect the ointment Mary had made up.

Helen was still toweling herself off when he returned. The activity had been slowed by the fact that she was trying to use a corner of the linen which was wrapped, toga-style, around herself. Hethe smiled slightly at the sight, apparently amused that she was suddenly so shy, when she had been splayed out naked before him earlier. Of course, she hadn't been comfortable then, either. Not exactly. And the possibility of their consummation suddenly seemed so much more likely. She turned away.

When, a moment later, he tapped her on the shoulder, she straightened immediately and whirled back to face him. As her eyes slid from him to the bowl he held, she forced herself to relax.

"Oh. Thank you." She held out a hand for the salve, but Hethe merely arched his eyebrows and shook his head.

"I told Mary I would apply it."

"Oh." Helen felt herself flush at the very idea. "There is no need for that, my lord. I can do it myself."

He took in her pleading expression, appeared about to acquiesce, then shook his head with a sigh. "You might be able to do your front, but there is no way you can do your back. Turn around and I shall apply it there. You can do the rest," he bargained.

Helen hesitated. Then, realizing there was nothing else for it, she reluctantly turned her thinly clothed back to him. Knowing that his eyes were roaming down her barely covered skin, she was as stiff as stone as she waited for him to start.

Chapter 14

ETHE hesitated, his gaze moving over his wife's body wrapped in the damp linen. He had seen her nude, her skin unblemished, on their wedding night when he had ordered her into the tub. He had also seen her dressed, prepared beautifully for their wedding ceremony. Now, he was staring at her standing before him, a wet linen clinging lovingly to her curves. Undoubtedly, this half-covered view of her was the most erotic. The cloth was extremely thin, turning transparent where it was damp, and it lay upon her like a gossamer web, driving his imagination wild.

Muttering under his breath, he dipped his hand into the healer's anti-inflammatory salve, then paused again. Where to begin? His gaze slid over his wife's bare shoulders, down over the linen hugging her damp buttocks, then to her bare calves and ankles where the fabric stopped. She had nice ankles. She had nice shoulders, too. And he was to rub all of her, not just her ankles and shoulders.

Shaking his head, he set the bowl of salve down, inserted a finger between the skin of his wife's back and the linen covering it, and tugged. The covering dropped away, pooling at their feet. He didn't miss the little gasp she gave before instinctively trying to cover her front. Fortunately for Hethe, he wasn't facing her front. He stared at her back and behind and gave a little sigh of pleasure. Had he really thought just a moment before that she looked sexier half-covered than she did in nothing? He'd been a fool.

Wee Hethe raised his head in agreement with that thought, and Hethe glanced down at his tenting breeches with a frown.

Helen bit her lip and stared at the fire before her, waiting in an agony of anxiety for her husband to begin to salve her back. She had half a mind to stop him, but she couldn't find the voice to do so. It occurred to her that if he applied the salve to her, there was probably no way he would actually want to consummate their marriage then, and get all sticky himself. Part of her thought that was a grand thing. The other part really didn't want to suffer all this again; it wanted to stop him from applying the balm and delaying any further.

The cowardly side of her won. Helen held her tongue and nearly sagged in relief as he began to smooth the cool cream over her shoulder. She was safe. Her deflowering would be put off for another night.

Of course, Templetun would not be pleased about that—but he did not have to suffer being poked by an ungreased pig!

Hethe finished applying salve to her shoulders, and his hands slipped down to slide over her back. Hands? Aye, he was using both, and she could feel them spreading the cream around. The decision was good of him, really, as it would be done much quicker this way. Unconsciously, she relaxed and leaned into his touch. It was really very nice. The salve was soothing what few itches still remained after her bath, and her husband's touch was firm and warm, almost causing her to melt beneath it. She let her eyes drift shut, absorbing his caresses as his hands slid down her back and up her sides. His fingers brushed lightly over the sides of her breasts, and her breathing gave a little hitch, but then they slid past, rising right up beneath her arms. A moment later, in descending, his fingers brushed again past her breasts.

A little shiver running through her, Helen leaned further backward and sighed slightly. His hands clasped her waist briefly, then slipped down over her behind, massaging and kneading as they went.

Helen blinked her eyes open, some of her relaxation leaving, but quickly his hands were gone. She heard the wooden bowl of ointment scrape a small ways across the floor; then his hands were back again, and he applied fresh cool salve to the backs of her ankles. It was only then that Helen realized that the salve had grown liquid in his hands from the heat of his touch.

She was distracted from such unimportant considerations by the way his hands were soothing and caressing her lower legs, slowly making their way upward. He spread the salve over the skin of her calves, and Helen almost giggled at the ticklish sensation; then he moved on and began to work on the backs of her upper thighs. She felt herself tremble, and her breathing seemed to turn shallow as his fingers ran along the inside of her thighs and skimmed upward. The oddest little tingles were set off between her legs, and Helen felt herself grow alarmed, but then he stopped again.

She waited tensely, listening to the quiet movements behind her, then released a sigh of relief when cool cream again touched her back. Apparently he hadn't finished there. She shivered as his breath skimmed her shoulder and stirred her hair. He had moved closer. *I can almost feel the heat from his body*, she thought vaguely; then his hands ran up her sides again. This time, however, they did not skim the sides of her breasts; they slid right under her arms and closed over the generous mounds.

Arms dropping away, Helen stared down at what he was doing, spreading whole handfuls of the salve over her breasts. This wasn't part of the bargain! *He was only to do my back*, some bit of her mind cried out, but Helen wasn't listening. Her eyes were glued to his hands as they massaged and caressed, squeezing so lightly that salve oozed through his fingers, then rubbing that excess on the undersides of her breasts. He was most meticulous, not missing an inch of skin. He even applied it to her nipples, rolling them between salve-covered thumbs and forefingers.

A soft "oh" slipping from her lips, Helen found herself leaning backward. It wasn't until she felt a hardness nudge her bottom that she realized he had removed his leggings and was applying the salve while naked. A sudden picture of how they must look popped into her mind, and Helen closed her eyes with a moan. Oddly enough, shutting her eyes only seemed to intensify her other senses. She was keenly aware of his chest rubbing against her shoulders, his legs brushing her own, his pelvis grinding gently against her backside.

As he suddenly stopped, she couldn't hold back a murmur of disappointment.

"Turn around."

Helen obeyed that husky order automatically, turned to find him squatting to scoop up more lotion. She felt a moment's discomfort when he raised his head and peered up the length of her naked body, then shifted to kneel before her and glanced down at her feet.

"Brace yourself on my shoulders," he ordered, then bent to lift one of her feet onto his knee.

She was grateful for her hold on those strong, wide shoulders a moment later as he began to massage the salve into her foot. It tickled and put her off balance, and she stumbled slightly, releasing a small giggle as he slid his fingers between her toes. Her laughter faded as his hands skimmed up her leg, gliding over her calf, her knee. Her hands tightened on him as those fingers slid higher up her thighs, his eyes following. She was terribly aware of how open and vulnerable to his eyes this position left her body.

A moment later, the side of his hand nudged against the center of her. She bit her lip and closed her eyes as a rainbow of startling sensations shot through her. Once again, she found herself startlingly disappointed when he stopped what he was doing and set her first foot back on the floor.

Opening her eyes, Helen watched him scoop up more salve, then catch and lift her other foot for the same treatment, applying the ointment to every bit of her foot, her ankle, her calf and upper leg. Then he started up her thigh. This time, however, when he reached the top, he did not stop. The hand on the inside of her leg continued higher, spreading salve before it. Helen gasped and stiffened as he massaged the very core of her, the salve seeming cool against her overheating flesh. She was so concentrated on what he was doing, she didn't even notice when he urged her foot off his knee, setting it back on the floor before rising before her. She did notice when his lips closed over hers.

Helen opened her mouth eagerly, inviting his invasion. He accepted the invitation with an ardor that increased her own, continuing to rub one hand between her legs, his fingers slick and hot.

She felt him cup her breast briefly and arched into that, even as she moved against his hand, but he released her and slid that hand down and around to cup her behind, squeezing and kneading there briefly. As his other hand slipped from between her legs to cup her other buttock, she groaned in disappointment, but it turned to a gasp as he lifted and spread her thighs, pressing her up and around him so that she straddled his waist as he crossed the room.

He tumbled them both down onto the bed, and Helen quickly realized that he was as slick and salve-covered as she. So, perhaps she had been wrong; he did not seem to mind getting messy. Their bodies slid across each other, their legs tangling, then untangling as he kissed her again and again, devouring her mouth with his own.

"Spread your legs," he murmured. Enraptured, Helen quickly did so, sighing and gasping when his hand slid between them. Oh, yes, she liked this, she thought vaguely as she raised her pelvis upward into his touch. Oh, yes. Yes, she—Oh!

She cried out in amazement as her body suddenly convulsed, her legs clamping instinctively around his hand and squeezing as a series of spasms rocked her body. She was aware of his hand slipping away, but was too wrapped up in the sensations convulsing her to care. Then he nudged her legs apart, slid between them and pressed into her.

Helen's eyes opened in shock at this sudden intrusion, and for a moment she feared he would not fit, but he pushed all the way in with one hard thrust that caused the tiniest pain within her. She glanced at his face to find him watching her; then he bent to kiss her again, and began to rock against her.

Pulling himself out, then pushing back in, he began to show her even more wonderful sensations than she'd known could exist. Helen clasped her arms around his shoulders and held on as he took her on a wild new ride.

The knock on the door sounded early. Too early. Hethe grunted, rolled onto his shoulder sleepily, and bellowed, "Go away!"

The knock sounded again, louder this time, and he shifted grumpily. "I said—"

Hethe paused, his mouth hanging open briefly, his eyes sharpening on the body in the linens next to him, his wife. Memories of the night before suddenly filled his mind, and his mouth closed, curving into a satisfied smile. He had performed magnificently, last night, if he did say so himself. And more than once. Aye. It had been rather impressive. They had made love all night and had not left the room once. They were well and truly married now, and there was no doubting it. Perhaps Templetun would finally leave him alone.

His gaze slid up the linens to the mass of golden tangles poking out of the top. There was no sign of a face, just those curly tresses poking every which way. Hethe's smile softened. His wife was so adorable. Sexy as hell, too, he added, his gaze sliding back along the curve of what he presumed to be her side and waist. Scooting forward in the bed, he pressed himself against her back, his hand resting on her hip and rubbing it through the linen.

She moaned and shifted against him sleepily, pressing herself against his erection which had suddenly sprung to life.

He knew the exact moment she woke up. Her body went quite as stiff as a board, then she flipped onto her back, tugging the linen down to stare at him. Hethe managed not to wince at the sight. Her face was streaked with dried ointment, and her hair, having dried while they slept, was a holy mess about her head. She gaped at him briefly, then tugged the bedclothes back over her face.

"What are *you* doing here?" she asked. Her hair trembled in syncopation with that muffled hiss from under the linens.

"I am your husband, and this is my bed," Hethe answered with a laugh, then slid his hand up her leg atop the linen, then along the inside of her thigh. His voice was husky when he asked, "Surely you haven't forgotten already?"

For a moment, she was as still as death; then she released a breath she had been holding, the linen billowing a bit as she did. "I did."

She pulled the cover down to peer at him consideringly. He arched an eyebrow as her gaze slid over his shoulders and chest, then across the bedsheet that still covered him from the waist down.

Hethe fancied he spotted a spark of desire in those blue eyes of hers as she found the bulge in the linens that signaled his own. She had opened her mouth to speak when another knock sounded impatiently at the door.

"Come in," he called out cheerfully, chuckling when Helen ducked beneath the linens again with a squeal of dismay. Rolling onto his back as the door opened, he eyed a timid Templetun with amusement. The man was hesitating by the open door, sniffing the air cautiously.

"You needn't worry," Hethe told the king's chaplain dryly. "The healer, Mary"—he made himself recall and say the girl's name; it was time he started being a proper lord around here—"she used some herbs in the bath that stopped the itching and removed the smell." His gaze slid to the lumpy linen beside him and he added slyly, "The girl appears to be much better than the healer employed by Tiernay."

An outraged squawk sounded from beneath the sheet, which Helen pulled down far enough to glare at him. "My Joan is as fine a healer . . . better even than Mary. Although," she added quickly, "while Mary needs more training, I am sure she will be as fine as Joan someday."

"Then why was *my* Mary able to get rid of your scent, whereas *your* Joan could not?" Hethe taunted.

"Perhaps Joan thought I wished to keep it," Helen answered sweetly, and Hethe burst out laughing. A small, reluctant smile tugged at her lips, too, before she glanced past him. She promptly flushed bright pink at what she saw, then ducked beneath the linen again.

Hethe glanced toward Templetun, his eyebrows rising as he saw that William was with the man. He supposed his first had been stuck out in the hall when the king's man had hesitated at the door, but Templetun had made his way cautiously into the room once Hethe had assured him there was nothing to fear. His first had apparently followed.

Hethe started to sit up, pausing when Helen immediately began to squeal and claw for the linens he was dragging with him. Biting his lip to keep from laughing, he shook his head and pushed the covering away, then stood up and grabbed for his breeches. "What are you doing here, William? I told Edwin to tell you—"

"Leicester and his Flemish mercenaries are captured. The king released us," William explained.

Hethe grunted as he pulled his breeches on, then straightened, picked up his tunic and headed for the door. "I needs must speak to Stephen."

"He is not here," William said.

At the same time, Templetun protested, "Now, just a moment, my lord."

Hethe paused and glanced from one man to the other. He decided to deal with Lord Templetun first.

"What?" he asked the man bluntly.

"Well." The king's chaplain appeared taken aback at Hethe's sharp, challenging tone. "W-we have not settled this yet."

"Settled *what?*" Hethe asked, turning his tunic about in his hands. The shirt was inside out from when he had tugged it off last night. He took the time to put it right side out.

"The bedding," Templetun snapped. "I must be sure—"

"Good God, Templetun!" Hethe interrupted, a little annoyed at the man's persistence. He was like a dog, sniffing about where he wasn't wanted. "What do you think I was doing up here all night? The minute Mary managed to remove my wife's smell, the problem was solved. The marriage is consummated.

Now let it go." He turned his attention back to his tunic, before glancing sharply back up to add, "Actually, now that I think on it, there is no need for you to waste your time here any longer. I am sure you must be eager to return to the king's side."

It was an invitation to leave Holden, and not a subtle one. Lord Templetun scowled slightly, then peered toward the bed. "Lady Helen?"

A moment passed; then she lowered the linens enough to peek out from them.

"Is the marriage consummated?" the old man asked quietly.

She nodded, her forehead and the tops of her cheeks turning pink with embarrassment. Templetun hesitated briefly, looking unsure whether to believe her or not; then his gaze suddenly sharpened and moved from Helen's salve-streaked face to Hethe's chest. He relaxed at once.

Glancing down, Hethe saw what had soothed the man's worries. His torso was streaked with dried salve. Hell, his whole body was probably streaked with the stuff, as was hers. The linens were quite a mess, too. They had been having a rather jolly romp, after all. Hethe looked over at Helen to see that she had also noticed the telltale marks of their activity. Flushing a bright red, his wife fell back, pulling the bedclothes over her face with an embarrassed groan.

"Very well," Lord Templetun conceded with satisfaction as he moved to the door. "William, you are my witness. These two both admit that the wedding is consummated. The marriage stands. I shall be leaving immediately after I break my fast."

"Have the servants bring up a fresh bath," Hethe called after the man as the door closed behind him. He was wondering if Templetun had heard and would do as he asked when William's shifting drew his gaze. The knight was sidling toward the door. "Where is Stephen?" Hethe asked abruptly, bringing the man to a halt.

Sir William grimaced. "I am not sure. He had something he said he had to take care of. I know he left the bailey on horseback," he answered slowly, his gaze moving between his liege's grim countenance and the lump on the bed. "Is there a problem?"

"Aye." Hethe crumpled up his tunic, tossed it on the foot of the bed, then began stripping off his breeches. As he had suspected, the dried salve covered him everywhere. He had to clean himself up. He couldn't go around looking like this.

"What sort of problem?" William asked, and Hethe scowled at the thought of his underling's treacherous actions.

"He has been doling out punishments unsanctioned by me."

"Nay!"

Hethe nodded at his first's shock. "That is what was behind Lady Helen's letters of complaint. He has been abusing his power here and blaming it on me."

"Stephen?" William asked doubtfully. Hethe could fully understand the man's incredulity at such a betrayal. It *was* hard to believe. But there was no reason for Helen to lie about what she'd told him. Besides, while he had not ordered those punishments given, Hethe did have a vague recollection of letters from Stephen mentioning the incidents she had listed, requesting directions on how to deal with them. He didn't recall what orders he had given the young knight, but *knew* it had not been to cut off anyone's hands, breasts or legs.

"Aye. Stephen," he answered solemnly. "I want to see him as soon as he returns to the keep."

"Shall I go find him? Bring him back to you?" William asked uncertainly. He appeared as troubled by the news as Hethe himself had been.

"Nay. It will wait until he returns," Hethe decided wearily, then glanced toward the bed. His anger faded somewhat at the sight of his wife lying there, so he turned back to his first. "Go on below and break your fast. I will join you shortly."

He waited until William left the room, then moved around the bed to Helen's side and gave her a light pat on the hip. Smiling to himself, he sat on the edge of the bed. When she pulled the linen down to peer at him questioningly, Hethe swooped in to press his lips to hers.

Helen remained still under his kiss at first, then relaxed against him. Her hands crept up to slip around his neck as she obviously remembered the night before and began to respond.

"Mmmm," Hethe murmured when he finally broke the kiss. "Good morning, wife."

"Good morning, husband," she said shyly, toying with the hair at the back of his neck.

He found himself grinning for no reason. She was just so adorable with her hair all over the place, her face salve-streaked and sleepy looking, and her lips swollen from his kiss. He raised a hand, caught the edge of the bedcover and dragged it down to her waist. His wife blushed but didn't protest, and he reached up to draw a finger between her naked breasts, then cup one gently.

"Your rash is nearly gone," he murmured, rolling her nipple between thumb and forefinger.

"Aye." She arched slightly to press her breast

more fully into his hand, her own fingers reaching out to slide curiously over his chest.

Hethe cupped her other breast, too, squeezing gently. "Did you sleep well?"

"Well, but not long," she murmured, eyes suddenly sparkling. "Mayhap we should go back to bed."

"Back? You have not left bed yet," he pointed out with amusement. He let one hand slide down over her stomach and smiled when it quivered in reaction.

"True," she agreed breathlessly, squirming slightly as his hand continued across her hip, ran lightly down her outer leg, then fluttered up the inside of her thigh. Her legs spread for him, her breath catching in her throat, and her eyes dilated as he pressed his hand against the core of her.

"Are you coming back to bed?"

Hethe chuckled at the plaintive question and the way she was now tugging at his head with her hand, trying to pull him down for another kiss. Giving in to insistence, he leaned forward, kissing her as she wanted to be kissed, his tongue plunging into her mouth as he slid a finger inside her. He could feel her flesh close around him and shifting beside her on the bed, he drew his legs up, resting one across her shins while fondling and kissing her.

A knock at the door interrupted them, and Hethe was breathing heavily when he broke their kiss. Raising his head, he glanced the length of their entwined bodies, then toward the door, debating whether to answer.

"Ignore them. They will go away," Helen gasped, trying to pull his head back down to hers, but Hethe resisted.

"It could be Stephen," he pointed out solemnly.

"And I have neglected that situation for far too long."

Helen released a little sigh of regret as her husband's hand slid away. She knew he was right, of course. It was morning. There were things for him to do. She was glad that he intended to take up his responsibilities here, but— Her thoughts died as the knock sounded again. Anxious, she drew the linen back up to cover herself as Hethe shouted out, "Enter!"

It seemed Templetun had heard the request for a fresh bath. The door opened to reveal servants bearing another tub. As they entered, Hethe remained seated on the bed, completely oblivious of his nudity as he watched them quickly fill the tub with fresh warm water. Once that was done, the servants emptied out the used water from the night before, then lugged their pails and the used tub out and away.

Hethe waited until the door had closed once more before he sought out Helen's hand and stood, dragging her up with him.

"What are you—"

"You don't expect me to bathe alone, do you?" he asked wickedly, urging her across the floor to the newly filled bath. Helen glanced from his sparkling eyes to the tub with dismay.

"But there is not enough room."

"Want to wager on that?" Stepping into the water, her husband settled down in it, then drew her closer with the hand he still held. "Come."

"But . . ." Her protest died as he gave her a tug. Shaking her head, she stepped cautiously into the warm water, then stood eyeing him doubtfully with one foot on either side of his upraised knees. "There really is not enough room—Ah!" she shrieked as he caught her other hand and pulled her down. Caught by surprise, she stumbled slightly, dropped to sit on his knees, then slid down to rest on his hip, her eyes wide. She could feel his manhood beneath her, a hardening shaft pressed between their bodies.

"See? There is room," he said huskily. Cupping water in both his hands, he lifted it to pour it over her breasts.

"Not much," Helen replied with some amusement as he dug around the side of the tub until he found the soap. Rubbing it between his wet hands, he built a slight lather, then reached for her chest. A moment later, each hand found a breast and began to massage it expertly, spreading suds everywhere.

"You can wash my back, and I shall wash yours," her husband murmured, concentrating on what he was doing.

"That is not my back, my lord," Helen pointed out on a near groan, leaning closer with each breath.

Hethe didn't bother to respond, merely continuing to touch and fondle and soap her. She almost protested when his hands finally slid away over her stomach and arms. Opening eyes she didn't recall closing, she snatched up the soap from where it landed between their two bodies and began to return the favor. She had barely finished covering him with soapy lather when he pressed her nearer, so that they were chest to chest, and began to soap her back.

Helen squirmed against him, then leaned back slightly to peer into his eyes. "I . . ." she began, but he silenced her with a kiss, devouring her mouth as his hands slid over her. After a moment, his hands dropped lower. Cupping her bottom, he urged her forward, pulling her along his engorged shaft. Helen groaned into his mouth as the hard flesh caressed her, aware but uncaring of the water slopping out of the tub, as they shifted. She continued to grind against him when his hands left her, making a sound of protest as he broke the kiss and leaned to the side, but then she glanced over to see what he was doing. He was reaching for one of several full water buckets the servants had left behind. She had just enough time to close her eyes and mouth before he spilled it over them both, rinsing the soap away.

"What?" she gasped, pushing her now damp hair out of her eyes and peering at him in confusion. Hethe stared at her chest and smiled, making her glance down curiously. "What?" she asked again.

"There was something I wanted to do last night, but was not sure if I should," he explained. He set the now empty pail he was holding back on the floor.

"What was that?" Helen asked huskily. He met her gaze, a fire in his eyes she was beginning to adore.

"To lick and suckle your breasts," he answered slowly. "But I was not sure if it was safe with the salve on."

"Oh." Helen's eyes widened, her breathing becoming shallow as she suddenly imagined his head bent to her breasts, his lips caressing her in place of his hands. The image was incredibly erotic. Helen closed her eyes to enjoy it more fully, then popped them open as she felt his lips close warm and firm around one nipple.

Oh, dear. The reality of it was even more erotic than the imagining, and a moan slipped from her lips as she peered down at the top of Hethe's head and arched into his caress. Oh, yes, this was very nice. She felt his hands slide around her waist to pull her closer, then sighed as she was again rubbed intimately across his lap.

She caught his head in her hands, knotting her fingers through his hair as he suckled at first one breast, nipping and tugging gently, before moving to the other. Then she felt one of his hands drop down over her back, slide over her bottom and between her legs from behind. Fingers brushed lightly over the center of her, but he was at an awkward angle. She wasn't surprised when he drew his hand away, sliding it between them instead, and lowering it between her thighs.

She moaned at his first touch. Her legs instinctively tried to close but were stopped from doing so by his body. Tightening her hands in her husband's hair, she ground against his hand as he caressed her, tugged his mouth away from her breast to kiss him, aggressively plunging her tongue into his mouth as he had done to her countless times. Her kiss became desperate as his caress became more forceful, and she rode his hand, her movements instinctive rather than practiced. He was driving her mad—and she wanted more. Letting go of his head, she reached down between them, leaning into the kisses he trailed across her cheek to her ear, then down to her neck as she sought, then found, his manhood. Hethe stopped kissing her and leaned his forehead into her neck with a groan as she firmly clasped it. Unfortunately, she didn't know what to do with it now that she held it, but it seemed enough for Hethe.

"Witch," he murmured, slitting his eyes open as she curiously squeezed him. "Enchantress."

Helen smiled wickedly, but her mouth went round when, with the hand that caressed her so intimately, he plunged a finger inside. The sudden explosion of pleasure caused her to stiffen in shock, but a moment later he withdrew the finger and shifted beneath her. Before she could ask what he was doing, he had taken her by the waist and was rising out of the water, lifting her with him as he went.

Scooping her off her feet once he was standing, her husband stepped out of the tub and crossed the room, dripping water everywhere. Helen hit the bed with a bounce, and he came down on top of her, his mouth covering hers briefly before it slid away, brushing her neck, her collarbone, then taking turns at each breast as his hand worked between her legs.

Moaning and writhing, Helen clasped his shoulders and twisted her head, her hips jerking even as her legs closed instinctively around his hand. She felt him replace his mouth with his free hand at her breast; then he was pressing little nips and kisses across her belly, then to the crease of her thigh. She didn't realize where he was headed until he was there, and then she didn't care as he pressed her thighs further apart and his mouth took the place of his hand between her legs.

Helen cried out in desperate desire, her fingers clenching in the linens she lay upon and her head twisting wildly on the pillow as he feasted on her with his lips and tongue, pleasuring her in a way she had never imagined possible. She felt his hand slide up her thigh, then felt a finger slip inside her again; she nearly tumbled them both from the bed in her excitement. Hethe chuckled against her heated flesh, and she felt it all the way to her toes and back. Her body shuddered and convulsed, and she called out to him desperately, clasping him to her as he slid up her body and pressed his arousal against her spasming flesh.

His hard heat filled her and his mouth closed over hers. She rode the wave he set her on, her body tightening around him. He stoked her fire with long, slow strokes that seemed to prolong her pleasure, intensifying it even after its climax.

Swept away, Helen couldn't tell where the first wave of ecstasy ended and the second began, for he continued driving into her. Her body was singing beneath him.

Suddenly he shifted, straightening enough to draw her legs up over his shoulders. Leaning against them left his hands free to cover her breasts, and he took advantage of that, fondling her as he drove deeper inside her, each stroke coming harder and faster than the one before until they both cried out and found release.

Chapter 15

LIGHT spilling across her face woke Helen up some time later. Blinking her eyes open sleepily, she peered toward the window. There Hethe stood, framed in the morning sunlight, wearing nothing but a pensive look. It was sexy, Helen thought with a self-conscious smile. They had drifted off to sleep after their little "bath"; she supposed they must have needed the rest. She felt much better now, had replenished some of her energy from the night's lovemaking.

Sitting up silently, she slid from the bed, retrieved and donned her chemise, then crept up behind her husband. She wrapped her arms around his waist and peered past him at the world beyond the window. The sun was high in the sky and shining brightly. It had to be near the nooning hour.

"Good morning," Hethe murmured, covering her hands with his own.

"Good morning," she answered, briefly pressing her cheek to his back. "It is a beautiful day, is it not?"

Hethe grunted in response, and Helen frowned. He seemed distracted and she wasn't quite ready to let go of the intimacy they had shared.

Helen smiled wryly at her fickle thoughts. At this time yesterday she could never have imagined feeling this way. But then, at that time, she had believed Hethe a cruel man and believed that the bedding would be unpleasant. She had learned a lot since. If what he had said was true, her husband was not the cruel bastard she had thought. And, as for his attentions being unpleasant, nothing could be further from the truth. She knew he had shown extreme kindness and gentle patience with her last night. Which had resulted in great pleasure rather than the pain her aunt had warned her about. Helen was grateful for that treatment, so grateful she thought she just might like to give him some pleasure back.

With that thought, she let one hand slide daringly down over his stomach until she found his manhood. It was flaccid again, and Helen turned her face into his back, pressing her smiling lips against his warm, salty skin as she recalled her reaction to her first sight of the member. She knew now, of course, that while it may not be very impressive in its relaxed state, once awakened, it could grow to rather intimidating dimensions. Just as it was growing now beneath her touch.

Hethe leaned back and groaned as she caressed him, letting the window covering fall back into place. Helen immediately slipped between him and the curtain, and she began to press kisses to his chest as she did. She wanted to do for him what he had done for her, but wasn't sure how to go about it. Deciding it couldn't hurt to try, she dropped to her knees before him and began to press kisses to his elongating shaft. For a moment she released her hold on it, though, and it popped up and hit her on the nose. Frowning, she grabbed the tip again to hold it steady while she nibbled along the side as if on an ear of corn. Hethe's shudder made her think she was doing it right, but after another moment, she noticed that the fleshy cob was shrinking.

Choked noises from above sounded suspiciously like muffled laughter. Pausing, she tipped her head up to peer at him, feeling foolish and useless when she realized that he was, indeed, laughing. She wasn't doing this right.

"Come here," Hethe murmured, obviously containing his amusement. Grabbing Helen's arm, he urged her to her feet before him and hugged her close. He pressed a kiss to the top of her head, then tipped her face up and kissed her lips. "Thank you."

"For what?" she asked unhappily. "I did it wrong."

"Nay, you just need a little practice," he assured her quickly.

"Shall I try again?" She pulled back to peer up at him. "If you told me what I was doing wrong, I could—"

"Another time," he murmured, then again drew her nearer. "Believe it or not, I have other things I must do."

"Stephen?" she asked quietly.

"Aye."

She was silent for a moment, her fingers moving absently over his hip. "But no one came to wake us. Does that mean he is not returned?"

"Aye. But there are other things to tend to as well. I have apparently neglected Holden for too long. I needs must find out if there is anything else that has gone awry while I was . . . absent."

Releasing her, Hethe turned and walked around the bed to collect his tunic and breeches. Straightening with them in his hands, he caught her yawning and faintly smiled. Seeing his amusement, Helen was suddenly aware that she must look a mess—with her hair all over the place.

Hethe dropped his tunic on the bed and began to pull on his breeches. "You are still tired. You should sleep a bit longer."

"Nay. I am hungry," Helen announced as he finished with his breeches and picked up his tunic. "I will dress and follow you below."

Hethe grunted in answer, tugging on his tunic, then straightening it about himself. He glanced her way again. "I will send Mary up to you, first. Your rash is nearly gone, but another application of her ointment may be a good idea."

"Hmm." Helen nodded in agreement as he collected his sword belt and dirk and moved toward the door.

She slid out of the bed as soon as the door closed behind him and went in search of a fresh chemise from the sack she had brought from Tiernay. She would wait for Mary, but would not take the time to have any more salve applied to her. That would have to wait until later. She was going to have something to eat, no matter what he said. She was absolutely famished. Starved. She felt as if she had not eaten for days. This being married business was hard work. Well, maybe not work, exactly. Not like running a keep.

Smiling to herself, she began to dress.

"When do you think we will be leaving?"

Hethe grimaced at his first's question as he lifted his mug to drink. William had assured him that Stephen had not yet returned, else he would have fetched him as ordered. Certainly there was no sign of his second's return. Hethe was finding the man's absence worrisome as it was, and now, considering his first's question, he sighed. He knew William would not be pleased with the answer. Where Hethe had always accepted battle as a necessary evil, a handy excuse to avoid a castle full of sad memories, William truly reveled in war. He would likely not be pleased to learn that Hethe intended to remain at Holden, to become the administrative lord he should have been years before.

"I have heard there is still trouble on the border," William said. "We could go up there and see if anyone needs our assistance."

"That is just rumor," Hethe said quietly, then cleared his throat and added, "It has come to my attention that I have been neglecting my duties here at Holden. It is time I took care of things, including my new wife. Besides, there will be peace for a while now."

William frowned, but overall took the news better than Hethe expected, merely nodding unhappily. Perhaps the man was mellowing. . . .

"Actually, you should consider marriage, William. You are not growing any younger," Hethe began. He nearly burst out laughing at the horrified expression that twisted William's face in answer.

Helen shifted fretfully and walked to the window to pull its covering aside and peer out. She was fully dressed now and had been for some time. She had even brushed out her long hair and fixed it atop her head. As she waited, her gaze moved slowly over the sunny bailey below and the people in it. A moment later, she let the covering fall back into place and turned away to pace toward the bed. Her gaze moved distractedly over its rumpled linens.

Mary still hadn't arrived, and Helen was growing impatient; worse, she was *hungry*. Spinning away from the bed, she returned to the window. She should just go below and find the girl. She could tell the woman there as well as here that she would rather eat before having any more salve applied—if she even needed it applied again.

Deciding she would give the woman another few moments, she again tugged the window's drapes aside, and leaned out to breathe in deeply of the fresh air. It was a beautiful day, but though the sun was shining brightly and there was only a slight breeze, she could smell rain in the air. A glance at the tree leaves in the courtyard below showed they were turning, preparing for a downpour. Aye, it would rain soon.

Helen was about to let the window covering slide back into place when a sight below made her pause. A man was crossing the bailey, and for one brief moment she thought it was her husband, but then realized it was Sir William. The two men truly were very similar in shape and form, she thought vaguely.

As she watched, a shout made William pause and turn back to wait for someone. Which made Helen lean further out the window and peer down toward the keep doors to see whom it had been.

Hethe! He started across the bailey toward William. Helen's gaze slid from one warrior to the other before she decided they were not so similar after all. Hethe was taller, a little wider, and had a proud bearing his first could not match, though the two men did have the same long-legged stride.

The sound of the bedchamber door opening drew Helen's glance to see Mary slipping inside. The girl hurried to her side.

"I am sorry I took so long, my lady. I had to send a messenger down to the village to—"

" 'Tis all right." Helen waved away the apology and glanced back outside at her husband crossing the bailey below. "I have decided I do not wish to put any salve on again until later if I must. I—"

She had been watching Hethe, but a sudden movement off to his side caught her eye. Peering closer, she saw it was a small wagon cart. But there was something wrong with the cart. The horse hooked up to it appeared to have gone mad. He was wildly rearing and pawing the air.

"Actually, I do not think you need the salve again," Helen heard vaguely as the healer examined her arm. "I think the one treatment may have been enough."

Helen hardly processed the words; her gaze was frozen on the scene outside. In the next moment, the vague alarm that had been forming in the back of her mind exploded into true fear. The cart horse slammed its hooves to the ground and charged forward as if all the demons of hell were chasing it— headed directly for Hethe. Couldn't he hear it coming? Her stomach lurching, Helen grasped the edge of the window and leaned out to shout a warning.

"What is it?" Mary asked, squeezing up to the window beside her as Hethe turned to glance up at where they stood. The healer spotted the trouble at once and breathed the words, "Dear God."

Ignoring her, Helen waved frantically, trying to turn Hethe's attention to his immediate danger. At the last second he spun the way she was gesturing only a bare moment before the damn horse would have run right over him. He had just enough time to throw himself to the side in an effort to avoid the horse and wagon, and he did save himself from the worst of it, but he couldn't avoid injury entirely.

Helen heard herself scream as she saw him knocked to the side. Then she whirled away from the window and raced from the room. Mary was right behind as they flew down the stairs and charged across the hall to the doors leading to the bailey.

A large crowd had gathered by the time Helen and Mary got to Hethe. Several people were standing silently in a circle. The two women had to push their way through to reach him. Sir William was already kneeling at his master's side, pale-faced and almost appearing to hold his breath as he stared down at him.

Ignoring the mud, Helen dropped to her knees on one side of her husband, while Mary urged William out of the way on the other. Both women peered down at Hethe breathlessly. His chest was rising and falling steadily, but his eyes were closed. Leaning forward, Mary quickly examined him. There was a cut on his forehead and a bump forming around it.

"There is another lump at the back of his head," Mary announced, and Helen winced. One was no doubt from hitting the horse, the other from hitting the ground. She took a deep breath and waited as Mary hurriedly completed her examination.

"His right leg also appears to be swelling, but I don't think it is broken," the young healer reported. "He must have twisted it while attempting to get out of the way," Helen murmured, squeezing Hethe's hand between her own anxiously.

"Is he . . . ?" William could not even finish the question.

"Nay. He will be fine," Mary said with calm confidence. It reassured Helen, and when she heard William release a pent-up breath she glanced up sympathetically at the man. She knew exactly how he felt. She had been holding her breath, too. How surprising that she had come to care for this man, she thought in an oddly detached way. This man who had been her enemy for so long.

"We should get him inside," Mary directed, and glanced around.

Had she thought about it, Helen would have expected several of Hethe's men to step forward, to take his arms and legs and tend to the matter. None of his soldiers were about, however, and none of the serfs and villeins making up the crowd around them appeared to want to offer their assistance. Her husband was not the most popular person at Holden . . . thanks to Stephen.

The situation didn't bother William, however. He merely bent and lifted Hethe into his arms with a grunt, then started back to the keep.

Scrambling to their feet, Helen and Mary hurried after him. Once they neared the main doors, Helen rushed ahead to open one. Much to her relief, Mary jumped forward as well to tug open the other, and William did not even have to slow or turn sideways to carry Hethe's limp form into the keep.

"I shall just fetch my medicinals and follow you," Mary called out and disappeared.

Helen scampered ahead of William and hurried up the stairs to get the master bedchamber door open for him. The knight stumbled into the room behind her and went straight to the bed. He nearly collapsed there, dropping to his knees to set Hethe on the bed.

"Thank you, William. Are you all right?" Helen asked.

Sucking air into his lungs, he nodded. He rose slowly, then moved aside as Mary burst into the room to join them.

Helen helped the healer as much as she could, assisting in undressing Hethe and helping to wash the blood away from his two head wounds. There didn't appear to be any other injuries needing binding. As far as she could tell, the injury to his lower leg was only a twisted ankle.

When they finished, she helped cover Hethe up and sat on the bed to hold his hand unhappily as Mary prepared a tincture for the pain for when he woke up.

If he woke up, Helen thought, then chastised herself for such gloomy thinking. She supposed that a day or so ago she would have hoped for just that, that Hethe would not wake up. It would have been extremely handy for a woman who didn't wish to be married to him. But Helen's feelings had changed somewhat. The man she was coming to know as Hethe of Holden, and the man she had known as the Hammer, were not the same man. The man who lay in the bed had withstood some rather mean efforts by her to avoid marriage, all with good cheer and little retribution. At least, she supposed, he hadn't done anything to her she didn't deserve.

Hethe, the Hammer of Holden, the man of those tales, the cruel bastard who ordered children's hands cut off and women's breasts removed, would never have withstood her pranks so well, she was sure. In fact, she had thought she was taking her life in her hands when first she had resolved herself to flouting his will. Yet, he had not hit her—or even threatened to—once.

Too, he was a sweet and gentle lover. Surely the man she had thought he was would not be like that. There was definitely something wrong, and she was beginning to believe that Hethe's second had truly behaved without sanction. But when she thought of the young, red-haired man in question she had trouble accepting that, too.

A groan from the bed drew her gaze, and Helen leaned closer as her husband's eyes opened.

"My lord?" she murmured, eyeing him with concern as he winced and drew in a long, hissing breath.

"My head," he moaned.

Mary was immediately there, tincture in hand. Helen helped her pull Hethe into a seated position, then watched silently as the healer urged him to drink. Her husband grimaced at the taste but swallowed the potion dutifully, then glanced at Helen as Mary took the mug away.

"What happened?"

"Do you not recall?" she asked anxiously, worried about damage to his brain. He had been thrown some distance.

He peered at her blankly for a moment; then his confusion suddenly cleared. "The horse cart."

"Aye," Helen breathed her relief.

"What . . . Why?" he asked.

Helen shook her head. She hadn't seen what set the animal off. Perhaps Sir William had, though she doubted it. His attention had been on Hethe, or so it had seemed. She glanced questioningly toward the knight who stood patiently at the foot of the bed.

"I shall find out," William vowed when he saw her look. And with that, he strode purposefully from the room.

"I need you to move your foot."

Helen glanced at Mary at those words. The healer was now by Hethe's swollen leg. Hethe twitched his foot, wincing in pain as he did, and the young woman nodded in satisfaction.

"Good. It is not broken. I did not think so, but . . ." She shrugged. "I think you had best stay abed for the rest of the day, my lord. Both your head and leg need a chance to heal."

Hethe scowled. "I will not spend the day abed. I have things to do."

"Whatever you have to do can wait another day or so," Helen said firmly. When he started to protest, she added, "William shall take care of whatever cannot wait."

Hethe grunted in disgust. "That was what I thought when I left Stephen in charge. You know how that turned out."

Helen's determination dimmed briefly, but after a glance at his forehead she straightened grimly. "This is different. You are here this time. Simply unable to traipse about."

"I—" Hethe began, but Mary interrupted.

"I fear that the tincture I just gave you for the pain in your head will not allow you to do anything, my lord. You shall be sleeping like a babe quite soon."

Hethe did not look pleased. His gaze narrowed and alternated from one woman to the other as if suspecting they were in cahoots. "I suppose this was my wife's idea? She was trying to lure me back to bed earlier, and now she has convinced you to aid her in the endeavor."

Helen's jaw dropped at her husband's accusation; then she caught the sparkle in his eyes and realized the man was teasing. Wrinkling her nose, she shook her head when Mary glanced at her uncertainly. She retorted, "I fear you may have suffered brain damage, after all, my lord husband. Surely you are imagining things if you think that I would want a scraped-up and dented specimen such as yourself in my bed."

Hethe started to laugh, as she knew he would, then stopped abruptly, wincing in pain. "Oh, my head," he groaned, clasping his hands to either side of it.

"It serves you right," Helen snapped, but inside she felt a brief twinge of concern.

Giving a great sigh, Hethe lay back in the bed and glanced at Mary. "Did you send someone to fetch your mother back yet?"

Helen widened her eyes in surprise, looking at the healer for an answer.

"Lord Holden sought me out this morning and told me my mother was needed here," the girl explained. "He said he never intended or ordered her to leave, that I was to have her move back." She grinned shyly. "She will take her rightful place again, and I won't have to go running to her with questions all the time."

"Oh, 'tis marvelous," Helen murmured.

"Aye," the young healer agreed. She spun back toward Hethe, telling him, "She was here this morning when you told me to request her return. She checks up on me from time to time because—" She paused, flustered as she realized what she was saying.

Helen patted the girl's shoulder sympathetically. "She came to make sure the Hammer of Holden wasn't stringing you up by your thumbs, or something else equally heinous . . . all for some minor offense," she murmured with a hint of amusement at her husband's expense. He was looking terribly disgruntled at his ogrish reputation. "'Tis all right, we understand. So you were able to tell her the good news yourself."

"Aye." Mary beamed at them both. "She is down in the village collecting her things now. Otherwise, you would have had her to tend you instead of me."

"You did well," Hethe said reassuringly, obviously struggling to push aside his irritation. "Never think I am bringing your mother here because you are inept. You are very skilled, but—"

"But she is more so," Mary finished, without taking insult. "I am not offended. I am grateful to have her near and to be able to learn from her. And she is grateful as well, my lord."

"Aye . . . well . . ." He shifted about in the bed, looking as uncomfortable at the praise as he had at being thought an ogre. "I am just sorry that she was thrown out in the first place. I truly did not order it." He scowled. "I considered having all the old servants returned to the castle, but I don't have the first idea who they are. And then there is the problem of what to do with the young women who replaced them."

"No doubt most of the women have found new positions elsewhere," Helen answered. She knew that a couple had found work with her. Hethe's expression said he suspected that might be the case.

Shrugging wryly, she glanced at Mary. "Perhaps, if you know of anyone, or your mother does, who hasn't yet found work, you might have them report to me during the next couple of days."

"I will be happy to, my lady," the girl assured her sincerely, then began to collect her medicinals together. She was at the door before Helen recalled her hunger.

"Mary?" she asked. The girl paused and swung back questioningly. "Would you please have Cook send up something for me to eat? I have not yet even broken my fast."

"Certainly, my lady." And with that, the healer was gone.

"You needn't stay here with me," Hethe murmured as the door closed behind her.

Helen glanced down at the man to see that Mary's tincture was already taking hold. He was starting to look as if holding his eyes open was a struggle.

"Tired of me already, are you, my lord?" she teased lightly.

He forced his eyes open to peer at her and gave a grunt. "Not likely." His expression turned serious. "Do you regret that our marriage is final, wife? Do you wish you had found a way out of it?"

Helen peered down at her hand. It rested in his. She, or he, she wasn't sure which of them had done it, but one of them had sought the comfort of the other's touch. It might have been her. Watching him being struck by a horse had scared her silly. She still felt shaky from it. She shouldn't, really; she hardly knew the man. Or did she? She had not known him long, but she had seen his response to many situations over the past several days. She had watched him wage their silent war with humor and good spirits. Had watched him keep his temper in the face of some unfair attacks. She had witnessed his wit and charm. And she had truly enjoyed his love-making.

"Helen?" he asked, but she was saved from answering by a tap at the door. Slipping her hand from his, she moved to answer it, stepping aside to allow two young maids to enter. She started to direct them to the chest by the fireplace, but Hethe overrode her, ordering the girls to place the food and wine on the chest beside the bed.

Following them reluctantly, Helen watched the serving women set out the food, noting with some interest that they were sending tentative smiles toward Hethe as they did. Helen suspected that the news was making the rounds. Mary would have passed on the fact that Hethe denied having ordered the harsh punishments and removal of all but the pretty serving girls. They would also have learned that he had asked that Mary's mother come back, that he was searching for Stephen to straighten out the matter. She had not seen their response to Hethe before this, but Helen suspected from his pleased reaction that these were the first servants' smiles he had received in a long time. She waited until the maids had left to comment.

"They appear to be willing to give you the benefit of the doubt," she said as the door closed behind the departing pair. She settled onto the edge of the bed near the chest where the women had set the food and wine.

Hethe gave a crooked smile. "As ashamed as I am to admit it, I never really noticed their fear and resentment of me. Looking back, I realize they were hardly welcoming, but I was here so rarely—"

"Why?" Helen asked, eager to avoid her husband recalling his earlier question. She was not sure how she felt about this marriage. Though her feelings seemed mostly good now—she was definitely beginning to see Hethe as a human being—they were too new for her to wish to dwell on. Keeping on some other topic seemed a good idea.

Hethe was silent so long, she thought he would not answer. Glancing over curiously from pouring some wine, she saw uncertainty and unhappiness pass over his face. When she offered him the goblet she'd filled, he refused and closed his eyes. She had just decided that he had drifted off to sleep when he spoke.

"When I was younger," he began slowly, "I hated it here."

Helen raised her eyebrows at that confession. Holden was a large gloomy castle, true, but it needn't be. It simply lacked the finer touches that could make a keep a home, tapestries and the like. It had been neglected, and felt like it. But surely it had not always been so? When his parents had lived?

"My mother died when I was still quite young, and my father was a hard man," he answered as if she had spoken aloud. "I was a great disappointment to him."

Helen started to argue that that couldn't be true, but he waved away her attempts to comfort him.

"It's true. In fact, he brought both William and Stephen into the schoolroom with me to shame me into trying harder. He thought the competition would do me good. That I would try harder to do better than 'two village brats,' as he called them. It did not turn out quite the way he had hoped." His mouth twisted wryly. "I *was* trying, you see. But no matter how hard I tried, I always seemed to have difficulty. William and Stephen, rather than becoming competition, covered for me. We became firm friends. Of course, I could never let my father know that, else he would have removed them. So we pretended to hate each other when he was around—which, thank goodness, was not often. Then when it came to training for knighthood, he kept me here and had them train with me. They became two of his best soldiers."

"And your best friends," Helen murmured. He nodded.

"As soon as I was old enough, I ran away to war, and they came with me."

"Your father must have been livid."

"Oh, aye." He gave a short laugh. "He did not give me all that training and education to have me slaughtered on the field for the king's greed," he quoted dryly and shook his head. "The first time I returned home, he arranged for my marriage to Nerissa. He wanted to see me wed, to get an heir from me before I was killed on the battlefield."

"But that was not the only reason?" Helen guessed from his tone.

"Nay. In truth, he wanted Nerissa's dower. She was still young—barely twelve, too young for marriage—but our land needed the coin. My father pushed for the wedding."

"And Nerissa's father?" Helen asked curiously.

Her husband gave a brief bitter laugh. "The man was eager for the title. They were a wealthy merchant family, but were common. They wanted to be one of us. Nobles."

"So the wedding went forward."

"Aye." Hethe sighed, and opened his eyes briefly,

glancing around at the tapestries overhead. "I tried to convince them that we should wait at least a year or so to consummate the marriage, but they would have none of it." He was silent for several moments and she was sure he was remembering. She could see the anger and frustration. The regret. "Nerissa died nine months later in childbirth. It lasted three days." He paused, and a haunted look crossed his features. "Sometimes I can still hear her screams."

He seemed to fret over that for a moment, then his gaze suddenly raised to hers with horror. "Dear God, I forgot all about that! I was so distracted—first, with trying to accomplish the task, then with the doing itself—that I did not think to take precautions."

"Precautions?" Helen asked, both confused and made anxious by his obvious upset.

"I should have withdrawn or . . ." Regret filled his face. "If you are with child because of my—"

"I am not Nerissa, my lord," Helen interrupted quickly, her heart warming at his worry. "I am not a child. I will not die on the birthing bed," she assured him, though she really couldn't guarantee such a thing. Her own mother had not survived her second child. But Helen would not have him fearing such a circumstance.

Deciding their original topic was a safer one, she prodded him back to it. "So, after Nerissa's death you went back to avoiding Holden?"

"Aye. And neglected my castle and my people . . . and they have suffered for it."

Helen reached out to touch his hand tentatively. The guilt in his voice was agonizing to hear. She wanted to comfort him, but could not find the words. Besides, in her heart of hearts, perhaps she held him to blame. At least a bit. Being a lord, or a lady for that matter, came with a great deal of responsibility. The lives of every person on your estate were, in the end, in your hands. He had failed his subjects miserably by trusting the wrong person, and for that he was terribly in the wrong.

They were both silent for a moment; then Hethe shrugged impatiently. "Father died a couple years later. His chatelain continued as mine, but he died just a few months before your father did. I replaced him with Stephen, whom I thought I could trust." His mouth tightened bitterly; then his gaze seemed to focus on her hand where it still lay on his. He twisted and clasped it firmly. "I was wrong. I won't allow it to happen again."

He seemed almost to be making a vow to her. Helen opened her mouth to speak, though she wasn't sure what she intended to say, but a tap at the door made her remain silent.

"Enter!" Hethe called, and the door opened.

It was William, and he wasn't alone. He held a small boy by the scruff of the neck and pushed him into the room ahead of himself. The child couldn't be more than five or six, she saw, and she was swept by a wave of both concern and curiosity.

Hethe frowned from the obviously terrified boy to his first. "What is this?"

"The culprit behind the charging horse," Sir William announced grimly. "It seems young Charles here likes to throw rocks. He hit the horse in the back flank, and the horse charged." The knight gave the boy a shake. "Tell him."

"Aye, milord. I am sorry, milord," the boy gasped, hardly able to breathe. "I didn't mean to hit that horse, milord. But my aim ain't so good."

Helen peered at the child and felt her heart squeeze tight. He was pale and shaking, his voice trembling as he spoke. She had a vague recollection of him standing among the circle of adults who had surrounded Hethe when she had reached him. She remembered his pale, shaken face from then, too. He surely hadn't caused all this trouble on purpose.

"Let him go, William," Hethe said after a long moment. Helen felt herself relax.

"But—"

"Let him go. I imagine he has learned his lesson. He will not be throwing any more rocks. Ever. Will you, lad?" Hethe asked heavily.

The boy's eyes widened at the threatening tone, and he shook his head quickly.

"See?" Hethe smiled slightly. "Let him go."

William hesitated, scowling at the boy, but then released him. Being a smart lad, the child promptly scrambled out the door and fled. Hethe's first watched him go with discontent. "You were too easy on him, Hethe. You always are. We might have lost you . . . and all because of one boy's stupidity."

"We didn't," Hethe pointed out gently.

"Nay." William's shoulders slowly relaxed.

"I planned to go search for Stephen. I guess I will not be able to do that, now. Will you tend to it?"

"Aye. Of course."

"Good. If you find him, bring him to me. If not . . ."

"I shall let you know, either way," William assured him and left the room.

The moment he was out the door, Helen turned a grateful smile on her husband and squeezed the hand still holding hers. "Thank you, my lord."

He turned to her, obviously surprised to see the relief and pleasure on her face. "For what?"

"For not punishing that boy."

"I can hardly punish a boy for bad aim. He was just playing." His eyes narrowed. "Did you truly believe I could be so vile? Did you still believe that I was the one to order those punishments on my people?"

"Nay," Helen protested, then realized it was too quickly. She sighed as her face flushed with guilt. "At least . . . I was not sure."

He seemed to struggle internally for a moment, then asked, "Are you sure now?"

Helen considered seriously, then nodded her head. "Aye."

"Then you are content to stay married to me?"

Back to this? she thought. Helen paused to ponder her feelings. Married to Hethe, properly and forever—or at least until death parted them . . . She tried to imagine the future, but all her mind could do was draw up images of their relationship so far. His horrified face each time she had shoved a baby into his arms that day of the picnic. Aye, he had looked petrified and completely at a loss as to what to do with each child, but he had not shoved them back, or dropped them in irritation. And the day of the boat ride. Water was an old childhood fear, but he had summoned the courage to face it—if only so that he would not show weakness before her. And then there were his kisses. Her body began to hum just at the memory of his caress.

"Helen?"

She glanced up with a start. It was the first time she could recall that he had used her name without including "Lady" before it. She liked it. And she liked the fire in his eyes as well. It sent shivers down her back.

"Do you wish the marriage to stand?"

"Aye," Helen breathed, knowing that her agreement now was more binding than the actual marriage vow had been. She just hoped she wasn't making a mistake.

Chapter 16

HELEN was settled in a chair before the fire in the great hall, mending a small tear in the gown she had worn for the journey to Holden. It was an old gown, faded and a bit tattered. The rend might even have been in it when she had first donned it, but smelling as she had at the time, she hadn't wished to risk ruining any of her newer gowns with the scent. Now, it was the only extra gown she had. Ducky had thrown only one dress in the bag she had brought below—as Templetun had ordered, Helen thought with irritation, but wasn't really very angry about it. She supposed the king's man had not thought she would be away from Tiernay long. No doubt he had expected Hethe to return to his war-mongering and her to be returned home immediately. Such was not the case, however. She was Lady Holden now.

That thought brought her husband to mind, and Helen glanced toward the stairs to the upper level. Hethe had fallen asleep not long after she had agreed to let the marriage stand. It was a deep sleep and he snored and snuffled in it, pausing to mutter sleepily every once in a while. He was really rather adorable, Helen had decided as she peered on his sweetly innocent face in repose. But she had tired of that sport after a while and had come below to do her mending and ponder her changed circumstances. She was still there, her mind racing, when the great hall doors opened and William walked wearily in.

Her husband's first moved toward the stairs to the upper floor, but paused when she called out to him. He turned and moved in her direction.

"No luck?" she asked curiously when he stood before her.

"Nay. Is he awake?"

Helen shook her head. "Mary said that he should sleep for a little while yet."

William nodded, then glanced at the chair opposite her. After a hesitation, he moved to sink into it with a sigh.

"It must be upsetting for you."

"What?"

"That Stephen has behaved so. I know Hethe is unhappy."

"Aye." William nodded and glanced toward the fire. Helen had asked one of the servants to build it up to fight off the chill in the air. The coming storm she had sensed this morning hadn't yet broken, but the air was heavy and damp. "We are all very close. Well, we used to be. I guess Stephen has changed these last five years, what with being left behind all the time.

"'Tis odd . . ."

"Hmm?" William glanced pointedly at her when she hesitated.

Shrugging, slightly embarrassed, she hesitated, then said, "The day we arrived here, I mistook Stephen for Hethe when he first stepped out of the keep. Today I did the same with you when I saw you cross the bailey. True, it was from the bedchamber window, but you all have the same build. And, while Stephen does not, you even have Hethe's coloring. The three of you could almost be related."

"That's because we are."

Helen glanced up sharply, catching the alarmed look that crossed the knight's face. He hadn't meant to say that.

"I mean—"

"Nay," Helen interrupted, knowing he was going to try to equivocate. "Tell me."

William hesitated, then sighed. "We are half-brothers. We all have the same father, just different mothers. Stephen's mother was the village lightskirt; mine was the blacksmith's daughter."

"I see," Helen murmured. "And the three of you were raised here in the castle together?" It was a logical conclusion, she thought. After all, she knew that the three of them had studied chivalry here together.

"Oh, nay." He gave a slight laugh at the idea. "Though Stephen and I were brought into the classroom, then onto the training field, we both continued to live in the village. Our father only paraded us around to try to shame Hethe into being a better student. He did poorly at his lessons."

"Aye. He told me so," Helen admitted, then shook her head. "I never would have guessed that. He is intelligent and speaks well."

"Oh, aye. He is intelligent," William assured her quickly. "He always did well in languages and such, so long as it was done orally, but he had difficulty with actually writing. He formed his letters backwards sometimes and—" William shook his head, seemingly at a loss to explain. "One of his teachers claimed he had come across it before, that the best thing to do was to teach and test Hethe orally and forget about the written word. But our father simply tossed the man out on his ear." He grimaced. "To his way of thinking, Hethe just needed more beatings—to inspire him not to be so lazy."

Helen had heard as much from Hethe, and it had disturbed her. She liked it even less now. She didn't like to think of her husband as a child being abused. She decided a change of topic was in order. "It must have been hard on you and Stephen. Living in the village and yet being forced to come up to the castle for lessons."

"Aye, sometimes," William admitted. "But Hethe always made us feel welcome. He was glad for the company, though our teachers never let us forget where we belonged. And the children taunted Stephen horribly about his mother—about being a bastard. About putting on airs and taking lessons in the castle."

Helen frowned at the thought. Children could be so cruel.

"You maybe shouldn't let His Lordship know I told you this," William said suddenly, looking uncomfortable. "He might be angry."

About to speak, Helen caught a glimpse of the man in question making his way down the stairs. Eyes widening with alarm, she quickly stood. "Hethe!"

Head jerking around, William caught sight of his lord limping down toward them. William was out of his chair in a flash and hurrying after his master's wife as she rushed toward the staircase.

"What are you doing? You could fall and break your neck!" Helen cried, rushing up the stairs. She saw that he wasn't so much limping down as hopping on his uninjured foot.

"I am fine," her husband grumbled as William caught up and gently urged Helen out of the way. Despite his protest, the knight then drew Hethe's arm over his shoulder and helped him down the rest of the stairs. Helen followed, her hands caught anxiously in the folds of her skirt.

"Besides, I was bored up there by myself," Hethe went on as William helped him cross the floor to the chairs by the fireplace.

"You are supposed to be resting your leg," Helen reminded him grimly.

"And I am. I have not put any weight on it. I hopped to the stairs."

"And halfway down them. You might have hurt yourself."

Hethe rolled his eyes and glanced at his first. "See what you are missing by not being married, William? We really have to find you a wife."

William merely chuckled as he settled his friend in the chair he himself had been occupying only a moment before. Helen promptly moved to seize the chest beside the chair in which she had been seated, and began to drag it around in front of Hethe, but William was there to finish the task for her.

"What is that for?" Hethe asked in surprise.

"To put your foot on. You should be keeping it elevated."

Hethe grumbled, but he allowed her to lift his injured appendage onto the chest. His gaze slid to William. "Did you find Stephen?"

"Nay," his first admitted, shaking his head in apology. "I looked everywhere I could think. I asked around the village, I even sent men out in various directions to question farmers, but no one has seen him. It is as if he rode out of the bailey and disappeared."

Hethe sighed, looking weary. "That does not bode well."

"Nay," William agreed reluctantly. "He should not be gone from the keep for so long."

"He could be injured, or . . ."

Hethe's voice trailed away unhappily, but Helen saw him glance up sharply when William added, "Or he fears you have discovered what he was up to."

"How would he know that?" Hethe asked.

"Well, Stephen was never stupid. Besides, there is Lady Helen here."

"Me?" Helen asked, eyes wide. "What about me?"

"Well, he must know you two would eventually talk, that things would come out."

"Aye," Hethe said thoughtfully.

Helen picked up the gown she had been mending and reclaimed her seat. She saw her husband's eyes fall on what she was doing, recognizing the fabric as that of the frayed, ugly dress she had worn at Tiernay on her last day as its sole master.

"Why are you bothering to mend that gown?" he asked irritably as she began to stitch. "Surely you have others?"

"Aye," she agreed calmly, knowing his testiness was merely due to concern about Stephen. "At Tiernay."

"At Tiernay? Do you mean to say that the dress you are wearing and that one are the only clothes you have here?" he asked with dismay.

Helen gave him a look. "Lord Templetun was in a bit of a hurry. He told Ducky to put one gown in a bag and bring it below, then he rushed me out."

"Damned idiot man," Hethe muttered, shifting

impatiently in his chair. "Well, we shall have to rectify that. We shall make a quick journey to Tiernay. It is probably for the best, anyway. Your aunt is most likely worried about you. I am sure she will be relieved to see you alive and well. No doubt she fears I have killed you by now," he added grumpily.

"No doubt," Helen murmured with amusement. "She is most likely preparing for the funeral as we speak."

His eyes shot to hers, his mouth opening for a retort. Then he caught the laughter dancing in her eyes and he slowly relaxed, a smile curving his lips. "Aye. We can attend it, perhaps. See how well done it is, then give her notes for future reference."

Helen laughed softly and bent her head to her sewing. Hethe was silent for a moment. She could feel him watching her; then he addressed William. "We will leave on the morrow. After midday."

Helen glanced up in time to see the knight nod. "I will see to the arrangements. How many men do you wish to bring?"

Hethe pondered briefly, then shrugged. "Ten and yourself should do well enough. It is not a long journey."

Nodding, William started to move away, but before he could, Hethe added, "Send Johnson in. I will be leaving him as chatelain. I must instruct him on how I want him to behave with the people here. And on how to deal with Stephen if he returns while we are gone."

William acknowledged the order with a wave, then continued out the keep doors.

"Why not William?" Helen asked. When Hethe peered at her blankly, Helen explained. "Why are you not leaving William as your chatelain?"

Hethe looked puzzled for a moment, then shook his head and shrugged. "William is always with me. He is my first."

"Aye, but—"

"Besides, he does not have the patience to be a chatelain. He is already growing restless here, and after only a few days. This little trip might perk him up some."

Helen accepted his words silently, then said, "Do you not think we might do better to wait another day or two before going?"

"Wait?" Hethe frowned.

"Aye. It would give your ankle more of a chance to heal before the journey, and perhaps Stephen will return in that time."

He considered that briefly, then said, "But you only have two gowns."

"Hmmm. That is a problem," she agreed solemnly. "I suppose I shall just have to wear them as little as possible." Meeting his gaze, she gave him a shy smile, then winked.

Hethe's eyes widened incredulously. "Was that . . . Did you just—" He took in her blushing cheeks and paused. She had. His wife was flirting with him. Throwing sexual taunts his way. Damn, he thought with amazement. Maybe this marriage would work out. Perhaps the unfortunate beginning they had known would give way to a successful union. If she turned all of that passion and creativity she had used to torture him toward finding ways to please him . . . The very idea aroused him.

"I believe I am swelling again," he announced abruptly, almost smiling when her blush receded and concern at once spread on her face. He felt anticipation rise within him as she quickly set her sewing aside, got to her feet and moved to bend over his leg resting on the chest.

"Are you sure? Is it sore?" she asked, peering at his hurt leg. "I can get Mary and see if she—"

Her words died on a startled gasp as Hethe grabbed her by the hips and pulled her into his lap. "Mary can't help me. It was Wee Hethe I was speaking of."

"Wee Hethe?" She peered at him with confusion even as she struggled to get off of him, then suddenly stilled as he shifted beneath her, pressing the swollen appendage in question against her bottom. Her eyes rounded, her earlier blush returning in full force. "You mean . . . ?"

"Aye." Hethe wasn't surprised to hear the huskiness now in his voice. "Aye. Just thinking about you being naked for the next few days has me swelling to painful proportions. And I fear only you have the cure for that."

"I see."

Much to Hethe's pleasure, his wife's voice was now as husky as his own, and there was a fire coming to life in her eyes that made his mouth dry with anticipation. She settled into his lap, then reached out a tentative hand to caress his cheek.

"Would a kiss help, do you think, my lord husband?"

"I do not know. Why do you not try and see?" Hethe murmured the words into the palm of her hand, delighted when she turned his face and leaned forward to kiss him. Despite her blushes and tentative touch, this was no demure kiss. While she was not yet skilled at pleasuring him with her mouth in other areas, as her sweetly clumsy attempts that morning had proved, his wife had definitely got the hang of kissing. She laved his mouth, then when he opened to her, let her tongue slide inside to find his.

Aye, she definitely had learned well there. Within moments, she had him panting and kissing her back with an excitement that Wee Hethe's amazing growth was proving. And he, himself, wasn't the only one affected. Helen was moaning and making sounds deep in her throat, her body shifting and rubbing against his in ways that were increasing his swelling tenfold.

Eager to see if she was as affected, Hethe slid a hand under his wife's skirts and quickly up her leg, ignoring her startled jerk. When she broke their kiss in protest and turned her head away, he merely let his lips trail over her cheek and ear as his fingers continued up her thigh.

"Husband, I do not think—*Oh.*" She stiffened even further as he reached the apex of her thighs, the arm she had wrapped around his shoulders tightening convulsively. The hand she had used to try to stop him, grabbing at his through the material of her skirts, clenched over his, no longer trying to pull away as he found the warm wet depths of her.

Aye, the kisses had excited her as well. And his touch was doing even more. She turned her head back and caught his lips again, kissing him almost desperately. Satisfaction rose within him at the knowledge of how he affected her, but that was quickly nudged aside by an eagerness to do more. He wanted to be inside her and briefly considered shifting her to straddle him so that he could have her right there, but the great hall would not afford the privacy he needed for all the things he wanted to do.

They would have to adjourn upstairs. But even as

he thought that, he slid a finger inside her, smiling against her mouth when she clenched her legs around his hand and arched into the action. She was making little strangled sounds of pleasure in her throat, and they were exciting him. He nearly spilled himself where he sat as she suddenly pulled her mouth away and bit desperately into his shoulder, shifting on his lap so that she could find and press one hand against his manhood through his clothes.

"Upstairs." Hethe gasped, feeling complete sympathy with her when she groaned in disappointment. He retrieved his hand from between her legs, knowing he should have stopped it sooner, should have made the suggestion they move when they had first kissed. But they would go there now. Urging her off his lap, he got to his feet, wincing as he forgot his injury and set his weight on it.

Helen, of course, did not miss the look. She became concerned at once, some of the passion leaving her face. "Maybe we should—"

"Upstairs," he said firmly, turning her in that direction. Still, she hesitated.

"Mayhap we should have William come help you up the stairs," she suggested anxiously, and Hethe felt his pride sting a bit at the suggestion that he needed assistance like an old man.

"I can manage," he said testily. She didn't look wholly convinced, but she didn't argue further. Instead, she took his arm with the intention of helping him, but Hethe shook off her hand and took her arm instead. He was a man, a warrior. He didn't need help. And to prove it, he made sure to support her arm rather than lean on it as he hopped quickly to the steps.

They managed the stairs and had reached the

door to the master bedchamber when Hethe lost his balance. Helen shifted to try to save him, but ended up being trapped between his solid weight and the wooden planks of the door.

Hethe rested against her briefly, then gave a breathless laugh. "This is right where I wanted you. Almost."

Lifting his head, he peered down into her face and found himself touched by the concern in her eyes. There had been points during these last many days when he had doubted that he would ever see such a tender feeling for him in her eyes.

Swooping down, he caught her lips with his own in a passionate kiss that revealed that his earlier intentions were still alive and well, despite their most unromantic hopping trip up here. He wished he could sweep Helen up in his arms and carry her to their bed, but he knew that was beyond his abilities at the moment. Straightening, he pulled her away with one hand, reaching past with the other to open the door at the same time. Helen started for the bed the moment he released her, but Hethe had different ideas. He hopped to the chair by the fire.

"What are you doing?"

Pausing before the chair, he leaned against it briefly to catch his breath, then turned to face her as he removed his tunic. "Come here."

His wife watched the garment hit the floor, confusion on her face, but came forward as he ordered. Pausing before Hethe, she watched curiously as he undid the tie of his breeches. When he moved to push them down, she knelt to accomplish the task for him. The moment he was free of the material, he sank into the chair and gestured for her to move between his spread legs.

Smiling at her continued bewilderment, he quickly
undid the ties of her gown, then pulled the loosened
material down over her shoulders. A sigh of pleasure
slid from his lips as the fabric dropped to hang around
her waist, leaving her sweet, firm breasts bared to his
eyes.

"Should we not move to the bed, my lord?"

Hethe grinned. While the question sounded uncertain, her voice was again becoming strained with
passion. Reaching out with both hands, he covered
her breasts. They were warm and round in his
hands, a pleasure to touch. Much to his gratifica-
tion, she responded at once, her breath catching in
her throat, and her nipples hardening under his
palm even as she arched forward. She allowed him
to fondle her briefly, then bent, seeking his lips with
hers, her hands clasping his shoulders for balance as
she showed him her excitement. She was aroused,
but not as frantic as she had been in the great hall,
and Hethe would settle for nothing less.

Releasing her breast, he clasped her by the waist
and tugged her down to kneel on the chair, so that
she was straddling him with his manhood pressed
flat between them. Then he kissed her. He felt her
hands slide up over his shoulders and smiled against
her lips as her small fingers delved into his hair,
brushing the nape of his neck, his skull, then along
the back of his ears.

Tearing his lips away from hers, Hethe pressed
kisses along her neck, then urged her up so that he
could catch one rigid nipple in his mouth. She was
moaning again, her hands clasping his head and
holding him close as he laved her silky skin. Reaching
between them, he began to fondle her as he had in the

great hall, caressing the nub at the center of her excitement with his thumb, sliding a finger into her.

It was apparently too much for Helen for, pulling her breast free of his mouth, she sat abruptly on his lap, then shifted herself and reached between them until she found Wee Hethe. In the next moment she had impaled herself on him.

Hethe clenched his teeth and squeezed his eyes closed as her flesh closed hot and slick over him, her muscles tightening around him in a glorious embrace. A moment later, he grasped her hips and helped direct her as she rode him until they both found glorious satisfaction.

Chapter 17

THEY waited several days for Hethe's leg to heal before they headed to Tiernay. Stephen, however, did not return.

Helen and Hethe spent the time getting to know each other better. They played chess, made love, talked, made love, argued, made love. Hethe caught up on events at Holden with his steward. Helen got to know the household staff. William grew more impatient and eager to leave, but, by the time they left, the rest of the people of Holden were starting to relax around their lord and lady. They had begun looking less tense, and there had even been a tentative smile or two, Helen thought with satisfaction as they entered the gates of Tiernay and rode across the bailey.

They had just reached the foot of the steps when the keep doors flew open and Aunt Nell and Ducky stepped out.

"Child!"

Helen grimaced at her aunt's shriek and quickly dismounted as the woman raced down the stairs toward her with the maid hard on her heels. She managed to get her feet on the ground and turn just in time to be captured by the two women and nearly squeezed to unconsciousness by their hugs as they cried out their relief and pleasure at seeing her. She had been gone for less than a week, but she would have thought that she had been away for years. Or that they had not expected to ever see her again.

Helen glanced apologetically toward Hethe, embarrassed on his behalf for the evil thoughts the women had obviously been harboring, but he was only shaking his head, looking a touch amused. Which was a pleasant change from the pained face he had worn throughout the last part of the trip here. The ride had not been kind to him. It was impossible to ride a horse without being jostled and bounced about. Hethe's ankle had begun to pain him during the last part of the way here, she knew, though he had been too proud to say.

"You look well," her aunt said, drawing Helen's arm through her own and urging her up the stairs as Hethe dismounted and directed the stablehands as to the care of their horses. Nell's obvious amazement at her health only verified Helen's suspicions that the woman had been imagining all sorts of awful ways the Hammer had been punishing her for their earlier high jinks.

"Aye," she admitted, then grinned. "I am *very* well."

"Do tell." Aunt Nell's eyes widened with interest, then she asked in a quiet voice for only Helen and Ducky to hear, "I take it there is still the possibility of an annulment, then?"

"Oh, nay." Helen blushed bright red.

Her aunt glanced at her sharply, then, "Nay?" she and Ducky gasped together. Helen grimaced.

"There is much for me to explain. But—" Turning

back, she glanced at her husband with concern as he limped toward the stairs, William at his side.

"What happened? Did *you* do that to him?"

"Ducky!" Helen gasped, shocked that the maid might even think such a thing. Then she remembered . . . "Nay, of course not. He had an accident."

"Hmmmph." Aunt Nell shook her head, then again took her niece's arm to urge her forward once more. Hethe and William started up the steps behind them. "Come, you had best tell us what is about, and if there is anything *special* we needs must do."

Helen grimaced at that, knowing that by "special" her aunt meant things like befoul the food or flea-bait Hethe's bed. Which was no longer necessary, of course. In fact, she was now aware that it hadn't been necessary to begin with. It had been fun, though, she thought, then smiled as her aunt pushed her into the keep.

"My, my, my," her aunt commented as they approached the trestle tables. "There must be a lot for you to explain. That is a terribly happy smile. I take it the man is kinder in the bedchamber than he is as a lord?"

Helen's jaw dropped at her aunt's crudeness. "I cannot believe you said that."

"Aye, well, I shall say a lot more, should you not soon explain what is about. Only days ago you were nearly kicking and screaming as Lord Templetun dragged you out of here. I have been worrying ever since. Now you return looking like the cat who ate the cream."

"Lord Hethe did not order any of the punishments the people of Holden have suffered these last five years," Helen announced abruptly to prevent her aunt from speculating on the carnal origins of her change in mood.

"Oh?" Aunt Nell did not look impressed. In fact, it was obvious the woman didn't believe her niece at all. Ducky looked much the same. Neither of them would accept Hethe's innocence easily. The two women both peered at her with doubt and pity, obviously convinced that Hethe had pulled the wool over her eyes.

"It is true," Helen insisted. "He was horrified when I told him what has been going on at Holden while he has been absent. He has been away, fighting for most of these last ten years, you see. Stephen, his chatelain," she explained, seating herself with a sigh once they reached the trestle table bench. "*He* has been running Holden these last five years. And that is when the trouble started, if you will recall. The man was doling out unsanctioned punishments."

"He was, was he?" Aunt Nell exchanged glances with a hovering Ducky. "And did Lord Holden punish the man?"

"Nay. Stephen rode out the morning after Templetun brought Hethe back, and he has not returned. No doubt he fled for fear of Hethe's wrath."

"Hmmm." Nell seemed to consider that seriously, and Helen felt herself begin to relax. At least her confidantes' doubtful expressions were easing somewhat. They were considering that what she claimed might be possible.

Turning, Helen glanced toward the two men slowly crossing the hall toward them. She didn't like to see her husband in pain. There must be something they could do for him. "Where is Joan?"

* * *

"Good morning, my dear."

"Good morning." Helen bent to press a kiss to her aunt's cheek, then slid onto the bench beside her.

It was the morning after their return to Tiernay. Helen had spent the better part of the previous afternoon and evening explaining things and reassuring first her aunt, then Ducky and finally Maggie that Hethe wasn't the monster they thought he was. Maggie had been the hardest to convince. She had been insistent on believing that Hethe and not Stephen was the true devil of Holden. Helen still wasn't sure she had fully convinced any of them, but at least they had stopped protesting and agreed to consider the possibility.

"How is the Ham—your husband this morning?"

Helen smiled wryly at her aunt's slip, but merely said, "I left him sleeping. He had a restless night. His leg was painful and kept waking him up."

"Hmmm. He should have let Joan give him one of her tinctures."

"Aye," Helen agreed absently, her gaze moving to the staircase as she recalled the grumbling and cursing that had woken her up repeatedly throughout the night. The man really should have let Old Joan give him a potion, but he had said that it would just make him sleep, and he hadn't wanted to. Actually, he had sounded a good deal like a protesting child, she thought with amusement, her mouth curving into a slight smile. He was so adorable when he was grumpy.

It took Helen a moment to realize what she was seeing. Her gaze was trained on the stairs, but she was really hardly taking them in when movement tore her mind from her thoughts. When she discerned that the movement was a body tumbling down the stairs, she gasped, her hand rising to her chest. Then she recognized whose body it was, and she leapt to her feet.

"Hethe!" Helen flew toward the heap at the bottom of the staircase, her heart skittering wildly inside her chest. He was dead. She knew it. She knew he was dead. He had to be. No one could crash down stairs like that and live. He was dead. Helen was positive of it when she reached the still and twisted form of her husband. Collapsing to her knees beside him, she hesitated, then reached out to touch him tentatively, a relieved hiss slipping through her lips when he weakly moaned.

"Is he alive?" Aunt Nell gasped, catching up to her, the majority of the great hall now crowding about.

"Aye. Fetch Joan," Helen ordered, shifting to turn her husband over. He didn't make a sound as she flopped him onto his back. Helen would have felt better if he had, but it appeared that the first moan was the only indication she was going to get as to his life.

"I am here, my lady," Old Joan spoke up, pushing her way through the crowd to kneel at Hethe's other side. "Took a tumble down the stairs, did he? I told him he should stay off that leg for a bit!"

"Aye, well, it appears he doesn't take direction well," Helen grumbled. "He is hardheaded."

"That may be a good thing in this instance." The healer's answer held some slight amusement as she ran her hands quickly over his head. "Two bumps back here, one on the side, and this one on his forehead."

"The one on his forehead is likely from his accident earlier," Helen explained. "As is one of the lumps on the back of his head."

Nodding, Joan let her hands trail quickly over Lord Holden's body, checking his arms and chest and legs. "Doesn't appear to be any broken bones."

"Amazing," Aunt Nell breathed from where she hovered over Helen's right shoulder.

"He must have hit his head at the start of the fall," Joan guessed. "Only a limp body can take a fall like this and not end up a pile of broken bones. Breaks usually happen when a body tries to save or brace itself. It's why drunks rarely break a bone despite stumbling about. They're too soused to tense up."

Helen frowned. "But he was not 'soused.' It is morning. He has had nothing to drink and refused to take your tincture—"

"Nay." Joan shook her head. "That's why I say he must have hit his head when he first fell. It probably knocked him unconscious and saved him during the rest of the way down."

"Oh."

"He'll be a sore mess of bruises soon, though." Joan glanced at Helen. "We should get him up to bed."

"Aye." Helen glanced about, relief covering her face when she saw William pushing his way to the front of the crowd.

"I shall carry him," the man murmured, stooping to pick up his liege and half-brother.

"Thank you, William," Helen said.

Lifting him with a grunt, the knight nodded and turned to make his way up the stairs. Helen immediately followed, aware that her aunt, Joan and Ducky were trailing.

Once inside the master bedroom, the women made quick work of stripping Hethe. Joan's prediction that he would be well bruised proved true. Great, ugly discolorations were already beginning to form on several parts of his body. His right hip. His left shoulder. His upper right arm. His left leg and each of his sides. Helen took in each new bruise with a wince. Hethe was going to be terribly stiff and sore when he woke up.

Helen gave up looking at her husband and quickly pulled the linens up to cover him. She glanced at Joan. "Are you going to give him something for the pain?"

The woman frowned down at her patient thoughtfully, then shook her head. "He took a nasty knock. I'll see him awake before I mix up a tincture."

"Oh." Helen wasn't too happy with the pronouncement, but she didn't disagree. While she didn't like to think of her husband in pain, she knew that head wounds were a tricky business.

"I will sit with him," Joan announced, glancing around until her eyes settled on the chairs by the fire. She had already started toward them when Helen spoke.

"Nay. You go on down and finish your meal. I shall sit with him."

Joan hesitated, then nodded and turned toward the door. "Call me when he wakes, milady."

"Aye," Helen whispered as the door closed behind her. "When he wakes." Then she glanced to her aunt and Ducky. "You two can go eat, too. I will be fine with him."

"Are you sure you would not like company?" Nell asked, but Helen shook her head.

"Very well," Aunt Nell agreed, and with that she and Ducky left her alone.

Helen sighed as the door closed behind them,

then glanced from the empty space in the bed beside Hethe to the chairs by the fire. She supposed it would be better to sit in one of those than to possibly disturb him by sitting on the bed. Walking over, she tried to lift the nearest of the chairs, but it was solid wood and extremely heavy. Wincing at the racket she made, she grimly dragged the chair back to the bed, then dropped into it with a sigh.

"Are you trying to kill me?"

She gave a start at the husky question and leaned quickly toward the bed. "Husband?"

Hethe moaned in agony, one hand lifting weakly to ward her away. "You *are* trying to kill me."

Helen covered her mouth guiltily. It seemed her enthusiastic response to his awakening had proven too loud for his poor head. She waited until the pain eased from his face and he let his hand drop weakly away, then whispered, "I shall go fetch Joan."

"Nay." He winced at the sound of his own voice, but caught her hand before she could move away. "Who was it?"

Helen peered at him blankly. "Who was what, my lord husband?"

"Who was it that hit me?"

Helen could hardly conceal her shock. "What? Someone hit you? *That is* why you fell down the stairs?"

"I fell down the stairs?"

They stared at one another, each absorbing different bits of information; then Helen sank onto the side of the bed and eyed her husband with concern. "Did someone hit you?"

Hethe grimaced. "Aye. I had just reached the landing at the top of the stairs. I heard a sound, started to turn and . . ." He winced and shrugged.

"Something smashed into the side of my head. Felt like my brains exploded. That's the last thing I remember." He took in her unhappy expression. "I take it I fell afterwards?"

Helen nodded solemnly. "Fortunately, you did not break anything. Joan said it was because you were unconscious. She thought that you must have hit your head on your first tumble," she added hopefully, but he shook his head grimly.

"I was hit before I ever started down. . . ."

"But who would . . . ?" She paused abruptly at the solemn way he was eyeing her. "Surely you do not think that I—?"

"Nay." He smiled faintly at the idea. "You can be troublesome when you are fighting for something you want—or do not want, as the case may be—but you are hardly a murderer."

"Murder?" Helen's voice rose with her alarm, and her husband winced. She immediately muttered an apology, then asked in a hiss, "Surely you do not think someone was trying to murder you?"

"What would *you* call it?"

Helen was silent for a moment, her expression troubled. Murder. Someone here at Tiernay had tried to murder her husband? She simply could not seem to grasp that possibility. Her people would not do that. Realizing that she was clutching his hand rather desperately, she promptly released it, then gave it a pat as she rose. "I shall fetch Joan up here. She may give you something to help you sleep."

"Nay." He caught her back again. "Nay. I want none of her tinctures. I want my wits about me. Besides, I need to get to the bottom of this." He began to push the bed linens aside in preparation of getting up.

Helen promptly put her hands on his shoulders to hold him there. "Nay, husband! You need to rest to heal."

"I need to find out who hit me so that it doesn't happen again," he argued, but winced in pain and allowed her to push him back in the bed, one hand going fretfully to his brow. "Damn. I am not pleased to be waking up with another headache."

"No," Helen murmured, pulling the sheets back up to his chest. Opening his eyes, Hethe scowled at the action and pushed the bedclothes away impatiently.

"I am not staying abed, wife. I have to sort out this mess. Someone tried to kill me."

"Yes. But, should you not wait until you are feeling better?"

"Oh, you would like that, would you not?" he snapped, glaring at her. "Lie here and wait for them to try again, to succeed this time. Then you wouldn't have to stay married to me. A state you did not want in the first place."

Helen stiffened at those words, hurt by them despite knowing how cranky men got when they were ill. Her father had been worse than a baby when not feeling well. It appeared Hethe wasn't much better. But she could hardly believe he would suggest something so cruel after the intimacy they had shared. Surely he didn't really think she would rather see him dead than be married to him?

No, of course not, she assured herself. Head injuries could leave a mind confused and . . . well, confused. That must be it. Which just proved her point. He really shouldn't be up and about right now. He would probably bluster his way right into whomever had pushed him down the stairs and get himself killed. She couldn't let him do that. But what could she do?

Straightening, Helen glanced toward the door, her hands unconsciously catching in the skirt of her gown and twisting it. She needed to get a sleeping tincture into him so he would sleep and regain his strength. She needed him in fighting form to face whomsoever had done this. And she needed to post a guard at the door to keep him safe while he regained that strength.

"Damn." Helen glanced back at that exclamation to see Hethe half upright, his head clasped in his hands, his face contorted with pain.

"Perhaps Joan has something for an aching head that would not affect your wits," she suggested tentatively. When he opened his mouth in what she suspected would be an automatic refusal, she quickly added, "I should call her up here just the same. I want her to check you over to be sure that you are all right."

Hethe looked fretful for a moment, then lay back with a small sigh. "Very well. Fetch Joan back with something for an aching head. Bring William back, too."

Nodding, Helen moved quickly for the door before he could change his mind. She would have Joan give him something for his aching head, something that would make him sleep. Then she would post a guard at the door to keep him safe while she sought his would-be murderer. Tiernay had always been her home. The people here were her responsibility. And if one of them had tried to kill him . . . Well, as embarrassing as it was to admit, they might very well think they were doing her a favor. She quite clearly recalled the day Templetun had given them the news of the upcoming wedding—Ducky's suggestion that Maggie knew "this and that about herbs," or Joan "might know of something we could give him to—"

Kill him, she now finished what she had stopped her maid from saying at the time. Dear Lord, there probably wasn't a person here at Tiernay who wouldn't think they were doing her a favor by killing Hethe, and it was partially her own fault. His reputation as a cruel ruler was probably part of it, but it didn't help that she had made her wishes on the matter so clear with her smelly potions and rotten food.

Which put her in a terrible spot. She had to keep her husband safe from her people, and her people safe from her husband, until she could sort the whole mess out.

Chapter 18

"How is he doing?"

Helen gave a start at the question and turned from closing the bedchamber door to find her aunt approaching down the hallway from her own room.

"Fine. I left Goliath to guard him. He's still sleeping. But I think he will need another dose of Joan's tincture soon."

Aunt Nell raised her eyebrows and gave Helen an amused look as they started toward the stairs. "Just how long do you intend to keep drugging him?"

Helen grimaced as guilt consumed her. Since Hethe had refused to willingly take any sedatives, she'd had Joan give it to him in place of the potion for his aching head that first morning. But Helen had continued to keep him drugged these last two days, pouring the potion down Hethe's throat any moment he showed signs of stirring. She had salved her conscience by convincing herself that it was in his best interests, that his injury had obviously left him confused, else he wouldn't have said those awful things about her being happy were he to die. But, the truth was she had hoped to sort out this problem of someone trying to kill him before he was up and about and vulnerable again. It wasn't that she did not think Hethe could take care of himself, but there were so many people here who could be behind the attack, so many who had suffered under his rule.

Helen had spent a good deal of the last two days subtly asking any and everyone if they had seen or noticed anyone on, near, or going up the stairs before the accident. No one had seen anything, of course. She was no closer now to sorting the matter out than she had been when he was hurt—and in good conscience, she could not continue to dose Hethe. He had slept for two days and his bruises were beginning to fade. No doubt the aching in his head would be gone by now, too. She would have to find another way to see him safe.

Sighing, Helen glanced unhappily over the people gathering for the evening meal as she and her aunt reached the bottom of the stairs and started across the great hall toward their seats. One of these people had pushed Hethe down the stairs. One of her own subjects. Her gaze slid over the faces again, recognizing many refugees from Holden. Serfs and villeins she had taken in after horrible abuses. Abuses most still thought Hethe had ordered. Any one of them might be harboring enough anger and resentment to wish him dead. She could even understand their rage. So many had suffered so much. Who could blame them for wanting revenge?

She felt a chill run down her back. Suddenly, people whom she thought she knew well—some for years, some all her life—didn't seem as harmless as before. Feeling a sense of danger closing in on her, she clenched her hands at her sides. She had to find a way to be sure none of her subjects would try to kill Hethe again. Could they? Those who were angry enough to kill would remain silent, and if any of her subjects knew of a plot, they were keeping it to themselves—and she supposed she could not really blame them. She might have protected Hethe's would-be assassin herself before she had learned that he was not the one behind the sadistic reign of Holden Castle and its lands. The thought made Helen pause.

"Of course," she whispered, her mind racing. She need not find the culprit. She needed only to pass the news around that Hethe was not the one behind the abuses and mutilations that had occurred. Surely, whoever Hethe's attacker was would then realize he had made a mistake and leave him alone.

"Child?" her aunt prompted.

"I will stop dosing him now," she said, in answer to the question her aunt had asked her upstairs. "He has healed enough."

Hethe opened his eyes slowly, an instinctive reaction to the pain pounding through his head. A remnant from last night, he realized and grimaced. He should be grateful that a headache was all he was suffering. He could easily be dead. It had been a nasty tumble he had taken. An angel must have been cushioning his fall when he had pitched down those stairs.

He didn't feel very grateful though. Oh, he was sure he would be glad to be alive in a day or so, but at the moment his pounding head made death seem a peaceful respite.

"You are really in a bad way," he told himself grimly and closed his eyes. He heard a soft whine from the foot of the bed; then a moment later something warm and wet slopped across his face. Hethe's eyes popped open and he found himself gaping into the smiling, slack-tongued face of Goliath.

"Dear God," he moaned, pushing the foul-breathed beast away, then glanced toward Helen's side of the bed to complain. He found her side of the bed empty. Scowling, he sat up slowly, groaning at the stiffness in seemingly every part of his body. Good Lord, he felt as if he had been trampled. Glowering, he glanced at himself and grimaced at the bruises coloring almost every inch of his body. Which explained his pain. Shaking his head, he eased from the bed and swayed dizzily. He felt as weak as a baby. Damn. Starting forward, he was forced to push Goliath away when the dog stepped into his path.

"What are you doing here, anyway?" he asked irritably as the dog again stepped before him, almost as if trying to stop him from getting up. "I thought you trailed your mistress like a shadow, hmmm?"

Goliath whined, then paced to the door and back.

"Abandoned you, too, did she?" he asked dryly. Moving to the chamber pot to relieve himself, he added, "Well, I shall let you out in a minute. Just let me—" *Sweet Jesu*, Hethe realized. *I am talking to a damn dog.*

"Must have knocked my head harder than I thought," he muttered, finishing with his business and hastening to pull on his clothes.

Goliath was waiting patiently by the door when Hethe was finally ready and made his shaky way to it. He fully expected the beast to bound out and race below to find his mistress as soon as he opened the door, but the dog didn't. Instead, it kept apace of

Hethe, walking him down the hall to the stairs, then accompanying him down those as well. Hethe found himself feeling some affection for the beast.

As he descended into the great hall, Hethe started toward the head table, only to pause halfway there when he realized that while her aunt was there, his wife was not.

"Where is she?" he called out to Lady Shambleau. Goliath promptly set out for one of the side tables. Hethe hesitated, then followed the beast. The dog led him directly to one of the lower boards. There, he found his wife seated, chattering away. She was so distracted with what she was saying, she hardly seemed to notice Goliath's arrival, merely reached down to absently pat the dog as she continued speaking to the young woman beside her.

Intrigued, Hethe stepped closer to listen.

"Oh, my, yes. It *is* true. He did not order Stephen to do *any* of those things. In fact, he tried to confront him on the matter while we were at Holden, but the man has disappeared. Which is an admission of guilt if I ever heard of one. Do you not agree?" Before the woman could respond, Helen added, "Oh! And he has tried to rectify some of the things that his second did. He has brought back as many of the older women as he could to the castle, and he wants to settle a pension on some of those who were unfairly maimed or—"

"Wife," Hethe interrupted.

Helen stiffened at his voice, then shifted abruptly on the bench to gape up at him. "Husband! You are awake. How do you feel?"

Launching herself from her seat, his spouse hurried to his side to peer at his forehead with concern. Hethe seized the opportunity to take her arm and hustle her over to the fireplace, out of earshot of Tiernay's people. Goliath followed at a happy lope, dropping to the ground by their feet as Hethe paused and turned to face her, not releasing her arm.

"What are you doing?"

"Standing, talking to you," she answered cagily.

He narrowed his eyes at her. "What was all that blather you were spouting to that woman? And who is she?"

"Oh, that is Gert," his wife answered quickly. "And I was just . . . talking," she ended lamely.

"You were just gossiping about my private business," he corrected. "And I want to know why."

Helen bit her lip, hesitated a moment, then admitted reluctantly, "Gert used to be from Holden."

"Oh?" He felt his stomach tighten. "And?"

"And there was some trouble."

Hethe looked back to the woman, surveying her more closely. "She does not appear to be missing any limbs," he said with relief.

"Oh, nay." Helen glanced back at Gert, too, and seeing the woman looking their way, she offered a smile, then turned back to Hethe. "Well, you cannot see her ears, of course. She wears her hair to cover it."

"To cover *it*?" Hethe asked reluctantly.

"Aye," his wife said apologetically, obviously sorry to have to impart another tragic story. "She was a laundress at Holden."

"And?" he prompted, knowing he really didn't wish to hear.

"And the beau of one of the other laundresses started paying too much attention to Gert. The girl was jealous and accused her of stealing linens to sell in the village. Stephen sent someone to check her cottage and found evidence. Now, Gert swears she did not take anything. She confided to me that she suspects the other girl planted it before accusing her."

"And?" Hethe asked bleakly. "How was she punished? Stephen cut off her ear?"

"Nay. Well, not exactly," Helen said solemnly, regret in her eyes. "She refused to confess, so they put her in the pillory. She stood there for days. Then Stephen claimed he got the order from you to urge the matter along. He nailed her ear to the pillory. She eventually pulled free but lost a good portion of ear to the effort."

"Oh, God," Hethe breathed in horror.

"Aye."

They were both silent for a minute; then Hethe peered at his wife and slowly shook his head. "I do not understand how he could have hidden such a monstrous streak. Stephen was always the quiet and peaceful one. 'Twas why I left him at Holden. He did not care much for battle."

Helen patted his arm sympathetically. "He seemed a perfectly nice man to me, too. And I am usually a very good judge of character," she added, as if that would make up for the fact that she, in moments, had not seen what he had missed with years of opportunity.

"You should have something to eat, my lord," she said when she saw him sway. Taking his arm, she urged him toward the head table. "You will feel better after you do."

Hethe knew that food would not help in this instance, but saw little else that would. Shaking his head, he started toward the head table. He had taken several steps when he realized that Helen was not with him anymore. Scowling, he swung around, wincing as the abrupt action sent pain shooting through his head. It did not help when he saw that, indeed, his wife was headed in the opposite direction.

"*Wife!*"

She paused at his call and turned back questioningly. "Aye?"

"Where are you going?"

"Oh, I was just going to . . ." Her voice trailed away, and the hand she was waving vaguely toward the other tables sank slowly to her side. Sighing, she moved back to join him. "Nothing. It will hold till later."

Eyeing her suspiciously, Hethe took his wife's arm and escorted her to their seats.

"How did you sleep?" she asked solicitously as they took their places at the head table.

"Like the dead," Hethe muttered. When she looked disturbed by the remark, he amended, "Very well, thank you."

"Oh, good." Helen's response was distracted and apparently unhappily so, it seemed from the tone, as a servant placed a trencher before each of them. Another servant followed with two mugs of ale. When Hethe started to raise his, she quickly snatched it away and handed him her own.

"What are you doing?" he asked when she handed his full mug to a passing servant.

"Nothing," she answered innocently, removing his trencher and sliding her own between them.

"Helen?"

She widened her eyes at his plaintive tone. "It is in the marriage contract, husband. You had it put there. We are to drink out of the same mug and eat out of the same trencher. There you are." She pushed her dish a little closer, encouraging, and Hethe scowled.

"There is no need for that now. That was just to prevent you from giving me bad ale and rancid meat," he pointed out. "You are not doing that anymore."

Helen shrugged and plucked a piece of cheese from their plate, avoiding his eyes. "'Tis in the contract."

"Yes, but . . ." He paused, and she glanced at him warily. He saw the fear in her eyes, and his mind made the necessary leap. "You are not worried about bad food; you are worried about poison!"

"Who? Me? Poison? Do not be silly."

He glared at her. "What were you saying to that woman?" When she shrugged and avoided his eyes again, he thought back to everything he had heard, then slammed the mug he had just raised down on the table. "You're still being forced to tell them I am not an ogre!" Just how long would he be cursed for having made a poor decision in choosing his second? He was not such an awful man, and it was wearing on him to be seen as such. And to have people trying to kill him because—

"I just thought it would be good to spread the word that you were not responsible for the punishments *Stephen* inflicted."

For a moment more he was furious; then he released his breath on a sigh and forced himself to relax. She had been trying to help. Catching a movement out of the corner of his eye, Hethe glanced over his shoulder to see Joan approaching.

"Good evening, my lord. How are you feeling?" the old woman asked, her eyes examining him closely.

Hethe almost snarled in response. "Like hell, actually. My head is pounding like the blacksmith's hammer."

"Your head?" Helen asked, then glanced at Joan. "Should his head not be better by now? It has been two days."

"It is probably from the tincture," the healer answered. "Several days' use can cause headaches."

"Oh." Helen relaxed somewhat, then caught a glimpse of her husband's shock. She gave another "Oh!," this one a little guilty.

"Did you say two days?"

"Oh, dear," Helen breathed.

"And what tincture? I did not take any tincture." He glared at Joan, who was peering at Helen.

"I told you you should not slip it into his drink that way," Lady Shambleau murmured, drawing Hethe's gaze to her before it shot to his wife in accusation.

"You dosed me without my knowledge?" he roared.

Helen jumped slightly. Her hands picked nervously at their trencher as the entire great hall went silent.

"You needed to rest and recover," she whispered, flushing under all her subjects' eyes.

"I told you I did not want any damn tincture! How long . . . two days!" He answered his own question as he recalled what Helen had said a moment before. "You have been dosing me for two whole days?"

"Now, husband," his wife anxiously replied. "I was just—"

"I do not want to hear it!" Hethe snapped, rising.

"Where are you going?" she asked.

He heard her gasp in alarm as he turned away;

then, pausing, he swung back and snatched a chicken leg out of her trencher. "For some fresh air. I need to think. By myself," he added coldly when she started to rise. He needed to be alone.

Helen sank slowly back onto the bench and watched unhappily as her husband left. At least, his anger appeared to have energized him. His pace was steady and strong. He no longer swayed as he strode away.

"You know, I do believe you may be right," Aunt Nell said, from beside her. "He did not react at all to the news that you have been drugging him as I would have expected. Perhaps he really did not order those punishments."

"I *told* you he did not," Helen snapped.

"Aye, but . . ." Aunt Nell paused, her gaze moving past her niece.

Turning curiously, Helen was shocked to find Maggie. She hadn't seen the woman for the past two days, as Maggie's daughter had gone into labor the morning after Hethe's tumble down the stairs. The mistress of chambermaids had gone down to the village to help out, first with the labor, then in the tavern while her daughter and the baby recovered.

"Hello, Maggie," Helen began. "Is something wrong?"

"Nay, nay," the maid assured her quickly, then frowned. "Well, I am not sure. As you know, I have been helping out in the tavern these last two nights . . ."

"Aye, I know. That is fine. We will make do till your daughter can manage on her own again."

"Aye. Thank you, but . . ." She hesitated, then blurted, "Stephen was in the tavern the night His Lordship took that tumble."

"What?" Helen stiffened with alarm.

"Aye. I wasn't going to tell you, but it kept bothering me. Then, when I learned today that His Lordship didn't fall down the stairs but was bashed over the head and tossed down them, well . . ."

"How did you know about . . ." Helen whirled to glare at her aunt accusingly. Nell was the only one she had told.

"Well," the older woman said with an apologetic look, "I went down to see the baby and it just sort of slipped out."

"Anyhow," Maggie continued, "I just thought you should know that Sir Stephen is around. I should get back now. It was busy when I left, but . . ." She shrugged and turned away.

Helen watched the old woman go with a frown. Stephen had been in the tavern the night of Hethe's accident. Had he been at Tiernay during the day, as well? She had to tell her husband and warn him.

Hethe leaned against the castle wall, his gaze roving over the star-studded sky. Much to his relief, the headache with which he had awoken was passing as he breathed in the fresh air. A few more minutes and it would be completely gone. It must have been caused by the tincture, as Joan had suggested.

Hethe grimaced at that reminder of his wife's perfidy. The blasted woman had dosed him with the potion, sneaking it into his drink despite her knowledge of his wishes. He shifted, grimacing at the stiffness in his shoulder and side. Even after two days, he was terribly sore, and for a moment he was grateful he hadn't been awake.

He laughed at himself wryly. So, was he angry or grateful? A little of both, he supposed. The woman was too smart for her own good. He rather liked that about her, but at the same time found it frustrating as hell.

The scuff of a foot was the only warning he got. Stiffening, Hethe started to turn when he was struck. Blinded by the stabbing white lights shooting through his head, he stumbled under the blow, then felt himself lifted and pushed. Air rushed past him. He was falling, flying through the air. He heard a shout, then a splash as he crashed into water and sank into darkness.

Helen was halfway across the great hall when the keep doors crashed open. Pausing, she turned curiously, her eyes widening when William and her man Boswell stumbled in with a sopping, sagging Hethe held upright between them.

"What happened?" she cried, rushing forward.

It was Boswell who answered. "He tumbled off the wall into the moat," her chatelain said breathlessly, shifting Hethe's arm which he had draped over his shoulder to help hold the unconscious Lord Holden up. "I heard what sounded like a shout and glanced up in time to see him falling through the air and into the moat."

"What?" Helen cried in disbelief.

"Aye, I was returning from the village when I saw it." Boswell added, "Had to run and pull him out. He swallowed a good bit of water before I could get to him, though."

"Do you want us to take him upstairs?" William asked pointedly, and Helen realized she was blocking their path. She stepped out of the way at once, then followed when they dragged him forward.

She was silent, her mind racing until they reached

the bedchamber and William and Boswell moved her husband toward the bed. Then her practicality reasserted itself.

"Nay!" she shrieked as they went to lay him on it. Both men froze and turned to her questioningly. "He—Here, just set him in the chair until we get him cleaned up."

She glanced around, relieved to see that her aunt and maid had followed. "Ducky, have a bath brought up, please."

"Aye, my lady." The maid fled.

"Where do you two think you are going?" Aunt Nell demanded when Boswell and William started moving toward the door. "We will still need some help with bathing him."

"You want us to bathe him?" Boswell asked in surprise, and Helen caught the way her aunt rolled her eyes.

"Nay, you need not bathe him," Helen said patiently. She began tugging Hethe's sodden tunic up his stomach. "But we will need your help getting him in and out of the tub. In fact, you can help me strip him while we wait for the water."

"I can strip myself."

Helen glanced down sharply at her husband at those husky words. "Husband, you are awake."

He lifted his head slowly, revealing open eyes that were a little dazed. "Aye. More's the pity. I feel like hell. And I smell worse."

"Aye, you do," Helen agreed, then smiled apologetically when he grimaced at her. "What happened? How did you end up in the moat?"

He lifted a hand to his forehead, frowning in concentration. "Someone knocked me in. Hit me over the head first."

"Again?" Helen cried in alarm. How many times had her husband suffered an injury to the head lately? Was it three times? And the man still lived. He obviously had a skull as thick as the castle wall.

"Aye. Again. And it is all your fault," Hethe snapped, catching Helen's attention and drawing a gasp of outrage from her.

"Mine?"

"Aye. If I had not still been a little fuzzy-headed from your potions, I would have heard the man approach."

Helen gaped at him for the accusation, then her eyes narrowed in fury. "Well, then it is a good thing you are such a hard-headed bastard."

Aunt Nell gasped in horror, and William and Boswell both shifted uncomfortably as silence filled the room. In response, Hethe asked with deadly calm, "And just what is that supposed to mean?"

"Nothing," Helen said sweetly. "Nothing at all. Though I should like to point out that you went completely unharmed while you were sleeping. However, since you won't continue to rest and recover up here where it is safe, perhaps you should wear your helmet should you intend to wander about anymore. It would appear you need it."

"You—" Hethe began furiously, but Aunt Nell saved Helen from his words by asking quickly, "Did you see who hit you?"

Hethe paused and glanced over at her. He started to shake his head, winced in pain, then said, "No," instead.

Her anger dissolving at seeing his pain, Helen released her pent-up breath on a sigh and reached out to caress his cheek. "Do you hurt anywhere besides your head?"

Hethe hesitated, then apparently decided to take the olive branch she offered. He reluctantly admitted, "My chest and my throat."

"The chest and throat must be from swallowing moat water," she explained. Glancing at his damp, matted hair, she was disgusted to see something move in it. She wasn't sure, but it seemed better to bathe him before checking for any more head wounds.

"You mean I swallowed that filth?" Hethe asked with horror.

Helen nearly laughed at his expression, but managed to swallow it back. "I fear so." She glanced around as her maid came back into the room, leading a contingent of servants carting a bathtub and pails of water. "Ducky, could you get a servant to fetch up some ale?"

"Aye, my lady."

Aunt Nell stopped her, saying, "Nay. I shall do it. Helen may need your help with bathing Lord Hethe." She was gone before anyone could protest. Not that such seemed likely.

Helen turned back to Hethe. "Perhaps we should get you out of those clothes and into the tub."

Boswell and William immediately moved forward, and Hethe scowled from one man to the other. "I said I can do it myself."

"Aye," William agreed soothingly. "We'll just stick around in case you're needing a strong arm to get you to the tub. Better one of us than you sully Lady Helen's clothes, too."

Hethe seemed to notice then that both men were as wet and filthy as himself. He turned an inquisitive look on William. "Did you pull me out?"

"Boswell got there first and did most of the work. I just helped."

"Oh." Hethe glanced to the man and nodded solemnly. "Thank you, Boswell."

Helen's man shrugged uncomfortably, but managed a grim "Milord," when she nudged him.

"Shall we get you into the tub now?" Helen prompted. The servants had finished their business and filed out.

Grunting, Hethe pushed himself to his feet . . . and nearly tumbled onto his face. Boswell and William each grabbed an arm to steady him, then began to help him undress, despite his protests, which grew fainter as the moments passed. It was rather obvious that he was growing weaker by the moment, and Helen was relieved that the men ignored his assurances that he could manage alone.

A servant arrived with the requested ale just as they helped Hethe to the tub. The girl handed it over to Helen, informing her that her aunt had arranged for baths to be prepared also for Boswell and William, so that they might clean up as well. Thanking her, Helen waited until Hethe was settled in the water, then passed on the news about the baths.

As the two men left, Helen moved to hand Hethe the mug of ale. He was so weak, he nearly dropped the drink in the water, but he refused to allow her to "feed him like a babe." Holding it with two hands, he gulped down some of the liquid, then handed the mug back.

Helen set it on the floor, then with Ducky's help began to bathe him. They washed his hair first, grimacing at the bits of slime and ooze that came out. Everything and anything got dropped into the moat, from animal carcasses to the contents of chamber pots. Both women did their best not to think too hard on that as they scrubbed. Once

Hethe's hair was clean, Helen examined his head until she found the spot where he had been hit. The skin was split, and another goose egg was forming on his scalp. He was getting quite a collection.

'Tis a good thing he is so hardheaded, she thought dryly, pleased to see that he appeared to have fallen asleep.

Working as gently and quietly as they could to keep from disturbing him, Helen and Ducky continued washing him until he was once more pink and healthy looking. Or as pink and healthy looking as they could hope, considering his past few blows to the head.

"Ducky, mayhap you had best go fetch the men back to help us move him to the bed," Helen instructed, but Hethe promptly stirred, his eyes blinking open.

"Nay. I can manage," he said stubbornly.

Helen rolled her eyes at the foolish pride of men, but there was little she could do. Shrugging at Ducky's questioning gaze, Helen, who had been kneeling beside the tub, slowly straightened and offered him her hand.

Ignoring it, Hethe braced his hands on each side of the tub and hefted himself up. Much to Helen's amazement, he did gain his feet. Barely. But then he began to sway like a sapling in the wind, and Helen and Ducky both moved forward to brace him from either side. Afraid he would not be able to stay on his feet long, they left drying him off for later and helped him stumble out of the tub and to the bed. He collapsed there with a small sigh, his eyes immediately closing.

"Go make sure Sir William and Boswell are not waiting around to help. He is abed," Helen said to

Ducky. As she set to work drying her husband, she heard the door close behind the departing maid. She turned her attention to Hethe's feet and legs, then slowly moved her way upward. When she reached his thighs, her eyes widened. Her husband might be out of it, but his manhood was wide awake. She closed her linen-wrapped hand around it and squeezed gently, smiling when Hethe's eyes popped open and he growled.

"If I were not half dead, I would take you up on that invitation," he murmured.

Helen smiled and widened her eyes. "Invitation, my lord?" she asked innocently. "I am merely trying to dry you." She slid her hand along his growing arousal then, and his breath came out as a sigh of pleasure.

"Dry me well then, wife. You would not want me catching the ague."

Helen chuckled softly at his words, but moved on with her toweling. Despite the interest the lower half of his body was showing, her husband's eyes were again drifting wearily closed and she knew he wasn't really up to anything. Finishing a moment later, she tossed her cloth aside and pulled the bed-clothes up to cover him, then gently brushed a lock of hair off his forehead. She had intended to tell him about Stephen, but it would have to wait until the morrow. There was something she had to take care of that could not wait, though.

Straightening, she moved silently to the door, eased it open and slid out as soundlessly as she could.

Chapter 19

$\mathcal{H}$ETHE's head was pounding something fierce when he awoke—a state he was becoming used to, unfortunately, he decided as he turned his head carefully to peer at his sleeping wife. His wife who wasn't sleeping and wasn't there, he saw with irritation. Did she ever rest?

Scowling, he glanced toward the window. The covering was drawn shut, making the room dim except for the light from a small fire in the fireplace. Hethe couldn't tell what time it was. It could be midnight or midday. Muttering under his breath, he sat up carefully, then shifted to sit on the side of the bed. There he paused to rest his elbows on his knees and clasp his head in both hands. He felt like hell. Dear Lord, waking up one day without a headache was sounding like heaven. He never used to wake up every single morning with a sore head like this, not till he consummated his marriage. If this was the cost of bedding one's wife . . . Well, he supposed it was worth it.

Smiling slightly at his thoughts, he glanced around for his clothes, then realized that those he had been wearing the day before were no doubt off being cleaned. Grunting in annoyance, he turned to the chest by the bed and bent over to open it. He didn't get halfway before his head felt as if it were about to explode and bile rose in his throat. Straightening, he quickly pressed his hands to either side of his head, trying to hold it together until the pain eased. He released a breath of relief when the pain at last abated. Moving carefully then, he slowly knelt before the chest, and kept his head upright as he opened and rifled through it. Finding a pair of fresh breeches and a tunic, he cautiously straightened and sat on the bed to don them.

Much to his disgust, he was weak and weary by the time the task was done. Hethe decided he was in pitiful shape. Just pitiful. He actually briefly considered lying back down for a bit till he felt better, but, recalling that that was exactly where his wife felt he belonged, safe and snug in bed like a defenseless child, he pushed the thought quickly away. He was no defenseless child or feeble old man. It was bad enough the people here at Tiernay thought him some sort of ogre; he would be damned if he was going to add weak and cowardly to their list of his sins. He was a warrior. Strong and capable and well able to take care of himself. And he was determined to prove that to them . . . even if it killed him.

Grimacing at the thought, Hethe pushed himself off the bed where he sat to don his boots and slowly made his way to the window. He wanted to know what time of day it was before he staggered downstairs, and a glance outside should answer that question.

He shifted the window covering, gasped as pain shot through his head, then let it drop closed again.

It was daylight. Bright daylight. The light stabbed through his eyes and into his head like needles. Well, that answered his question, anyway. Judging by the sun, the great hall would be filled with people partaking of the midday meal. He would walk down there and join them and prove to one and all that he was hearty and hale.

Ignoring the weakness that had his legs trembling with every step, Hethe made his way to the door, pulled it open, then jumped quickly back as a body fell into the room at his feet. Blinking through the pain coursing through his head at his sudden movement, Hethe glared at the young soldier who had been leaning against the door. The fellow scrambled quickly to his feet, flushing brightly.

"Good morning, milord," the man-at-arms said quickly and in far too loud a voice.

Wincing at the discomfort it caused him, Hethe scowled at the lad. "What were you doing?"

"Guarding you, milord," the boy answered promptly. Rather proudly, too.

"Guarding me?" Hethe nearly bellowed. He had never needed a guard in his life. Not since he had earned his spurs. The fact that his wife had set one on him just seemed to prove how weak she now saw him. After his fall down the stairs, she had left only the dog with him; now she had him guarded. Where was that dog, anyway? he wondered irritably. He was not at all pleased to find himself abandoned by both his wife and her idiot dog, and left in the care of a wet-behind-the-ears boy. How low had he fallen?

"Who exactly would you be guarding me from?" he asked in grim tones.

The soldier shifted from foot to foot, looking

uncertain. "Milady felt since someone had tried to kill you—"

"Where is she?"

"Who?"

"My wife," Hethe snapped impatiently. "Where is she?"

"Oh. She went downstairs to have a word with Lady Shambleau."

Growling, Hethe stepped past the man and started for the stairs, pausing to turn back and scowl when the soldier started to follow. Hethe's eyes widened when he saw that his guard had multiplied. There were now two. "Who the hell are you?" he asked the new fellow.

"Garth, milord."

"Nay. I mean, where did you come from?"

"I was at the end of the hall. I was to stay there and back up Robert here in case of trouble," he explained.

Hethe blanched at the explanation. Not one guard, but two? Lord love 'em! "I do not need a guard," he snapped.

"Aye, milord. I mean, nay, milord," both men agreed in unison.

Hethe's eyes narrowed at their patronizing tone. "I said, I do not need a guard. You are released. Go do something else."

The two men hesitated, then exchanged glances.

"What do you think?" asked the young one who had been leaning against the door.

The other shook his head, then urged his friend a few feet away. Presumably, he thought he was out of earshot. He was wrong. Hethe heard every word he said.

"I'm thinkin'," the guard began, "that he knocked his head pretty good in the fall. And I'm thinkin' Her Ladyship said to guard him. Therefore, guard him we should."

"Aye, but he's the lord. Don't we have to listen to him?" the younger man asked, his higher voice carrying even better than the other guard's, adding to Hethe's building rage.

"Well, now, not iffin he ain't in his right mind. Then we have to obey Lady Helen. And I'm thinkin', like as not he ain't in his right mind—else he'd appreciate a guard. The man is hated here. There's more than one person who'd like the chance to slit his throat."

Hethe had heard enough. He was so furious it almost seemed to be choking him. Worse yet, it was a free-floating fury. He couldn't be mad at his wife for caring enough to post a guard. He couldn't blame these men for doing their duty. He couldn't even blame the people here for hating him for what they thought he had done. He was responsible for all of it. Stephen was his man. Had been his friend.

Turning on his heel, he strode down the hall at a fast clip, his anger eating away at him and intensifying the ache in his head. This time he ignored the men when they fell into step behind him. He acquired a third guard at the top of the stairs. The man had obviously been set there as a backup for the other two. Hethe spared him a glare, then started down the stairs, knowing without checking that he now had all three trailing him.

He had obviously judged the time wrong, he saw as he stepped off the stairs and started through the empty great hall. Helen wasn't there. Neither was her aunt, unfortunately, or Hethe would have asked the woman where his wife was. He tried the kitchens next, not really expecting her to be there, but hoping that maid of hers may be able to tell him something of use. Unfortunately, Ducky wasn't there either, which annoyed Hethe, but not as much as the fact that he found himself tripping over his guards as he turned to leave the steamy rooms. Glaring at the trio, he headed out of the keep and paused on the steps to survey the bailey. They clanked to a stop behind him.

Spotting Helen walking across the grounds with Goliath at her side, Hethe promptly started down the stairs. His escort followed. He could hear the crunch of their footsteps as he hurried across the bailey, and found the sound terribly grating. It didn't help that the headache he was suffering seemed to be amplifying the sound in his head. He sped up. They sped up. He started to jog and could hear them running behind him. He was out of breath and out of patience by the time he reached his wife.

"Husband!" she cried in surprise when he caught her arm and drew her around to face him. That surprise gave way to concern as she took in his flushed face. "Are you sure you should be up? Really, it is too soon. You need your rest to heal. Which is why I was drugging you—"

"Wife," Hethe interrupted grimly. "I realize you have run Tiernay for years on your own and are used to giving orders, but pray stop giving them to me."

Her eyes widened, a wounded look appearing, and Hethe was momentarily sorry he snapped. But then there was the sound of skittering stones as his guards arrived and slid to a halt behind him, and he felt himself grinding his teeth.

"Make them go away," he ordered through his clenched jaw. Confusion replaced her hurt look.

"Who?"

"Who? Them, that's who!" He jerked a thumb over his shoulder at the three men.

"But they are to guard you, Hethe. Someone is trying to kill you." She was speaking in a reasonable tone meant to soothe him, but it was having the opposite effect. The fury that had been growing in Hethe began to bubble and boil at this further proof of her seeing him as weak.

"I can take care of myself!" he snapped.

"I know you can," she said soothingly. "But you no longer need to. You have a wife, and a family, and everyone here at Tiernay to—"

"Kill me?" Hethe interrupted coldly. He had found himself softening when she had said he no longer needed to do things alone, that he had a wife and family now. It had brought a warm squishy feeling rising up in him . . . until she had added the part about the people here at Tiernay. They hated him and he knew it. The warmth drained out of him to be replaced by rage.

His wife frowned at his interruption, then said quietly, "I should have told you this sooner, I suppose, but you were injured. However, as you seem to think you are ready to be up and about now, you should know that it may be Stephen who—"

"Stephen?" he interrupted in a bellow. "You cannot blame these attacks on Stephen. They did not even start until we came to Tiernay. It was one of *your* people who pushed me down the stairs, one of *your* subjects who tossed me off the wall."

Helen stiffened, her eyes narrowing to slits, and she asked coldly, "Isn't it more likely that it was one of your own people who has been staying here for protection?"

Hethe felt as if she had punched him. His head actually drew back, the sudden movement sending pain through his skull. He was still reeling from it when she added, "Besides, Stephen was spotted in the village tavern the night you fell down the stairs. It is likely not one of *my* people, after all."

Hethe felt the rage explode within him. Pain, frustration and a sense of failure were all suddenly whirling within him, and he clenched his fists to keep from lashing out. He wanted to hit someone. Anyone. And keep hitting them, and—

Shaking his head like a dog trying to shake off water, he turned abruptly and started away across the bailey.

"Where are you going?" Helen called out in alarm. She hurried after him, his guards hard on her heel.

"I do not know. Anywhere but here." His words were sharp and cold.

"You are running away again?" she cried in dismay.

He stiffened, then whirled on her in a fury. "I have never run from anything in my life!"

"Well, you never stay and face things, either! You told me yourself that you are forever running off to battle. No doubt 'tis easier to play at war than to deal with reality." Helen's voice was sharp, full of anger. The fact that he planned to just leave was like a knife to her heart, and she was reacting like a wounded animal, snapping and snarling at him.

"Well, at least in battle you know who your enemy is. You do not have to worry about someone sneaking up behind you to slit your throat!" He turned away, then suddenly whirled back, his cold gaze shooting to the three guards. "If these three know what is good for them, they will stop following me." The threat in his voice was unmistakable. He turned then and continued on across the bailey.

The men hesitated, their questioning gazes shooting to her. She released them with a slight shake of her head. Nodding with obvious relief, they turned and strode in the opposite direction, leaving her alone to watch her husband walk to the stables. Her heart sank like a stone as he came out a moment later, leading his horse.

Mounting up, Hethe "the Hammer," Lord Holden, turned the horse toward the gates and rode away. *Just like that*, Helen thought faintly. *Get on a horse and go.* Taking all her hopes for a happy marriage with him.

Hethe rode quite a while before his anger cleared enough for him to start thinking coherently again. The argument he had with his wife cycled through his head. The part that bothered him the most was her dismayed, "You are running away again?"

He scowled as the tiff replayed itself. He was not running. Running was cowardice, and Hethe was no coward. The fact that he ran off to battle should prove that he was no coward. Hethe frowned as he considered his own words. The fact that he ran off to battle? That didn't sound very good. Surely he wasn't *running* to battle, was he?

Well, you obviously aren't staying, some part of his mind pointed out logically. He grimaced. Aye, but there was a difference between going and running, he reasoned. But he couldn't manage to fool himself.

Dear God, he *was* running. Had been running for a long time. The realization rankled. Hethe had always prided himself on his courage. His bravery in

battle was really all he had to be proud of. He
hadn't exactly been a stellar son, husband or lord.
And he hadn't even noticed his deficiencies in the
lord part until recently. Now, the knowledge that his
courage in battle was a result of his fleeing something else seemed to take away from all he'd done.
What was it he was fleeing? Unpleasantness?

Nay, that couldn't be it, he decided. Battle was
terribly unpleasant, yet he never fled that. Was it
fear, then? Hethe considered that seriously, but it
did not seem right. He hadn't fled Tiernay because
he feared his wife, or because he feared whomever
was trying to kill him. He was aware of the threat
and felt confident he could guard against it . . . now
that he was sure it wasn't a mistake.

"So, why are you not back there sorting it out?"
he muttered to himself in frustration. With a sigh, he
forced himself to calm down and think clearly. The
answer probably lay in the first time he had run off
to battle. He considered that time now, allowing the
memories to wash over him. He had had an argument with his father. Well, he supposed calling it an
argument was a bit misleading. Mostly it had been
his father shouting, roaring and criticizing him.

Just remembering it made the old fury build
within Hethe, and he suddenly knew the answer. He
had been fleeing his own anger. He had stood there
that day, growing more and more enraged as his father tore at him. His fists had clenched, a buzzing
had sounded in his ears, and his blood had seemed
to boil. He had wanted to strike out. He had wanted
to tear his father limb from limb. It had been a killing rage. And that had terrified him. He had left
Holden that day and headed for battle, where he
could work off that urge productively. And he had

done it every time that rage had reappeared—which was pretty much every time he had returned to Holden while his father still lived.

Then there was Nerissa. But she had not caused rage in him. She had been sweet, and innocent and soothing. It was her death that had affected him badly. It had turned his rage at his father toward himself. He had failed her. Her death had been a result of his failure to postpone the consummation. He could clearly recall his own frustration and fury at her death. His desire to hurt someone as he himself hurt. He had headed right back to battle.

He supposed he was doing that now, too. His anger and frustration were consuming, as was his guilt over what had been happening at Holden these last years. Again he had held people's lives in his hands, and again he had failed to protect them. Hethe had left Tiernay intending to ride until he found the king's men, someone engaged in battle in which he could bang some heads. Which, he realized suddenly, was what had left his people at Holden vulnerable to Stephen's cruelty.

Worse, looking back, was the fact that none of the times he had fled to battle had made him feel better. In truth, his rage and anger had remained the same over the years, a cold, hard lump in his chest that burst into flame every time it had the chance. He had found no peace by fleeing, because he could not escape himself, the rage built in him by his father but stoked by himself over many years. It was time to let the fire go out.

I should turn around and go home to my wife, he thought, and a picture of her laughing face rose up in his mind. His mouth eased into a smile, and he actually felt soothed by just the thought of her. Then he recalled her hurt and anger in those last moments before he had left, and Hethe felt an ache in his heart in response. He hadn't meant to hurt her. He also hadn't expected hurting her to pain him. But it did. Oddly enough, making her happy made him happy, too. He slowed his mount as these thoughts coursed through his mind, and for once he knew exactly what they meant.

He loved her.

The thought didn't surprise him. He had liked and admired her from the first time they met. Love wasn't a large jump from there, and she was definitely a woman worthy of such devotion. But was he a man worthy of her love? The question caused a small ache in his heart. Then he recalled their love-making, their laughter, her pride and beauty—and her caring. She had shown him more of that since the night they consummated their marriage than his father had in all the years of his life. But then, she was a special woman.

They had talked some the afternoon they had consummated the marriage. After that first mating, they had moved to the chairs by the fire, to eat the food and drink the wine that the servants had left behind. Helen had been wrapped in her linen, Hethe had been naked, and they had eaten in an oddly awkward silence at first. Then the wine had loosened her tongue. Then Hethe had begun to ask her questions and draw her out.

He had learned about her childhood, the loss of her mother, how her aunt had taken that role in raising Helen. She'd told him of the death of her father and the burden of responsibility that had become hers upon his death. She took that responsibility very seriously. And he had felt shame as he had listened.

She held great affection and responsibility for her people. She knew their names, their jobs, their woes and joys, their strengths and weaknesses. Lady Helen of Tiernay had been—was—truly noble.

Hethe thought back with two minds. One focused on the similarities between him and his wife. While she never said so, he heard in her stories how little attention her father had paid to her, how cold and indifferent he had been. Not unlike his own father, who, when he had bothered to speak to Hethe at all, had only done so to criticize. Their mothers had both died while they were young, and where Helen had seen her widowed aunt step in and fill that void, Hethe had known William and Stephen.

Also, both he and Helen had been disappointments to their fathers—Hethe because of his difficulty with writing and reading, and therefore with much of his lessons, and she because she was not the boy her father had hoped for.

Aye, there was much that was similar in their backgrounds. But there were also differences. The stories she had told had pointed out how whenever there was a problem or conflict, she had rolled up her sleeves and confronted it. As she had when Templetun arrived with the king's order of this marriage. Despite thinking Hethe a cruel butcher, who could have done harm even to her, she had not fled to the safety of a nunnery and hidden behind vows. She had decided to stand and fight, to devise a plan and carry it out. Which was just the opposite of what Hethe had always done. He had always turned and walked away, leaving all his responsibility in Stephen's lap and retreating to the emotionally distant safety of warfare. He could see that now, though he hadn't at the time.

He wasn't going to flee again, he decided now. It was time he stopped reacting like a child and started acting like a man. Time to face up to his responsibilities, no matter how inadequate he felt to deal with them. He could not do worse by trying than he had by fleeing. Aye. He would return to Tiernay and tend to matters there. He would also, he decided, do his damnedest to make his wife return his love. Oddly enough, that determination to face things, to confront his fears, gave him a sense of purpose. It also seemed to remove the last embers of the rage that had been burning in his chest.

Hethe drew his mount to a halt and had started to urge it to turn when the pain hit. Dragging in a shocked breath, he glanced down sharply at his chest and saw the arrow protruding there even as he started to slide off his horse. Everything was numb, he realized as his hands and body refused to obey his commands. He hardly even felt it when he slammed into the ground. He heard the noise though and heard his horse's panicked snort before it charged off, leaving him lying alone in the path.

He sprawled half on his side, his cheek pressing into the ground at an angle that allowed him to watch his life's blood leak out of him. Staring, he saw the ground eagerly soak it up and distantly thought that it was really rather a shame. Now he would never get to tell Helen that he loved her.

"My lady!"

Helen blinked her eyes open and forced herself to sit up on her bed. She had come upstairs to lie down after Hethe's leaving. Not right away—she had tried to act as if nothing had happened and to go about her business at first, but had found the effort too much after a while. She had come up and lain, dry-eyed, for a good long while before at last dropping off to sleep.

"My lady!" The second cry sounded just before the door burst open to let Ducky inside. Her panicked expression had Helen on her feet at once.

"What is it?" she asked, hurrying to meet her maid.

"His Lordship! Injured! Again!" The maid drew the last word out in a sort of horrified disbelief, and Helen felt her chest tighten painfully.

"Not another head wound?" she asked in despair.

Ducky didn't get the opportunity to answer: William and Boswell stumbled into the room then, bearing Hethe between them. Helen took one look at the arrow protruding from her husband's chest and felt the blood leave her face. A head wound would have been preferable. At least she knew the man was thick-headed enough to survive that. But this? She took in his blood-soaked torso and swayed weakly on her feet.

"Set him on the bed," Joan ordered, bustling into the room with Aunt Nell on her heels. "Be sure you don't jostle him too much."

"What happened?" Helen asked faintly, moving to the bedside. She was only barely aware that she was clutching Ducky and being held up by the woman as she moved forward.

"Some fellow just rode up to the gates and set him down," Boswell answered, shaking his head.

"Who?"

The chatelain frowned. "A red-haired fellow. Didn't stop to give his name, just set him down, then turned and rode off."

"Red hair," Helen murmured.

"'Twas Stephen," William said grimly.

Helen closed her eyes, and then, letting go of her concerns about who had done what and how, she turned her attention to doing what she could to help Joan mend her husband. The weakness that had gripped her since they brought Hethe in suddenly disappeared, replaced with purpose. She hardly noticed when the men moved out of the room.

For the next half hour the women worked frantically, stripping his blood-soaked tunic from him, cleaning the blood from the wound, removing the arrow, then washing and sewing the wound. Helen held Hethe up while Joan poured a potion meant to give him strength down his throat; then, having done all they could, the healer and the other women left.

Helen moved a chair next to the bed and sat down to watch over her husband. She watched him through the rest of that day and night, hardly noticing when her aunt or Ducky checked in. Afraid to leave him, she waved away all offers of replacing her, even those so that she might sleep or eat. She nodded off occasionally in the night, only to awake with a start and reach out to feel Hethe's forehead. His skin was cool and dry each time she checked, and Helen fervently thanked God that at least he had no fever.

When her aunt joined her at dawn, Helen gave her a distracted smile, then quickly returned her gaze to her husband. It was almost that she was afraid he might stop breathing, or suddenly develop fever after all, should she take her eyes off him.

"Has he stirred at all?" Nell asked after they had sat in silence for several moments.

Helen shook her head and tried not to think if

that might be a bad thing. Her concern up until now had only been with infection, or fever. A fever could kill no matter if the actual wound hadn't. Now she began to worry that his long, deep sleep was a bad sign.

"He probably needs the rest," her aunt murmured soothingly.

"Aye," Helen agreed. "Has anyone gone out to search for Stephen?"

"I believe Sir William sent some men out yesterday, right after bringing Hethe up."

"Where is Sir William?"

"In the great hall. He has not left there since going below. He just sits at the tables, fretting and asking if there is any change each time Ducky or I come from checking up here."

Helen nodded. "I hope to God that they find Stephen. I cannot take another incident like this."

"You believe it was Stephen who did this, then?"

Helen glanced at her aunt with surprise. "Of course. William recognized him."

"Aye. William saw him bring Hethe here and leave him at the gate, but he did not see the man shoot an arrow into him."

"Well, aye, but—"

"Does it not seem odd that Stephen would shoot Hethe, then bring him here for help?"

Helen sat back, confused. That really didn't make much sense. "You are thinking it was not Stephen?"

"I am thinking it would be hard for someone with carroty-red hair to walk through the bailey, into the castle, and nearly kill your husband, then walk out through the bailey again without being noticed. Twice. And then bring Hethe for assistance."

Helen considered that briefly. "Perhaps my guards are protecting Stephen."

"Helen," her aunt said firmly. "They may not like or think much of Hethe, but they love and respect and are loyal to *you*. They would not lie. Besides, their opinion of Hethe is starting to change. Word is spreading about his not knowing what was going on, and most are willing to give him the benefit of the doubt."

"But if it is not Stephen, then who? And why has he been hiding?"

"Maggie simply said he was at the tavern the other night. Perhaps he was not hiding."

"Then why did he not come back to Holden while we were there? And why did he not stay when he brought Hethe back?"

Aunt Nell was silent for a moment, then said, "I noticed there was rather a lot of blood on the back of Hethe's tunic."

Helen remembered it, and she nodded.

"But the arrow did not go through to his back," Aunt Nell reminded her.

Helen's eyes widened. "You think Stephen was injured, too."

"Hethe would have been seated on the horse before him, his back leaning against Stephen's chest."

"A chest wound," Helen murmured, then stood abruptly.

"Where are you going?"

"I have to sort this out. I have to find him."

"Nay, Helen," she cried in alarm. "Send Sir William or—"

"Nay. William is so mad at Stephen, he would kill him without learning the truth."

"But—"

"Aunt, he may be injured. He may need help. And we owe him that for helping Hethe." Seeing the uncertainty on her relative's face, she added, "I will be careful. I will take Goliath. Watch Hethe for me. Let no one near him but William. I will return as quickly as I can."

Chapter 20

WITH Goliath's help, Helen easily found the spot where Hethe had been felled; the dog, who had been jogging along happily a few feet in front of Helen's mount, stopped dead at the spot and sat down. Drawing her mare to a halt, Helen got down and moved carefully forward, her gaze sliding past the seated dog to where he was sniffing. The dirt path was a dry cinnamon brown everywhere else, but the spot in question was soaked a much darker, richer brown—Hethe's blood. Kneeling, she examined the leaves and bits of debris lying about, and saw several splashed red with dried gore.

Helen felt tears swim to her eyes as she took in the scene. The stain was rather large. So much blood. She hadn't known he had lost so much. She suddenly realized she could lose him. The thought was a painful one. She had grown quite used to his presence in her life.

Liar, her heart cried out. It was more than that she was used to his presence. She liked it. She enjoyed his ready wit and amusing company. His very presence sent little shocks of sensation through her. She felt electric when he was around. Felt energy zip through her like a small inner storm whenever he was near. He made her feel alive. Whether they were having a war of wills, a battle of wits, or making love, she felt unique around him. She felt competent, beautiful, special. He made her feel that. He looked on her with admiration and approval, and she felt herself bloom beneath his gaze like a flower under the sun.

She loved him.

Helen felt that admission resonate deep in her soul and knew it was true. She loved her husband, the Hammer of Holden. She could not lose him. And she would not, she assured herself grimly. Joan had said that the true danger had passed. He would survive this latest attack. And Helen herself would make damn sure there wasn't another.

Taking a deep breath, she straightened slowly, patted Goliath on the head, then glanced around. The ground had been muddy from the rain the night before when Hethe had ridden here. The prints were clear and easy to read—even for her. She saw the evidence of two horses. One was Hethe's, coming from Tiernay; the other seemed to lead from the opposite direction, toward Tiernay.

Helen frowned. Stephen had been spotted at Tiernay a day ago. Why would he have been coming from Holden?

She peered at Hethe's horse's prints again, noting that it looked as if he had started to turn back. Perhaps he had seen his attacker coming and had tried to turn away and run. But that did not seem right. Hethe was not the sort to flee from a battle. A verbal battle, perhaps, she thought dryly, but a physical one? Never.

Putting the mystery aside, for the moment, she

carefully peered over the tracks. She could see quite clearly that someone had come from Holden. Stephen? Those tracks met up with Hethe's, then continued toward Tiernay, sinking deeper in the muddy ground. It would have been Hethe's added weight that caused that. Then a third set of tracks appeared off to the left, also headed from Tiernay. They continued on toward Holden where Hethe had been headed. Helen felt in her bones that these were Stephen's tracks, from his return journey.

Grabbing her mount's reins, she walked past the spot where Hethe had fallen, digging his tunic out of the sack she had attached to her saddle. Folding it so only the back of his shirt, where there was blood she was sure was not Hethe's, she called Goliath to her side and offered it to him. The dog sniffed the shirt briefly, then began to nose around the ground. Several moments later, he barked and pawed the earth.

Pulling her horse behind her, Helen moved to his side to see what he had found, her eyes narrowing on a splash of blood. She was in luck. Stephen had been injured. He had left a trail of blood. Whirling back toward her horse, Helen remounted and collected her reins.

"Go," she ordered her hound from her mare's back. "Find."

The dog set off at once, following the trail for some ways, then turning off it onto a lesser traveled path she would never have noticed on her own. They traveled this new track for quite a while, and Helen knew they were onto Holden land when the path suddenly gave way to a clearing surrounding a small cottage. Trotting to the door, Goliath sat down patiently to wait.

Helen drew up her mount and surveyed the clearing warily. There was no sign of a horse. Or people, for that matter. Shifting on her steed, she glanced nervously back the way she had come. She hadn't been afraid when she had set out, determined as she had been, but now she was suddenly aware of how alone she was.

Goliath's whine drew her gaze back around. She *wasn't* alone. It was time to settle this, she told herself and slid from her mount's back.

Pausing, she pulled a dirk from her sack—she had not come unprepared—and clasped it firmly in hand, then walked to the door. Stopping, she caught her dog's collar with her free hand and opened the door awkwardly with the one holding her weapon. Pushing it open swiftly made it crash against the wall. Light spilled through the doorway around her, splashing across the small interior of the one-room cottage and illuminating the naked man rising from the bed.

"Lady Helen!" Stephen gasped, then collapsed.

Hethe opened his eyes and stared at the bed curtains overhead. He felt like hell and had to wonder what was the matter with him now. He felt dried out, his mouth as though it had been stuffed full of wool for several days. It was like that time he had been struck down by fever. Was he sick? He searched his memory, trying to find the last thing he recalled, when a movement drew his gaze to the side.

William stood with his back to the room, peering out the window. His hands were balled into fists that were propped on his hips. His expression— what Hethe could see of it—was grim and furrowed his forehead in lines of discontent.

"You look unhappy." Hethe had meant to speak the words, but they came out as a parched rasp. *I need water*, he thought impatiently. But, whispered or spoken, the man heard his words and sharply turned.

"You are awake." His first sounded startled by that.

"Aye. More's the pity." Hethe started to shift, then winced at a pain in his shoulder. Glancing down, he saw the bandages covering him there and closed his eyes. He had been shot, he recalled. How had he managed to get back here to Tiernay? The last thing he remembered was thinking he would die out there in the woods without ever having told Helen how he felt about her.

William moved to the bedside, drawing Hethe's attention away from thoughts of his wife. His first peered down at him, a disturbed look in his eyes. Something was obviously bothering the man. No doubt it was Stephen's betrayal, Hethe decided unhappily. They had grown up together, the three of them, as close as brothers. He himself had certainly trusted Stephen like a brother. And through all those years, there had never been a sign of a cruel streak, or of the betrayal that would come. Not one. The man hadn't even liked violence; he certainly never seemed to care for battle as William or Hethe himself did. He had fought at Hethe's side when necessary and fought well, but he had always preferred the running of Holden Castle and its estates to warfare. He had never seemed at all to mind being left behind to tend to the estate while William and Hethe had ridden off to battle. In fact, he had seemed to prefer it, claiming battle too bloody for his tastes. Had Stephen really preferred the unconscionable maiming of helpless serfs and villeins to a fair fight?

Shifting impatiently as he was besieged by his bitter feelings of betrayal, Hethe started to struggle against the linens and furs covering him, trying to sit up.

William hesitated a moment, searching Hethe's face as he struggled, then brought his feeble efforts to a halt with a hand on his shoulder. "You are too weak to sit up. Just rest."

Hethe gave up his attempt to regain some dignity with a sigh and allowed his weak muscles to relax. They hadn't been succeeding anyway, had been set to trembling by the very attempt.

"So," he sighed, after a moment to regain his breath. Just trying to sit up had left him gasping. "Why so bleak? Am I going to die?"

William hesitated, then shrugged. "You survived again, it would seem. You are the luckiest bastard I know."

Hethe grimaced, not feeling particularly lucky. After all, he'd been nearly trampled, knocked out and tossed down the stairs, knocked over the head and tossed off the wall, then shot in the woods and left for dead. He supposed it was all a matter of perspective. His gaze moved to the chest beside the bed, alighting on the pitcher and mug there. "Is there anything to drink?"

"Aye." William busied himself pouring the liquid from the pitcher to the mug, then helped Hethe to sit up somewhat, lifting him with one arm and holding the mug to his lips. It was water, pure and cool. Hethe drank a bit, forcing himself not to gulp, then gestured that he had had enough. William eased him back onto the bed and set the mug aside.

Hethe sighed. "So, what were you thinking when you were looking out the window? What makes you so grim?"

William peered down at him solemnly. His eyes were burning slightly as he admitted, "I was thinking that it is well past time this mess was resolved."

"Aye." Hethe felt himself overwhelmed by sadness at what must be done. "It is well past time. Next time he may succeed at killing me."

"He?"

"Stephen."

"Better?" Helen asked, easing the glass away from Stephen's mouth and leaning back to peer at him warily.

"Aye." Stephen nodded, then grimaced. "My lady, I am sorry to have received you like this." He gestured to the fur she had drawn up over his nakedness. "I heard your horse and feared William had found me. I had to know if it was him."

Helen frowned at the man's formal tones. He wasn't acting like a crazed killer. She decided it would be best to get right to the point. The man was in no condition to be much of a threat to anyone. She had seen the bandages wrapped around his chest and the blood seeped into them. He was obviously weak and even a touch feverish.

"Are you the one who shot Hethe with the arrow?"

"Nay!" he cried, obviously shocked by the question. "I would never do that. I collected him and brought him back to you, so you could mend him."

"Ripping your stitches and ruining all my hard work while you were at it, too."

Helen glanced around sharply at those irritated words. An attractive older woman stood in the open door, glaring at the man in the bed with displeasure. Her hair was red, like the man's in the bed, but streaked with gray. Her face was freckled like his, and her eyes were the same bright green, though hers were spitting fire at the moment and his were tired and glassy. Stephen's mother? Helen wondered. The young man's next words answered that question.

"I could not just leave him lying there in the path, Mother."

The woman's mouth tightened, but she merely shook her head and moved to drop near the fireplace the wood she carried. Apparently she had been out collecting it when Helen arrived.

"If not you, then who shot him?" Helen asked, glancing back to Stephen. Her gaze narrowed when he avoided her eyes.

"I did not see. I was headed for Tiernay to talk to Hethe. I found him lying on the path—already wounded." He gave her an innocent look that was in no way convincing.

"You may not have seen, but you have an idea who it was," she guessed. When he flinched, she knew she was right. "Who?"

Stephen shook his head. "I must talk to Hethe first."

"*Who?*"

"William." The answer did not come from Hethe's second.

"Mother!" he bellowed, and Helen glanced sharply at the woman as she straightened from feeding the fire. Their gazes met, and the older woman nodded. "He was always the bad one of the three."

"He was not bad," Stephen amended. "He was just—"

"Mean," his mother finished. "Spiteful. Always picking on those smaller than him."

"*He* was the one always being picked on," Stephen argued. "The other children in the village made fun of him—because his mother was a lightskirt. They were jealous because of our father, because we were being taught with Hethe."

"But I thought your mother was the light—" Helen cut herself off as she realized what she was saying and in front of whom. When Stephen frowned at her, she flushed and said apologetically, "William told me that his mother was the blacksmith's daughter."

"*I* am the blacksmith's daughter," Stephen's mother announced dryly.

"Oh." Helen glanced from one to the other, then felt a moment of fear. If Stephen was not the power-mad man who had caused so many wrongs . . . "Did Hethe order you to punish George by cutting his legs off or not?"

"I do not know."

Helen was torn between shock and annoyance. "What do you mean, you do not know? Did he order you to or not?"

"I received those orders, aye. And they were signed by Hethe."

Helen felt as if her heart had been ripped out. She heard the lost sound in her voice as she murmured, "Then those orders came from him after all."

"I do not know."

She peered at him in confusion. "But you just said—"

"That those orders were written on the messages Hethe signed," he repeated carefully.

Helen shook her head in confusion. "Then he must have—"

"Unless William was writing down things he wished to happen, things that Hethe had not ordered."

"William? Why would William write Hethe's messages to you for him?"

"Hethe cannot write. Nor can he read."

"What?" she cried in amazement.

"'Tis why his father brought us to the schoolroom to be taught alongside him," he explained. "Hethe could not read. Our father thought it laziness. The teacher tried to tell him that he had encountered it before, that it wasn't lack of effort, that Hethe needed special lessons, that he sometimes saw the letters backward and such and needed assistance . . . But Lord Holden would not listen. He tried to use us against him."

"So you covered for him," Helen murmured, remembering what William and Hethe had both told her. Neither had said that Hethe could not read or write, though, just that he had difficulty with it.

"Aye. William or I were always with him. One of us reads for him and writes. He merely signs his name."

"He can write his name?"

"Aye. He can read some, too, but it takes him a long time and is laborious. It is easier just to let us do it."

"So he never actually wrote any orders to you?"

"Nay. William did."

"Dear God." She sank to sit on the side of the small bed. "It has been William all along."

"I fear so, yes." He sighed unhappily. "When the orders started coming in to do those things, I . . . Well, it did not seem like Hethe to me. But I could never ask him. He was so rarely at Holden, and when he was there, he was usually tired from battle or his journey and would put me off. Then he would either leave at once, telling me to write if I had any concerns, or William would send me on some task or other and—" He shrugged helplessly. "He claimed the orders were always from Hethe. I could not refuse. I had just started to suspect that William was deliberately keeping us apart when everything got out of hand."

Helen raised her eyebrows, and he explained. "The morning after Templetun brought first you, then Hethe, back to Holden, William returned. He sent me to the village on a minor task as soon as he arrived. Then he showed up and stopped me on my way back to the castle. He said he was concerned about Hethe's mental state, that he was growing more and more cruel. He said he wished to talk to me. I thought we were finally going to get to the bottom of things. He suggested we ride a bit and discuss the situation, and I agreed. We had not ridden far when he attacked me. I did not see it coming." He shook his head. "He left me lying there in the woods for dead."

"But you did not die," Helen said.

"Nay. I was able to regain my mount and head here."

"He was near dead when he arrived," his mother piped up. "I didn't think he'd survive."

"But I did, thanks to you." Stephen gazed at his mother with love and gratitude for a moment, then went on. "By the time I had healed enough to return to Holden—"

"You were *not* healed enough," his mother snapped.

"Mother heard news that Hethe had taken you to Tiernay," Stephen continued, ignoring her.

"So you went to Tiernay, too."

Stephen's eyebrows rose. "How did you know?"

"Maggie recognized you in the tavern."

"Maggie." He sighed, obviously recalling her. "How is she? Is she making out all right?"

"Aye. She is fine. Why did you ride to Tiernay? To talk to Hethe?"

"Aye." He grimaced. "But I was warned by an old Holden tenant that Hethe was looking for me. That he thought I had been doling out unsanctioned punishments. Which I suppose I was, really." The young man looked so troubled that Helen took the time to soothe him, despite being impatient to hear the rest of his tale.

"You did not know that. Besides, they were sanctioned. His signature was on them even if he did not know what he had approved."

"Aye." He gave her a grateful smile that turned wry as he admitted, "Anyway, I left at once. Fled in a panic, I guess. I realized my mistake almost at once and was going to return, but decided I needed a plan. But when I returned the next morning, it was to hear that he had fallen down the stairs and was abed. I decided to give him a couple of days to recover before returning. The next time I headed to Tiernay was when I found him in the road. He was unconscious and badly wounded. I knew I had to get him to help, else he would surely die. So I pulled him up before me on my horse—"

"Reopening your wound," his mother added irritably.

"Well, I could not just leave him there," Stephen repeated wearily, and Helen suspected he had said it a hundred times in response to the woman's complaints.

"Why did you bring him to Tiernay, though? Holden was much closer to the spot where he fell."

"I suspected William was the culprit. I could hardly take Hethe back for William to finish the job, so I brought him to you."

"But William is at Tiernay. Not Holden. What made you think he was at Holden?"

He appeared surprised at this news. "I just assumed that Hethe would leave him to act as chatelain."

Helen shook her head. "Hethe said William has not the patience for such a position. He left Johnson as chatelain."

Stephen considered that briefly, then nodded in approval. "Johnson is a good choice. He—Wait! Did you say William is at Tiernay?"

"Aye."

"Alone with Hethe?"

"Nay, of course not. There are hundreds of people there, too. My aunt, the servants, the—" She frowned suddenly. "Surely William would not try anything with all those people around?"

"Is there someone staying with Hethe? Guarding him?"

"Aye. My aunt is sitting with him. I told her to let no one near him but . . . William." Helen groaned and saw her own horror reflected in Stephen's eyes. She was on her feet almost at once. "I must get back to him."

"I am coming, too," Stephen announced, shoving his coverings aside and stumbling from the bed.

"Over my dead and bleeding body!" his mother roared, rushing forward to stop him. Helen paused to glance back as the woman added, "I am not sewing you back together again. You just get back in that bed now!"

But Stephen was not listening to his mother. He was already pulling a pair of bloodstained breeches on. Some of it was likely Hethe's blood, she realized unhappily. "Perhaps your mother is right, Stephen. You are in no shape to—"

"I am going," Stephen insisted, wincing and stumbling toward her as he pulled an equally bloodstained tunic on as well.

"But," Helen began even as his mother snapped, "Don't be an idiot! Get back—"

"Where did you put my horse, Mother?" Stephen ignored them both.

His mother glared at him helplessly for a moment, then sagged and hurried to the door. "I hid him behind the cottage. I shall get him for you. Put your bloody boots on."

Helen hesitated as she watched Hethe's second find and then struggle to don his boots. She wanted to leave him there and just go, but could not. Muttering under her breath, she rushed back to help him. She had his boots and swordbelt on quickly, but his mother was quicker still. She had brought his horse around and sat mounted on him when they came out of the cottage.

"What are you doing?" he barked, seeing her.

"I am going, too. Someone has to keep you on this great behemoth of a horse."

Stephen opened his mouth to argue, then seemed to think better of it and merely moved silently forward. Between his mother's pulling from her perch on the mount and Helen's pushing from the ground, they managed to get him into the saddle. Helen then hurried around to her own horse and mounted it. Remembering Goliath, she glanced around. She had left the dog outside upon seeing that Stephen was too weak to be a threat. He was nowhere to be seen now. Helen called for him, whistled, and finally relaxed when the dog loped out of the trees.

"Come," she ordered, snapping her mare's reins. And with that, they were off.

Chapter 21

S TEPHEN." Hethe repeated the name unhappily. "You know he must be the one behind this, right?"

"Oh, aye." William reached out, absently spinning the mug where it sat. "Who else? I doubt any of the servants or villagers are practiced at archery."

"Aye." Hethe watched his first's actions, but his mind was on Stephen and his perfidy. Then he admitted, "I fear I can see no other answer, myself. I just do not understand why he has taken this so far. I could have forgiven his cruelties to the serfs and villeins . . . well, perhaps not forgiven them, but given him a punishment and the opportunity for him to right the wrongs he has committed. I do not know why he had to take things to this level. What does he hope to gain?"

"Perhaps he hopes to gain all you have," William murmured.

Hethe gave his first an angry look. "Killing me will not give him that," he said harshly. "Holden would go to my cousin Adolf should I die."

William stilled, then nodded slowly. "Aye. So it would."

"So why would he wish me dead?"

"Perhaps he hates you."

Hethe froze. "Why?"

"Well, you have everything a man could wish for. A rich, powerful estate. A lovely young wife. The king's ear. And he has nothing."

Hethe frowned. "I inherited it all from my father. It was a matter of—"

"Chance."

Hethe scowled, but William continued. "Stephen has the same father as you. But his mother was the blacksmith's daughter. Had your mothers been reversed, he would have been lord and not you. You did not know, of course."

"No." Hethe frowned, his gaze dropping and shifting around the room as he considered. Stephen was his half-brother. Impossible. He had never even suspected. Well, of course he hadn't. "He looks nothing like me. He has red hair and green eyes. You look more like me than he does. Are you sure—"

Hethe paused, his gaze riveted on his first. William did look more like him than Stephen did. William was the same height as him, had the same dark coloring, the same blue eyes, the same mouth—a mouth that was at the moment curving up with amusement.

"Our father was quite prolific," William said, then allowed a moment for it to sink in before continuing. "As for Stephen, his mother was a green-eyed redhead. He took her coloring. But he inherited our father's size and shape—as we did. He also has the same straight nose and strong chin."

Hethe gaped at his first. Two brothers. He had *two* brothers. All these years he had thought himself an only child and—"Why was I never told?"

"I suppose our father never bothered telling you because he did not feel it significant enough. He never acknowledged us openly, after all. And Stephen did not know."

"But you did."

William shrugged. "I was taught that it was something not to be discussed. I was never really sure if you knew or not."

Hethe was silent for a moment, then shook his head. "But if Stephen did not know—"

"He learned it once he was older. *I* told him." William began to spin the mug in place again, his gaze turning away from Hethe and concentrating on it. "We discussed it at length. I know it has preyed on him since. He found it hard to accept that, but for chance, he might have been Lord of Holden. He could have sat at tables with kings, have married a lady. He would have answered to no one."

Hethe frowned at those words. "It is not all as wonderful as it sounds. You know that, and so should he! I have to answer to the king, if you will recall. In his position, Stephen must only answer to me. He is fortunate. The king can be very demanding. And as for marrying a lady, just look at how I was ordered to marry Lady Tiernay. I hardly would have chosen her to wife."

"But all worked out well. You seem pleased with her."

"Aye," Hethe agreed, his expression softening.

"Well, Stephen likely envies you that, too."

Hethe grimaced. "Then he is a fool. Not that my wife is not worth envying, but why waste his time on such silliness? It will get him nowhere. And, as I said, should I die, Holden will go to Adolf."

"But Tiernay would return to Helen."

Hethe blinked. "Aye. I suppose it would. We have not been married long, and there are no children to inherit. Most likely Tiernay would remain with her and the king would see her remarried."

"So, perhaps your assassin plans to woo and marry her. She might turn to him in her grief to help with managing Tiernay. It will be easy for him to ingratiate himself with her." William smiled, and Hethe felt a chill run through him. "Especially with Stephen still running loose out there."

"It was never Stephen," Hethe realized.

"Stephen was never smart enough to come up with anything approaching a plan."

"He is smart enough, but he is loyal."

"He is a fool."

"*You* were sending those instructions to Stephen. You were the one mutilating my subjects in my name!"

William shrugged. "You obviously did not have the courage to do what needed doing. You have always been the weak one. Too stupid to learn how to write, too—"

Hethe lunged upward, grabbing up the pitcher on the table and slamming it into the side of his first's head. The blow was one of desperation, with little strength behind it, but the surprise was enough to send William backward, shaking his head.

Hethe tried to bolt from the bed, throwing himself toward the door. He was not a fool. William would never have so calmly confessed had he intended Hethe to live. The man planned to kill him. He had been trying all this time, trying to make it seem an accident. Hethe doubted that this time he would fail. He was too weak in his condition to do battle. His only hope was to get out into the hall and summon help.

Alas, his desperation was not enough to save him. His body, still weak and atremble just from swinging the pitcher and plunging from the bed, gave out on him as soon as his feet hit the floor. He started to pitch forward, but suddenly William was there, pushing him back onto the bed in disgust.

"Now, what the bloody hell was that supposed to be?" the knight snapped, shoving Hethe back beneath the linens and again covering him with furs. "You are in no shape to be prancing around."

Hethe watched warily as the man straightened and surveyed him unhappily. Then his first sighed.

"I really do not want to kill you, Hethe. In fact, I thought I had taken care of matters when I stabbed Stephen and left him for dead."

"You stabbed Stephen?"

"Aye. Well, I could hardly have him telling you that he had been following your orders. You might have figured it out, then." He pursed his lips unhappily. "I truly thought the situation resolved, that things would return to normal. I was always content to serve as your first. You would return to your old routine as soon as you wearied of your wife. Things would be fine."

"What changed your mind?" Hethe asked through a dry mouth.

"Actually, it was that accident with the horse cart. I had no intention of killing you until then. In that moment, when I feared you were dead, I realized that Helen would be alone. Tiernay would be lordless. Everything would be up for the taking. And I realized how much I wanted it. I wanted it all, and I deserve it as much as you ever did.

"Of course, then I had to figure out how to get it, and it did seem that the only way was to see you dead. So I started to make my plans, but decided to wait until we arrived here to set them in motion. I knew that everyone would assume it was a vengeance killing by one of the villeins."

"Or Stephen."

"Aye. Well, at the time, I thought he was dead." Hethe's half-brother shrugged, then said almost kindly, "Were there another way to get what I deserve, I would surely have gone another route. But you are standing between me and Helen, and she can give me everything I want and deserve."

"She will never marry you," Hethe said quietly.

"Of course she will," William argued as if explaining something to a child. "I get all your leftovers. Besides, I will be charming and remind her of you. She will marry me out of her confused love and loss. She will even think it is her own idea."

Love and loss? Despite the situation he found himself in, Hethe perked up at those words. Did Helen love him? William seemed to think so. He savored the idea for a moment, then realized that it might not be a good thing if William were right. If she did love Hethe, she might just marry William, if he caught her at a weak moment, if he used her grief against her. His expression tightened, and he lifted his head slightly. "So, how do you plan to kill me?"

William made a face. "In truth, *that* was what I was contemplating when you awoke to catch me staring out the window. If I had it my way, the arrow would have killed you. Other than that, a sword cleaving your head from your body is my preference. That would be painless, but it would of course give away the game." He smiled wryly. "Poison would have been my next option. I would just say you never awoke. But I have none on my person at present and cannot risk leaving you alone. So I guess it will have to be smothering." He picked up one of the furs that had fallen to the floor and began to bunch it up as he spoke. "It is slow and unpleasant, but I really do not have many options." He paused in his bunching and cocked his head. "Any last requests or comments?"

Hethe closed his eyes briefly, rage rushing through him, followed closely by despair. He silently cursed the weakness that made him such easy prey, then opened his eyes. William had moved closer, but paused when their gazes met.

"Well?" he asked.

"Why did you order Stephen to cut that peasant's legs off?" When William appeared thrown by the sudden question, Hethe reminded him. "George. He was accused of poaching. Did you really think it a just punishment, or were you really punishing him for that time he beat you silly when we were boys?"

William's upper lip curled slightly, his hands tightening on the fur he held. "He had no right to touch me. I was the lord's son."

Hethe nodded slowly. An idea had just occurred to him, sparked by William's arrogant expression. It had reminded him of when they were children and William would raise his chin and glare defensively at the other children. That, of course, had not gone over well with the others. Taking his defensive attitude as arrogance, they had often beaten him, and Stephen and Hethe had often had to wade in to help. The worst had been the time George had taunted William for putting on airs, teasing him about only being a lightskirt's son, a woman anyone could have. He had just had her and it had only cost a groat, he had claimed.

William had charged the other lad, but swiftly regretted it. George had been a big boy, brawny and strong. He had beaten William senseless. Thinking of that had made Hethe wonder if the poacher, George, was that lad grown up. It seemed he was. Now he wondered about the others.

"And Bertha?" he asked, thinking of the alewife who had had her breasts cut off. "What did she do to deserve what she got?"

"She was always teasing me, taunting me about thinking I was above myself."

"And Adam? Surely that seven-year-old was too young to have bothered you."

"His mother was a worse slut than my own. She spread her legs for everyone and never charged. But when it came to me, she said she'd have no bastard between her legs."

"So you punished her by maiming her son?" Hethe sighed, his eyes closing. Stephen's doling out unsanctioned punishments had not made any sense. Unfortunately, William's reasons did. He had been using his position to wreak revenge.

A rustling sound made him open his eyes, and he saw that his first was moving forward, raising the furs as he did.

"Where is my wife?" Hethe asked, to stall him, some hope forming that she might suddenly appear and save him.

"She is resting, I think." The other man seemed surprised by the question. It was obvious he hadn't considered her whereabouts. His gaze slid to the door and he hesitated briefly, then shook his head.

"Aye, she is most likely resting. She has spent a great deal of time at your side—what with your sudden tendency to get injured." The man glanced back at Hethe and shrugged.

"Well, we had best get this finished, ere she decides to check on you," he commented easily. And with no further ado, he stepped to Hethe's side and leaned down to press the fur firmly against his face.

Hethe struggled, his hands reaching out, first, to try to push the fur away, then searching for the face of the man smothering him. If he could gouge William's eyes, or reach his throat, he thought desperately. But the other man, strong and unhampered by injury or weakness, avoided him easily.

Hethe felt his lungs begin to burn from lack of oxygen. He felt his head begin to swim and knew he was dying. He had a vague recollection of himself asking, "Why so bleak? Am I going to die?" and the other man's shrug. He *had* been going to die. He just hadn't realized it.

"My lady!" Ducky rushed forward when Helen burst into the keep, Goliath hot on her heels. "Is something amiss? Do you—Who is that?"

Helen paused and glanced over her shoulder to see Hethe's second struggling up the stairs behind her, with his mother's aid. "That is Stephen. Is my aunt with Hethe?" She prayed Nell was, but Ducky was stuck on the first part of the conversation.

"Stephen?" the maid asked, eyes wide with alarm. "Here? But he—"

"Nay, he did not," Helen said quickly. "*William* did."

"William?" If anything, Ducky looked even more horrified.

"Aye. Where is he?"

Ducky paused, eyes wide with horror. "He is sitting with His Lordship. Your aunt was nodding off in her chair, and he suggested she take a nap. He said he would watch Hethe for her."

"Sweet Jesu," Stephen swore, arriving in time to hear her explanation. Helen didn't say a word, just whirled toward the stairs and made off at a dead run. Stephen, his mother and Ducky promptly chased after her, but she left them behind on the stairs as she raced ahead.

Hethe gasped in shock, sucking air into his lungs with relief as the fur was suddenly removed from his face. For a moment, he was too busy filling his lungs to care why it was gone. Then the buzzing in his ears receded and he became aware of a good bit of screaming and banging. Opening his eyes, he glanced around until his bleary gaze settled on a hunchbacked William turning in crazed circles in the center of the bedchamber. Another moment later, he was able to see that William hadn't suddenly gone hunchbacked. The hunch was his wife.

Lady Helen was hanging from William's back, one arm around his neck choking him, and the other hand tugging viciously at his hair. She was screaming like a banshee. He had suspected from the first that Lady Helen of Tiernay was a dangerous enemy to have, and here was his proof, he thought proudly. He cried out in fury and alarm when William managed to cast her off his back, sending her tumbling to the floor in a heap.

If that were not bad enough, William pulled a short, sharp blade from his waist. Hethe felt his blood run cold. Suddenly, fury fired through him and he shot from the bed. Of course, he didn't have much more energy or strength than the last time he had tried the maneuver, and he tumbled forward as soon as his feet hit the floor, but he managed to grab William's ankle and hold on fast. He tugged the man weakly this way and that, trying to overset him, bellowing the whole while. It took him a moment to realize that another enraged roar had joined his, another pair of boots stepped into view. He looked up.

"Stephen," he gasped as his second lunged for William's knife. The man managed to hook his arm over William's and hung weakly from it, restricting its movements. Then an older, red-haired woman joined the fray, leaping over Hethe to grab and swing from his first's other arm.

William gave a bellow of rage.

Hethe had not seen Ducky step up for her turn, but she must have run around the other side of Stephen, for Hethe heard the conk as she slammed a chamber pot over William's head. It was not empty, and Hethe instinctively released his hold on his enemy and tried to move out of the way. The pot's contents flowed down over his would-be killer. Stephen and the redhead were also rather quick to get out of the way, leaving William turning in stumbling circles, slashing out blindly with his knife as he tried to see through the muck oozing over his face. Hethe's heart nearly stopped in his chest when the man turned on Helen. She had regained her feet and was trying to get out of his way, but was cornered by the wildly stabbing man.

A growl from the door drew Hethe's attention then, and an idea came to him quickly upon spotting Goliath. He didn't know what order the dog

had been trained to respond to, or even if he had
been trained to attack. However, he did know one
command the beast had been taught lately. Reaching out, Hethe tapped William's ankle and shouted,
"Look, Goliath, it is Lord Holden!"

The large wolfhound was on the man at once,
clasping William's waist and humping for all he was
worth. Hethe's first bellowed at the attack, slashed
at the dog, then instinctively tried to save himself as
the weight of the animal started to tumble him to
the floor. William twisted in the air, trying to break
his fall with the fist holding the knife, but such was
folly. A grunt of air slid from his lips as he crashed
down, impaling himself on his own blade.

No one moved, all eyes frozen on the inert body.
They all knew it had been a killing wound. The
dagger had caught him at the throat, going right
through. A pool of blood was fast forming around
his body.

"Well," Helen murmured after a moment of silence had held the room. "It is obvious that the
chambermaids are growing lax while Maggie is
away helping her daughter. That pot should have
been emptied yesterday."

Hethe's gaze slid to his wife. Suddenly a smile
tugged at his lips, then a hysterical laugh bubbled
up from his chest. He shook his head. "Dear God,
woman, I love you."

The words were spontaneous and not at all how
he had intended to tell her, but there they were.
Hethe waited for her response, a disappointed sigh
slipping from his lips when all she managed was a
tremulous smile as she got to her feet. She moved to
Goliath, who had not moved from where he had
landed next to William. Hethe frowned in concern

at the pained whine the beast gave when his wife
sifted through his fur.

"Is he all right?" he asked, shifting weakly to a
sitting position and leaning against the bed in an effort to get a look at the dog over Helen's shoulder. It
was damned frustrating being so weak.

"He is cut. I do not think it is too deep, though.
Ducky, come help me get him on the bed."

Hethe watched helplessly as the women coaxed
the injured dog to half walk to the foot of the bed,
then got him up on it.

"Should I fetch Joan?" the maid asked.

"Aye. And find a couple men to remove . . . him,"
Helen ordered, giving a shudder of disgust as she
peered over her shoulder to where William lay covered in waste. Ducky nodded and quickly left.

Hethe watched as his wife straightened from the
dog. She glanced from a swaying Stephen to where
Hethe sat on the floor beside the bed, then said to
the little redhead, "You get Stephen, and I shall handle my husband."

Nodding, the redhead promptly moved to Stephen and took his arm. She led him toward the
chairs by the fireplace.

Helen paused next to Hethe and said, "Nay, bring
him to the bed, instead." After a hesitation, the
woman did as she'd been bidden.

Helen knelt to offer her assistance to Hethe. Now
that the crisis was over, he was pretty much out of
strength. He did his best to help, but knew his wife
was doing most of the work. When he finally collapsed on the mattress, it was to find the other side
occupied by an equally weak Stephen.

"Ducky said I was needed," a voice cried out.

Hethe looked up to see Tiernay's old healer rush

into the room. She took one look at the three injured males crowding the bed, then made straight
for Hethe. He was quick to wave her away, however.

"I am fine. See to Goliath. He has a fresh wound;
I merely need re-bandaging." He was amused to
note the surprise in her eyes before she turned her
attention to the dog at the foot of the bed. Hethe
turned to the man beside him, noting only then the
bloodied bandages covering his half-brother's chest.

"What happened to you?" he asked with a frown.

"William," his brother answered.

"Me, too."

Instead of speaking, Stephen grunted in pain as
the redheaded woman began to remove his ban-
dage.

Hethe glanced toward his wife as she began to
undo his bloodied wrappings as well, then he looked
back to the redheaded woman.

"Who is she?" he asked curiously.

"My mother," Stephen answered through gritted
teeth. The woman in question was poking and prod-
ding at his wound.

"Oh. Pleasure to meet you," Hethe said politely.
The redhead ignored him.

"She is mad at me," Stephen said, excusing her
rudeness apologetically. Then, he added, "And you."

"Why me?" Hethe asked in dismay, hardly wincing as Helen began to examine his injury, so distracted was he with the news. *Everyone always
seems mad at me*, he thought with irritation.

"She blames you for reopening my wound when I
found you in the woods and brought you here."

"That was you?"

"Aye."

"Thank you."

"You're welcome."

They both fell silent then and cast sympathetic glances Goliath's way as the dog whined. Joan continued cleaning his wound. Helen and Stephen's mother began to re-bandage them, and Hethe tried to think of a way to broach the subject that had consumed so much of his thoughts since his discussion with William.

Finally, he just blurted, "So, I hear you're my brother."

"Aye."

"That's nice. Never had a brother before."

"We had another," Stephen pointed out sadly. They both glanced over at William's body. For a moment they were both silent, recalling many memories—mostly good.

The sound of footsteps clomping up the hall preceded the entrance of two of the men who had been guarding Hethe earlier. Ducky was with them, and she directed them to the body. The two burly men considered the mess they were being forced to clean up. One of them muttered in disgust.

"I wish . . ." Hethe cut the words off. It was useless to wish that things had been different, that he had known they were siblings, that he had recognized the depth of William's need to make a name for himself. Perhaps if he had seen it, he might have helped him. Things might have ended differently.

"There was nothing you could do."

Hethe met Stephen's understanding gaze and shrugged uncomfortably. The man knew him too well.

"William chose his own path," Stephen added quietly.

"Did he?" Hethe asked bitterly. "Do any of us?"

"Yes," his brother said firmly. "You chose yours . . . and have now chosen to change it." When Hethe glanced at him sharply, Stephen let a smile tug at his lips. "I have known you nearly all your life, Hethe. And you have always carried a heavy mantle of rage about you. Some of that anger appears to have abated."

"Aye," Hethe agreed, his gaze turning to his lady wife who, along with Ducky, had turned their attention to cleaning up the mess on the floor. There was no doubt in his mind that Helen was the major reason behind the change in him.

"Well, William had his choices, too. He made the wrong ones. You, I think, have made the right one."

"Aye. I think I have, too," Hethe murmured. He cleared his throat and gave the man a crooked smile. "So," he joked, attempting to lighten the mood. "I guess with William gone, that makes me your favorite brother."

Stephen gave a laugh that ended on a moan of pain as he touched his bandaged chest. Letting his breath out cautiously, he grimaced and glanced at Hethe. "So long as you do not order me to perform any more harsh punishments."

Hethe winced, knowing how it must have pained the man to carry them out. "I swear it."

Stephen nodded, a smile tugging at his lips as he took in Hethe's expression of combined guilt and apology. "Just *how* bad do you feel about what you put me through?"

Hethe's eyes narrowed at the amused look that had suddenly entered the other man's eyes. "Not enough for you to get away with whatever you're planning."

"Ah, well." Stephen sighed with feigned regret. "I suppose you are my favorite brother, anyway."

The two men grinned at each other.

Hethe awoke slowly to a complete lack of pain and could hardly believe it. He was so used to blinding agony every time he opened his eyes, this was a feeling to be savored.

A rustle at his bedside made him glance to the left to find his wife there, fussing with his bandages. "What are you doing?" he murmured curiously.

She glanced at him briefly, then turned back to what she was doing. "I am preparing to change your dressing. We must get you healthy again so that you can run off and get yourself killed in battle for the king, mustn't we?"

Hethe sighed at her sarcastic tone. So, she was holding the day he was shot against him. Well, he supposed he deserved it. Had he stayed at Tiernay, things might have turned out quite differently. Still, many good things had come of that ride.

Reaching out, he took her hand and drew her to sit on the edge of the bed. "You need not fear that happening ever again. In fact, it would not have happened that day. I was intending to return. I have given up running; I shall fight no more except in defense of my home."

Her gaze narrowed on him suspiciously. "Truly?"

"Aye. In fact, that is probably what saved my life. I was turning back to Tiernay when William loosed his arrow. Elsewise, I am sure he would have hit my heart. The man was an excellent shot," he told her, then sighed. "I meant it when I said I love you. I do. I realized that on my ride that day. I also realized that I was running, as you said. But from my own anger, and you cannot run away from yourself. So in the future, while I might need to go for a walk or ride once in a while to let my temper cool, I will never run off to battle again. In fact, the king may have trouble getting me to fight at all anymore. Because I love you."

"Oh!" Helen released her breath on a sigh, and leaned down to kiss him. "I love you too, my lord. You are a very special man."

Smiling, Hethe kissed her, putting considerable passion into it. His wife relaxed against him with a sigh, only to pull away and glare at the man who had been asleep beside her husband when she had entered, but who was now trying to slip undetected out of the bed. "What are you doing, Stephen?"

"Oh. I, er, thought you had forgotten I was here," he admitted with embarrassment.

"Well, I had not," she assured him. "Lie down, sir. You will be reopening that wound again if you don't, and then your mother will have fifteen fits. Besides," she added with a laugh, "Hethe is too weak to do anything untoward."

"I will never be too weak for that, wife," he said, squeezing her hand. "Never in a million years."

Epilogue

"J-OHN, f-ive bales . . . hay. Gee-orge, four—" Hethe lowered the scroll with disgust and scowled at his wife. Not that she noticed. She lay on the fur next to him, flat on her back, dressed only in her chemise, her eyes closed and her face tipped up to the sun, a sweet smile curving her lips.

His expression softened. Life had changed amazingly since their marriage. And not just for him. The people of Holden were happy now. All fear had left them, and they were as content and relaxed as their lord.

Helen and Hethe had split their time between Holden and Tiernay, enjoying their stays at each. Strangely, if anyone asked, Hethe would have had to say that, of the two castles, he preferred his childhood home to Tiernay. Holden no longer resembled the cold, stark castle of his youth. Helen had set her hand to turning it into a home. Colorful tapestries splashed the walls there now. The great hall's once-bare tables sported linens, and the floor's rushes had flowers strewn in them to add a sweet scent to the air. She had made the place seem cozy.

Besides, Hethe enjoyed spending time there getting to know Stephen as his brother.

While Helen's aunt, Lady Shambleau, acted as chatelaine during their absence from Tiernay, Hethe had reinstated Stephen as chatelain again at Holden. He was perfect for the position, especially now that he was no longer forced to perform mutilations or other cruel punishments. The man's mother had even moved back to the village.

A bark drew Hethe's attention to the river's edge. Goliath was splashing along the shoreline, barking excitedly at the ducks paddling further out. The animal, like his master, had healed completely from the wound William had caused.

"You have stopped reading."

Hethe scowled down at his wife and complained, "'Tis boring."

"I know 'tis boring, but we cannot always read fun things like *Beowulf*," she said. With a grin, she reminded him cheerfully, "Besides, you need read only five more entries and I will remove my chemise."

Hethe peered over her in the skimpy undergarment, imagining her naked under the sun, then turned back to his list with renewed enthusiasm. His wife had decided to teach him to read. It was an effort on her part to be sure that no one could ever again take advantage of him as William had. Hethe agreed. He didn't want anything of the like occurring again, either. The people of Holden were now as plump, happy and apple-cheeked as the people of Tiernay. He intended on making sure they remained that way.

Actually, learning to read this time around was

not the chore it had been when he was a child. Helen made it a pleasure. She never criticized or cursed him. She encouraged and aided him. She also had an amazing motivational technique, he thought as he read the fifth entry.

Lowering the list, he expectantly turned to watch his wife.

Her smile widened; she knew that he was looking. She stretched languidly, then sat up. Getting to her feet, she turned to face him, then slowly, painfully—for Hethe at least—bent to grasp the hem of her chemise and draw it up her body. Hethe ogled her calves, her knees, her thighs. His gaze paused, and he almost groaned as her delicate triangle of golden curls came into view. His eyes rose to the hem of the gown again, and he found himself licking his lips as she skimmed it up over her breasts. She pulled it over her head, held it out to the side and very deliberately let it drop.

Hethe swallowed hard as she eased back down on the fur again, a veritable feast laid out before him. She closed her eyes and squirmed deliciously in the warm breeze, then sighed and said, "Only five more entries and you can remove them."

Hethe blinked at that reminder, then glanced down at himself. His tunic had gone several entries ago. Now he sat leaning against the tree trunk in only his breeches. Five lines and he could remove them. Then the lesson would truly get interesting. He turned his gaze back to the Tiernay accounts, and ran through four more entries in rapid order. He was reading the fifth when her hand on his waist made him pause. Glancing up, he took in her slow smile and almost sighed with anticipatory pleasure.

"Keep reading," she instructed, trailing her fingers

across his stomach, watching curiously as the muscles there rippled in response.

He repeated the entry he had been reading before she touched him, his voice going husky as she began to run her hands lightly over his chest. He started on the fifth line. "J-ohn-son. Six . . . oh, God." He groaned as her fingers slid down and found the bulge of his manhood through his breeches.

"Six oh-Gods?" Helen asked with amusement, releasing him and untying the laces of his breeches.

Sighing, he opened the eyes he had squeezed closed and quickly scanned the page before his nose, knowing that if he stopped for too long, she would stop as well. He didn't want that. She was a wonderful teacher, he thought with a smile, lifting his hips to help her as she removed his leggings, leaving him as naked as she.

"Six?" she prompted, setting his leggings aside, and Hethe forced himself to focus.

Six . . . six . . . six. Six what? *Make something up*, he thought frantically, eager for the return of her hands on his flesh.

"Six bales of hay," he said quickly and relaxed as she returned to running her hands over his skin. Then he forced himself to look over the lists seriously. But it was impossible to concentrate. He lowered the accounts again.

"How many?" he asked, his voice husky and strained.

"How many what?" his wife asked innocently, her hand sliding along his hip.

"How many entries must I read before I can touch you?"

A slow smile slid across her face, then she arched an eyebrow. "Why do we not try a new method?"

"New?" He eyed her with interest.

"Aye. You can touch me so long as you keep reading."

Bull's-eye, Hethe thought happily, a grin breaking out on his face as he reached for her. But she caught his hand before he could touch her warm skin and nodded toward the list. "Read."

His grin dissipated somewhat but didn't die as he glanced back at the list. Holding the sheet in his left hand, he began to read again, even as his other hand felt for her. He found her shoulder at the end of the first entry, followed it down to her breast with the second, and was cupping and kneading it as he read the third. Then his voice broke. She had started to touch him again. Her hand was on his staff, warm and firm.

Clearing his throat, he continued on, only to pause abruptly when she leaned forward, her lips closing over his erection. Dear God in heaven, she was a *wondrous* teacher, he thought happily. She was a marvelous student, as well. Her technique had improved amazingly this last year. She no longer nibbled on him like he was an ear of corn; she—

Helen stopped suddenly and raised her head to peer at him. "You have ceased reading again."

"Nay," he lied glibly. "I was reading to myself. You did not say it had to be aloud when we made this bargain," he pointed out. Chuckling at the vexed expression which filled her face, he tossed the list aside and pulled her onto his lap.

Helen sighed as her husband's mouth covered hers. For one brief moment, she considered breaking away and forcing him to return to his reading, but he had done well today. Besides, she really didn't want him to stop. She was as eager for this as he was, she admitted as he tumbled her onto her back and covered her.

He made love to her in the open air with a passion that had not waned during the entire last year. If anything, their need for each other only seemed to increase with time. With each day, they learned more about each other and about how to pleasure one another.

When it was over, they lay entwined as they recovered. Helen rolled onto her back and peered up at the sky, watching the clouds drift by. She saw one that looked like a bird, another a dog. Then she spotted one that reminded her of the skinny, spindly Lord Templetun, and she grinned.

"What are you smiling about?"

Rolling back toward him, she rested her chin on his chest. "I was just thinking of Templetun's visit."

Hethe grunted at the mention of the name. The man's temporary position as the king's chaplain had ended some weeks ago. Henry's usual man had recovered from his ailment and was back at his sovereign's side. Templetun had stopped in on his way home to see them and whine about the unfairness of the situation. While the king had been pleased at first with the way things had worked out between Hethe and Helen, he had lost some of his appreciation once he realized what it had cost him.

Oh, aye, he was no longer pestered with their mutual complaints, but he also no longer had Hethe at his beck and call, eager to aid him in battle. Once he had realized such was the case, Henry had been furious, and had known just where to lay the blame. He had made Templetun's life miserable those last few months of service, which Templetun had thought terribly unfair.

"The irritating clodpole," Hethe muttered, and Helen glanced at him in surprise.

"Do not be so mean, Hethe. Were it not for Templetun, we should not have married."

"Ha! I would have found my way to you eventually," he said firmly. Her husband was unwilling to give the old man any credit. Especially not for giving him Helen, the greatest gift he said he had ever received. He shifted impatiently. "Besides, when he was here, the man had the nerve to ask me to return to battle so that the king would not be so irate."

"What?" she asked, dismayed. "You did not agree, did you?"

"Of course not." He frowned, which made her feel better. Still, she realized that this year had not made her forget the day he had ridden away, determined to flee once again to battle.

"Helen," he said gently. "I have told you; I have no interest in living like that anymore. I shall serve my time under the king as everyone must, but that is all." He ran a finger lightly over the furrows on her forehead, gently smoothing them out. "I told you. I am content here with you. I will not be running away anymore. I have a home now."

"You have two," she corrected.

"Nay. I have one. Wherever you are. And it would be useless to try to run away from that home, because I carry you in my heart." With those words, the last of her doubts dropped away. She relaxed, a smile beaming across her face, and she hugged him tightly.

"I am glad, husband."

"Are you?" he murmured, running his fingers lightly through her hair.

"Aye. Because if you did ever try to run away

again, I would have to hunt you down, drag you back, and chain you to our bed."

Hethe grinned at the threat, then teased, "And torture me with garlic? Or have Joan give me a potion to make me sleep?"

Helen made a face at his words and shifted to lie on her side, her head in the crook of his arm so that she could run her fingers lightly over his chest. "Neither, my lord. That garlic was torture to myself as well, and sleeping would make you useless to me." She emphasized that statement by reaching down to grasp his manhood. Much to her surprise, while Wee Hethe did show signs of reawakening at her touch, large Hethe's response was to laugh. She tipped her face up to peer at him questioningly and he hugged her tightly, a softness in his eyes as he stared down at her.

"Do you know, I think the day the king decided we should marry was the luckiest day of my life?"

"Mine, too," Helen said softly, a smile widening her lips.

"You didn't think so at first," he countered. "Unless having Goliath hump me was your way of showing affection."

Helen laughed merrily as she recalled that day, then quickly sat up to climb onto his lap. Once straddling his hips, she pushed her golden hair back behind her ears and smiled at him slyly before asking, "How else would the Tyrant of Tiernay show her affection?"

Hethe gaped. "You knew what we called you?"

"Of course, I knew." Helen laughed at his surprise and shifted herself to slide against his stiffening manhood. "What I didn't know was that being married to the Hammer of Holden would be so . . ."

She let the words trail off, looking thoughtful, and Hethe prompted, "So *what?*"

"Well." Helen turned her gaze back to his and shrugged. "Let us just say that I thought there would be a little more hammering." She thrust against him abruptly to let him know what sort of hammering she was speaking of.

A laugh slipped from Hethe's lips and he reached up to clasp her breasts. "Do you know, wife, I have found that there are definite benefits to having a tyrant for a wife," he announced. Rolling her onto her back under the shade of the tree, he proceeded to show her just what some of those benefits were.